INTRIGUED

out of the

OFFICE

Office Intrigue, Book 2

By Nicole Edwards

The Alluring Indulgence Series
Kaleb
Zane
Travis
Holidays with the Walker Brothers
Ethan
Braydon
Sawyer
Brendon

The Austin Arrows Series
Rush
Kaufman

The Bad Boys of Sports Series
Bad Reputation
Bad Business

The Caine Cousins Series
Hard to Hold
Hard to Handle

The Club Destiny Series
Conviction
Temptation
Addicted
Seduction
Infatuation
Captivated
Devotion
Perception
Entrusted
Adored
Distraction

The Coyote Ridge Series
Curtis
Jared

The Dead Heat Ranch Series
Boots Optional
Betting on Grace
Overnight Love

By Nicole Edwards (cont.)

The Devil's Bend Series

Chasing Dreams
Vanishing Dreams

The Devil's Playground Series

Without Regret
Without Restraint

The Office Intrigue Series

Office Intrigue
Intrigued Out of the Office
Their Rebellious Submissive

The Pier 70 Series

Reckless
Fearless
Speechless
Harmless

The Sniper 1 Security Series

Wait for Morning
Never Say Never
Tomorrow's Too Late

The Southern Boy Mafia Series

Beautifully Brutal
Beautifully Loyal

Standalone Novels

A Million Tiny Pieces
Inked on Paper

Writing as Timberlyn Scott

Unhinged
Unraveling
Chaos

Naughty Holiday Editions

2015
2016

INTRIGUED out of the OFFICE

Office Intrigue Duet, Book 2

NICOLE EDWARDS

Nicole Edwards Limited
PO Box 806
Hutto, Texas 78634
NicoleEdwardsLimited.com

Intrigued out of the Office – An Office Intrigue Duet Novel is a work of fiction. Names, characters, businesses, places, events and incidents either are the products of the author's imagination or used in a fictitious manner. Any resemblance to actual persons, living or dead, or actual events is purely coincidental.

Cover Image: © Wander Aguiar | wanderbookclub.com
Model: Olivia Korte @ Brisebois Agency
Cover Background Image: © enki | 123rf.com

Cover Design: © Nicole Edwards Limited
Editing: Blue Otter Editing | www.BlueOtterEditing.com
ISBN (ebook): 978-1-939786-86-9
ISBN (print): 978-1-939786-85-2

BDSM Romance
Mature Audience

ONE

BOSS MEETING

LANGSTON

FOR POSSIBLY THE FIRST TIME in my life, I didn't like the holidays one fucking bit.

The thought of not seeing Luci bothered me. Not only the fact that I was thinking about it too much, but also the fact that she would be away from me. I wanted more time with her, not less.

And, fuck, that bothered me, too.

By the time we got a table at a nearby restaurant, I was trying to read minds. I could tell by the look on Ben's face that he knew something that Landon and I didn't. As much as I wanted to grab him by the collar and insist he tell me what it was, I managed to refrain. I was nothing if not controlled. It was what made me a damn good Dom. I couldn't even remember the last time I'd lost control.

Okay, that wasn't true. It was the day I'd come into the office to find Luci at her desk and not naked in my office like I had requested. I'd lost it that day. After I'd spent so much time anticipating having her all to myself, seeing her not where I'd instructed her to be had set me off.

However, I did at least have the common sense to let some time pass before I had punished her for her transgression. I derived absolutely no pleasure from punishment that wasn't associated with playing. However, I would dole it out as it was necessary to maintain the balance between a Dom and a submissive.

"All right," Justin said after we'd received our drinks. "Go ahead and tell them what Luci told you."

I knew it.

Ben glanced at me and Landon. "I asked what her plans were for the holidays. I got the sense that she was not looking forward to them because she would be spending it alone."

"Why would you assume that?" I narrowed my eyes, trying to read him. "What about her parents?"

"She said they went on a cruise," Ben explained. "Won't be back until after the first of the year."

"According to Luci," Landon offered, "she doesn't spend much time with them anyway."

Well, fuck. Why didn't I know that?

"And Kristen?" I asked Landon.

He shrugged. "No idea, but that does explain why she's hesitant to go home when I tell her to."

"She doesn't want to be alone," Ben offered, which was the same conclusion I'd drawn.

"Was anyone planning to spend time with her over the holidays?" Justin asked.

I glanced at Landon. I hadn't spoken to him about it, but I had intended to see her. No way could I go two fucking weeks without seeing her. I'd probably go out of my mind.

And that honestly had nothing to do with the fact that I wouldn't get sex otherwise. Although I was hesitant to act on my attraction to Luci, that didn't mean I could ignore her entirely.

"I was going to call her," Landon admitted. "I haven't nailed down anything at this point, but I was going to see her. Or try, anyway. Take her to dinner or something."

Justin glanced at Ben, then back to me. "Unfortunately, we've got a lot going on. I'm not sure we can see her much until after Christmas."

Ben took a sip of his drink before speaking. "I'm willing to change some things around. I'm spending Christmas Eve with my momma, but I'll be available before and after."

As I sipped my drink, an idea came to me. I glanced at my brother and he nodded, as though he had read my mind. Sometimes I thought he could actually do that.

"Let me call our folks," Landon told Justin and Ben. "See if they'd be willin' to do somethin' different."

"Like what?" Justin was obviously curious.

Fortunately, my brother didn't show his hand before he was ready to play it. "Give me until tomorrow mornin'. Then we'll let you know."

"As long as someone's going to take care of Luci," Ben said firmly. "Otherwise, I'll shift what I have to. I don't like the idea of her spending the holidays by herself."

I didn't like the idea either, but if it came down to it, I would rather be the one to spend time with her. Well, Landon and I. That was my possessive streak coming out, though.

"She won't be spending them alone," I assured them.

No matter what my brother and I came up with, Luci would not be spending the holidays by herself.

I would make damn sure of that.

TWO

WHEN I WOKE UP ON Friday morning, after getting a solid eight hours of sleep, I felt a little better. I wasn't ready to face the holidays alone, but I did feel as though I could take it day by day. Apparently, I'd needed a good night's sleep. It went a long way to lifting my spirits.

Instead of thinking about my bosses and the fact that I wouldn't get to see them for two weeks, I decided I would do some last-minute Christmas shopping. I probably could've waited until the day after Christmas and gotten everything on sale, but I had procrastinated long enough and I had too much time to kill.

Rather than shower, I simply pulled my hair up into a ponytail and donned a pair of jeans and an oversized sweater with my Uggs. I didn't look like a supermodel, but I didn't look homeless either, so I considered it a win.

I headed for the mall and fought the crowds in an attempt to find something that my mother might actually use. Seemed no matter what I had bought her over the past few years, she seldom used it, and sometimes, I even found my gift still in the bag, tucked in one of her guest room closets. Jim was easier to buy for because he collected hunting knives, so I had purchased his gift months before, finding the perfect one online. I ended up buying my mother some bath bombs and other goodies from Lush, hoping that she would at least get some use out of them.

After I'd made the required purchases, I did a little shopping for myself. I ended up buying a tiny fake tree that I could set on my kitchen table, along with a couple of cute little Santa and Mrs. Claus figurines that would brighten up the living room. It wasn't much, but I was doing my best. Unlike usual, I did not buy any clothes or shoes, although I was tempted. Fortunately for my bank account, there were just too many people to make the trip enjoyable.

Once I'd escaped the throngs of overzealous procrastinators, I stopped for Chinese takeout, then headed back to my apartment and changed into yoga pants. At that point, I wasn't really hungry, so I stashed my lunch in the refrigerator and settled in with some popcorn and decided to watch movies to keep my mind off everything.

It worked for a few hours and I cuddled up in a blanket on the couch, enjoying my alone time. Or, rather, pretending to. It became nearly impossible not to check my phone every twenty minutes to see if someone had texted me although I knew they hadn't. Finally, I broke down and texted Kristen.

Luci: *Missed you at yoga last night.*

Kristen: *Aw. I wish I had been there. We're at Tim's parents until Christmas Eve. Then we were planning to go see my dad for a couple of days.*

Luci: *Maybe when you get back to town we can hang out. You have plans for New Year's?*

Kristen: *Nothing final. But I'd love to get together. Maybe the three of us can go out on the town.*

I wasn't fond of being the third wheel, but it sure as hell beat sitting at home by myself.

Luci: *I'd love to do something. Hit me up when you get back.*

Kristen: *Will do. And Merry Christmas!*
Luci: *Merry Christmas to you!*
And just like that, I was alone once again.

•

While I was flipping through channels that afternoon, debating on whether to heat up the Chinese food or come up with something else to fix for an early dinner, there was a knock on my apartment door. I figured it was my neighbor. Mrs. Idlemann was known to make cookies, using them as an excuse to stop by from time to time just to chat, and I figured since I had been holding odd hours, she was curious as to where I'd been.

Without looking through the peephole, I yanked the door open, ready to cheerfully greet Mrs. Idlemann, when I came face-to-face with…

My head snapped up and I was peering into intimidating hazel eyes. "Master." My eyes darted to the other man. "Landon."

"Sir," Landon corrected, a beaming smile on his face. "From here on out, you can call me Sir."

Master and Sir? *That* was going to get interesting.

"Okay…uh…Sir."

They both grinned, and let me just say, the things that those smirks stirred inside me should've been illegal.

"What are you doing here?"

They didn't wait to be invited in before they gently nudged me out of the way and stepped inside, closing the door securely behind them. Of course, I wasn't at all surprised by this because, hey, I had already admitted that I wanted to submit to them. They knew me. This wasn't exactly a boundary they were pushing.

I liked it.

Once inside, Sir made a beeline for my bedroom. I had no idea what he was doing, but I didn't get the chance to go after him because Master pulled me into his arms and fused his lips to mine.

Needless to say, I was shocked.

And definitely not disappointed.

I moaned into his mouth as his tongue dominantly sought mine. The kiss was rough and sexy and…over way too soon.

"What's going on?" I asked, the words said breathlessly as I fought to get air into my lungs. "I thought…I thought I was on holiday until next year."

"We're kidnapping you."

He said it so matter-of-factly I actually believed him.

Now, I'd never had a fantasy like that, but I could admit, the idea sounded deliciously kinky.

I jumped to my next question. "Where are we going?"

"That's a secret."

"But what if I don't want to—"

Master jerked me to him again, slamming his lips over mine and making me moan. I melted against him, completely pliant, and he likely knew from that move alone that I would do anything he wanted.

When he was finished plundering my mouth, Master gripped my hair and pulled my head back. The sensual sting shot down my spine, making my pussy clench. I met and held his stare, waiting eagerly for him to tell me what was going on. I was so happy to see them, it didn't really matter, but I could tell they had a plan.

"From this point forward, no more questions," he commanded, staring down into my eyes. "At least not until we get there."

I started to speak, but he cocked one dark eyebrow.

"No questions, pet. You'll find out everything you need to know when we're ready to tell you."

I grinned. "Yes, Master."

His smirk was wicked.

Landon—I meant, Sir—stepped into the room and my eyes shot to his as he held up a suitcase. "She's all packed."

"I'd prefer she go without clothes," Master stated, deadpan.

"Trust me, she'll be naked a good amount of the time."

Mmm. I never thought I'd enjoy hearing that, but coming from them, it was nice.

Master released me and I turned to face Sir. He set my suitcase down on the floor, then reached for me.

"One day," he said softly. "We didn't last one whole day."

"No, we didn't." I was including myself in there because I'd been going crazy without them.

Sir jerked me into his arms, his lips locking with mine and kissing me as passionately as Master had. I couldn't resist gripping his shirt in my fist as I moaned, eager for more. I hadn't realized it was possible to miss someone as much as I'd missed them in such a short amount of time.

"You trust us, sweet girl?" Sir rasped when he pulled back and looked into my eyes.

"Of course I do."

"Good. Then I suggest you go change. And don't bother with panties or a bra. They won't be necessary. And though we're not in the office, the rules still apply. No pants."

I was long past trying to hide the grin that had overtaken my face. "Do I have time to shower?"

He glanced at his watch. "You have one hour. We have to run an errand, but we'll be back. I expect you to have the door unlocked and to be kneeling here, waiting for us. Understood?"

"Yes, Sir." My heart swelled and I felt dangerously close to bursting. The thought of submitting to both of them was...more than I ever could've hoped for.

Master turned me toward the bedroom, then swatted my ass, making me yelp.

I had one hour and I was going to be ready when they returned.

Ready and waiting.

THREE

I WAS READY AND WAITING a good ten minutes before my hour was up. After they left, I had started the shower water and returned to lock the door so I didn't have any unexpected guests while I was naked and wet. I then took what might've been the fastest shower of my life while still managing to pay special attention to every detail. After drying off, I donned a maroon maxi skirt and a flowy, black, off-the-shoulder sweater and a cute pair of black boots. I went with minimal makeup and left my hair down, letting it dry naturally in long, wavy strands.

I had even grabbed my coat, then checked my suitcase, tossing in my makeup and my birth control pills before grabbing my phone charger and placing it all near the door, which I then unlocked as Sir had requested.

The elevator dinged in the hallway and my heart picked up speed as I waited, kneeling by the door, eagerly waiting for them to return. I was still slightly shocked that this was happening. I hadn't expected it and my excitement couldn't be contained.

They were here.

For *me*.

When the door opened, I kept my gaze down, my palms up, paying attention to how I appeared to them. If Master and Sir listened closely, they could probably hear the solid pounding of my heart against my sternum. I could certainly hear it and it was loud enough to drown out almost everything else.

Two hands rested on my head briefly and a tingling sensation trickled down my neck, through my torso, and straight to my belly. No doubt about it, I was impatient.

And hopeful.

Definitely hopeful.

"Stand and greet your masters," Sir instructed, his voice warm with approval.

Masters. That was music to my ears.

I got to my feet, then stood in front of them, glancing from one to the other. It took a tremendous amount of willpower not to bounce on the balls of my feet. I was so excited, my cheeks already starting to hurt from smiling so much.

"Stunning, as always," Sir said, his eyes roaming over me.

"Thank you, Sir."

His face sobered and he met my gaze. "While we're away, you belong to us. Only us. You will do everything we ask of you and you'll do it with a smile."

"Of course."

"For this experience, you are our submissive, Luci. Not our employee, not our office plaything. Our submissive. Do you understand?"

"I do."

"Good." He brushed the backs of his fingers down my cheek.

"Are you ready, pet?" Master held his keys in his hand, his eyes locked on me.

"Yes, Master."

"After you," Sir said, motioning toward the door.

Master took my apartment key from my hand, then locked the door. He didn't give it back and I thought nothing of it. I willingly gave myself to these men. I knew without a doubt that they would take care of me and the fact that I could do so was such a freeing feeling. I'd never experienced anything like it and I never wanted it to end.

Sir kept me close to his side as we got in the elevator and headed down. Master opened doors and waited for us to exit. It was well choreographed, as though they'd thought it through completely. I'd never given much thought to what it would be like to be in a relationship with two men. And no, I wasn't jumping ahead of myself; however, Sir had said I was their submissive, which meant, for the time being, I belonged to both of them.

I was surprised when we approached a sleek black town car idling in the parking lot. Sir opened the door and allowed me to climb inside while the driver took my suitcase and placed it in the trunk. I moved to the middle and then was flanked by both men in the back seat. A few minutes later, we were pulling out of the apartment complex and I was on the verge of bouncing up and down with excitement. It was a hard urge to quell, but I managed. Barely.

The same couldn't be said when we arrived at a private air strip a short time later and I noticed a private jet waiting for us.

I peered over at both of them, then back out the window. My gaze jumped around as I took it all in. Questions burned my tongue, but I remembered what Master had said. Holding back wasn't easy for me, and they both obviously knew that.

"Patience, pet," Sir mumbled against my ear as he brushed my hair back. He kissed my cheek.

"I'm trying, Sir."

"After takeoff, we'll have to ensure she has something to do with her hands," Master stated with a wicked smirk.

He seemed much more laid-back than usual. Sure, he still had that overwhelming dominance that he had long ago perfected, but I sensed that something was different. I liked this side of him.

Warmth pooled between my legs as we walked toward the stairs that led up to the plane, both men's hands on the small of my back. I wasn't nervous about flying, which was likely because I was too excited about where we were going. The fact they weren't telling me made it that much hotter.

Once we stepped onto the plane, my eyes were wide as I took it all in. This was one of those jets you saw in movies. All decked out with fancy seats and tables. Nothing like a commercial airliner. If I had to guess, I'd bet good money there was a bedroom on this thing.

Not that I got to look around. Sir guided me to a chair and I sat, my butt cradled by the buttery-soft leather. There was another chair beside mine and two directly across, facing me. There was a good three or four feet that separated the chairs. Sort of like a lounge area, not at all like a regular commercial plane.

When I stopped moving around, Sir buckled my seat belt, then kissed my lips before going to the front to have a conversation with a young man who had greeted us when we stepped on. In an effort not to appear as though I was trying to eavesdrop, I found myself looking at Master, who was standing near a small bar, adding ice to two glasses, then pouring an amber liquid in both.

His gaze shot over to mine. "Would you like something to drink? Scotch? Water? Pretty much anything you could want."

"No. Thank you." I wasn't thirsty and I didn't want alcohol to muddle my experience.

Sir returned a few minutes later and Master passed him a drink before they both took the seats directly across from me. I wasn't sure what to do or say, so I kept my mouth shut.

"Once we've leveled off, we won't be bothered for at least an hour," Sir told Master, sipping his drink as his eyes skimmed over me.

Master smirked. "I think our pet is about to burst. Is there a question you'd like to ask, little one? That *doesn't* pertain to where we're going?"

I had a million and I wasn't sure where to start. Figuring everything I wanted to know was related to where we were going and how long it would take to get there, I finally shook my head. "No, Master. I don't have any questions."

He chuckled, seemingly amused by me.

"Well, in that case…" Master reached for something on a table beside him.

I watched, noticing he was holding out a stack of papers. I instantly recognized them as the limits I'd originally listed for him.

"While you have a few minutes, you can review your limits, make sure there're no changes. And for those you marked that you needed more information, you'll see that I added notes."

I glanced down at the papers, then back up at him and smiled. "Thank you, Master."

He nodded, then leaned back in his chair and continued to watch me.

When the captain announced that we would be taking off, I leaned back against the leather seat and peeked out the window. I'd been in first class before, but this… There was nothing compared to the extravagance of being on a private jet.

And I had the feeling there would be nothing compared to all that would happen on this private jet once we were at cruising altitude.

•

I was on the last page of the limits, having gone through them twice since takeoff because I wanted to review all those that Master had elaborated on and make the correct selection for me. Considering I was looking at this list through submissive eyes this time, I felt as though my answers were slightly different. Plus, with Master's detailed descriptions—some far more detailed than even I cared to know—I had a better understanding of what I was looking at.

I felt as though I'd grown a little where this lifestyle was concerned. I had learned a lot in the previous weeks I'd spent with them, experienced some, and I felt it was appropriate to consider that as I was reviewing my answers. As I was scanning the last line— which pertained to watersports (still a definite hard limit for me)— a large hand appeared.

"I think you need to take a break."

I looked up, taking a second to realize that Sir was the one standing before me. He had removed his glasses, which was my go-to determining factor. However, I had realized not too long ago that Sir had a small scar on his left eyebrow, which made it easier to determine who was who.

He placed the papers on the table, then took a seat in the chair beside Master again.

"Are you doing all right?" Master asked.

My smile ratcheted up a notch. "Perfectly well."

Master smiled in return and I could see he was pleased by my answer.

"We didn't even ask if you had an aversion to airplanes."

I shook my head. "Not at all. This is the first time I've been on a private plane."

"You like it?"

I giggled. "I love it."

"Still need something to do with your hands?"

I grinned even more. "I wouldn't be opposed to it."

Master glanced at Sir, then gave a slight nod.

"Stand up, pet," Sir instructed.

I unbuckled my seat belt and got to my feet.

Master pointed to the floor between them. "Remove your sweater, then kneel."

With their full attention on me, I removed my sweater, loving the heat that consumed me as their eyes grazed my bare chest. No matter how I felt about my body, they had the power to overrule any body image issues with their heated stares alone. They made me feel beautiful, sexy.

Once I was topless, I knelt on the floor between their legs, resting my butt on my heels while my skirt covered my bottom half.

"Move a little closer," Sir said, his tone slightly raspier than before.

I inched forward, close enough that my breast came into contact with the hand Sir was holding out. He caressed my left breast, cupping it, squeezing gently while Master did the same with the right.

"You have beautiful tits," Sir said, continuing to stroke my nipple with his thumb. Their combined touch scorched me, my nipples hardening into painful points as they teased my flesh.

Master's hand retreated first, then Sir's.

"I want you to cup your breasts," Master instructed.

I did as he commanded, curling my hands around my small breasts while I watched them both intently, awaiting further instruction.

"Squeeze lightly," Master continued, "then pinch your nipples between two fingers and tug."

While I watched them, I did as Master requested. Normally, my breasts weren't that sensitive. However, as with other parts of my body, they were overly sensitive just from being instructed, from having them watch as I followed their orders to the letter. Admittedly, it was a unique feeling, not something I'd ever thought about. The idea of someone being in complete control of my pleasure and theirs left me aching for more.

"Pinch harder," Master stated. "As hard as you can without pushing beyond what you're comfortable with."

That wasn't as easy to do, but I focused my attention, whimpering when I pinched just a little too hard.

"Do you like pain?" Master inquired.

"Some," I admitted, the word rushing out. "More than I thought I did."

To have both men watching me made my insides quiver, my pussy throb. If I wasn't careful, I would come from touching my breasts, something I'd never had happen before.

"You've come a long way in a very short time, pet." Master's voice was pitched low. "We're both impressed with your progress."

"Thank you, Master."

"I like that you don't try to hide from us, that you're willing to trust us."

The former was something I had to consciously work on because my natural instinct was to hide my nudity. But I had learned in the past couple of months that they instructed me to do things that would please them. And that was my main focus.

"Don't stop," Sir snapped when I moaned, my hands slipping.

I instantly returned to teasing my own tits, tugging on my nipples as I tried to ignore the residual ache that was building inside me. I continued for several minutes until I was unknowingly squirming, the need for friction on my clit overwhelming.

"I think she likes touching herself," Master said.

"Do you, sweet girl?" Sir's eyes never left my chest. "Do you enjoy playing with your tits?"

"Only when you're watching me," I admitted around another moan.

"Oh, we're watching," he assured me. "When you're present, it's hard to do anything but watch you."

I was still squirming, my desperation ratcheting up a few degrees. I wanted to feel their hands on me, their mouths.

"Stop," Master barked.

I dropped my hands, my breaths coming rapidly.

"What else do you enjoy doing?" Sir asked as they both freed their cocks from their slacks.

My mouth watered with the need to taste them. "I enjoy…sucking your cocks."

Never in my life had I thought I would be turned on by dirty talk. Not coming from my mouth, anyway. It was one thing for a man to talk like that, something else for me. However, I could tell they enjoyed it, which made me want to do it more.

"We enjoy that as well," Master said, his hand gliding up and down his shaft. "Those sweet lips wrapped around my dick…"

"Give me your hand," Sir insisted.

I offered my left hand. He planted it on his thick cock.

Master took my right hand without giving me instruction and wrapped my fist around his length.

"Stroke us," Master ordered. "Slowly. And don't stop until we tell you."

I started out slow, focusing all my attention on giving them equal pressure, my hands caressing their velvety smooth skin. They hardened even more beneath my ministrations.

Until I had met my bosses, I'd never thought of a cock as being beautiful, but when it came to Master's and Sir's, I could understand the terminology. They were long and deliciously thick with smooth skin and wide, bulbous heads. My body knew exactly what they were intended for and the need for them to fill me was intensifying.

Not wanting to rush, I kept my pace slow, then added a twist on the upstroke, my thumbs grazing the tips, slipping through the pre-cum that pooled there. They were both intently focused on me, which only made the encounter that much hotter.

"Mouth or pussy?" Master asked Sir.

My body stirred as I realized what they were intending.

"Mouth." His eyes met mine. "I want those lips wrapped around my dick, want to feel the tightness of her throat as she swallows me."

"Stand up, pet," Master instructed, getting to his feet.

I stood, then moved directly in front of Sir, who also got up from his seat.

"Put those sweet lips on my cock, Luci. Suck my dick like you crave it."

That wasn't going to be hard to do because I did crave it.

Sir reached for me without hesitation, guiding my head down to his groin, pressing his cock past my lips. Bent at the waist, I sucked him in deep, relishing the taste of him. He smelled like sin and it made my pussy drip. I was on fire, my body desperate for release.

Strong hands toyed with my ass, cupping and kneading after lifting my skirt out of the way.

"Such a perfect little ass," Master groaned from behind me.

He gripped my hips, then answered my silent prayer, guiding his cock into my pussy. He nudged me open with the thick crest, then pushed in deep, pulling me back against him. It was an amazing feeling, his cock brushing greedy nerve endings.

And there I stood, one cock in my mouth, one in my pussy as they filled me.

"Now fuck us both," Sir demanded, his hand resting on my head.

It wasn't as easy as it looked, but I managed to rock forward and back, impaling myself on Master's cock, then taking Sir's between my lips. I had to focus in order to maintain a steady pace.

When Sir grabbed my head, pulling me down on his cock, I opened wide, taking him as deep as I could. Then Master slammed into me, driving Sir's cock deeper into my throat, making me gag.

"No teeth," Sir said, his tone not nearly as demanding.

I made sure to avoid grazing him with my teeth while still trying to bring him as much pleasure as possible. When they took over, I submitted, allowing them to take me roughly. It felt naughty to be fucked on both ends by the sexiest men on the planet and I loved every second.

Sir groaned loudly. "Aww, sweet girl. I'm gonna come down your throat."

I moaned, urging him to do so. I wanted to taste all of him.

Master's hips slowed while Sir's picked up speed. He used my mouth, his cock pulsing in warning. I sucked harder, then swallowed every drop that burst onto my tongue as his cock twitched.

I didn't have a second to get my bearings, because the instant Sir pulled back, Master slammed into me, grabbing my hips and jerking me back onto his cock. Sir dropped down into the chair and placed my hands on the armrest, giving me something to hold on to.

The next thing I knew, I was hovering on the verge of climax, my body being pummeled by Master's rough thrusts.

"May I come, Sir? Master? Please...oh, God! I need to come."

They both answered with a gruff yes and I let the sensations overtake me, my orgasm rippling up from deep in my core.

"Fuck...yes," Master groaned, driving his cock as far as possible as he held me there, pulsing as he came inside me.

I couldn't deny, my induction into the Mile-High Club was not something that I would ever forget. Not if I lived to be two hundred.

FOUR

AFTER OUR IMPROMPTU EROTIC AIRPLANE session, Sir helped me put my sweater back on while Master took care to clean us both. Then they settled me back in my chair and tucked me in with a blanket.

"It'll be a while before we get there, pet. Why don't you rest for a bit?" Master pressed his lips to my forehead, then fixed the blanket once more.

For a few moments, I didn't think I could possibly sleep, but the lull of the plane had me closing my eyes, my body sated, my mind finally at ease. I hadn't given much thought to how tired I was, but due to the fact that I passed out shortly thereafter, I had to assume they had worn me out.

In the best way possible.

I probably could've slept for several more hours if it weren't for Sir waking me before we started our descent to our destination.

"How long did I sleep?" I wiped my eyes and noticed it was dark outside.

"Four hours."

I jerked upright. "Really?"

Master seemed genuinely amused by my reaction. "Really."

Holy shit. Obviously, tired was an understatement. Which was odd, now that I thought about it. Before they'd arrived at my doorstep, I had spent most of the afternoon chilling on the sofa. Then again, I'd spent the morning at the mall.

Rather than dwell on that, my brain latched on to the fact that we had flown for approximately seven hours based on my calculations. I had no idea where that put us, but it could've been almost anywhere in the United States. As for outside of the U.S., I wasn't sure.

As the three of us sat there, I stared out the window into the darkness. There were twinkling lights down below, but not as many as I would've expected had we been over a big city. When I looked up, I noticed they were watching me.

"Can I ask where we are now?" I directed the question at both of them.

"U.S. Virgin Islands," Sir said simply.

Well, there you go.

"Are we going to St. Thomas?" I inquired. I'd never been, but I'd heard a lot about it. A beach holiday. Wow. That would be awesome.

"Private island," Master replied.

Why I was surprised, I wasn't sure. These men obviously had money. And I was pretty sure that the private jet belonged to the company, and quite possibly the island as well. It seemed to make some sense considering what they did.

Not that I really cared. In fact, I would've been happy wherever they took me, just as long as I was spending time with the two of them.

I knew I was getting in over my head, but it was hard not to. After all, they had showed up at my apartment and whisked me away on a private jet to a private island. Somehow, I'd hit the Dom jackpot. I considered myself pretty damn lucky.

We landed without incident, but since it was dark, I couldn't tell where we were or how big the island was. I knew that many of them weren't much more than five to ten acres.

Not that any of that mattered.

We were at our destination and now I was anxious to find out what they had in store for me.

•

Turned out the house on the island was far nicer than anything I would've expected. It was an eclectic mix of rustic and modern. Like the melding of all four of my bosses, which led me to believe that they did in fact all own the place.

"Are you hungry, little one?"

I turned to Master as I gauged my stomach's reaction to the thought of food. It rumbled softly, making me chuckle. Then again, it was late and I hadn't eaten dinner. I'd also bypassed most of my lunch, and popcorn didn't go a long way.

I nodded. "Would you like me to make something?"

"No need. We have a cook who'll handle all of that while we're here. This is a vacation; therefore, you are not to work unless we specifically assign you a task."

I was curious as to what tasks they might assign.

Master spoke to Sir, then disappeared from the room. I took a moment, checking it all out. The living room space was overly large, with vaulted ceilings and two solid walls of windows that I guessed would likely overlook the ocean. I couldn't wait for morning to find out.

The furniture was cozy, nothing pretentious in this place. It all seemed to get some use, which I took to mean they frequented the island.

Sir moved over to the sofa and took a seat. His gaze followed me around the room, but he didn't say anything. That seemed to be their M.O. And I liked that they watched me; it let me know that they had an interest.

When I had satisfied most of my curiosity, I walked toward him.

Sir pointed toward the spot by his feet.

"Kneel."

I nodded, happy that he'd requested for me to do so. It probably seemed unusual to some, but it felt natural to me. After all, it wasn't the first time they'd asked me to kneel.

I knelt by his feet, and Sir put his hand on my head, pulling it toward his thigh. He brushed my hair back from my face and caressed my cheek. Although I had never knelt at anyone's feet until I met Master and Sir, I found something uniquely soothing about the act. Sure, it probably wouldn't be the same if they didn't touch me. However, they did, and through that small interaction, I felt cherished.

"It's late," Sir said softly.

I hadn't checked my phone, but I figured it was close to midnight. And it had been a very long day, both mentally and physically.

"Still tired?" he asked.

"A little." I had no idea why, since I'd taken a long nap.

"We'll have dinner, then hang out in the hot tub for a bit."

I lifted my head. "There's a hot tub?"

Clearly my genuine surprise at all the details was entertaining them to no end.

He chuckled, then gently urged my head back to his knee and continued to pet me. It was a foreign sensation, both soothing and comforting. I found all the tension I'd felt since I left work yesterday afternoon had disappeared entirely. I still couldn't believe that I was here with them.

Master reappeared. "Dinner'll be served on the back patio in five minutes." His eyes dropped to my face. "I expect you naked before you join us. In fact, whenever we're alone here, I expect you to be naked."

"We're alone?" I thought he'd said they had a chef.

"For the most part. So, let me clarify. As long as we don't have guests, I expect you to be naked."

I lifted my head. "Yes, Master."

I hadn't been sure what the dynamic would be with both Master and Sir taking charge. However, it seemed that they worked in tandem, neither of them feeling the need to overrule the other. I wondered if that was something that happened naturally when there were two Doms or if it was merely the way they chose to handle things. I thought about asking, then realized I would save that for later.

"May I freshen up before dinner, Sir?"

"Yes, but come here first."

I crawled into his lap when he tugged on my arm. He pulled me in close, then fused his mouth to mine. The kiss was exploratory, not rushed or frantic. My body reacted all the same, eager to get closer, desperate for his touch.

He cupped my face with his hand, and I melted against him.

When the kiss ended, I pulled back, staring into his eyes. "Thank you, Sir."

I could see the smile in the hazel depths, although there wasn't one on his mouth.

"Go freshen up." He motioned toward the stairs. "Your bedroom is the first one at the top. And remember to strip before you return."

The first thing that caught my attention was the fact that I had my own room. Did that mean I wouldn't be sleeping with either of them? Was that how they handled it when they shared a submissive? The night I'd spent with Master, we had stayed in the guest room. But here they were relegating me to my own room?

I wasn't sure what I thought about that. But I would have to deal with those particular emotions later.

Not wanting to be late and risk punishment, I rushed up the stairs, coming to a stop in the giant bedroom. The king-sized bed with mosquito netting pulled neatly back on all four posts stood in the middle facing one wall that was made up of sliding doors that appeared to retract all the way. I could imagine being in that bed with the warm ocean breeze blowing over my skin...

Shit.

I was wasting time.

Hurrying to the bathroom, I found all my toiletries had been laid out for me. I quickly used the restroom, washed my hands, then brushed my hair. Removing my clothes was becoming second nature; however, I was concerned that there were other people in the house. What would they think if they saw me walking around with my bare ass on display?

"Doesn't matter," I mumbled to myself. That had been Master's instruction and I had no choice but to obey. Because I wanted to. The thought made me smile.

Although I was comfortable with the command, I was still a little hesitant to traipse through the house naked, so I paused at the door and listened. When I heard nothing, I turned the knob and stepped out into the hallway before darting down the stairs. I wandered through the living room and found my way to the back patio.

Sir and Master were standing near a railing that overlooked the water. The moon was bright enough to light up the waves gently crashing against the shore. I noticed they had both changed out of their cold-weather attire and were now wearing shorts, which allowed a delicious view of their muscular calves and their broad backs highlighted with T-shirts.

It was a good look for them here in...

Paradise.

Yep, that's where we were.

Master was the first to turn and his gaze met mine. He smiled, something that he seemed to be doing more of.

"Have a seat, little one," he urged, motioning toward the table before pulling out my chair for me.

"Thank you, Master."

When they joined me, some of my nerves eased up. It helped that I didn't see anyone else milling about.

"Tell us about your mother and your stepfather," Master prompted as we ate.

Although I'd never actually thought I would be having dinner with two Dominants while completely naked on a private beach, I could guarantee, if I had, it definitely wouldn't be when having a discussion about my parents.

I stalled for a few minutes, situating the food on my plate before looking up again, my eyes darting between the two men. My gaze dropped back to my plate and I wiped my mouth with my napkin. "I'm not sure what there is to say."

"I told you she'd say that," Sir said, glancing over at Master.

"Since there's plenty to say," Master said to me, "come up with a better response."

I stared at him.

He lifted one eyebrow, then promptly launched into a question. "You mentioned before that you don't see them often. Are you close to them otherwise?"

I shook my head. "Not really, no. I guess I'm closer to my stepfather than my mom. He's been a part of my life for as long as I can remember. He adopted me when I was six, but it wasn't until I was ten that I actually understood what that meant. At first I'd been excited."

"At first?" Master did not seem pleased by my response.

Sighing, I resigned myself to telling them the rest. "I remembered thinking that it was great that my stepfather wanted me to be his daughter. Or at least that's what I initially thought it meant. My mother not so kindly clarified that it had been for legal reasons only. She was never the type to mince words, nor did she sugarcoat anything. Ever."

Master and Sir glanced at each other briefly.

"Please," I urged. "Don't feel sorry for me. It's not like they were abusive in any way. I simply learned early on that my mother didn't want children. If you looked at it that way, she did the best she could, considering."

"Ben said they went on a cruise for the holidays?" Master said when I didn't say anything more.

Well, that explained a lot about why they'd shown up at my apartment. Apparently, Ben had taken it upon himself to talk to Landon and Langston. I briefly wondered if they did feel sorry for me and that was the reason they'd brought me here.

Apparently reading my mind, Sir reached over and touched my hand. "Don't go making up reasons for why things happen. We invited you here because we wanted to spend time with you, Luci. The information Ben gave us simply spurred us into action faster."

Feeling a little better, I answered honestly. "That's what my mom does. She works hard all year long and doesn't take any time off until the end of the year. Then they tend to travel."

"During Christmas." It wasn't a question.

I nodded anyway.

"And they don't invite you?"

I chuckled, but it held no humor. "No. I'm a grown woman and I can take care of myself." Not wanting to go into depth about the strained relationship with my mother, I attempted to redirect. "What about your parents? Will you be seeing them for Christmas?"

I had no idea how long they intended to be here, but considering Sunday was Christmas Eve, there was a good chance they would be missing the holidays with their parents because of me. I didn't like knowing that.

"We will," Sir confirmed, his eyes locking with mine. "They'll actually be down here tomorrow."

My jaw fell open and I nearly choked on my food. "Here? Like in the house, *here*?"

Master chuckled. "Probably wouldn't be wise to force our mother to sleep on the beach."

No, probably not. However, this was not good news. Not for me, at least. I wasn't sure how I was supposed to act around their mother. Would she approve of me? Did she understand their lifestyle? Could I merely hide in my room for the duration?

"She's thinking too much," Sir told Master in a mock whisper.

I couldn't stop staring, stunned to the roots of my hair by this news.

"Ask a question, pet," Sir ordered.

"Does your mother... Does she know about your lifestyle?"

Master chuckled, picking up his drink. "I'd hope so. Considering our father's her Dom."

My eyes were as round as saucers. "Really?"

"Well, technically, he prefers to be called her master," Sir clarified.

My jaw practically unhinged.

"What?" Sir said with a chuckle. "Did you think that generations before ours were strictly vanilla?"

Well...actually, I *had* thought that. Maybe not outwardly so, but it had been an assumption. Clearly, an ill-conceived one.

"Don't worry, pet," Master said, his tone soothing. "You'll enjoy the company of my parents and they won't make you feel awkward."

"Will I be naked?"

Sir smirked. "Of course not."

Well, that was a relief.

However, my thoughts took on a life of their own. I could picture their *mother* wandering around naked, which would be uber-creepy and wrong on so many levels. How had they grown up in a house like that? I'd never given it much thought, but now that I had, I was a little creeped out by the idea.

Sir exhaled loudly as he leaned forward. "Look at me, Luci."

My gaze shot up to his face.

"Our parents will arrive tomorrow. They'll be here for two days. We'll have a regular dinner. Then, we're having a party on Christmas Day. No, it's not the traditional holiday gathering, but I guarantee you'll enjoy it. We'll have a number of guests arrive that morning and they'll be leaving that night." He grinned. "While our parents are here, we'll keep it very vanilla, if you will. And they'll leave before the dirty stuff takes place on Monday."

I nodded, trying to make sense of it all.

"Do they…?" I grabbed my glass and took a gulp of water. "Do they know that I'm here?"

"They do. We've told them about you."

That warmed me. It was unexpected and it eased some of my tension.

Master pointed at my plate with his fork. "Now finish your dinner. We'll soak in the hot tub, then get a good night's sleep. The next couple of days will be the same mundane stuff that most families enjoy on Christmas. And then on Monday, we've got some interesting things planned for you."

"BDSM things?" I asked.

"Well, of course." Master chuckled. "After all, testing your limits is something we enjoy."

Grabbing my fork, I focused my attention on my food as I tried to wrap my head around it all. Testing my limits seemed tame compared to having to spend the next two days with their parents. What if they didn't like me? What if they thought I was all wrong for their sons?

What if…what if…what if…

It was all too much.

FIVE

FOR WHATEVER REASON—WHETHER BECAUSE they knew I was having some reservations or simply because that was how they intended it—I slept alone last night.

After spending an hour in the hot tub, Master took me to my room, then tucked me into bed. Sir came in a short time later and kissed me good-night. And it wasn't one of those platonic kisses either. The room definitely heated a few degrees.

But then they both left.

And I was alone.

At first, I was disappointed because the thought of sleeping between them was something I'd pondered for quite some time.

Unfortunately, that hadn't happened.

For some strange reason, it didn't bother me as much as I thought it would. Simply knowing they were in the same house was enough for now. However, now that the sun was rising and I was alone, I *felt* alone. I didn't know what to do, where to go, what to say, so I remained in the bed, staring out at the brilliant blue water that seemed to go on endlessly.

It wasn't until Master came in that I stretched and turned, smiling up at him.

"Good morning, pet."

"Good morning, Master."

To my surprise, he crawled, fully dressed, into bed with me. It was a move I never would've thought him capable of. The man was always so proper, so well put together. Gone was the hot tub attire from last night. Instead, Master was sporting a pair of black linen pants and a lightweight white shirt. It just seemed off that he would willingly wrinkle his clothes to be next to me.

But pleasant at the same time.

He pulled me against him, wrapping his arms around my naked body and pressing his lips against my neck. I inhaled his sexy scent, relaxing into his hold.

"Our parents'll be here shortly."

I stiffened as soon as the words registered.

He chuckled. "Considering it's already ten in the morning, it's not that early for company."

Company, no. But his parents weren't company, they were…his parents. Crap.

"Talk to me," Master urged.

I sighed, then rolled onto my back and stared at the ceiling, enjoying the warmth of Master's arms around me.

"What if they don't like me?"

Master chuckled and as always it surprised me to hear it. He was the man who rarely smiled and didn't laugh all that much. Although, now that I thought about it, Master had changed somewhat in the few months I'd known him. He wasn't quite so…pretentious. At least some of the time, anyway.

"My mother is like any other mom, pet. Only, she has a broader viewpoint than some. You'll find that a lot of people in this lifestyle are less judgmental overall."

"So, you don't think I have anything to worry about?"

He kissed my neck again. "No. I don't. She's gonna like you. What's not to like? You're smart, beautiful, and you know how to make people feel welcome."

Wow. I hadn't expected those compliments. But I would take them.

"However, there is something you should know."

Of *course* there was.

The way he said that had the hair on the back of my neck standing on end. I turned my head so I could see his face.

"My mother is more than a sexual submissive. She doesn't merely offer sexual submission to her Master, she gives up total control," he explained. "Do you know what that means?"

"She's a slave?" I knew there was a difference between a Dominant/submissive and a Master/slave relationship, but I didn't truly grasp everything that it encompassed.

"In the realm of BDSM, yes." Master nodded. "My father was an experienced Dominant when he met my mother more than forty years ago. They hit it off right away." He kissed my nose. "I'll let her tell you the story, but I want you to have the opportunity to see a rare dynamic between a Master and a slave. Their love is their greatest bond and her submission is what fuels them both."

"Master, what's the real difference between a slave and a submissive?" I'd read so much and some of it I understood, some of it I didn't. One thing I'd noticed, there were a lot of people who attempted to define this lifestyle, a lot of them having never experienced it for themselves.

"A submissive willingly gives up control. Sometimes only in the bedroom or during a scene, sometimes more often, but they generally have limits and they're involved with negotiations with their Dom. A slave gives up total control and with this, they empower their Dom to make all the decisions, often without negotiations or limits."

Oddly enough, I was now anxious to meet them, to witness the relationship they shared. From what I'd read online and the groups I'd explored, I knew I did not want to be a slave. I needed the opportunity to make my own decisions about certain aspects of my life. Plus, the idea of not having limits was not appealing to me in the least. I knew for a fact there were things I was not willing to do, no matter what.

Not that I would judge another person for what they needed, because it wasn't my place. I just hadn't had the opportunity to see a real-life Master/slave relationship.

Master shifted on the bed. "Now, I'll give you two options this morning."

Needing his dominance, I turned to face him.

"You can either suck my cock, allowing me to come down that tight little throat, or you can let me eat your pussy until you flood my mouth."

My breaths slammed roughly in my chest, the raunchiness of his words enough to make me forget about everything else except my master's pleasure.

"I'd like to do what pleases you."

He nodded and got to his feet.

"Turn over onto your back."

I rolled onto my back as he pulled the blankets off the bed.

"Pull your knees against your chest, then spread them wide and hold them open for me. I want to admire your pretty pussy before we begin."

I was instantly wet, my arousal fueled by his dirty words and his dominance.

I got into position, which put my pussy on display for him. He stood at the end of the bed, simply staring between my legs. Although it turned me on, I also felt a modicum of modesty. I had to fight the urge to cover myself.

"You have a beautiful pussy, little one. Don't ever feel the need to cover it. It pleases me to see those puffy lips and soft, pink center."

His praise melted me.

He proceeded to remove his shirt as he spoke. "Mostly, it pleases me to see you wet and eager for my mouth."

Well, he was getting that in spades.

My attention drifted to the hard planes and angles of his chest. My fingers itched to touch, but I didn't dare move, not wanting to break the spell. I wasn't sure if this was the prelude to a sexy blow job or if he was going to feast on me. Either way, I was enjoying it.

When he started moving toward me, my legs trembled. And when his knee rested on the bed, my blood surged in my veins. My pussy was so wet I could feel the trickle of my juices. I craved his tongue on my clit, but I kept that to myself.

"I'm gonna feast on you for a while. Only when you think I've had my fill are you allowed to come."

Oh, crap. That seemed like a tall order. How in the world would I know when he was ready for me to come?

The warmth of his breath fanned the eager place between my legs, and I inhaled deeply, trying to prepare myself for the pleasure of his wicked mouth. Master took one long lick between my legs, pulling a moan from me. The soft rasp of his tongue was heaven.

He took his time, licking and nipping, not giving any attention to my clit whatsoever. It allowed my arousal to slowly build. When Master's tongue finally flicked my clit, I jerked and twitched, the powerful sensation making my insides quiver. The more he did that, the more time he spent tormenting my clit, the harder it became to hold back. I couldn't tell if he was ready for me to come, and I wanted to please him. Considering the overwhelming pleasure he was gifting me with, I felt it was only fair.

Master's hands pressed down on the insides of my thighs, forcing me open even more as he pressed his mouth fully between my legs, his lips suckling my clit. Unable to move, I couldn't stop the pressure from building inside me.

"Oh, God!" An electric current of energy shot from my clit to my womb, then radiated out in all directions as I came hard and fast.

When Master lifted his head and licked his lips, he looked pleased.

"Thank you, Master," I said on a rush of air. "That was…amazing."

"My pleasure, pet. My absolute pleasure."

•

Per Master's instructions, I showered, then did my hair and makeup. He had mentioned laying my clothes out, so I donned a towel while I did all of that, then went into the bedroom to see what he had selected for me. Knowing I was going to meet their mother and father, I was curious as to what he considered appropriate for that encounter.

I smiled to myself when I saw the short, flirty black skirt and the sexy off-white sweater. Well, it wasn't really a sweater because it was so lightweight, but it was cute. I knew instantly that these hadn't come from my wardrobe, but they obviously knew me well.

The ensemble lacked a bra and panties, which I hadn't really expected. However, there was a teeny tiny black and white bikini, which made me giddy. There also weren't any shoes, but this was an island and there was a beach, so I was hoping this meant I would get to feel some sand between my toes.

After pulling on the outfit, I took a quick look at myself in the mirror. I liked what I saw. Not merely in the physical sense either. These past few months had taught me some things about myself and I believed my confidence level was growing, which allowed me to accept some of my flaws while focusing more on my strengths.

I owed my four bosses for that, I knew.

Realizing I couldn't stay in my room forever, I took a deep breath and ventured downstairs. I could hear people talking down below and I hesitated halfway down.

"Come down here, pet," Sir ordered.

His command made me smile. It also made me feel as though I'd been caught with my hand in the cookie jar.

Straightening my posture, I continued down the stairs, hoping to appear graceful. When I got to the bottom, all sense of decorum shot right out the window when I saw the man and woman sitting on the sofa in the living room.

The man was a spitting image of Master and Sir, only older with a head full of salt-and-pepper hair. The woman was likely the most stunning woman I'd ever seen. She had dark brown hair that was an inverted bob, longer in the front, shorter in the back. She didn't look a day over forty at best, but based on my calculations, she had to be close to sixty and that was if they'd gotten together when she was twenty.

"Over here, sweet girl," Sir instructed. "I'd like to introduce you to our parents, Melanie and Jeremy Moore."

I had absolutely no idea how I was supposed to handle myself in front of these people. Master had informed me that their father was a Dom. Did that mean I was supposed to bow to him? Avert my gaze?

"The first rule of a good submissive is to be polite to your guests," Master said, coming up behind me.

I squeaked, surprised by his appearance.

He chuckled and took my hand. "Mom, Dad, this is Luciana Wagner. Pet, meet our parents."

Be polite to your guests.

For some reason, that comment broke me from my stupor and I realized that Mr. and Mrs. Moore were no different than me in the fact that they were humans and I was to treat them with the general respect I treated everyone with.

Mrs. Moore glanced over at her husband. I noticed his subtle nod before she placed her hand softly on his thigh. It seemed like a thank you gesture to me. Once she stood, she moved over to me with a beaming smile on her beautiful face.

"It's wonderful to meet you, Luciana." She leaned in and hugged me.

She was tall, quite a few inches taller than me, in fact.

"Oh, please call me Luci," I muttered, enjoying the warmth of her embrace. It was such a motherly thing to do and I felt a hint of longing, wishing my own mother treated me as kindly. I couldn't remember the last time my mother had hugged me.

When Mrs. Moore pulled back, she fluffed a long strand of my hair and smiled. "She's as beautiful as y'all said she was."

She had the same twang as her sons.

I felt myself blush. "Thank you, Mrs. Moore."

"Please call me Mel."

Smiling, I nodded.

"Come over here, Luci."

My eyes widened at the gruff command coming from Mr. Moore. He was in full Dom mode. Or perhaps that was the setting he was always on. It made sense, considering what I knew about Master and Sir. Although Sir was a little more laid-back at times, Master was always on, always in command.

"Yes, sir," I said, trying to keep some level of confidence in my tone.

I stopped in front of him, unsure what to do.

Mr. Moore seemed amused. His gaze shot over to his sons. "She's a wild one, huh?"

"That she is," Master agreed.

I frowned. I had no idea what that meant.

"A wild one refers to an untrained submissive," Melanie explained.

Oh. That didn't sound good.

Melanie chuckled. "It's not a bad thing, sweetheart. We all have to start from somewhere. And honestly, I believe that every Dom must experience a wild one before he can consider himself ready to be a full-time master. They will learn as much from you as you from them."

"My kitten is quite wise," Mr. Moore said, grinning.

He got to his feet and I found myself looking straight up into intense hazel eyes that reminded me so much of Master and Sir.

"It's a pleasure to meet you, girl," Mr. Moore said.

"The pleasure is mine, Mr. Moore," I choked out.

"Please, you may call me Jeremy."

That felt strange to me. As though I wasn't giving him the respect he deserved. He must've noticed my reservations because he tilted my head back by pinching my chin, then studied my face momentarily.

"You'll need to work on merging your vanilla world with this one, girl. We're not as formal as you may think." His eyes shot to his sons. "However, it's always a Dom's preference as to what they would like to be called."

I nodded.

"So, today, you'll refer to me as Jeremy and should you ever see me in a non-vanilla setting, you can refer to me as King."

I swallowed hard. "Yes, s—Jeremy."

"Come here and relax, pet," Sir commanded.

It broke me out of my spell and I moved toward the couch. He motioned for me to sit between him and Master. Again, I felt a little uneasy.

"Sweet girl?" Sir prodded. "Is there a problem?"

I swallowed down the anxiety and forced a smile. "Sir, would you mind if I...knelt at your feet?"

It might've sounded strange, and I hoped it didn't bother Mel and Jeremy, but I was more comfortable there. I didn't know why and I was sure it wouldn't always be allowed, but I needed it to calm my nerves.

Both Master and Sir shifted their legs, leaving room for me to kneel between them.

Only then, when I was situated at their feet, did I feel the tension ease from my shoulders. What might've seemed weird to others was quite comforting for me.

Like coming home.

SIX

"THE BOYS TOLD ME YOU did a phenomenal job on their quarterly meeting," Mel prompted as we were lying on towels down near the water.

"I enjoyed it," I told her with a grin. It made me feel good to know that Master and Sir had really spoken to their parents about me. "It was a challenge, but I think it went fairly well."

Mel chuckled. "Well, I can tell you, those boys complain about that meeting every time it comes around. They never know what to do to keep everyone happy."

I peered over at her, shielding my eyes with my hand. "I'm not sure it's possible to keep everyone happy." I looked up at the sky. "I went into it wanting to do what was best for my bosses. They work hard and the people who work for them admire them for what they've built. I wanted everyone to get a chance to see that, to get some face time with them." I glanced her way again. "What is it that you do?"

Her smile was huge. "I'm a lawyer."

I turned onto my side. "A lawyer? Really?"

"Really."

"Do you have any partners?" I knew very little about law firms, but I remembered the guy from my yoga class mentioning he was going to be a junior partner.

"There are only two of us," she said. "King and I branched off years ago, opening our own firm."

Wait.

"You and King are…both lawyers?"

She smiled. "I can see that brain of yours working," she teased. "And yes, I know what you're thinkin'. I'm his slave, how could I possibly be a partner in a law firm?"

"I…uh…" God, it sounded so shitty when I thought about it, but Mel was right, that was what I was thinking.

"Don't worry, honey. I'm not offended. We live a lifestyle that not many people understand. By day, I'm an independent woman who takes care of my clients, and at night, I take care of my Master."

I swallowed hard. "I didn't mean… I'm sorry." Sighing, I rolled onto my back on my towel. "I have so much to learn."

"I think you'd be surprised by what you've learned so far. Do you want to know the last time my boys introduced me to one of their submissives?"

No, actually, I really didn't.

"Never," Mel answered.

I turned my head again. "Really?"

"Really. Luci, I know you're new and you don't understand a lot about this lifestyle you're interested in, but you should know that you don't have to be up-to-date on all the terminology or what's trending right now. You're doing it right by being true to yourself. You're a natural submissive."

"Is it obvious?"

She chuckled. "It is. And that's not a bad thing. In fact, that's what a true Dominant wants. He's not looking for a woman he can mold and shape and train. He wants a woman who's open to exploring her desires, a woman who's eager to please. You can train anyone to be a submissive, but she's not going to succeed if it isn't what her heart wants.

"More importantly, a Dominant wants a woman he can see himself spending his life with. What most people don't understand is that you can't simply handpick someone to be your Dominant or your submissive. There is no list to choose from. You don't get to walk into the hardware store and point at a person and say, 'You're mine.' It doesn't work that way. As in any relationship, you have to find someone you're compatible with. Someone you find appealing, who you can hold conversations with, laugh with."

Mel smiled over at me. "You have to determine what it is that *you* want. Not what someone else wants you to be."

"I never thought I was submissive," I admitted, staring up at the clear blue sky once again. "Honestly, it's not something I ever thought about, period. Until I went to work for the firm, I didn't have a clue there was an entire lifestyle dedicated to this."

"They introduced you slowly," Mel stated knowingly.

I had no idea how much she knew about my relationship with my four bosses and I didn't feel comfortable talking to her about it, but I could tell she understood.

"They did," I confirmed. "And it was so natural I didn't think anything of it."

"Is this what you want?" she inquired.

"To be a submissive?" I asked, wanting to make sure we were on the same page.

"Yes."

"It is."

Regardless of how things turned out with my bosses, I knew without a doubt that I was submissive and this was something I wanted to pursue.

•

That evening, Master and Sir surprised me with a huge artificial Christmas tree that they brought in from God only knew where. It looked brand new and I figured it likely was because what were the odds that they spent Christmas on an island every year?

"Go on, girl," King prompted. "It won't put itself together."

I felt like a little kid finally getting the opportunity to put up the tree. My mother didn't have a tree in her house. I couldn't remember a single Christmas decoration growing up. I would stare out my bedroom window, admiring the lights on all the neighbors' houses, wishing that we had some of our own.

Getting to my feet, I felt a little self-conscious as I opened the box and stared at all of the greenery that was smashed inside.

Master and Sir both chuckled and I looked up to see that they were watching me. It was clear I had no idea what I was doing, but I was bound and determined to give it my best shot.

Half an hour later, I had managed to drag all the pieces out of the box. It hadn't been easy because it was one of those trees that only had a few sections. They would all be pieced together to make one tall tree and the lights were already attached.

According to the box, it should've been easy, but it wasn't.

"All right, boys," King said gruffly. "Stop makin' the poor girl work so hard. Get on up there and help her."

Master and Sir joined me, and within minutes, they had it put together. It had to have been at least twelve feet tall and I laughed when I saw the monstrosity that filled a good portion of the living room. No way would I have been able to do that myself.

"Your turn," Master said, cupping my face and kissing my lips. "All that greenery has to be fluffed."

My eyes widened as I stared over at the tree. That was going to take hours.

•

By the time dinner was ready, I'd managed to get at least half the tree to look relatively decent. Mel had helped, which made it all the more embarrassing. Clearly, we weren't cut out for this sort of thing.

"Come on, ladies," King called out. "That's enough for one day."

Mel and I washed up in the kitchen, then joined the men on the back patio. Dinner consisted of pot roast with potatoes, carrots, and baby onions, along with honey cornbread. I had to wonder if the chef was responsible for this, or if it was a dish that Mel had made. It wasn't something I'd ever tried, but it smelled heavenly.

The conversation revolved mostly around Laura, Master and Sir's sister, as well as Laura's four kids. Apparently, once Mel and King left the island on Christmas Day, they would be flying to Kentucky to spend the rest of the week with them.

After the food was consumed, I offered to help Mel clean up the kitchen and we worked diligently to get it all taken care of. Shortly thereafter, King retired to the bedroom with Mel in tow, leaving me alone with Master and Sir.

For a few minutes, we sat on the sofa and stared at the Christmas tree.

"It looks terrible, huh?" I asked, smiling to myself.

"It's definitely not gonna win any awards," Sir confirmed.

"I only have a small tabletop tree at my apartment," I admitted. "And I only bought that when I was at the mall yesterday." Had it really only been yesterday? It felt as though it'd been a month since then.

No one said anything for the longest time, and finally, Sir got to his feet and held out his hand to me.

"Come on, let's get you up to bed."

Getting to my feet, I allowed Sir to lead me up the stairs while Master followed us. Once in the bedroom, Master closed the door while Sir opened the balcony doors, letting in the warm breeze coming off the ocean.

I had no idea what to expect, but when Master and Sir came over and sandwiched me between them, I knew it was going to be a good night.

Surprisingly, they didn't ask me to strip; instead, they handled that part themselves. While their mouths trailed warmth all over my neck and shoulders, they easily removed my clothes, along with their own. I could do nothing more than hold on to them, basking in the warmth of their skin against mine.

There were no commands issued, yet they dominated my every move, positioning me how they wanted me as they kissed and licked every inch of my body. I took the rare opportunity to touch them, my hands roaming, seeking. Every now and then, I would elicit a moan from one or both of them.

"Come here, sweetness," Sir urged, pulling me on top of him.

Within seconds, he was seated deep inside me, his mouth brushing mine. I kissed him like a woman starved. This was what I needed, being with both of them at the same time. Although I enjoyed them separately, it was this moment when I knew I was complete. It felt right to me, as though I was exactly where I belonged.

While I rocked my hips, Sir's thick cock lodged deep inside my pussy, Master moved behind me. I knew what they were going to do and I welcomed it. I wanted to feel them both at the same time. Especially like this. They weren't in a rush, didn't seem to be desperate to make me lose my mind. We were simply three people existing in that moment.

Several minutes later, Master's cock was tunneling deep inside my ass. I groaned as the pain lanced me. They were patient, taking their time as they filled me to capacity.

My heart squeezed in my chest. There was something different about them tonight. This wasn't merely domination and submission. This was…more.

"Sit up," Sir instructed, urging my chest off of his.

I couldn't move far because I was sandwiched between them, but I did as he requested.

"Put your hands behind your back, pet," Master commanded.

He then took my wrists in his hand and held me there, effectively restraining me with my arms behind me.

Sir cupped my breasts in his big hands, holding me up as they began to thrust into me, picking up their speed, rocking me between them.

I moaned in earnest, loving the way they handled me.

"You're beautiful, Luci," Sir whispered, his eyes locked with mine.

Master's lips pressed against my neck. "So fucking beautiful," he echoed.

And then they were fucking me, driving in deep, retreating. They had a rhythm of their own and it was perfect. As though the three of us were made for each other. It didn't take long before they detonated my orgasm, sending me flying higher and higher as they continued to impale me over and over.

"Another," Sir insisted. "Come for us again."

I was so lost in the sensation, I didn't think it was possible, but they didn't let up. I was inherently aware of the way Master gripped my wrists tightly, pulling me closer to him as he slammed into my ass, while Sir firmly kneaded my tits, squeezing and pinching my nipples.

"Come for us," Master growled. "Right now."

As though they had a finger on the button, another orgasm rocketed through me, making the hair on my body stand on end. It was exquisitely brutal, slamming through me at the same time they both stilled. Our combined grunts and groans echoed in the space as they came with me, filling me at the same time.

As I drifted off to sleep a short time later, wrapped securely in their arms, I knew without a doubt that I was falling in love with these two men.

Sure, I was probably a glutton for punishment, because I knew that my love was not what they were seeking, but it didn't matter.

It was no longer my choice.

I was giving it to them freely.

Expecting nothing in return.

SEVEN

THE NEXT DAY, I WOKE up in the arms of the two men I'd fallen asleep with.

I was surprised to find them still in bed, but I was thankful all the same. While they slept, I watched them, admiring their beauty and the peace they obviously found in sleep.

They must've sensed me watching, because it wasn't long before they were both awake, using their fingers to drive me right over the edge as a form of punishment for waking before they did. If that was how they were going to handle things, I vowed to always wake up before them.

The rest of the day was spent outside. Master took me for a walk on the beach after lunch. Then Sir spent a couple of hours with me down by the water. I enjoyed spending time with them separately, knowing that the other was nearby. And surprisingly, it hadn't been awkward having their parents there with us. In fact, Melanie and I spent plenty of time chatting.

All in all, it was one of the best Christmas Eves I could remember having.

Later that evening, I ended up stuffing myself full of a traditional Christmas dinner complete with turkey, dressing, cranberry sauce, green bean casserole, and even pecan pie. Whoever was responsible for the meal had done a fabulous job. I couldn't remember the last time I'd had such fantastic food on any given holiday. Like I'd said, my mother wasn't into the festivities, but this helped to make it feel more like a holiday for me.

After dinner, Melanie and I were dismissed to the living room, where she regaled me with tales of her boys when they were younger. She mentioned that Master had always been the more serious one, taking after his father. And Sir was very similar to her in regard to their sense of humor.

It was interesting because I saw so much of both Master and Sir in their parents. They were a perfect blend of both. And despite the fact that I'd been ridiculously nervous, the weekend had turned out to be much better than I'd thought it would. Then again, that was partially due to the fact that I got to spend so much time feeling as though I had a family. No, I wasn't getting too wrapped up in it, being mindful of the fact that it was only temporary, but I did allow myself time to enjoy.

If it were up to me, I would never leave this place or these people.

"Oh, my goodness," Melanie said, her hand going to her heart. "I remember the first time Langston found one of King's paddles…" She chuckled softly. "My stern little boy hadn't been happy about it, accusing King of being mean to me."

I grinned. "How old was he?"

"Four." She giggled. "He had no idea what it even was, but King sat him down and informed him that sometimes people did things that required them to be disciplined." She waved her hand dismissively. "We never used corporal punishment on any of the kids, so he had no clue what King was talking about."

"So, was it…difficult raising children while living as Master and slave?"

Melanie beamed. "As with anything in life, if you want something, there's always going to be compromise. Sure, when our daughter was born, we had to change some of the things we did when it came to play. We could no longer have parties at the house because we didn't want her to stumble upon something she was too young to see. Instead, we started spending our date nights at the club when it was possible. So, when the boys came along, we'd already adjusted quite well."

"But you live the life twenty-four seven, correct?"

"I do. I've willingly given my master complete and total control over me, including my decisions."

Except when it came to work, I knew. She was a truly independent woman in that regard.

I frowned. I was sure Mel had encountered many people who couldn't grasp the idea of what it meant to be so totally devoted to someone else. When I thought about those who had been cruelly enslaved—not by choice—I couldn't help but shudder. The hell they had endured was not something anyone should ever face. Granted, I knew the kink world had a different definition, but still.

"The key there, honey, is I was willing. I wasn't forced. It was a choice and one that I thought long and hard about. In the end, it was necessary for me to be happy."

Some of it I understood, sure. I mean, I was willingly offering up my body and my trust to these men, believing wholeheartedly that they would care for me and keep me safe.

Melanie smiled. "And I'm sure all three of our kids realized early on that I wasn't like other mothers out there. But I was *their* mother and they knew that King and I loved them unconditionally. I expected they would ask questions eventually."

"Did they?"

"Of course. And we explained it to them the best we could using terms they would understand. I think our daughter realized, but chose to pretend otherwise. I think she was embarrassed by our choices. Then, when the boys were teenagers, they started to figure things out on their own, knew that their parents were definitely different from their friends' parents. So, when they turned fifteen, King sat them down and explained everything."

Oh, God. I could only imagine what I would've done if my parents had shared that sort of information with me. As it was, I did not want to think about my mom and Jim having... Yeah. I didn't want to think about it.

"One thing to understand, Luci, is that communication is the most important part of a relationship. Whether it's in the vanilla world, D/s, or M/s. It doesn't matter. Without communication, you have nothing. We felt it was important for the boys to know so they could make their own decisions."

"Were you surprised when you found out they'd taken after King?"

She smiled widely. "No. Not at all. And I feel as though they're better Doms than King was at their age."

"Because they had him as a mentor?"

"Precisely."

I was curious about Master's and Sir's take on growing up in a household like that. I bet it was interesting.

"Kitten. Girl."

I looked up at the sound of King's booming voice. I found it oddly endearing that he'd given me the pet name *girl* and had used it whenever he spoke to me.

"I think it's time for this old man to hit the hay," King announced when he joined us in the living room.

Melanie reached over and squeezed my hand. "Looks like I'm being summoned."

"Thank you for today and yesterday, Mel. It's been a pleasure meeting you. And thank you for sharing your stories with me."

"Oh, honey, the pleasure's all mine. I'll see you in the morning. King and I will be around before the others arrive, but then we'll be heading back. As much fun as those things are, there's only so much a mother can do when her sons are in the same place."

I giggled, understanding completely.

I got up and hugged her. "Good night."

"Good night, honey."

I watched as Melanie walked into King's arms before retreating to the downstairs bedroom at the back of the house.

Easing back onto the sofa, I stared at the space they had occupied. I couldn't remember a time I'd had so much fun simply talking to someone. I secretly wished my mother and I could have conversations like that. Well, maybe not *exactly* like that. Unfortunately, my mother was too opinionated and I'd become too standoffish for that to ever happen.

Something else I'd enjoyed about the last two days was seeing how people who were immersed deeply within the lifestyle interacted. It was no different than in the vanilla world. Mostly. There was the fact that Mel asked permission or King gave it freely before she did just about anything. It seemed she needed his direction in order to be content. And he didn't seem to mind giving it. But for the most part, they were normal, everyday people.

I wasn't sure how my expectations had been skewed or why I thought it would be drastically different, but I had.

It was definitely easier to relax when your expectations were set. Knowing that Master and Sir would command me in the event they wanted something specific, my only responsibility, as in any relationship, was to be attentive to them.

"What's on your mind, pet?" Master asked when he joined me in the living room.

I smiled up at him. "Just thinking how great today was."

"It was nice, wasn't it?"

"Absolutely. Your parents are wonderful. It was an honor to meet them."

"Funny, my mother said the same about you."

He took a seat beside me, balancing his drink on his knee.

"Can I ask you a question?"

Master nodded.

"Was it weird growing up in a house knowing that your parents were in a…nontraditional relationship?"

He stared at the tree. "Until I was a teenager, I didn't recognize there was really a difference. They were my parents and I wasn't familiar with things being done any other way."

Well, that made sense. "But once King told you?"

He smiled. "Sure, it was weird. I don't think there's a kid out there who wants to know what their parents do in the bedroom. Hell, I still don't want to know." Master chuckled. "However, my father laid it out for us in technical terms and he managed to relay the information in a way that didn't make us uncomfortable. Not too much anyway."

"Did you know you wanted to be like your dad in that regard?"

Master shook his head. "It made sense to me as I got older. But it wasn't something I questioned."

"So, did you look to him for answers?"

"On some things, sure. I was able to get information from him on discipline and such."

So, they really did use King as a mentor.

We sat like that for several minutes before Master got to his feet. He held out his hand and I instantly took it, allowing him to help me up. He led me out to the balcony that overlooked the water. Sir joined us a few minutes later.

Both men set their drinks on a small table near the cushioned chairs, then turned to face me.

I swallowed hard, seeing the intent in their eyes. Whatever they were thinking was likely going to result in me being naked and probably enjoying an orgasm or two.

"Slowly remove the top," Sir instructed, referring to the bikini top I'd kept on when we returned from the beach, with a skirt over the bottoms. "As though you're unwrapping a gift just for us."

I would never tire of him saying things like that. The command in his tone alone was enough to have my heart rate increasing and my thighs trembling.

I leaned my back against the railing, then reached behind my head and untied the string. Rather than free my breasts instantly, I slowly ran my fingers over my shoulders, down my chest, keeping the ties firmly in my hands. When the fabric dipped just below my nipples, I lifted it slightly, watching them as I did. I could tell they were enjoying the show, so I revealed one breast, allowing my fingers to play over my nipple, making it pebble. I then did the same with the other before reaching behind my back and releasing the bottom clasp.

Neither man moved and I waited with bated breath for what they instructed me to do next.

EIGHT

I COULD FEEL MY ANTICIPATION growing as my two masters stared back at me, heat making their hazel eyes sparkle.

"Now the bottoms, but not the skirt," Master instructed, his voice slightly rougher than before. "I want you to turn around and show us your pretty pink pussy as you lower them down your legs."

I'd never performed a strip tease for anyone, but I was definitely enjoying this. It was a rush to know that they desired me, that they found my body appealing.

Turning away, I spread my legs apart, then lifted my skirt in a flirtatious move as I glanced back at them over my shoulder. Feeling goose bumps rise on my skin from the heat I saw in their eyes, I slowly closed my legs, pushing the bikini bottoms down as I remained bent over so they could still see my most private parts, then shimmied out of them. After discarding the bottoms, I spread my legs farther apart and shook my ass playfully.

A solid smack landed on my ass, making me squeal.

"Now the skirt," Master commanded.

I did the same, teasing them as I went, feeling my pussy getting wetter by the second.

Once I discarded the skirt, Master patted the railing. "Get that cute little ass up here."

A frisson of fear shot into my bloodstream when I peered over the side of the railing.

"We won't let you fall," he assured me.

There was only a second of trepidation before I accepted that I trusted them. I knew they wouldn't endanger me. Plus, it wasn't like it was *that far* of a drop. Maybe eight feet. Into sand. Surely I wouldn't break a bone if—

"Up. Now," Master barked softly.

I jumped, then scurried to hop up onto the railing, noticing that Sir was heading into the house.

"On your stomach."

With Master's help, I managed to lay myself out flat on the railing. It was probably a good eight inches wide, maybe more, so it wasn't like I was balancing precariously on it.

"Put your hands on this rail." He guided my hands down, waiting until I had wrapped my fists around one of the decorative wood rails that ran vertically from the bottom rail to the top.

I felt a measure of relief when he didn't take his hands off me. He slid them down my back, holding me still without applying too much pressure. When he got down to my legs, his warm hands curled around my ankles.

I heard footsteps, but I didn't look up, not wanting to chance falling to the ground. I assumed Sir had returned.

His legs appeared in my line of sight.

"Do you know what this is?" Sir asked, holding something in his hand.

It was long and thin with a flattened end. "A miniature paddle on a stick?"

"It's a crop."

Looked like a miniature paddle on a stick to me.

He moved and I felt the coolness of leather as it slid down between my shoulder blades, then farther down my spine before caressing each of my ass cheeks. I was trembling with anticipation. It was the not knowing that got me. I wasn't sure if he was going to spank me with that thing or if he was simply going to caress me until I couldn't take any more.

A second later, I found out his intentions.

Smack.

My body jerked from the stinging impact and I squealed, squeezing my hands tighter around the railing to keep from falling. I could feel the firm grip of Master's hands on my ankles.

"Be very still, pet."

I gave Sir a jerky nod.

Smack.

Another squeak escaped me as my body lurched again.

Warm hands slid between my thighs, inching higher before teasing my lower lips. The stinging on my butt cheeks dissipated as the sensual caress became my focus.

"Her ass turns a pretty shade of pink," Master said absently. "Let's see how red we can get it."

The crop moved over my left thigh, then my right before grazing my ass again.

Smack.

"Oooh!" I didn't mean for that to come out as a moan, but it did.

"Color, pet?" Sir asked.

"Green," I said without hesitation.

"Good girl."

Warmth infused me at his approval.

Smack.

I twitched again but kept my hands firmly on the rail as the pain exploded on my right butt cheek.

Smack.

Then the left, this time a little harder than before.

Sir's hand traveled between my legs again, teasing me briefly.

"Very nice, pet. I like to feel your pussy dripping on my fingers."

I wasn't sure how it was even possible, but Sir was right. My pussy was wet and growing more so by the second. Between lying out on the railing naked with Master's warm hands on my legs, the danger associated with my position, and the biting sting of the crop, my arousal was growing.

"Now I want you to remain extremely still for this next part," Sir said. "Keep your hands on the rail."

Oh, God.

I had no idea what he was planning to do, but the hint of fear that his command invoked seemed to turn me on even more.

The leather traveled down my left leg, all the way to my ankle, then up my right. It was soothing.

Smack.

And then it wasn't.

Smack.

Smack.

The stinging blows were delivered on the backs of my thighs and along my calves. The rapid succession didn't allow me time to breathe, much less move.

Smack.

Smack.

Smack.

By the time Sir stopped, every slap landing on a different part of my leg, I was practically vibrating. It hurt so good.

A warm hand dipped between my legs, this time through my wetness and into my needy pussy. One finger, then two. I assumed it was Sir who was fingering me and I whimpered, wanting him to continue.

Of course, it stopped too soon for my liking.

"Time to turn over," Sir told me. "Don't move until we help you."

I waited, not relinquishing my death grip on the rail until Sir wrapped one arm around my torso, holding me against his body as they easily turned me over, positioning me on the rail.

Sir adjusted my arms above my head and fixed my hands so that I was gripping the flat top rail. With my elbows pointed toward the sky and my breasts thrust upward, I imagined I made quite the sight.

At least from this vantage point I could watch what they were doing.

Sir traded places with Master, taking up the position at my feet and securing my ankles while Master glided the crop from my shin to my nipple and back down.

"You'll learn that my brother's not as into pain as I am."

I shivered, my eyes meeting Master's.

"Do not move, pet." His eyes narrowed, his expression serious. "Not an inch. No matter what, do not remove your hands from the railing."

Okay, so the warning was ominous, which increased my fear. I realized it was the good kind of fear. Similar to watching a scary movie or riding a roller coaster. The anticipation made it that much greater.

My eyes trailed the crop as Master moved it over my belly, then pulled it back. I expected the stinging blow to land near my navel, but he changed course, slapping the outer curve of my left breast.

I arched my back as I cried out and his hand was instantly on my stomach, holding me in place.

When I relaxed once again, he released me, the crop brushing over my mound.

Smack.

My pussy burned from the impact and once again I jerked.

His eyes met mine.

"It's obvious you can't stay still, so we're gonna do this a different way."

Both men helped me down, then Master wrapped his arms around me, offering me support. My legs were weak, trembling from all the endorphins flooding my body.

I heard the rustle of clothing. Master turned me around so that I was facing Sir, watching as he stripped.

He really was a masterpiece. Long limbs and hard muscle. Just looking at him made my body throb with need.

"On my lap, sweet girl," Sir instructed as he took a seat on one of the lounge chairs.

My legs wobbled as I stepped toward him, but Master kept a hand on my arm.

Sir spun his hand, signaling for me to turn around.

I faced the opposite direction and he gripped my hips, then guided me onto his lap.

"Bend your legs and put your feet by my hips."

I did, which left me straddling his thighs, kneeling on the chair.

He pulled me back, then guided his cock inside me and pulled me down onto him.

I groaned as he filled me. "Sir…that feels so good."

He wrapped one arm around my rib cage and pulled me back so that I was resting against his bare chest. Sir was warm and hard and made me feel incredibly safe. His hand then trailed down between my breasts, over my belly, before he rested one finger on my clit. With slow, circular movements, he tormented me with his sensual touch.

I moaned again, trying to move my hips, but unable to in the position he held me in.

"Grab your feet."

Okay. So this was new.

I was sitting on Sir's cock, my back against his chest, my legs curled beneath me, my ankles pressing against Sir's hips. Because I was grabbing my feet, my breasts were thrust forward, ready and available for anything Master desired. I wondered what it looked like to him, how appealing my submissive position was. I was stuffed full of Sir's cock and practically laid out before Master.

"Now don't move, pet. I plan to pick up where I left off."

My nipples hardened in anticipation. I felt the flex of Sir's cock inside me and I moaned softly.

The crop trailed from my chin down to my breastbone before Master pulled back. I watched as the crop made impact with the underside of my right breast.

I hissed as the pain shot through me.

"She definitely liked that," Sir said. "Her pussy's nice and tight."

It appeared Sir was gauging my reaction by the way my pussy milked his cock.

Master must've approved, because he began a string of stinging slaps over my breasts, my nipples, and my belly. Every time the crop made impact with my skin, Sir teased my clit and I whimpered with need.

It wasn't long before I was panting, hanging by a thread, ready to be launched into the abyss. Every time I thought Master would send me over, he eased back. When I tried to rock on Sir's cock, he held me still, keeping me completely immobile yet impaled by his thick cock.

"Please...please, let me come," I pleaded, tears dripping down my cheeks as I was held on the razor-sharp edge of release by two sadistic Doms.

Master seemed to consider this before nodding. "One more."

I nodded, willing to take anything he wanted to give me just as long as they would let me come.

"This one'll be on your clit."

My eyes widened as I stared up into his face. The thought of that thing smacking my clit...it scared me and thrilled me at the same time.

Sir's hand moved to my hips, holding me in place.

As though in slow motion, Master placed the crop over my clit, then pulled it back and smacked me. It was possible that it was harder than the others, or maybe it wasn't. Either way, the impact made me scream, my body shuddering as I came in a furious rush. It was mind-blowing, shattering my senses and leaving me reeling.

"So fucking beautiful," Master declared as he dropped the crop and unbuttoned his jeans.

The next thing I knew, Sir was fucking my pussy and Master was driving his cock into my mouth as he held my head in his hands. Another orgasm—or quite possibly the same one—made my body twitch and jerk as they continued to use me for their own pleasure.

Master groaned, gripping my head firmly as his cock pulsed against my tongue, while Sir's fingers dug into the flesh of my hips, his cock throbbing inside me as they came at the same time.

I had never expected that something like that could be such a rush.

And I certainly hadn't expected that I would want more.

NINE

I WAS AWOKEN WITH THE sun warming my skin, shining in through the open doors.

Last night, after Master and Sir had their wicked way with me on the deck, Sir had carried me to my room, then they'd both joined me in bed, curling up against me on either side. It was the second night in a row that I'd slept with both of them at the same time, and I wouldn't lie, if I could know that feeling for the rest of my life, I would be one happy girl.

However, as my senses awakened, I realized I was alone in my room. I stretched, feeling the familiar ache of my body. It no longer surprised me, but rather made me feel better. Remembering the way they pleasured me and took theirs in return was an intoxicating feeling.

I turned my head toward the door and noticed a small piece of paper on the nightstand.

Join us for breakfast when you wake up. No need to shower. We'll take care of that later. ~Sir

"Mmm." My stomach rumbled at the thought of breakfast.

A few minutes later, I managed to force myself out of bed, then made my way to the bathroom. I used the facilities, then brushed my teeth and pulled my hair back into a ponytail. I grabbed a pair of shorts, but didn't bother with panties. I did, however, put on a bra beneath my T-shirt.

When I made it downstairs, I heard Melanie's voice coming from the kitchen. I headed that way and the sweet woman greeted me with a warm hug before handing over a cup of coffee.

"Did you sleep well?" she asked, sipping from her own cup while she regarded me with a smile that made her eyes sparkle.

"I did." I smiled sheepishly. "And you?"

She grinned. "There's nothing quite like the sound of the ocean and the warm night breeze blowing in through the open doors."

It took a moment for me to understand what she was saying. A blush stole over my face as I realized that with the doors to their room open last night, they would've heard everything that took place out on the deck.

"Oh, don't worry, honey. Your secret's safe with us."

That certainly didn't help.

Only when Melanie chuckled did I smile, although it was forced.

"Come on, let's join the men for breakfast."

I followed Melanie into the dining room, noticing Master, Sir, and King were talking while enjoying bacon, eggs, and pancakes.

My belly rumbled in anticipation.

Sir nodded toward the chair between him and Master, so I moved that direction. Before I could take a seat, Sir gently circled his fingers around my arm and pulled me down for a kiss.

"Good morning, pet."

"Good morning, Sir." I smiled, enjoying the way he welcomed me.

Master followed suit, kissing me before pulling out my chair and helping me into it.

"Good morning, girl," King greeted, tipping his coffee mug to his lips. "You look well-rested."

"Thank you. I slept very well last night."

King's hazel eyes darted to each of his sons. "That's a good thing. Considering what you've got planned for her today."

No one said anything for a moment and I waited with bated breath for them to elaborate.

They didn't.

But they did laugh at my expense. I felt more color infusing my cheeks but I managed to smile. I was still thinking about how their parents had heard us last night. Well, in all fairness, it was probably more me than them. Okay, and *that* didn't help at all.

"When do your friends arrive?" King asked.

"The boat'll be here around ten," Master stated, sipping his coffee.

King nodded. "We'll be taking that boat back for our flight home. Or rather to your sister's so we can spend some time with the brood."

While the conversation went on around me, I focused my attention on the food. I was starved and I knew that I would need my energy for whatever they had in store for me today.

My biggest question though...

Who were the friends that Master and Sir had invited?

•

After breakfast, I said my official good-byes to Melanie and Jeremy just in case they left before I was finished. Once that was out of the way, I went upstairs to shower and get ready for the day, per Sir's request. He instructed me to put the utmost care into preparing myself for my Doms and he suggested that I start with a long soak in the tub.

I didn't have any issues with relaxing before the festivities started, so I eased into a hot bath. Once immersed in the water, I leaned my head back and closed my eyes, allowing the memories of last night to slip back to the forefront of my mind.

I still couldn't get over how I'd reacted to last night's scene. It seemed as though I was turned on by the slight fear they'd woven in. Between the balancing act on the railing and the sting of the crop, even my memories caused my belly to flutter. It was intense.

It made me wonder how Master and Sir came up with those types of scenes. It seemed like a lot of work, having to find creative ways to push a submissive's boundaries.

When the water finally cooled, I took a shower, running through my routine. After that, I applied lotion to every inch of my skin, then applied my makeup and did my hair. By the time I was finished, two hours had passed. When I walked into my bedroom, I found the cutest little red-velvet dress trimmed with white fuzz. It was strapless and short and definitely festive.

There was no bra, which wasn't surprising; however, beside the dress was a pair of sexy red panties with the words *Santa's Helper* on the back.

Oh, yeah. This was going to be fun.

It took no time at all to dress and when I was finished, I twirled around, allowing the flirty skirt to lift and show off the cute undies. Yep, I was definitely looking forward to the party.

A knock on the door had me squeaking as I spun around to see Sir stepping into the room. His eyes did a slow perusal from my head to my toes, then gradually back up. Of course, I took my own little peek at him, admiring the black slacks and crisp white shirt. Looked as though the beach attire had disappeared and they were back in what I considered Dom mode. His sleeves were rolled up, revealing his thick forearms and the dark hair that covered them.

When I looked up into his eyes, I saw that he was staring down at my cleavage, what little of it there was. I was tempted to show him my underpants but decided against it. I figured he'd see them soon enough and if he knew what they looked like, then I was hoping he'd be thinking about them in the meantime.

"I'm not sure who's responsible for the dress, but thank you, Sir."

"The dress was Langston's idea," he informed me. His eyebrow lifted. "However, I'm the one who picked out the panties."

"Well, thank you for the thoughtful underwear, and I'll be sure to thank Master for the dress. Has the boat arrived yet?"

"It's on its way."

I moved closer. "If you don't mind me asking, what exactly will be taking place during the party?"

"It's a play party," he informed me. "Very similar to the environment of a club."

I had yet to go to a club, so I had no frame of reference; however, I still looked forward to it.

"Unfortunately," Sir continued, "we require the assistance of some of the guests before we can finish setting up, so I'd like you to go with me to greet them when they arrive."

"I'd be honored, Sir."

He reached for my arm and pulled me closer. I stepped right into his embrace, planting my hands on the hard planes of his chest as I gazed up into his eyes. "Thank you for inviting me here, Sir."

He cupped my face. "I'm the one who should be thanking you for coming."

I giggled at the direction my dirty thoughts wandered.

Sir obviously recognized where my train of thought derailed and he smirked.

"You'll be doing plenty of that today, too," he said in a deep, low rasp that had my body warming nicely.

"Well, I'm looking forward to whatever you and Master have in store for me."

His expression sobered. "I want you to remember that everyone who's here today is part of the lifestyle. And though you might be a little surprised, they understand the need for discretion. Also, we're not entirely certain how things will go, but should your assistance be needed in another scene, we intend to loan you out."

I frowned. I did not like the sound of that.

He brushed his knuckles along my cheek. "You have to trust us, pet. We will not put you in harm's way. You also have to remember that we're incredibly possessive, so the opportunity may not arise."

That piqued my curiosity, but Sir didn't elaborate.

"Now let's get downstairs so we can meet the guests when they arrive."

My eyes shot down to my feet. "Should I wear shoes?"

Sir looked at my feet. Coincidentally, my toenails were painted a festive red, which matched the dress.

"No. Barefoot is a good look for you."

After he brushed my mouth with his lips, we headed downstairs. In the time it had taken me to get ready, they had decorated the majority of the house, including fixing the sad excuse I'd made of the tree. I couldn't hide the wonder on my face. It was the most beautiful Christmas setting I'd ever seen.

There was the huge tree decked out with white lights and a variety of silver and blue ornaments. The decorative blue and silver skirt flowed out from the wide base, the ripples causing the light to bounce off the velvet. Candles—I noticed they were flameless—had been strewn about to create a romantic ambience. I figured by the time night fell, the room would be a fantasy come true, but at the moment, most of the lighting was lost in the sunlight streaming in through the windows.

"What do you think?" Sir asked as he took my hand and led me down the stairs to the main floor.

"It's stunning," I told him, still taking it all in. "Like a fairy tale."

"I'm glad you like it."

Master met us at the bottom of the stairs. I paused on the last step and he slid his hands up the backs of my thighs, inching higher until he was cupping my ass.

"The dress suits you," he whispered in my ear. "Very...festive."

I wrapped my arms around his neck and kissed his cheek chastely. "Thank you for the dress, Master."

"Well, enjoy it while I allow you to wear it," he said with a smirk.

"I definitely will."

"The boat's here!" King announced as he stepped into the house. "We'll be heading out shortly."

Melanie made her way over, hugging Master and then Sir before taking my hands and staring back at me.

"You look beautiful, honey. I hope you enjoy the day." She glanced over at her sons. "You be sure to keep them in line."

Sir snorted and I giggled. I didn't think anyone could keep them in line.

"I'll certainly give it my best shot," I told her, then returned her hug.

"Come on, pet," Sir said, taking my hand and linking our fingers. "Let's greet the guests and move them around to the back deck. Langston can handle things in here."

With my hand held securely in his, I found I would've followed Sir anywhere.

TEN

WITH A SMILE ON MY face, I followed Sir outside and down to the path that led to the dock. The sun was shining, the sky a vibrant blue, and although I was already happy, I felt my spirits lift even more simply because of how beautiful it all was. This truly was paradise.

From our spot in front of the house, I could see that people were already disembarking, making their way down the pier and onto the sandy shore. I couldn't make out the faces due to the distance, but I was eager to find out who my masters had invited.

The first person I recognized was TJ Arlington. Well, him and the harem of women who were following. I noticed three extremely attractive ladies wearing matching spaghetti-strap sundresses of green, red, and gold, who were remaining close to him, while several others were trailing behind.

Sir greeted TJ first, using his first name and offering his hand to shake while I stood there, confused about what to do. The last and only time I'd been introduced to the man, I had been...an ornament. That day I hadn't even had a name. I wasn't sure how to act. Was I supposed to look at the ground? Keep my mouth shut?

"These are my girls," TJ said with a flourish of his hand. "Catarina, Isabella, and Maria. Ladies, this is one of our hosts, Master Moore."

The three women offered polite smiles and tilted their heads down.

I couldn't help but stare. They were all strikingly beautiful and very, very different in physical appearance. While Catarina—the tallest and thinnest—had bright red hair, emerald-green eyes, and legs that went on for miles, Isabella was shorter than me with big, brown doe eyes and long, silky blond hair. Similar to me in stature, she had small breasts and narrow hips. Then there was Maria, quite possibly the most beautiful of them all. Her curvy figure—big breasts and wide hips—was what caught my attention first, but her long black hair and bright blue eyes were what highlighted her round face. Needless to say, they were going to attract a lot of attention.

"TJ, I'd like you to meet our pet, Luciana Wagner."

In a move that shocked me, TJ took my hand and smiled down at me. "It's a pleasure to officially meet you, Luci."

I wondered if Master or Sir had talked about me considering he referred to me by my nickname without being told. He didn't seem like the type of man who would merely make assumptions.

"Thank you, Master Arlington," I said, trying to look anywhere except in his eyes. I wasn't sure what the protocol was.

TJ chuckled. "The wild ones are always cute."

Sir pulled me to his side. "We like her." He motioned toward the house. "Langston's inside waiting for you. He'll help you get everything set up."

"Perfect." TJ turned to his submissives. "Ladies, please take your pets inside. Get them set up and then return to me when you're finished."

"Yes, Master," they all said cheerfully before dutifully following his instruction.

There were at least a dozen or so women and a couple of men who followed the three women toward the house.

"While we wait for the decorations to be finalized, we'll be relaxing on the back deck," Sir informed TJ. "There're refreshments waiting."

"I'll make my way over. Thank you."

We were then met by several men, all introduced to me as Dominants. I could tell by the way they spoke to Sir that they were close friends. One of them had hooked a leash to a woman's collar as they approached. I found that interesting, something I had yet to see thus far.

After the brief greetings, Sir informed them to head toward the back deck.

I was smiling as I watched the group of men walk away, which was the only reason I didn't see who was coming toward me.

"Nothing better than a trip to the island on Christmas."

I jerked my head around. "Jordan?" My eyes widened and a smile formed on my face. I couldn't believe he was here.

"Hey, kiddo," he said with a wide grin. "You're looking mighty festive."

I curtsied. "Thank you."

"Master Moore, you remember my boy."

"I do," Sir agreed, shaking Jordan's hand. He nodded toward Jordan's boyfriend. "Nice to see you again, Dale."

"Thank you, Sir," Dale replied softly.

I found it extremely shocking to see Jordan acting in such a dominant manner. It went against everything I thought I knew about him. For one, I had absolutely no idea he was into the lifestyle. And two, based on his demeanor, I would've pegged *him* as the submissive one in his relationship.

"Luci, this is Dale. Dale, Luci."

I smiled at Dale, still fighting off my shock.

Jordan peered up at Sir. "I do enjoy seeing people's faces when they realize my role."

It was the oddest thing. Jordan sounded the same, he even acted the same, yet there was something distinctly dominant about his presence. I had never noticed it before.

"Assumptions can be damning," Sir said, grinning.

"That they can." Jordan smiled at me. "You and I have a lot to chat about when we get back to the office."

"I'll say," I teased.

Sir advised them to make their way around to the back of the house as more people approached.

The two men who sauntered up needed no introduction.

"I am liking the dress," Ben noted. "Let me guess." His eyes went to Sir's. "Langston?"

"Of course."

"Figures."

Sir turned to me. "Pet, please greet Master Snowden and Master Parker appropriately."

I had no idea what that meant, but I stepped forward. Thankfully, Ben took control and leaned in and kissed me. It wasn't a simple kiss either. It was enough to steal my breath and make my knees weak.

Once he was finished, Justin did the same.

When I stumbled back, Sir wrapped his arm around me and pulled me close. It felt almost possessive, as though he wasn't quite as comfortable with sharing me with my other two bosses as he usually was. I wondered what that was about.

"Everyone's out back while the rest of the decorations are being added."

"I'm intrigued," Justin told him. "It's not like you to go all out."

"What can I say," Sir joked, his eyes darting to me. "I'm evolving."

Justin's eyes cut over to me briefly before he looked back at Sir and smirked. I had no idea how to interpret that look, but it sure seemed as though they were silently referring to me in some way.

"We'll see you in a bit," Justin told Sir before leading the way to the back deck.

I vaguely recognized the next man to approach. He was alone, but I figured he wouldn't be for long.

"Master Chaos," Sir greeted. "This is our pet, Luci. You might remember her."

"Oh, yes, I definitely do."

Oh, my God.

It was the man who had watched me pleasure myself during the quarterly meeting. The one Ben had verifying I did as I was told.

"It's a pleasure to see you again," he said kindly.

"Thank you, Master Chaos."

Sir gave him the same instructions he'd given the others.

I was watching him walk away when I heard a familiar voice say hello to Sir. I turned to see Kristen standing there. She looked absolutely *nothing* like I was used to seeing her. The outfit she had on was sexy and sleek, even the heels that her boyfriend (sub?) was in the process of removing for her.

Holy shit. What was going on here?

"I'm glad you could make it," Sir stated.

I couldn't have formed words to save my life.

This was my friend.

She was…not the same woman I knew.

"Yes, well, I figured why not. I am a bit curious as to how your little submissive is doing."

Oh, my God! And she knew about my submissive relationship with these men.

"There may be a few things she doesn't know about me," Kristen clarified, her eyes dancing with amusement as she peered over at Sir.

A few? Try *everything.*

Kristen offered me a conspiratorial wink. I, however, didn't respond. I had never seen her like this and I wasn't really sure how to react. I wasn't sure why, considering I'd just witnessed Jordan in his Master role and I had been able to converse with him without a problem.

I glanced over at her boyfriend, noticing he was standing just behind her and to the right. His head was down and he was wearing a collar around his neck. And now that I thought about it, he looked nothing like he had the few times I'd interacted with him over the years. While he normally appeared quite confident, he seemed very…submissive.

How in the world had I known this woman all this time and I didn't know this about her? This was huge. Like monstrously huge.

I frowned. She and I were going to have to talk, because she had a lot of questions to answer.

Sir instructed them to go around to the back of the house and Kristen offered me a smile. I was still staring at her in awe, unsure how to act around her.

No matter who else showed up, I knew that this was going to be a very interesting party.

•

After all the guests made their way to the back deck, Sir and I walked Melanie and King out to the boat to see them off before we returned to the house. As we made our way up the back steps, Master was walking out onto the deck. His eyes searched the area until they landed on me. It made me feel good to know he was seeking me out.

Sir steered me around to where Master was getting everyone's attention. The various conversations died off as everyone turned their attention to Master.

"First, we want to thank you all for joining us today. We realize it was a spur-of-the-moment invite and we appreciate you all changing your plans to be here. Second, we're here to enjoy ourselves, to relax, and ultimately to have fun. If you're a sub, follow your master's rules. If you're a Dom, well, do whatever the fuck you want." He grinned as the Doms laughed in unison. "And beyond all that, my brother and I truly had an objective when we scheduled this last-minute party. Our submissive is currently transitioning—slowly, I might add—from the vanilla world into kink. We wanted the opportunity to show her that despite the differences, there are a vast amount of similarities. The biggest distinction"—Master smirked—"our parties are more fun."

"Hear, hear!" someone cheered.

I couldn't stop staring at Master. There was one key point I seemed to be hooked on. *My brother and I truly had an objective when we scheduled this last-minute party.* Was he saying what I thought he was saying? That they had put this party together on a whim? For me?

"Now, come here, pet," Master commanded me, pulling me out of my stupor.

I moved toward him and warmed when he cupped my face.

"Merry Christmas."

I smiled. "Merry Christmas, Master." I sighed. "Did you…" My eyes darted around us. "Did you do this for me?"

He didn't answer one way or another, but I could see the gleam in his eyes. They *had* done this for me. And that…that was probably the most generous thing anyone had ever done where I was concerned.

Master's voice lowered as he leaned in. "Now kiss me, little one. I want to show all these other Doms who's king."

Unable to resist, I wrapped my arms around him, went up on my toes, and planted my lips on his.

ELEVEN

BOSS MEETING

JUSTIN

I KNEW WHEN I GOT the invite to the island that I wasn't going to be thrilled with what was going on. However, that didn't stop me from accepting and showing up. I was curious, wanted to understand what exactly was taking place.

And in an effort to get to the bottom of it now, I urged Langston and Landon to meet with me before the party got fully underway.

"For the record," Landon offered when we stepped into the small office downstairs, "it's incredibly rude for the hosts to disappear like this."

"I'm not going to keep you," I told him. "I simply need to know what's going on."

"As we told you," Langston stated, "we altered our holiday plans to spend more time with Luci."

"Obviously," I huffed. "However, you didn't mention you were whisking her away to the island."

"Does it bother you that we did?" Langston countered.

I could tell he was in full control mode. He was the king of this castle, so to speak, and he intended to make sure everyone else knew it.

Good thing I wasn't one to cower to other Doms who had a superiority complex.

"What's the protocol while we're here?" I growled, crossing my arms over my chest.

"We've informed Luci that she's our submissive," Landon said, motioning between him and his twin, "while we're here on the island." Before I could speak, he held up his hand. "However, we are still abiding by the office agreement. She will not have sex with anyone else."

Well, that was a given. I knew better than to think she would, for the simple fact that Landon and Langston were far too possessive to let that happen. They had all but claimed the woman indefinitely.

And that was what pissed me off the most.

"During the scene, we would appreciate if you and Ben maintained some separation," Langston stated, glancing between the two of us.

"I'm fine with that," Ben said, looking over at me.

"As long as you do not utilize anyone else for a scene," I told him.

Landon frowned. "Of course not. Should we need assistance, we would only use you or Ben."

"Me," I clarified. "For the time we are here, Ben will be my submissive. He will not be acting in a Dominant fashion."

"Understood."

It was a power play, I knew. One I didn't generally succumb to, but I couldn't deny that I was disappointed with the way things were going. I wasn't willing to let Luci go. And I certainly wasn't willing to stand back and not fight for her when I knew good and damn well that Langston had no intentions of collaring her. Had I thought he was looking to go that route, I would've willingly stepped aside.

However, I could tell that nothing had changed in that regard. For one, she wasn't wearing a collar. Not even a temporary one, which would've made all these people realize that Luci had been claimed. Had I been in charge of the party, she would've at least worn a protection collar, signaling to every other Dom that she was not to be touched.

I had no fucking idea what Landon and Langston were up to, but I knew Luci was still being strung along. Not that she looked upset. They were obviously caring for her the way she deserved. Even I could tell she was quite content to be here.

"We would like to ask that the two of you stay tonight," Landon said. "Once the party winds down, everyone will be taking a boat back. However, we would like to continue to play with Luci while the two of you are here."

At least we were being included somewhat. I nodded in agreement.

"If there's nothing else"—Langston narrowed his eyes—"we have a room full of people who we need to attend to."

I nodded. "Fine. But should anything change, I expect to be notified immediately."

Langston shook his head as he turned toward the door. "I told you, nothing's changed. I'm not sure why you keep harpin' on it."

He didn't let me get a word in before he stepped out of the room, leaving the rest of us behind. Landon followed him, which then left me and Ben.

"Master? Is there anything I can do for you?" Ben offered when I turned toward the window, looking out over the ocean.

I shook my head. "Not at the moment."

However, I was sure I would think of something.

Eventually.

TWELVE

OKAY, I COULD ADMIT THAT there were, in fact, plenty of similarities between the vanilla world and the kink world. Most of which pertained to interactions, conversations, and the ability to laugh and joke regardless of role.

I spent the first half hour after Master's speech mingling with the guests outside while enjoying fruity cocktails that were being poured by one of TJ's additional band of submissives. The atmosphere was relaxed, the conversations spirited, and I was truly enjoying myself. It was a bit easier not having to worry about what was coming next.

Plus, I got to spend time with my masters, relishing the conversations and getting to know them a little better. For instance, I learned that Master had a penchant for the flogger, and at one time, there had been a line of submissives at the club wishing to spend time with him. I also learned that Master preferred steak to chicken, beans more than rice, and would rather hire someone to cook for him so that he didn't have to spend time in the kitchen. Well, I actually knew that last part.

As for Sir, I learned that he was a stickler for punishment, but he preferred his submissives to stand in the corner or kneel or withhold orgasms over any sort of physical punishment. However, he would do whatever was appropriate in the moment. It was also brought to my attention that Sir read at least four books a week, sometimes more, and he was a fan of old gangster movies.

I liked learning new things about them because it made me feel closer to them.

"The decorations are complete, Master Moore," one of TJ's submissives informed Sir after waiting for him to acknowledge her.

Sir placed his hand on my back. "Shall we?"

I wasn't sure what it was he wanted to show me, but I nodded. Then, with his hand curled comfortingly around the back of my neck, Sir guided me into the house. It looked the same as it had earlier, the romantic Christmas ambience in full effect, only now there were...additional decorations. In the form of submissives, both women and men.

Unlike when Master and I were at TJ's house, I found this new discovery interesting. Perhaps that was because I had permission to actually look at them.

"Some submissives find this exciting," Master explained when he joined us. "The fact that they are used as an object can be quite stimulating."

Personally, I did not see the appeal. Being set aside and ignored was definitely not my thing.

We walked directly up to a naked woman who had been painted with blue and silver paint from her head to her toes. Her body was arranged in a way that exposed her pussy and her ass, although no one seemed to be paying her any mind at the moment. I wasn't sure exactly what her purpose was, but I figured someone would get a kick out of her eventually.

There was another naked woman positioned at the end of the sofa. She was on her hands and knees, her back perfectly straight, her head held high as she faced the opposite direction of all the people. I noticed she was wearing a decorative plug in her ass and someone had set their drink on her back. I assumed that meant she was a table. I respected her ability to remain completely still. That glass had to be cold.

"Are people allowed to...um...touch them?" I asked Master and Sir.

"Yes. And the submissives were made aware of that before they took their positions. As with any other play, they have safewords should they feel the need to use them," Sir explained. "This is actually TJ's preference with his own submissives. And he offers training for both collared and uncollared submissives and slaves. Being invited to train at his school is quite a privilege."

That was an interesting notion. The idea of a school for submissives… It piqued my curiosity. Granted, I had no intentions of ever going to a school. I much preferred to be trained by Master and Sir.

Master turned me around. My gaze searched the room for what he was directing me to look at. That was when I noticed one of the submissives was being used as a platter, very similar to the setup at Master Arlington's home. She was laid out flat on a long table while lettuce leaves and various finger foods decorated her body.

"They are trained to remain absolutely still, no matter what. Should they move, make a sound, or come, it's grounds for punishment, which they will receive when the party is over."

That sounded incredibly painful. And not the punishment part. I wasn't sure I'd be capable of remaining still, certainly not if I was being teased. I watched two of the unattached Doms carry on a casual conversation while one of them fingered the woman's pussy, the other tweaking her nipple. I had to admire how well she was doing, because there was no way I would be able to obey the rules.

All in all, there were six women and two men, all from the harem TJ had brought with him, who were posed and decorated as various pieces of furniture and décor.

I glanced between my masters. "Is this something that turns you on?"

"It can be an interesting experience," Master stated as Sir nodded in agreement.

"The main reason you're not set up similarly is because we wanted this to be a learning experience in other ways," Sir explained. "Plus, we're not allowing anyone to touch you without our permission. Like I told you earlier, we're still abiding by our office agreement."

Oh. Well, thank goodness for that.

I also took that to mean that my four bosses would not be having sex with anyone outside of our little group. I'd admit, I liked that.

Still trying to take it all in, I surveyed the room, admiring everything taking place around me. My attention was drawn to a Dom who was leading his submissive around by a leash. It probably wouldn't have seemed odd except the submissive was on her hands and knees, crawling behind him. She was wearing a pair of cat ears and a long, furry tail coming out of her...ass.

Well.

Sir chuckled. "Pet play is quite popular. Especially in our circles."

The man carried a bowl over to the sofa, then set it on the floor before he took a seat. At his instruction, the woman leaned down and began lapping at whatever was in the bowl. He proceeded to casually pet her as he struck up a conversation with Master Arlington.

"However, it's not our thing," Sir stated, clearly picking up on some of my tension. I did not want to be someone's *actual* pet.

It all appeared relatively casual, as though their interactions weren't forced. I wondered, if I went to their houses, if this was the way they lived on a regular basis.

Nonetheless, it made for some noteworthy observations.

•

A couple of hours passed while I made my way around the room. I was able to spend quite a bit of time with Kristen, watching the interactions between her and her submissive. Admittedly, I found it hot that he referred to her as "Mistress." I'd spent my fair share of time with Tim and Kristen and never had he referred to her in such a manner, so it was different.

Not that I wanted to refer to her as such, but the dynamic between the two of them was not something I would've expected. Considering what I knew of her, and all the time we'd spent together, it still shocked me to see this side of her.

"If your tongue falls out of your mouth, that'll be a symbol of disrespect," Kristen said teasingly.

My gaze darted up to her face and I felt my blush creep up to my forehead. "I'm sorry. It's just…weird."

She laughed, waving her hand to encompass the room. "Weird is subjective, is it not?"

That made me chuckle because she was right. There were many types of kink and what was weird for one certainly wasn't weird for another.

Someone whistled from the other side of the room and all eyes turned, including mine. I noticed Master Parker waiting for everyone to look his way.

"We will be opening gifts in ten minutes. So, please, grab your drinks and make your way into the living room."

Gifts?

My eyes darted to the Christmas tree, but I didn't notice any gifts there. However, I did notice that additional seating was being moved in and space was being cleared within the circle. Someone brought in a table and set it directly in the middle. It was similar to the table in the conference room at the office. Low to the ground but large enough for…someone to be laid out on it.

No one seemed concerned, so I tried not to be. If I was expected to have a gift for someone, then I was in some serious trouble. Figuring I wasn't going to find out unless I asked, I made my way around the room in search of Master and Sir. I found them talking to Master Arlington in the kitchen. Both their eyes lifted when I walked into the room.

"Are you ready for gifts?" Sir asked, motioning me to join them.

"I'm not sure what it entails," I admitted, glancing between them. "I didn't bring a gift."

Master smirked. "No worries, pet."

There was a twinkle in his eyes that said I wasn't completely understanding and he seemed to find it amusing.

Before I could ask, the three men started back to the living room, where everyone was already gathering around the table. I noticed the Doms were sitting in the chairs and the submissives were kneeling beside them. There was a group of unattached submissives also kneeling in a row in front of the tree.

When Master and Sir took their seats, they directed me to kneel before them. I did so without question, trying to take it all in and make sense of what was about to happen.

A few minutes later, the conversations died down and Ben appeared carrying a small glass bowl with sheets of paper folded inside.

"Every Dom shall choose a number. That will be the order in which the gifts are opened. Remember, you are only allowed fifteen minutes to open your gift, although ten minutes would be more appropriate if possible."

Ben carried the bowl around, allowing the Doms to select. I noticed that Master did not pick a number, but Sir did.

Justin stood up and then, to my absolute shock, Ben knelt beside the chair Justin had vacated.

"Who has number one?" Justin asked, glancing from one Dom to the next.

"I do," one of the men I didn't recognize stated. He did not have a submissive with him.

"Congratulations, Master Edge. Since you're rolling solo this time, feel free to select one of the gifts beside the tree."

Again, I was trying to find these mysterious gifts he was referring to.

When Master Edge walked over, then held out his hand to a pretty blonde, it all clicked into place. *We* were the gifts.

Holy shit.

"Thank you for choosing me, Master Edge," the woman cooed as he led her over to the table.

He held her hand as he had her step onto the top. Once she was standing on the table, he made a slow circle around her. I couldn't tell what he was thinking, but it intrigued me nonetheless.

"Remove your clothing," he instructed. "But do so slowly. Remember it's all about presentation."

The submissive nodded her head, then reached for the hem of her dress. Her eyes remained fixed on Master Edge as she slowly raised it, revealing her creamy thighs, then higher. I was surprised to see she was wearing a pair of gold, see-thru panties.

Seconds later, the dress came off and she allowed it to fall to the floor on the side of the table.

"Very nice," Master Edge said approvingly.

She smiled, then wiggled out of her panties.

"Now assume the inspect pose."

My eyes widened as I watched. That was the first time I was hearing a named position.

The woman gracefully spread her legs shoulder-width apart, went up on the balls of her feet, then laced her fingers behind her head, her elbows pointed outward. It left every part of her body open and...well, available for inspection. Plus, it defined her calf muscles, lifted her breasts, and accentuated the lines of her body.

It was certainly intriguing.

Master Edge moved around her, his eyes grazing every inch of her skin. He paused when he was behind her, slipping his hand between her legs.

"You're very eager, aren't you, slave?"

"Yes, Master Edge."

"What do you consider your most appealing physical attribute?" he asked the woman.

She answered without hesitation. "My breasts, Master Edge."

He moved around in front of her, tweaking her nipples firmly. "I'll agree, they are very nice." Master Edge lifted his eyes to hers. "Now which part of your body are you offering up as your gift to me?"

"Whatever pleases you, Master Edge."

"Very good answer." He smacked her ass. "Now kneel on the table."

The submissive quickly yet gracefully knelt on the table. Her back remained straight, her big breasts dangling downward, her legs slightly spread so her pussy was visible.

"I'm going to take your mouth as my gift," Master Edge informed her as he unbuttoned his pants and freed his cock.

I noticed he was partially aroused already. That seemed to change quickly as he used her mouth for his pleasure. I found it interesting that he didn't touch her, didn't try to pull her mouth onto him. He simply rocked his hips, fucking her face. I could tell she was doing her best not to move, remaining in that perfect position.

Yes, I found it hot.

"I'm going to come in your mouth, slave. Close your lips around me and suck hard."

The woman did as he instructed, and after several more forceful thrusts, Master Edge came down her throat with a long grunt.

When he was finished, he helped her to her feet, then led her over to his chair before pulling her onto his lap. It was nice that he didn't send her back to the tree, choosing to hold her in his arms. I imagined that made her feel better.

"Thank you for sharing your gift with us, Master Edge," Justin said. "Who has number two?"

"I do," Kristen said, getting to her feet.

She led her boyfriend over to the table, then waited while he stood on the top.

"Please undress for me, sub," she commanded.

Surprisingly, Kristen did not give him any instruction as to how, but he seemed to know what would please her. He slowly removed his shirt, revealing an extremely hard body and a surprising number of tattoos. I noticed that the submissive gifts were all watching intently from their spots near the tree. I couldn't blame them. The man was impressively built.

When he removed his pants, my eyes widened. His cock was huge. Like…really freaking huge. On top of that, he was pierced. His penis! His freaking huge penis had a barbell through the end. I shivered as I thought about how painful that must've been to do. Still, I couldn't look away because he was…huge.

And I'd thought Ben was the most well-endowed man I'd ever seen.

Kristen trailed one blood-red nail over her submissive's cock, making it twitch from her touch. "Please lie down on your back on the table." She motioned to one end. "Put your head down there."

She turned her attention to those around them.

"Is anyone willing to loan me their submissive for a few minutes? Keep in mind, my slave will be touching her and she will be instructed to come. However, there will be no penetration."

To my absolute horror, Master offered me up.

Kristen smiled down at me, then held out her hand. Her fingers were soft against my own and I slowly got to my feet. She led me around to the end of the table near her slave's head.

"If you're wearing panties, please remove them."

Feeling extremely out of my element, I stumbled when I removed my panties, letting them fall to the floor. I couldn't stop looking over at Master and Sir, noticing they were watching me intently.

"Sub, I don't think it's necessary to ask what your most impressive physical attribute is," Kristen said with a chuckle as she once again ran her finger over his huge dick. "However, I would like you to tell me what part of your body your Mistress is most fascinated with."

"My pierced tongue, Mistress," he said softly, his eyes focused upward.

His tongue was pierced, too? Holy crap.

"Very good."

Kristen's eyes lifted to meet mine. "Please turn around and lift your dress to your waist."

It wasn't easy, but I managed to do as she instructed, all while trying to block out all the eyes I knew were on me. I had no idea what was about to happen.

"Sub, please make her come with only your tongue. And if you can do so within three minutes, you have my permission to come as well. But you aren't allowed to touch yourself."

"Your pleasure is my pleasure, Mistress."

I felt heat flood my face, knowing that everyone here was going to watch Kristen's submissive make me come. With his tongue. The mere thought of coming in front of all these people was terrifying, but I tried to block it out, tried to pretend we were in the office and…

Yeah. It wasn't helping.

Big, warm hands wrapped around my thighs, urging me backward until I was standing above the man laid out on the table, my legs spread wide as I was forced to bend my knees because of the width of the table. It was actually the perfect position, although it wasn't the most comfortable. My thighs burned from holding myself up. Kristen's submissive shifted, taking some of my weight on his forearms, which made relaxing a little easier.

A second later, a gentle rasp caressed my slit, then her submissive fused his mouth to my clitoris. His wicked tongue—piercing and all—was as good as Kristen said it was and it wasn't long before my legs were trembling and I was moaning in earnest, my eyes closed tightly as I continued to block out the rest of the room. My orgasm remained just out of reach and I thought for a second he was going to miss his deadline. I should've known he had everything under control. When he lapped repeatedly over the sensitive bundle of nerves, it shot me closer to the edge, only to be forced right over when he relentlessly flicked my clit with only the tip.

I cried out as I came and as I was standing up straight, trying not to fall over, I heard him groan his own release. I turned in time to see his cock jerking and twitching as his seed spurted all over his belly. The most amazing thing was he hadn't touched himself, hadn't been incited in any way. Until that moment, I didn't know it was possible for a man to come like that.

"That's a very nice trick," one of the Doms said to Kristen. "Must've taken a lot of training."

She smiled. "He's a very good boy."

Kristen held out her hand to me, then escorted me over to Master and Sir. I knelt on the floor as Kristen's submissive handed my panties over to Sir before cleaning himself with a towel that his mistress handed him.

"Who goes next?" Justin asked as one of the submissives used disinfecting wipes to clean the table.

"That would be me," Master Arlington said proudly.

I figured things were about to get really interesting.

THIRTEEN

I COULDN'T DENY THAT WATCHING all the interactions as the Doms opened their gifts and used their toys was getting me all worked up. Since the time the gift opening started, I'd seen pretty much everything in the kink spectrum. For example, a female submissive fucking another female submissive with a strap-on; a master decorating his submissive with a variety of wax, coloring her breasts and her pussy with the warm liquid; another master unwrapping his gift only to tie her back up with jute, creating an impressive design with her body and the rope.

Admittedly, I'd been captivated by Justin inserting a thick plug into Ben's ass before punishing him with a wide, wooden paddle until he came. It appeared that some people preferred punishment as a means to achieve orgasm. Who would've thought?

As of now, almost everyone else had gone, with only Master, Sir, and Jordan remaining. I wasn't sure who would be next, but I was hoping it would be me. Then again, the thought of watching Jordan master his own submissive was intriguing in its own right.

"Thank you, Master Chaos," Justin said. "Who's next?"

Adrenaline shot through my bloodstream when no one said anything. I could tell they were purposely holding back, probably wanting to keep me and the other submissive on edge. It was working.

"I'm next," Jordan finally said as he got to his feet.

I wasn't sure what he was going to do, but I was almost as eager to see it as I was to participate with my own masters. And for some reason, even the idea of coming in front of these people again wasn't as nerve-racking as I'd originally thought. Maybe because I felt as though I knew them at this point, I wasn't sure.

It didn't take long for Jordan to have his submissive disrobe, then lie flat on the table. His boyfriend's cock was already standing at attention, which wasn't surprising. Everyone was likely worked up from the show. However, men didn't have the ability to be as discreet as women when it came to hiding their arousal.

"Some of you might be familiar with the violet wand," Jordan began, pulling something out of a case.

I frowned. I'd only read about it on the limits list Master had provided me. I had gone with curious as my selection after Master had given a definition. The static electricity sounded stimulating.

"For those who aren't familiar, this is not a painful tool. Some submissives enjoy the sensual stimulation, which some have likened to that of champagne bubbles along their skin."

I watched as Jordan had one of the submissives plug his wand into an electrical outlet, but my attention then redirected to the long glass tube that sizzled and sparked as Jordan ran his finger around it. He walked around to the submissives and Doms, asking if anyone wanted to get a taste of how it felt. Of course, I raised my hand, curious as to what it felt like.

Jordan held the tool an inch or so away from my skin. He was right, it felt almost like bubbles against my skin. I could see how that would be erotically charged under certain circumstances.

"My toy is quite fond of this tool. And for Christmas, I've decided to give him the gift of electrically stimulated orgasm."

I wondered if Jordan was going into detail because I wasn't familiar with it or if there were a lot of subs who hadn't yet experienced the violet wand. Whatever his reason, I was glad that he was explaining.

With the toy in hand, Jordan leaned over and kissed his submissive on the mouth. "You do not have permission to come until I tell you."

The man on the table nodded, his body trembling. I assumed he was excited, but I couldn't really tell.

For the next few minutes, Jordan trailed the glass wand over his submissive's body, arms, legs, hands, nipples. The glass never came in contact with his skin, but the static electricity could be seen arcing between the submissive's body and the glass. The purple glow was mesmerizing, as was the way the man's leg hair stood on end when Jordan came into contact with that part of his body.

The man on the table began moaning in earnest, as Jordan came closer to his cock and balls. It was evident he was enjoying himself and likely riding the fine edge of what I expected to be an intense orgasm.

"Color, pet?"

"Green."

"Good. Now I'm going to use indirect stimulation by applying a body contact to myself. It will electrify me and allow me to transfer the electricity with my touch."

I watched, my eyes wide as Jordan put down the wand, then picked up something else. I had no idea what it was he was doing, but the next thing I knew, he was holding his fingers over his sub's groin and an electrical current passed between them.

Holy shit. That was wickedly cool.

"I can also electrify him with my mouth."

My entire body heated when I watched Jordan take his sub's cock into his mouth. He proceeded to suck him, moving up and down the thick shaft as the man rocked and moaned on the table. I wondered what that felt like for Jordan. Did it have the same electrical stimulation? Or was that only for the sub?

Jordan released him from his mouth. "You have my permission to come."

"Thank you, my Knight," the man groaned.

When Jordan engulfed his cock once more, the man's hips shot up off the table, spasms shaking his body as he came.

I found it extremely intense and erotic to watch, and it even ratcheted up my own curiosity.

I was so caught up in what Jordan had done I didn't pay attention to the fact that he had cleaned up and taken his submissive back to his seat, where he was in the process of tending to him in a loving manner that made my heart swell. It was obvious Jordan and his partner were completely in love.

"It's our turn, pet," Master said as he got to his feet. "Please, stand on the table."

A sense of excitement drowned out the fear of getting up in front of these people. I was nervous but desperate for release, so it made the trip over to the table much easier than I expected. Sir held out a hand and helped me onto it. I was trembling even before Master began inching the dress down, officially "unwrapping" me in front of all the other guests.

My nipples instantly pebbled as the stretchy velvet lowered to my abdomen, freeing my breasts. It continued south, until it puddled at my feet. I stepped out of it and Master moved it out of the way.

"Are your nipples sensitive, pet?" Master asked, his tone ringing with authority.

"Yes, Master." They were at the moment, anyway. Likely heightened by the way they were looking at me.

"Good. We're going to test that."

Sir appeared in front of me, standing next to Master.

"Without touching any other part of your body, you are expected to come from nipple stimulation alone."

My eyes widened. Although my nipples were sensitive, I wasn't sure that was possible.

Sir turned. "Master Parker, we'll need your assistance for this."

Okay, so this might get interesting.

"We aren't taking her word for it," Sir explained. "If you'll please do what's necessary to confirm that she does in fact orgasm."

"It would be my pleasure," Justin said, moving around to stand behind me. His hands trailed from my shoulders, down my spine, over my ass, then between my legs.

I whimpered when he pushed two fingers inside my pussy.

"She's certainly wet."

Master smiled up at me. "She's about to be drenched."

The next thing I knew, Sir was placing a blindfold over my eyes, blocking everything out.

I focused on listening to what they were doing, but they were too quiet. That or my heart was beating too loudly.

I felt warm breath on my left nipple and I sighed as a mouth suckled me. Then the other nipple received the same attention. I was still aware of Justin's fingers inside me, but he wasn't moving, and the sensations on my breast soon became my main focus.

Between the gentle sucking and the erotic sting when they nipped me, I was enjoying everything they were doing. However, they weren't driving me any closer to orgasm.

A short time later, one mouth disappeared, replaced by something sharp. I sucked air into my lungs at the new sensation. It was a direct contradiction to the soft tongue grazing my other nipple. Then it switched.

"She's enjoying that," Justin said, my pussy fluttering around his fingers.

Master and Sir continued to tease, alternating the sharp sting and the gentle suction. Warm air blew on one pebbled nipple, cool air on the other. I shivered and moaned in response.

True to their word, they didn't touch me anywhere else and it was driving me insane. I needed something more to push me over. When I tried to move my hips, wanting Justin to fuck me with his fingers, a sharp slap landed on my ass.

"Be careful, pet," Master's voice rang in my ears. "You'll earn punishment for disobedience."

At the moment, punishment sounded more like a reward. They were teasing me with no chance of release and I was already worked up from watching everyone else.

Both mouths disappeared once again, replaced by more piercing pinpricks. I had absolutely no idea what they were using on me, but within seconds of the sharp pricks rolling over my nipples and breasts, I felt the real stirrings of my orgasm.

The mouths returned, my climax ebbing slightly. When they sucked my breasts fully into their mouths, applying delicious suction, I moaned again.

And when they bit down in unison, I cried out as wave after wave of pleasure coursed through my insides.

"Oh, yes. She's coming beautifully," Justin praised.

Hands were then on my hips, holding me still before someone lifted me off the table and into their arms. I curled against the warm chest, inhaling deeply. Although blindfolded, I knew it was Master who held me.

"So *fucking* beautiful," he whispered against my ear.

I loved when he said that. The words rang with wonder as though he was surprised by his reactions to me. And that in itself was the greatest compliment.

•

Not long after all the "gifts" had been opened did the party start to wind down. Master announced that the boat would be arriving soon and everyone except Ben and Justin would be leaving to stay at a hotel on another island before flying back home in the morning.

I was excited by the prospect of spending time with all four of my bosses. I'd been informed that we would be returning home tomorrow, too, but at least I had tonight.

Once I'd said my good-byes and thanked each of the guests for celebrating with us today, Master led me into the house.

"Where is everyone?" It looked as though they'd all disappeared.

"Probably making dinner," he said, taking my hand. "We all need some nourishment before we continue the festivities tonight."

The fact that they intended to play some more made me giddy. Sure, I'd come earlier, but it hadn't been enough to sate me. I felt a little depraved for wanting my bosses to use me in any way they saw fit. It felt as though this was the one opportunity to make it happen. The playtime in the office had to be limited due to the fact there were other people there. Granted, now knowing that Jordan was into the lifestyle, it didn't bother me so much that he might hear me scream from time to time.

"Did you enjoy today?" Master asked as he poured a drink.

"I did." I still couldn't believe they'd held the party for me. It made me feel as though I mattered to them. Then again, even without the party, I felt as though I mattered. Both Master and Sir made me feel wanted, even if they didn't feel as deeply for me as I felt for them.

"What intrigued you the most during the gift opening?"

I had given that some thought earlier and I knew exactly what I'd enjoyed the most. "Anytime one of the submissives was restrained," I admitted. "I liked the idea of being unable to do anything to stop what was going to happen."

"So, say we were to restrain you tonight," he mused. "What would you want to happen?"

I felt my face heat from my blush. "I'd like it to be rough." I couldn't believe I was admitting it out loud.

"Rough?"

"Yes. I'd like to know what it feels like when my masters unleash on me without holding back."

Master's dark eyebrow lifted. "Are you sure you're ready for something like that?"

I nodded. "I have this fantasy…"

Master nodded toward the sofa. "Have a seat and hold that thought."

I watched as he disappeared out of the room. I sat down on the sofa and breathed a little easier when he returned. He was holding a small notebook and a pen.

"While I help the others with dinner, I want you to write out your fantasy."

"Write it?"

"Yes. Be as detailed as possible with it."

I'd never thought to write down my fantasies, but I had plenty so I figured it couldn't be too difficult.

After Master passed over the notebook and the pen, I sat on the floor and used the table as my writing surface. I waited until he disappeared from the room before I started writing it out.

I'm pretty sure I could sit out here all day and all night. The sound of the waves as they lap at the shore is soothing and I can't remember ever being quite so relaxed.

Rolling onto my stomach, I glance around, noticing there's only a couple of people on the beach tonight and they're several yards away. The thought of removing my bikini and allowing the warm air to caress my skin has been something I've been contemplating for the past hour. If I don't do it now, I'm not sure I'll ever get the chance again.

With my gaze fixed on the two men, I reach around and untie the string at my back and let my top fall away, slipping it over my head and placing it within reach. The two men don't seem to be paying me any attention so I do the same with my bottoms, untying the strings on my hips, then pulling the fabric from beneath me.

Instantly the warm air brushes over every part of my skin, teasing me. It's arousing me to the point of distraction. I can feel my pussy getting wetter. I know I'm not supposed to be turned on by this, but I am.

I hear someone talking and I jerk my head around to see two men walking past. Their eyes trail over my naked back as they pass. I can see the interest in their eyes, but they keep going, but not without giving me second and third looks before they join the other two men who seem to be packing up to leave.

It's getting dark and if I don't head back now, it'll be impossible to see. That's my cue to go inside. Figuring it's pointless to get dressed now, I pick up my bikini, then wrap my towel around me and secure it in place before heading up to the beach house I'm renting for the weekend.

I hate that it's my last night here, but a week has passed and I have to get back to the real world. I've been a little disappointed that I wasn't able to make any new friends during my trip. The lack of personal interaction has left me wanting for something I can't quite put my finger on.

Not ready to go inside, I drop my bikini on the table, then light two of the torches to provide ample light to see by. Once they're burning, I lay my towel out on one of the lounge chairs and relax. It's my last night here; I might as well enjoy myself a little.

I think back on the men who'd been down by the water and I find myself fantasizing about them watching me. The idea turns me on, which then has my hand trailing down between my legs, my fingers grazing my pussy. I can almost picture them walking up on the deck and watching as I play with myself.

They know that I see them and the fact that I don't send them away seems to make them bolder. They slowly make their way up to the deck but don't approach me directly. They keep their distance, watching as my fingers dip deep into my pussy before returning to my clit.

Thanks to the light from the torches, I can see the outlines of their cocks through their shorts. It makes my arousal burn hotter, the thought of watching them stroke their own cocks while I play with myself.

"Why don't you move closer," I say in the sweetest voice possible. "Pull up a chair."

Only one man moves closer and my gaze trails to him. He doesn't move quickly, obviously trying not to scare me. But the thing is, the longer they stand there, the more I wish they would all move closer. The idea of having their lust directed at me is making my pussy wet, my nipples overly sensitive.

"Don't stop," the closest man says as I moan, my hand pausing in its quest for relief. "Let us watch."

I meet his eyes and whisper, "I don't want you to watch."

"No?" He doesn't sound as though he believes me, and I can't blame him since I haven't asked them to leave.

"No," I admit.

"Then what would you rather we do?"

I glance from one man to the next, finally stopping to meet the gaze of the man closest to me.

"Personally, I'd rather have you tie me up and do whatever you want."

"Is that so?"

I nod.

The closest man glances over his shoulder, seemingly seeking the input of the others. I can see their interest; it's reflected in the desire burning brightly in their eyes.

When he turns back to face me, the man smirks. "We won't be gentle," he admits.

I smile. "I don't want gentle." I pause for effect, shoving my fingers deep into my pussy. "I just want to be fucked. Hard."

"Hey, sweet girl, it's time to eat."

I looked up to see Sir watching me. Crap. I wasn't finished.

"I'm not done," I told him. There was so much more I wanted to add, like how the four of them descended upon me, roughly taking me in every way possible until…

"That's all the time you get, I'm afraid."

Glancing back down at the notebook, I sighed. At least I'd left off at a perfect place for them to pick up should they decide to indulge my fantasy.

"Bring it to me," Sir insisted. "And let's go eat."

Feeling both excitement and a slight amount of fear, I handed Sir what I'd written. He didn't bother to read it, choosing to head into the dining room. He passed the notebook to Master before holding out my chair.

"This smells delicious." I took it all in, from the place settings to the exquisite food decorating the table. "So, who's the master chef in this group?"

"That would be me," Ben admitted.

"It's true," Justin agreed. "Although I can hold my own, I don't hold a candle to Ben."

I noticed that Ben seemed pleased by the praise from his master. I couldn't blame him.

While I was dishing food onto my plate, I noticed Master start to read my story. Embarrassment flooded me as I thought about what he might think of me for having a fantasy like that. Part of me was ashamed that I would possibly enjoy the idea of being manhandled by strangers. However, I had to admit that I wasn't turned on by the fact that there would be strangers who would touch me. It was the idea of my masters playing out this fantasy that did it for me.

It didn't take long for Master to finish and his expression never changed. He then handed the notebook to Sir. The four of them passed it around as they ate and read, leaving me to watch them. I think they knew that my anxiety level was rising as I watched. Perhaps that was what they were aiming for, I didn't know for sure.

However, what I did know was that after dinner, my masters dismissed me to go down to the beach after Sir delivered a bikini that he'd obviously found in my dresser back at my apartment. It was the black one I had yet to wear because of how skimpy it was.

"Go change, then go down to the water's edge. There's a towel on the back deck."

"Does this mean we'll be acting out my fantasy?"

Sir smirked. "I expect the performance of your life."

I giggled, feeling both anxious and excited as I grabbed the bikini and headed for the bathroom to change.

"Oh, and pet?"

"Hmm?"

"Remember your safeword. There's a fair chance you might need it."

A tremor danced down my spine and my belly fluttered at the thought.

FOURTEEN

BECAUSE IT WAS ALREADY LATE, the sun had set, but it looked as though someone had the forethought to place a couple of torches down on the beach to provide light. I laid out my towel and got comfortable, relaxing as the water gently rolled up onto the sand. I had no idea how long I laid there like that, but it was long enough for me to get completely relaxed before I heard someone talking.

I glanced over to my left and noticed two men. One of them was Justin, the other could've been either Sir or Master. I was unable to tell from this distance. They were standing by the water, several yards away, not paying me any attention.

The fact that they were there was enough to make my pussy clench with excitement. Remembering my fantasy, I decided now was the perfect time to remove my bikini top. The breeze was strong, caressing my skin and making my nipples harden into points. Then again, it could've been my excitement that did it.

I waited a few minutes as I lay on my belly, carefree and lighthearted as I kicked my feet in the air, pretending not to notice that the men were there. Feeling brave, I then unhooked my bottoms and tossed them with my top. It felt delightfully wicked to be outside naked like this. Although it was a private island, it still felt as though someone might see me at any time and that made it feel exceedingly naughty.

While I lay there, enjoying the gentle lapping of the waves, I heard more people talking and I peered over my shoulder to see Ben and either Master or Sir—again, I couldn't tell who was who—walking slowly past.

"Cute little ass."

I recognized that voice. It was definitely Sir.

I grinned playfully, pretending that it was completely normal for me to be naked and alone on the beach.

They continued to walk a little ways away, but then Sir stopped.

"I'll be right back," he told Ben. "I'm gonna…go talk to her."

I tried not to giggle, loving the way he was giving my fantasy a life of its own.

"Hey," he said, sounding slightly hesitant—a definite difference from how he normally sounded. He was obviously in character. Since he was wearing a pair of swim shorts and no shirt, I didn't mind this character at all.

"Hi." I reached for the towel to cover myself, but he tsked me.

"No need to cover up," Sir stated. "It's a very nice view from where I stand."

I smiled shyly, which I didn't have to pretend.

When he took a seat a few feet away, I found myself watching him closely. I wasn't sure which direction this was going, but I was pleasantly surprised by the improvisation.

"You stayin' nearby?" he asked, making small talk.

"I am. Rented a place for the week." I pointed behind me. "Right up that way."

"How long are you here for?"

Brushing my hair over my shoulder, I kept my breasts covered by remaining on my belly. "Just until tomorrow. It's time to head back to the real world."

"You do any sight-seeing while you were here?"

"Not much, no. I thought I'd meet more people, but I'm realizing not many people go to the beach for Christmas."

Sir nodded toward the others. "My buddies and I headed down for a few days." He tilted his head in the opposite direction of the house. "We've got a place not too far from here, but the beach isn't as nice, so we thought we'd wander down this way."

I feigned a yawn and then covered my mouth. "I'm so sorry. It looks as though it's past my bedtime."

The expression on his face looked like real disappointment. "No worries. We were just gonna head back ourselves."

When I sat up, I grabbed the towel in an effort to keep as much of myself covered as I could. Sir got to his feet, then held out his hand and helped me to my feet.

"Thank you," I said coyly. "That was very sweet of you."

As I positioned the towel, Sir's hand brushed against my nipple, making it instantly pebble. He made it appear accidental, but I had to wonder.

"Well…" I held the towel a little more securely and reached down to get my bathing suit. "It was nice chatting." I glanced over at the others. "Have a safe trip home."

"You do the same."

As I started up toward the house, I glanced over my shoulder, noticing he was watching me. I gave him a flirtatious wave, then continued toward my destination, spotting the lit torches they'd set up around the space.

Once on the deck, I placed my towel on one of the chairs and then took a seat. I didn't have to pretend to be turned on. I most definitely was. My hands wandered over my breasts, my belly, then lower, easing between my thighs.

I heard someone clear their throat and I looked up to see Justin watching me. He'd come halfway up the stairs but stopped, his hand gripping the rail. He looked as though he was holding himself back.

Our gazes locked and I continued my efforts to tease myself, not rushing. The man looked delicious without a shirt and I realized it was the first time I'd seen him this relaxed.

"Deeper," he said, his voice gruff.

"What?" I acted as though I was confused.

"Push your fingers deeper into your pussy."

Feigning outrage, I narrowed my eyes at him and pulled my hand back. "I don't know who you think you're talking to."

"You," he snapped.

Just when I was going to refute him, the other three men walked up. None of them stepped onto the deck, but four sets of eyes zeroed in on me.

I felt someone dribbling lube on my ass, then something thick penetrated me, pushing in. I cried out, the sound muffled by Master's cock. My ass was stretched impossibly full, but I didn't have time to think about it when another cock pushed into my pussy. Then three men began fucking me, filling all my holes. They weren't gentle and it only took seconds before my first orgasm pummeled me.

Master removed his cock from my mouth and allowed me to catch my breath. However, he wasn't patient, shoving back inside while staring into my eyes.

"She's gonna take four cocks," Sir announced. "Four cocks fucking this sweet little body."

"You think you can handle four?" Justin asked, his tone still incensed as he continued to play the part.

I shook my head, but Master quickly stopped the movement.

"You can do it," Master crooned. "Be a good little girl and take all our cocks at once. Maybe if you're nice, we'll even let you come again."

Considering I only had three holes and they were all full, I wasn't sure what they were planning, but I knew it was going to involve at least a little discomfort. Probably a lot. Strangely enough, I was excited about the prospect of them pushing me beyond my limits.

There was movement as bodies shifted, then I felt more pressure as I was soon forced to take another cock in my pussy.

Holy fuck.

I had two cocks in my pussy and one in my ass. I felt as though I was going to be torn in two. It was too much. Part of me was grateful that they hadn't attempted to double fill my ass. It was already difficult enough having one in there.

Master's gaze was fixed on my face and I could tell he was trying to ensure I was okay.

"Green," I whispered, making sure he understood I wanted everything they were willing to give me.

Master nodded, then brushed the head of his cock over my lips.

Sir was the one to step closer. "Don't mind him," he said. "He's just a little...excited. Not often do we see such a lovely creature in all her naked glory."

I'd stopped teasing myself, but my hand still rested on my mound.

"Please, don't mind us," Sir stated. "We just want to see a beautiful woman give herself the appropriate attention."

"And what do you consider appropriate?" I countered. I purposely looked at Justin from time to time, as though making sure he hadn't moved closer.

Sir nodded toward the chair beside me. "May I?"

I gave him a reluctant nod.

Sir didn't rush upon me, instead slowly making his way to the chair. He didn't immediately sit either, but his eyes never left mine. "Please continue."

"What makes you think I want to?" I asked with a huff.

His eyes dropped to my breasts. "I'd say you're quite fond of being an exhibitionist."

I glanced down at my nipples and gave a shrug. "It's cold out here." It was a lie. It certainly wasn't cold.

Sir smirked. "Well, we can warm you up."

My eyes widened as the other three moved closer, all three of them now on the deck. I didn't know who to look at first.

"Little girl, you're getting in over your head," Justin said, his tone still rough but not quite as harsh as earlier.

"You don't know me," I quipped. "Maybe I like to live on the edge."

Justin's blond eyebrow lifted. "Prove it. Fuck your cunt with two fingers."

The command in his tone had me sitting back, my lust skyrocketing. I was definitely enjoying the game. The ability to be bratty and to push them was erotic.

Figuring I would have to give in sometime, I spread my legs wide, then pushed two fingers inside me. Of course, the friction caused me to moan.

"I could take over for you if you'd like," Sir offered sweetly.

I gave him a shy nod, encouraging him.

"Is that what you want?" he inquired with a devilish smirk. "Does the naughty beach brat want to give up control?"

"Maybe," I said meekly, glancing up at each of them from beneath my lashes. "It's just...it's been so long."

"Since...?" Master asked, moving even closer.

"Since I had a man please me," I admitted.

"Is that so?"

"Yeah. Not many men know how to...give me what I need."

"And what is it you need?" Sir questioned.

I let the question hang in the air for a second as I glanced from one man to the other. I pretended to be hesitant about how I wanted to answer. Before replying, I bit my lower lip. "I...uh...I like it rough."

"Are you sure about that, little girl?" Justin asked, still playing the sexy villain.

"I'm sure."

"You want it rough, we can give it to you rough."

Before I could say anything else, Master and Sir pounced on me. They each grabbed one arm, then dropped the chair so that the lounger was lying flat. Rough hands positioned my arms above my head, holding me securely. I expected them to tie me down, but they didn't. Still playing my part, I attempted to wiggle out of their hold.

When Justin straddled my hips and pressed his weight down on me, I stilled, staring up at him. The man was so incredibly sexy and the idea of him manhandling me was so hot I couldn't hide my desire for him.

He crudely grabbed my breasts, pinching and tugging on my nipples. I cried out as pain shot through me, but he didn't stop. I tried to jerk away, but he planted his hand on my ribs and held me still, continuing to punish my breasts before he pushed his finger into my mouth.

I bit down but purposely kept from hurting him. After all, I really did want to play.

Justin gripped my cheeks hard, holding my mouth. "Bad little girls need to have a cock put in their mouths. Why don't you give her a taste, pup?"

My eyes widened when Ben moved over me, stand
my chest, his feet planted on each side of the chair, blocking 1
of Justin. He was naked, his cock thick and hard as he strok
his fist. He smiled down at me. "Open wide."

I was about to argue, but he took advantage, shov
cock in when I opened my mouth. His hand fisted in m
pulling hard enough to send pain lancing through my s
yelped, but he continued to roughly fuck my mouth.

It was amazing and exactly what I needed.

I heard the rustle of clothes around me and assume
bosses were all stripping down. Then there were more hands o
shifting my legs back and exposing my pussy. I was sud
impaled by someone's cock, but I couldn't see who because Be1
blocking my view.

"My turn," Master growled.

Ben pulled his cock from my mouth and moved away, l
didn't have much time to draw in air because Master was takin
place, shoving his dick in, and gripping my hair in the same man

I sucked him, unable to help myself. This was exciting.

"Be a good girl," he growled. "Suck me hard while
brother fucks that pretty little pussy."

Well, at least I knew who was fucking me.

I was so caught up in pleasuring him I didn't notice at f
that Sir had retreated and I was being shifted. Then there was a h
body beneath me. It wasn't until Justin growled in my ear tha
realized it was him, his arms coming around me, his hands rougl
cupping my breasts.

"Gonna take one in every hole, aren't you, little girl?"

I couldn't speak because Master continued to fuck n
mouth. His grip on my hair didn't let up as he pushed his cod
deeper. For several minutes, he slowed, pushing in as deep as h
could, filling my throat before sliding back out. I could see the lu
burning in his eyes, knew he was enjoying this role playing as muc
as I was.

"Now be a good girl while we fill you with cum," Justin rumbled.

My moans came roughly as they all began fucking me. It was an overwhelming sensation to have so many cocks inside me. I was stretched beyond capacity, my body feeling as though I was being pushed beyond my limits. To my surprise, Master pulled his cock out of my mouth but continued to stare down at me while I was fucked hard and fast.

"Fuck, she's tight," Justin groaned. "I do like this little ass."

I moaned when someone's thumb pressed against my clit. They started to rub the little nub until holding back became futile. My release built until the pressure was too much to contain. I screamed with the force of my orgasm, feeling Justin's cock pulsing in my ass. Suddenly, there was less pressure as one of the cocks shifted out of my pussy as the other jerked inside me.

Strangely, I was hovering on the edge of another orgasm when that cock disappeared and another shoved inside. Then Master's cock returned to my mouth and someone pounded my pussy while Master took his pleasure from my throat.

When both men cried out at the same time, I realized Master and Sir were both coming, which then triggered another orgasm, leaving me completely boneless, yet with a huge smile on my face.

I couldn't lie, that was one fantasy I hadn't seen playing out that way. But I certainly wouldn't have changed a thing.

FIFTEEN

BY THE TIME NEW YEAR'S Eve rolled around, I was starting to go stir crazy. My apartment felt so small and I was desperate for something to do.

Although Master and Sir had taken me to their private island and showed me a world of interesting things I'd never experienced before, the fun hadn't lasted forever. The day after Christmas, we returned home and they delivered me to my apartment. After a rather sweet good-bye, I closed the door behind them and was left to my own devices.

At first, the silence was deafening. Having spent so much time in the presence of others, I feared that being alone was going to drive me slowly out of my mind. Oddly enough, I had needed the solitude to get in touch with my own thoughts and feelings. The weekend had been incredible, but the overstimulation wasn't something that I was used to.

While trying to get in touch with myself, I spent most of my time contemplating everything that had happened, alone with my thoughts. Fortunately, my four bosses mixed things up a bit, alternating between calling and texting throughout the six days since I'd seen them. It made me feel good that they were checking in on me.

Part of me had wanted to spend some time with Kristen, to force her to explain how she'd come into this lifestyle and how she had managed to keep it from me. Although grilling her sounded like a great plan, I had chickened out at the last minute. I wanted her to give me all the answers, but I was hesitant to talk to her about it. At least not until I could come to terms with it all myself. Maybe then it would make sense.

So, without my friends or family to pass the time with, I had counted down the minutes until the day came that I could go back to work. Unfortunately, there was still one more holiday before that would happen and I feared I would be ringing in the new year alone. Despite the fact that Kristen and I had made tentative plans, she had texted to let me know that something had come up at the last minute and they wouldn't be going out.

I had just decided I would spend the evening watching Netflix and eating Ben & Jerry's then going to bed before midnight when my phone chirped on the coffee table. At first, I thought it was my mother responding to my text from earlier when I'd asked her how the trip was and when they'd be home. It wasn't my mother. She hadn't responded.

But it was someone I had longed to hear from.

Master: *Your presence is requested tonight.*

I grinned, feeling giddy once again. I hadn't expected to hear from him until we were back in the office.

Luci: *At the risk of sounding lame, I do not have any other plans for the evening, so my presence could be arranged.*

Master: *I'm happy to hear that. In about twenty minutes, a car will arrive to pick you up and take you to the spa. We have scheduled you some time so you can relax and enjoy yourself. You don't need to bring anything with you except for your cell phone.*

Okay, so giddy was an understatement. As I read the text, I was standing up, bouncing on the balls of my feet.

Luci: *I'll be ready.*

Master: *Your masters look forward to seeing you this evening. Enjoy your afternoon, Luci.*

Yep. I knew this was going to be a New Year's to remember.

•

The limo arrived at my apartment a short time later, just as Master had said it would. I was also delivered to the spa without incident, where I spent a solid three hours being buffed and polished and utterly cared for. When the attendant arrived to remove the hot stones from my back, she informed me that I would be taken to a private villa, where I would be allowed to shower and get ready for my evening.

I was surprised to learn that I would not be going back to my apartment. I briefly panicked, thinking I wouldn't be able to do my makeup and hair. That was critical for a night out, right? How was a girl to look her best if she couldn't get to her makeup? I soon learned that wasn't necessary.

After I took a long, hot shower in the beautifully decorated villa, then wrapped myself in a big fluffy robe, two ladies arrived to do my hair and makeup. They were extremely professional and paid close attention to every detail to the point I felt like a princess. Admittedly, I enjoyed all of the attention, not to mention how incredibly beautiful they made me. Before they left, I was given a large red box and told I could get dressed.

It took everything in me not to rip into the box like a kid on Christmas. I managed to untie the bow and opened the box to find an exquisite silky black gown, a black G-string and matching strapless bra, along with a pair of sexy, strappy heels. I fought the urge to cry as I got dressed, not wanting to ruin my makeup.

When I was finished, I stared at myself in the mirror. I had never looked more beautiful in my entire life.

My phone chirped and I found myself giggling, my hands trembling from my nerves mixed with excitement.

Sir: *Are you ready?*
Luci: *Yes.*

There was a knock on the door and my heart leapt into my throat as I made my way over. When I opened it, my eyes widened when I noticed Master and Sir standing there, wearing tuxedos and matching smiles.

I'd seen these men in everything from shorts to jeans to immaculate suits, but nothing prepared me to see Master and Sir all decked out in formalwear. The sight of them made my heart skip a beat or two.

"You look beautiful," Sir said, his eyes scanning me from head to toe as he took my hand.

"Thank you." I felt beautiful. More so with them looking at me the way they were.

Both men gave me a quick kiss, careful not to muss me up, which I appreciated. I felt like a princess and I wanted to look the part for a little while longer.

After Sir handed me a black clutch that matched the dress, I tossed my phone and my apartment key inside, along with the lipstick the woman had left me with. They escorted me out of the building and down to an awaiting limousine.

"May I ask where we're going?"

"We're attending a party tonight," Master informed me. "But first, we're taking you to dinner."

I couldn't help but feel cherished that they had invited me. It had been a pleasant surprise, one I would likely never forget. In fact, I was sure I would never forget a single moment spent with these two men. Not as long as I lived.

•

Dinner had been at a high-end restaurant where we dined on exquisite pasta and fine wine. The conversation had been light and enjoyable. Most of the time I reminisced about our time on the island while they watched me with amusement.

Afterward, we got back into the limo and headed for our final destination. I had no idea where we were going or what we were going to do when we got there, but it didn't matter because I was with Master and Sir and they'd already made this a wonderful evening.

"The host of our party is TJ Arlington," Master relayed as the car came to a stop at a red light.

Okay, so maybe it did matter.

My eyes widened and I suddenly felt a cold chill race down my spine. I did not want to be an ornament tonight. In fact, I would've preferred to go back to my apartment and watch Netflix and chill before I wanted to walk one foot behind my masters while keeping my eyes down and my mouth shut. I was just about to tell him that when he cupped my cheek.

"Tonight's party is vanilla, pet. No ornaments, no naked submissives. We're going to enjoy ourselves. Maybe dance a little, have some champagne, and ring in the new year with friends."

Relief was instant, rushing out of my body on a breath I hadn't realized I'd been holding.

Master smirked. "We have been known to exist without bondage and discipline as the theme for the evening."

I smiled. "Thank you, Master."

"No, thank *you*, pet. Tonight is about the three of us spending time together and nothing more."

Sir turned my head to face him. "However, I can guarantee you will be naked before the sun is up."

I lifted one eyebrow, hoping he would enlighten me.

"We'll be spending the night at the apartment tonight. And unless you would rather go home, we would like you to join us."

"I would love to," I blurted.

"Good."

The limo came to a complete stop.

"Now let's go inside, enjoy ourselves and bring in the new year together. Then we'll go back to our apartment, strip you out of this sexy dress, and ravish you until you can't breathe."

Now that sounded like a fabulous plan.

The driver exited the limo first, coming around and opening the door. Sir climbed out, then held out his hand for me. I joined him and Master followed. Both men placed their hands on the small of my back and we headed inside. It was freezing, but they had thoughtfully brought a wrap that helped to ward off some of the chill. Thankfully, the walk to the front door only took a minute and then we were ushered into the warmth of TJ's house.

This time I got to look around, taking it all in, admiring the art that decorated the walls, the exquisite fixtures, the high-end everything. The house truly was a mansion fit for a king.

Speaking of king…

"I am so glad you could join us tonight," TJ Arlington greeted the three of us with a genuine smile.

"You look lovely, Miss Wagner."

I smiled. "Thank you, Master Arlington."

"Oh, no," he said with a grin. "Please call me TJ tonight." He glanced at Master and Sir. "I've been told I've forgotten the meaning of vanilla, so I'm going out of my way to prove everyone wrong tonight."

Master and Sir both laughed.

"Anything you need, one of my attendants can bring you." He lowered his voice slightly. "And if you're interested in ditching the vanilla, the dungeon is open."

"Of course it is," Master said with a smirk. "Couldn't go straight vanilla, could you?"

"Absolutely not. Unless it's the flavor of my vodka, vanilla bores me." The twinkle in the man's eye made me grin. "Anyway, I hope you have a lovely evening. I'm sure you'll know quite a few people here. I took your advice and invited other members of the club. It was my attempt to get to know them better."

I had yet to know what club it was they were all members of, but I soon learned that most of the people who had come out to the island were in attendance tonight. Including Kristen.

"Luci, I'm so glad you're here," she greeted me with a hug. "It about killed me to have to back out on you tonight." She glared at Sir. "But I was asked to keep my mouth shut. Which, as you know, isn't easy for me to do."

Well, that certainly explained something coming up that had thwarted Kristen's plans.

"I forgive you," I told her. How could I not when I got to spend the evening with Master and Sir?

"We appreciate your discretion," Sir said, wrapping his arm around my shoulder. "We wanted to be the ones to invite her out tonight and we wanted it to be a surprise."

My heart swelled in my chest at the knowledge.

Kristen huffed. "Doms. They can be such a pain in a girl's ass."

That made several people laugh, including Master and Sir.

"Come on, let us show you around," Sir said, guiding me away from Kristen. He called out to her over his shoulder. "You'll have time with her later, Kristen. Tonight she's ours."

Kristen winked as I was ushered away and led directly to a huge ballroom on the second floor. It didn't look like it belonged in a house, that was for sure. They had spared no expense with the decorations and there were dozens of people dancing in the center of the room.

"Care to dance?" Master asked, holding out his hand.

I glanced up at him, feeling my cheeks heat. "I don't know how to dance." I hated admitting that, but I didn't want to embarrass him.

"Let me lead and you'll be fine."

I would let this man lead me anywhere, so I took his hand and as he led me to the dance floor, I fell in love just a little more.

SIXTEEN

AFTER I DANCED WITH MASTER, Sir cut in and took my hand.

"I had absolutely no idea the two of you could dance so well," I said, slightly breathless from my dance with Master.

"There are some things we don't like to brag about."

I couldn't help but laugh.

We took a few more spins around the floor, weaving between other couples who were doing the same before we headed toward a table covered in white linen and decorated with beautiful white roses.

Sir had pulled the chair out for me and I was about to sit when I heard a familiar voice calling my name from behind me. I turned to see Jordan and his boyfriend moving my way.

"Fancy seeing you here," he teased with a huge grin on his face.

"Jordan," I said in a rush of breath. It was so good to see him. As it was, I'd been looking forward to going back to work just so we could have lunch together.

"Would you gentlemen mind if I steal your girl for a few minutes? I promise to return her after one dance."

I glanced over, noticing Master and Sir were both smiling. Master offered a curt nod and Jordan then led me back in the direction I'd just come from.

"As always, you look absolutely gorgeous," he said as he placed one hand on my hip, my hand curling over his other hand.

"You don't look too shabby yourself."

"This old thing?"

"This old thing" was a finely tailored tuxedo that made him look like a million dollars. I could only imagine what his closet looked like.

"So, I take it you're a member of the club?" I was unable to keep the question from coming out.

Jordan smiled, flashing white teeth. "I am."

"What's it like? This club?" I was more than a little curious.

He stared back at me. "I could tell you, but then I'd have to kill you."

"Top secret, huh?"

"Actually, it is. Well, not so much top secret as it is discreet. Unfortunately, I can't tell you much of anything about it, but I figure you'll get to see it for yourself one day."

I wasn't so sure of that. After all, we were going back to work the day after tomorrow, and I figured at that point things would get back to normal. And by normal, I meant that I would be spending more time with my bosses in the office and less out of it. I knew that these past two weeks had been a fluke. They were being kind to me, ensuring I wasn't spending all my time alone.

Don't get me wrong, I truly appreciated it. I enjoyed spending time with them outside of the office, but I wasn't naïve enough to believe that this was a forever sort of thing. Master and Sir weren't falling in love with me and they weren't going to whisk the princess away at midnight and make all her dreams come true.

Sure, they would probably make quite a few come true. Dreams I hadn't even known I had until I met them. Most of them would involve me being naked, I was sure.

"One of these days, I want you to come to my place for dinner. Dale keeps asking about you."

I smiled, glancing over at our table to see Dale conversing with Master and Sir like they were old friends. Perhaps they were. If they were all members of some club, then I was sure they'd spent some time together.

I turned my attention back to Jordan. "Why didn't you tell me that you were a Dom?"

"Would you have known what that meant?" he countered.

"No, probably not. Not until recently anyway."

"Sometimes, it's best to learn from experience, kiddo."

I didn't know about all that. Sure, I understood what he was trying to say, but it would've made things a lot easier if he'd come out and said, "Hey, I know exactly what you're going through. Let's chat."

And I was probably being unfair to Jordan. It wasn't his place to school me on Domination and submission, but I couldn't deny that finding out two of my closest friends were in the lifestyle and I never knew still bothered me.

The song ended and Jordan paused in the middle of the floor.

"Thank you for the dance, kind sir," I told him sweetly.

"And thank you, fair maiden."

I giggled. God, I had missed Jordan so much. I couldn't wait for our next lunch date. I wanted to get as much information from him as I possibly could.

·

The night flew by as we chatted with people, some I knew, some I didn't. It was lively and fun and everyone seemed to be having a good time. As promised, it was kept completely vanilla, even during the countdown to the new year, when Master and Sir took me out on the heated veranda and we watched a fireworks display at the stroke of midnight.

Or maybe the fireworks had been all in my head when both of my masters had kissed me until I was out of breath. I'd always heard that the person you kissed at midnight would be the one you spent the next year with. Since I had kissed both Master and Sir, I wondered what that would mean, other than possibly I would still be employed by the end of the year.

Fortunately, I didn't have time to dwell on it when Master and Sir decided to call it a night shortly after one in the morning. After saying our good-byes to TJ and his harem of submissives, the limo returned and we headed back to the city.

We finally arrived at the apartment a little after two and that was when the party resumed.

"So, what did you think of the vanilla evening?" Sir asked me.

"It was interesting." I smiled. "Although I'm curious how the two of you could last through such a dreadfully boring event."

Master smacked my ass, making me giggle.

"Boring, huh?" Sir teased.

"Absolutely." I pretended to be put out. "I mean, come on. No one was naked, there were no spanking benches or…or…torture tools."

"Torture tools?" Master sounded intrigued. "You're interested in torture tools, huh?"

"Me?" I pressed my hand to my heart. "Of course not. I'm a good girl, don't you know? Prim and proper. I would've been shocked to the roots of my hair by…torture tools."

Both men stalked me, the heat in their eyes evident.

Sir was the one to speak as he brushed my hair back over my shoulder. "It's been a long, dreadfully boring night," he said softly. "From the moment I saw you in this dress, I wanted to see you out of it."

I feigned exasperation. "You mean…naked?"

"I do." He fingered the thin strap on my shoulder. "I love seeing you naked, sweet girl."

Heat consumed me. Although I was trying to keep up the ruse of a fair maiden, it was impossible to do when these men made me want things I'd never thought I'd want.

Master moved in behind me. A multitude of sensations consumed me when he pulled my hair to the side, the long strands tickling my back as he pressed his lips to my neck. Sir slid the straps of my gown off my arms, then allowed the silk to slide down to my hips. They worked succinctly to strip me as I stood between them, my body temperature rising as they kissed and licked the skin that they bared.

I touched them both as much as I could as I fumbled with buttons in an attempt to get them as naked as I was about to be.

By the time they had worked their way into the kitchen, my dress, panties, and bra had disappeared. After setting me on the island, Master removed my shoes, then ran his hands from my toes up my legs, not pausing where I needed him the most.

"Your choice, pet," Master whispered as his mouth descended onto my breast. "We can keep things vanilla if you'd like. Just for tonight."

Although I had to agree that vanilla was boring, especially after the world they'd introduced me to, there was something delicious about it, too. There was a connection I felt from these men, something that transcended all kinks and fetishes, something that ignited at the core of my being. I wanted anything and everything they could offer me, and yes, vanilla was one of those things.

"Vanilla," I whispered, arching my back as Master scored my nipple with his teeth. "Vanilla works."

"Vanilla works," Sir echoed, coming to stand between my legs as Master laid me back on the island.

I palmed Master's head as he leaned in and kissed my lips at the same time Sir's mouth trailed up my thigh to my pussy.

I jerked and moaned as they feasted on me, torturing me with slow, sweet licks of their tongues.

By the time Master's mouth trailed down my neck, I was panting and moaning, begging for them to hurry. They didn't, proving no matter what I thought, they would always be in control of my pleasure. Which they gave me in spades using nothing more than their exquisite mouths and their fingers. They worked me over for what felt like hours, right there in the kitchen.

I was trembling with an orgasm just out of reach when Sir took my hand and helped me to sit up. He wrapped his arms around me and lifted me, forcing me to hold on, my legs going around his waist, my arms around his neck. And then he was carrying me out of the kitchen, through the living room, and down the hallway.

The room he stepped into wasn't the guest room I'd stayed in with Master. No, this room was more masculine with beautiful, dark wood furniture and a lamp that offered a golden glow over the brown suede comforter.

Within seconds, the comforter was ripped from the bed and then I was laid out on the cool sheets while I watched Master and Sir quickly strip the remainder of their clothing from their bodies. When they joined me, I couldn't resist running my hands over them, wanting to be as close to them as I could possibly get.

For the next few minutes, they lavished me with kisses, working me into a frenzy once more as their mouths skimmed my oversensitive skin until I was once again panting and pleading for them to hurry. I needed more. I needed everything.

Sir flipped me over onto my stomach, then dragged me to the edge of the bed. He didn't command me to get onto my knees, choosing rather to position me the way he wanted. Once I was on my hands and knees, Master knelt in front of me, holding his cock firmly in his hand as he guided my head down.

"Suck me, Luci," he growled softly.

I wrapped my lips around his cock, drawing him deep into my mouth. At the same time, Sir knelt behind me, pushing his cock deep inside me. They filled me from both ends, but neither seemed to be in a hurry, leisurely fucking me while their hands roamed over my skin, tangling in my hair, making my body hum as I inched closer and closer to the edge once more.

"Suck hard," Master commanded, his teeth gritted as he tightened his grip on my hair.

I sucked him more forcefully as Sir slammed into me, filling my pussy, the friction making me whimper as I got closer to the precipice. It wouldn't take much to send me over and it seemed they knew that because they both held back once again. They drove me crazy, alternating between a few punishing thrusts and the leisurely rocking of their hips.

"Make me come, Luci. I want to come in that sweet mouth."

I focused my attention on giving Master what he needed while letting Sir drive me closer to climax with the delicious friction of his cock inside me.

"Oh, yeah. That's it, baby. Just like…that." Master's hips stilled and his cock pulsed against my tongue as he came.

When he pulled back, my entire focus was on Sir as he drove into me again and again. I could tell he was holding back, but I wasn't sure why. I couldn't tell if he was trying to maintain control or if he merely thought this vanilla fucking was the only thing I truly wanted. None of it mattered a few seconds later because he reached around, his thumb working my clit, shattering my mind and my body at the same time as my release slammed into me.

I cried out his name as his fingers dug into the flesh of my hips, his body stilling as he followed me right over.

It took several minutes for me to come back to myself, and when I did, I realized two things.

First, the night had been amazing. Having both men focus their attention on me, making me feel like a princess while we existed in the vanilla world, something I could tell that wasn't their preference but they'd done for me, was such an incredible feeling.

And second...

The night was apparently over, because as I was coming to, as my mind fixed firmly back in place, I watched as Master strolled out of the room, closing the door firmly behind him as Sir crawled into bed and pulled me against him.

I wouldn't be sleeping alone; however, I wouldn't be sleeping with both of them either.

I curled up to Sir, relishing the warmth of his arms. And as I drifted off, content to be with this man, the one who held half of my heart, I couldn't help but wonder what I'd done wrong, why Master was abandoning me after what had quite possibly been the most perfect evening.

SEVENTEEN

THE SECOND I STEPPED OFF the elevator this morning was like coming home. The first thing I saw was Jordan's smiling face as he beamed back at me.

"Hello, gorgeous!"

"Jordan!" Although I'd seen him just two nights ago, it felt like ages since I'd been able to spend any real time with him, so my excitement at seeing him back in the real world was palpable. I knew he could tell by the way he stepped out from behind his desk and held out his arms to me.

I quickly hugged him, smiling from ear to ear.

"I've never met anyone quite so happy to be back at work," he said as he pulled back.

"What can I say? I love this place."

He pretended to gag. "We need to work on getting you a life outside of these walls."

"That we do."

We then agreed to meet for lunch to dish about everything now that I had nothing to hide from him. It felt good knowing that I didn't have to keep my secret anymore, that when he said he wouldn't judge me, he wasn't trying to simply get me to spill my guts.

Knowing there was a ton for me to catch up on, I headed for my desk, desperate for something to focus on. Ever since Sir had taken me home yesterday morning, I'd spent more than enough time thinking about what had happened during my holiday vacation. The island, the party, the way Master had retreated completely. It was a mixture of fond memories and chaos that had consumed me, but now that I was back at work, I knew I could reset and put the past behind me.

Ben arrived at nine with a smile on his face.

"Good morning," I greeted. "I've got coffee ready to brew."

"That would be fantastic," he said as he stepped into his office.

I hit the button on the coffeemaker and skimmed the calendar to see what was going on today. It seemed things would be relatively light, at least for the next few days. Probably because everyone was coming back from at least a few days off. It would allow me plenty of time to get through my email and figure out a plan for the coming weeks.

When the coffee was finished, I carried a mug into Ben's office and placed it on his desk. He was hanging up his phone, a frown on his face.

"Is something wrong?"

His smile was forced when he looked up at me. "Not at all. Just something I need to take care of."

He took a sip of his coffee, then turned his attention back to his computer. I slipped out quietly, curious as to what had made his smile falter in the few minutes he'd been there. I didn't get a chance to find out, because a few minutes later he was carrying his mug out of his office and down the hall. He took a right, which would lead him to the back conference room.

Again, I was curious as to what was going on, but I forced myself to focus on my work. It wasn't my place to drill my bosses about what they were doing anyway.

It wasn't until eleven o'clock that I realized none of my other bosses had come in. I didn't have any messages from them, so I called Jordan.

"Hey, have you heard from anyone? Do you know if they're coming in today? I saw Ben earlier, but he disappeared."

"Uh…"

I could hear the concern in his tone. "What?"

"Justin came in a couple of hours ago. Landon and Langston arrived shortly thereafter."

"No they didn't," I argued, looking around to make sure I wasn't mistaken.

"They did. They're…in the back conference room. They said they didn't want to be disturbed."

"Oh. Okay. Thanks." I hung up with Jordan and stared at the hallway.

What the hell was going on? Hadn't they done this once already? What in the world were they discussing that they had to be so secretive? So much so that they hadn't bothered to let me know they were in? That was just downright rude. Were they talking about me? Did I do something wrong? I mean, I knew something had happened with Master, the way he had gone missing after our vanilla evening, but surely that had nothing to do with this. Did it?

A million things went through my head and they all revolved around the time we'd spent together over the holidays. The island, the way Master and Sir had claimed me as their submissive during the time we were there. Of course, I couldn't forget New Year's or the fact that Justin and Ben hadn't been at the party. Did something happen to Justin? Was that what this was about?

I didn't get any answers to the questions, because no one came out to speak to me.

Rather than get all worked up about it, I focused on my email, then went to lunch with Jordan, grateful for the distraction.

EIGHTEEN

BOSS MEETING

LANDON

I HAD ABSOLUTELY NO CLUE why we'd all been called into this room again.

Well, that wasn't entirely true. I did know. However, I wasn't sure now was the time for us to be discussing this. We had work to do and the last thing we needed was to become a bunch of fucking harpies talking about feelings and shit. I had enough on my plate as it was. We'd been away from the office for two weeks and I was terrified to look at my inbox, knowing I would spend just as much time making up for the time I'd taken off.

"It's obvious things are changing," Justin declared, addressing all three of us directly. He'd been the one to call together this meeting, so it only seemed fair for him to begin. "It was brought to my attention that the two of you took Luci to TJ's party on New Year's Eve."

We had, but I wasn't sure what that had to do with anything.

"Yet no one filled me in," Justin continued.

Langston appeared as confused as I felt. "You were invited to the party. It's not our fault you opted not to go."

Justin glared at Langston. "I might've changed my mind if you'd have mentioned taking Luci."

"Why would that matter?" I asked, totally baffled about what the fuck was going on here.

Justin sighed heavily. "It would've mattered." He glanced at Langston, then back to me. "Regardless, it's obvious things have changed. The dynamic between the two of you and Luci isn't what we all signed on for originally."

Okay, fine. He had a point there.

"That does seem to be the case," I agreed.

Justin was right. Things *were* changing. As far as I was concerned, they were changing for the better. After the trip to the island, I'd made up my mind about what I wanted. The issue was in convincing my brother that it was time for us to make a move. Unfortunately, every time Langston took one step forward, he took two steps back. For example, the night he walked out of my bedroom and left me alone with Luci. He had retreated from her in a way that pissed me off, yet I hadn't bothered to call him on it.

"I think it's only fair that we figure out how to proceed," Justin said, his gaze bouncing back and forth between Langston and me.

"We could start by going to work," Langston snapped. "That's the reason we're here, right?"

Justin glared at him.

Ben cleared his throat. "I assume we're discussing our personal relationships with Luci? Not her working here?"

"That better be the case," Langston said, his tone hard as his attention cut over to Ben. "Her job isn't in question."

"No, it's not," I agreed. "Quite frankly, she's the best damn secretary we've ever had." The woman had gone above and beyond what anyone had expected. Not of her, but of the position. We all knew going into this that Luciana was a smart woman. She might've been messy at home, but she was organized and consistent. She kept us on our toes.

"I agree," Ben stated. "Which is the reason I wanted to clarify. If it comes down to whether or not she's staying on, there's no question. I'm ready to promote her to office manager, rather than merely a secretary."

"I think that's pretty much deduced," Langston said, his tone now bored. "She's far more than a secretary."

"However," Justin inserted, "I think she likes the title. It defines the job as she sees it, not necessarily how she handles it."

"Seriously? Is that why we're in here? To talk about her job title, because you can call her whatever the hell you want. Her position is still the same."

Justin sighed. "No, that's not why I called this meeting."

"So, enlighten us," Langston insisted.

"I saw the way you two were with her on the island."

Yep, I knew where this was going.

Justin's attention was fixed on Langston. "And I know you took her to TJ's house for dinner before that. As your submissive."

"I did."

"And you spent the night with her."

"Correct." Langston appeared uninterested in the conversation. "I didn't realize I needed to ask permission."

"You don't," Ben stated, glancing between the two men.

"No, you don't," Justin continued. "However, it seems you're looking for something more from her. And I thought we had all agreed to keep the others informed of our intentions."

"We did." Langston shrugged. "Where the hell are you going with this?" he grumbled.

I wanted to know that as well.

"It looks as though you've claimed her as your submissive." Justin's eyes darted over to me. "You, too." He frowned. "And not just on the island."

No one had *officially* claimed Luci, but Justin was right. Things were progressing and that was the path that I wanted to take. It was merely a matter of time.

"No one has claimed her," Langston stated, his defenses coming up.

"Maybe not yet," Justin snapped. "Goddammit, Langston. It's not an option. We have an agreement and I refuse to let you derail this while we're just getting to know her."

Just getting to know her?

Luci had been working here for three months. We'd all gotten to know her well enough at this point. At least, I thought we had.

Shit. I should've expected it to come down to this. From the day Luci walked into our lives, we'd been somewhat at odds with one another. My brother and I against Justin and Ben. That was the way things worked around here. Everyone knew that Langston and I would eventually settle down with one submissive. That had always been our goal.

And since Justin and Ben's relationship had been heating up, it was only safe to assume they would be following that path as well.

However...

As far as I was concerned, Luci belonged to me. No way was I going to step out of this completely and let them fight for her. She was mine. I'd known it from the beginning.

The only problem was, I knew Langston wasn't on the same page. Not yet. There for about a minute, I thought we were making progress, but then my asshole brother did what he always did and retreated from what he truly wanted. It never failed.

"So, what are you suggesting?" It was clear Langston wasn't happy about the topic.

"I'm suggesting that we continue on the path we *were* on. In the beginning," Justin explained. "You're more than welcome to spend time with her after hours, even have her spend the night, but not at the expense of the rest of us. You can't monopolize her time."

Langston didn't respond immediately.

"Are you wanting something more?" Justin asked, his eyes locked on Langston.

Again, Langston didn't say anything.

"Son of a bitch," Justin groaned.

"I didn't say I wanted more," Langston clarified, his voice deep and full of emotion. "However, I'm not ruling it out. As of right now, I'm content with the way things are going. However, I do intend to get closer to her." Langston looked at Landon. "My intention was for both of us to get closer to her."

I wasn't surprised by that statement. Not entirely. But my brother was still holding himself back. He seemed to want more, but he was unwilling to ask for it. I think it had a lot to do with how inexperienced Luci was. She was learning, but she still had a long way to go before she understood the true meaning of submission.

Perhaps it was her request for more vanilla that had thrown him off. Everyone knew my brother wasn't comfortable with that. He wasn't looking to wine and dine a woman, to spend the evening making love to her. He wanted to dominate her, and for whatever reason, he took the full-time D/s thing seriously. He didn't seem to know any other way to do it.

"Trust me," Langston clarified, "I'm not ready to move forward with her. I want to get to know her, but that's all I want. For now."

That bothered me more than I expected.

Justin looked pained.

"You need to make up your mind," Justin bit out. "I'm tired of wandering around waiting for the other shoe to drop."

"No one said you should wait," Langston argued. "Fucking go after her if that makes you feel better. I'm certainly not considering your feelings when I invite her somewhere."

Great. This was quickly going nowhere.

"You should collar her now and get it over with," Justin yelled.

"But…that's *not* what I want from her," Langston admitted.

I kept my mouth shut. It was exactly what *I* wanted from her and my brother knew it. As always, I was letting him lead because I knew that he was more practical when it came to shit like this. I tended to go after what I wanted, which, in this case, hadn't been easy because I'd been holding back so much all this time.

"But is that your plan? To eventually collar her?" Justin asked, his tone no longer strained.

"It's highly likely."

"What does that even mean?" Justin snapped. "Are you saying that the two of you intend to claim her for your own but you're biding your time? Or are you stringing her along?"

Langston's gaze slammed into Justin's. "Don't act as though you haven't noticed, Parker. From the moment I met that girl, I knew that she would belong to us."

"Yet you've been toying with her all along."

That seemed to piss Langston off. "I'm not toying with anyone. I'm merely letting her get her feet wet. She deserves to explore this because it's obviously what she wants."

"We don't know what she wants," I noted. "No one has bothered to ask her directly. We've only assumed based on her actions."

"So, why doesn't someone ask her?" Ben questioned, his irritation bleeding into his words.

"I think that's a brilliant idea," Justin agreed. "I think we should give her a chance to tell us what she wants."

Langston glared at Justin. "Fine. Call her in here. Let's get it over with."

"I'd like to think we should at least have some options for her before we drag her ass in here," Ben said, ever the voice of reason.

"I think the two of you are overstepping," Justin insisted. "That woman has a good head on her shoulders. If she wasn't interested in continuing this, she would've told us."

"Maybe," Langston agreed. "Or perhaps she doesn't want to step on any toes. The woman's a natural submissive."

"Well, no shit. We figured that out from the second she stepped into the office," Ben said flatly.

Justin took a deep breath. "I say we come up with a few options and let her decide."

"Y'all can do whatever the hell you want," I stated, feeling the need to get my two cents in. "I'm not willing to give her up. Not yet." Not ever.

Justin's tone was somber when he said, "I think we're all on the same page there."

Nineteen

I WAS BACK AT MY desk at two o'clock on the dot. I instantly noticed that none of my bosses had returned, and I didn't know what to think about that. They had been holed up in the conference room for hours.

Seriously? What did they have to talk about for *that* long?

About ten minutes till three, I looked up to see Sir walking toward me. He looked tense, but he managed to smile when he approached, though it didn't quite meet his eyes. I was shocked when he held out his hand to me, silently willing me to stand up.

"We'd like you to join us in the conference room, sweet girl."

I loved when he called me that. And I loved when he looked at me the way that he was. As though I was the only person he wanted to look at.

"Okay. I just need to tell Jordan I'll be in a meeting."

Sir stepped back while I grabbed the phone and hit the button to dial the front desk.

"I hope this is good news," he said by way of greeting.

"I'll be in a meeting for a little while. Please hold all calls or send them to voice mail."

"Yes, *ma'am*. And hey…good luck."

I chuckled at his excitement, then hung up the phone. We had spent our entire lunch hour coming up with reasons our bosses were hiding out. All of which were completely ridiculous. After all, I couldn't imagine it was anything serious. Things had been progressing quite well. And the more I had thought about it, the less tense I'd become. They were probably talking about work and now they wanted to have an impromptu Monday meeting…on Tuesday.

Sir was still waiting for me, so I turned to follow. He placed his hand on the back of my neck—a possessive move that stirred some sort of deep need inside me—and urged me toward the back conference room.

Once inside, I noticed that the blinds were open and Ben, Justin, and Master were still talking. They went silent when I joined them. There was tension in the air, something that I'd never felt before.

"Please," Master said, motioning toward the chair between him and Sir, "have a seat."

"Yes, Master," I whispered.

Once I was seated, Justin was the one to start talking.

"As you can see, we had some things to discuss today. And we wanted you here for two reasons."

I swallowed hard, then blurted out my fear. "Are you going to fire me?"

Despite all the fun and games, I had come to love my job and I didn't want to have to look for another.

"It's good, Luci," Ben stated softly. "There's nothing for you to worry about. Regardless of what decisions are made going forward, your employment here is secure. You've done a phenomenal job in that regard. I don't want you to think otherwise."

I was sure he meant to ease my fears, but he only made it worse. I had no idea what was going on. Everything had seemed fine when we left the island, but I could tell something was really off right now. And the issue appeared to be between the four of them. Did that mean I was at the heart of it? I had only briefly spoken to Justin and Ben since the island, so I wasn't sure how that could be the case.

Justin leaned forward, planted his elbows on his knees, and dropped his head into his hands. It was strange to see him look that way. Usually the man was so self-assured, so confident. He appeared almost…defeated.

"We were actually trying to find a way to make things less confusing around here," Sir explained when no one else spoke. "It seems that in the past couple of weeks, the dynamic has changed and we know it's going to affect things here in the office." He looked at me as he spoke. "I assume you've noticed it, too?"

I nodded. Things had changed. In a good way. Or so I'd thought. Now I wasn't so sure. Still, I responded with, "Yes, Sir."

Justin cleared his throat. "See, right there."

Sir's gaze shot over to Master, then to Justin.

I was scared to look at Master, worried what I would see on his face. The last time we'd been together, he had walked out of Sir's bedroom without looking back.

Instead, I continued to focus on Justin. He seemed to be the most upset out of all of them and I didn't know why.

He stood up and paced the room, all eyes following him.

A few tense moments passed, but then he took a deep breath. "We initially thought we'd give Landon and Langston the choice but then decided that wasn't fair. To you."

Choice? What choice?

I frowned, not sure what he meant.

"Initially, we were going to force them to either collar you or let you go."

Collar me? Master and Sir? Why would they do that?

My hand instantly went to my neck. I'd read about collaring, knew exactly what that meant. When a Dom claimed a sub as his, he collared her. I'd read numerous stories, some so deeply romantic it was a level of trust and love that I'd never known existed. In my opinion, it was far more revered than even the sanctity of marriage, which, if I looked at it rationally, seemed to be more about government and paperwork than about true love anyway. And wasn't the statistic something along the lines of one in three marriages ended in divorce? I mean, look at the divorce rate of famous people.

But that wasn't the point.

The point was Justin felt the need to push the issue. I mean, yeah, I thought we'd made progress during our time together, but Master and Sir had given me no inkling as to whether they wanted this to progress further than what it was. In fact, Master had made me feel the opposite when he walked out on us the other night.

"However, after considerable discussion, we decided to make the choice yours," Justin declared.

"Mine?" I didn't like the sound of this.

Justin came over and knelt down before me, his hand cupping my face as he stared into my eyes. I could see a torrent of emotion in the ocean-blue depths. It drew me in and I found myself leaning into his touch.

"You see, our reasons for hiring you weren't completely altruistic, Luci. Your friend Kristen…well, let's just say that she had some positive things to say about you. And not all of them were work related."

I pulled back, feeling as though someone had slapped me. "What does that mean?"

Justin returned to his seat and once again, I felt all eyes on me.

Sir sighed. "As you're aware, Langston and I know her. And after your time on the island, I'm sure you even know *how* we know her."

"No, not really." I had yet to get that detail.

Sir continued, "Kristen's a member of…the same club we are."

I glanced around, my eyes going to Justin and Ben. "Everyone keeps mentioning this club. What sort of club is it exactly?"

"BDSM," Ben explained.

My eyes cut back to Sir. "Okay." That explained a lot. "But what does that have to do with anything?"

"Kristen felt as though you'd be a good fit, not only for the position but for *us*."

I started shaking, the news hitting me like a two-by-four to the face. It almost sounded as though my friend had pimped me out to…her Dom friends. Why? Why would she do that to me?

Sir moved toward me, his hand cupping my face, forcing me to look at him. I sucked in air.

"We agreed to do the interview. But the day you showed up, not a single one of us can deny that we felt a spark, a connection with you. It might sound strange, but it happened. The decision to hire you was unanimous. We wanted to see where this might lead."

I took that to mean my resume hadn't played into it at all.

Which meant they hadn't hired me because they thought I'd be a good fit for the company, they merely thought...

I shook my head. I couldn't think about that. Not if I was expected to keep my cool.

I waited, relishing the feel of Sir's thumb as it brushed over my cheek. It was the only safe thing in the chaos engulfing me and I feared it wasn't going to last long enough. I didn't know what to think, what to believe, or even what to feel. This was rapidly spiraling out of control. Or maybe that was just my life.

I felt as though I'd been misled. I thought for some reason, they had...come to like me on their own. Not because my friend had convinced them I'd be a good fit for their kinky fetishes.

"Not all of us have had our fair share of you," Justin whispered from across the room.

I started to speak, but Sir pressed his thumb over my lips. "It's not your fault. It's ours. We were just getting comfortable with the way things were going but then..." His eyes lifted and he peered over my shoulder at his twin. "They changed."

When he looked back at me, I waited patiently for him to continue. He didn't.

I could see a torrent of emotion in his eyes as he leaned back in his chair.

"We aren't all on board with this change," Justin stated. "Like I said, we haven't all had the chance to explore where this thing is going."

I dared to look over at Ben, who discreetly nodded.

Justin continued, "So, we've decided that going forward the choice would be yours."

Oh, God. I seriously hoped they weren't expecting me to choose between them. That didn't seem fair at all. After the time I'd spent with Landon and Langston...I was scared where my heart was at. I'd given it some thought over the past couple of weeks and Sir was right about one thing. It was moving rather quickly, the dynamic changing into something that I didn't recognize. Something I wasn't sure I was even ready for. However, there was no doubt in my mind that I'd fallen in love with both Landon and Langston.

And maybe that was what the issue was. Did Justin feel slighted? As though I'd done this on purpose?

"We're gonna make this easy on you, sweet girl," Sir said, shifting so that he was facing me, his elbows resting on his knees. "As easy as we can, anyway."

"However," Master chimed in, "you are not to make the decision today. Once we lay out the options, we want you to go home and think about it."

Justin spoke up. "We're giving you tomorrow off. Paid, of course. And we want you to give it some serious consideration."

I was so freaking confused. How had we gone from having a good time on the island, then a party on New Year's, to me making a decision that could very well destroy what we'd already established? And what about my job? Why were they acting as though that was secondary to this?

"On Thursday morning," Sir said, "once we're all in the office, we'll reconvene to hear your answer. Of course, if you need more time than that, you simply have to ask. Remember, there is no wrong answer, Luci. No one will hold it against you, regardless."

I wasn't so sure about that. I'd heard something along those lines before. Like back in high school when I told Joey Williams that I only wanted to be friends. He told me that he understood. And though we'd spent the first three months of eleventh grade hanging out, he never spoke to me after that. Not one time.

So, no one could blame me for not buying into the whole *there is no wrong answer* bullshit.

However, I didn't think this was the time or place to explain that to them. Instead, I scanned the room, glancing at the others. They each nodded. The only one who looked remotely worried was Master. My heart ached at the thought of what options they might be giving me.

When I glanced back at Sir, he was still watching me.

"As I mentioned, the four of us wanted to hire you. We had our individual reasons, and over the past few months, you've gotten to know us. Some more than others."

My heart sank in my chest. I had a feeling I knew where this was going.

"As far as we're concerned, you have three choices."

Ben cleared his throat, so I looked his way. "Your first choice is to continue on the way things were in the beginning. The four of us sharing you, enjoying you here in the office with a few chance encounters outside the office. You will not answer to one person, and no one will monopolize your time. We'll keep it more interactive with the four of us present. More like a friends-with-benefits arrangement with no strings attached."

Who invented that term? No strings attached? Had to have been a man because it was stupid.

I frowned.

"Or," Justin said, my gaze shooting over to him, "we'll change things up a bit. We'll rotate so that you have one person to answer to every couple of weeks. We'll still share you, we'll still play, but you'll have more individual time with each of us. So that we can each get to know you on the level we originally intended."

"Your final option," Master noted, his voice rougher than I'd ever heard it. He cleared his throat and continued. "We'll move forward with me as your master. Only me. That means *I* will be responsible for you, for directing things as I see fit."

My gaze cut to Landon. Only Langston? What about Landon? I didn't want Langston without Landon. I thought they knew that. Why would they even make that an option?

"However, pet," Master said, drawing my attention back to him, "it's important you understand that I'm not in a position to collar you at this time. That's not the direction that I'm going. That doesn't mean I don't want you to be mine, it merely means we're not at that level yet. We could be someday."

Could be.

Wow. How romantic.

I wasn't sure he realized that with those few words, he had completely shattered my heart. Sure, I'd been second-guessing myself, but deep down, I was the kind of girl who was hoping for her fairy-tale prince (or two in this case) to come in and whisk her off her feet, declaring his undying love.

Clearly, my prince was not in this room.

I swallowed the lump in my throat, wanting to say something but not sure how to express what I felt. The last part pained me more than anyone would know. Considering my feelings for Master and Sir, it was devastating to know that they didn't feel the same.

"Do not answer now," Sir added.

I couldn't help but wonder why he wasn't giving me an option that included him. That was the only thing I wanted. He had to know that.

"We want you to go home and think about it," Sir continued. "We've agreed that we won't make direct contact with you until you've made your decision and you meet with the four of us on Thursday." He waved his hand. "Or whenever you're ready." Sir's gaze shot to the other three men. "That means no one is to contact her. Not by phone, text, or showing up at her apartment. This is her decision."

"Like we said," Justin added, "there is no wrong answer. We want you to make the decision that is right for you. And like Ben said, your job is not in jeopardy. Should you come back on Thursday and tell us all that you want nothing to do with this anymore, we'll understand that, too. It wasn't supposed to happen this way, Luci."

I nodded, unable to keep the tear from trickling down my cheek.

I don't think they understood how difficult this decision was.

Or how painful it was to know that no one truly wanted me. For their own.

TWENTY

I COULD SEE THE SHOCK on Jordan's face when he found out I was leaving for the day and would not be returning until Thursday. He knew something was up, and I assured him that I would be back and not to worry.

Granted, *I* was worried.

"Too late for that, kiddo. I'm already worried. Why don't you come over for dinner tonight? With me and Dale."

I stared back at my friend, then nodded. "Okay. What time?"

Without answering me, Jordan reached out and stole my phone from my hand. He quickly put in his number, then called his phone.

"Okay, now that I have your number, I'll text you after I talk to Dale."

I shook my head. "Jordan, seriously...I don't want you to go to any trouble."

He held up his hand. "Shut it. No one's going to any trouble. You come over, we'll feed you, and we can talk about whatever you want to talk about."

It wasn't like I wanted to argue with him. I honestly needed a friend right now and I found myself closer to Jordan these days than I was to Kristen.

"Okay. Just text me."

"Will do. Be careful. And call me if you need anything." He slowly sat down in his chair, watching me like a sad puppy dog as I backed toward the elevator. I offered a smile, then turned around.

I had a lot of thinking to do before I shared anything with Jordan, and I didn't have the faintest idea where to start. The only consolation was that they weren't firing me. If it turned out that I couldn't continue doing this with them, then at least I would still have my job.

And wouldn't that be freaking awkward.

•

After I returned to my apartment, I changed into yoga pants and an oversized sweatshirt, then made a cup of hot chocolate. I needed something to soothe my soul and this was the only way I knew to begin.

Soothe my soul.

Right.

Like that would ever happen.

Never in my life had I felt more like a punching bag than I did in that moment. These men were tossing me around as though it was inevitable that I would bounce back. Only, I wasn't sure I had any bounce left in me. This was nuts. One minute we were role playing on the beach, the next I was dancing at New Year's, and now I was being told I had to choose. But quite frankly, my choices sucked.

"Uggh!"

Before settling on the sofa, I grabbed a notebook and pen from my nightstand, figuring the best way to attack this was to start with lists. That was what I was good at.

"This is not gonna be easy," I muttered to myself, curling up with a blanket. "Not easy at all."

I figured the best thing to do was to start by listing what my options were.

I wrote the headings on three separate pages: *Back to the beginning; A little taste of everything; False commitment.*

Those seemed fitting for what my bosses said I could choose from. The idea of kicking them all to the curb, as Justin had hinted at, did not sit well with me. I was confused and a little heartbroken, but I wasn't ready for this to be over. So, I wasn't even considering it.

My first option wasn't all that appealing. Although I had enjoyed it in the beginning, even *I* could accept that I wanted more than to be a mere plaything for the four men to entertain when they chose to. Sure, I enjoyed it and I knew I would continue to enjoy it, but there was no ending, which made it feel too undefined, I guess was the right word.

The second option of being dominated by each of them randomly, while still being shared between them, was the least dreadful. I couldn't deny that. I enjoyed being with each man, but I also enjoyed having all their attention. It would give me the most options, the ability to get to know them better. And not just sexually.

And the final option, which was giving myself to Master, while not having him give himself to me in return, made my heart hurt. It was an abysmal option. For one, I cared about him, but I didn't want him without Sir. That I knew for an absolute fact.

And then there had been his declaration. He wasn't ready to collar me, but one day he might be? What kind of crap was that? I physically ached when I thought about what he'd said, how he wasn't ready but he *might* in the future. However, I couldn't deny that I had feelings for him and I wanted to please him.

On the other hand, I hadn't even known what collars were three months ago. Why would anyone assume I was ready or willing to wear one?

I huffed.

No, this certainly wasn't going to be an easy choice.

"Pros and cons," I muttered to myself. That seemed like a good avenue to explore next.

With my pen in hand, I decided three pros and three cons for each scenario was necessary, so I got to work.

BACK TO THE BEGINNING

Pros
- ✓ Enjoy the attention of all four men.
- ✓ Spontaneity.
- ✓ No stress.

Cons
- ✓ No structure.
- ✓ Lack of real intimacy.
- ✓ No future.

A LITTLE TASTE OF EVERYTHING

Pros
- ✓ Intimate encounters with each man.
- ✓ Spontaneity.
- ✓ Some structure.

Cons
- ✓ Delicate balance.
- ✓ Worry about pleasing everyone.
- ✓ No future

FALSE COMMITMENT

Pros
- ✓ Commitment.
- ✓ Spend more time with Master.
- ✓ Structure.

Cons
- ✓ Lack of true commitment from Master.
- ✓ Owned but not kept.
- ✓ Not having Sir.

Although the lists came relatively easy, I instantly knew that they wouldn't help in my decision. For one, I tended to follow my heart and not my brain, which meant this decision was more of an emotional one.

Dropping my pen and notepad onto my lap, I picked up my hot chocolate and stared at the wall. Anger began bubbling up inside of me and I wasn't sure where it was coming from. Perhaps I was upset that my bosses were making this so difficult for me. Up until this afternoon, I thought we were enjoying ourselves. I'm not sure what caused things to move in this direction, for any of them to make a decision that would alter the course of everything.

I wanted to blame one of them for being selfish, but I couldn't. For one, I had no clue whose idea this was. I suspected it was Justin, but I didn't know for certain. He seemed to be the one keeping the most distance between us. Or maybe Ben? What if he didn't like the way things were going between me and Justin? Or hell, maybe it was Landon.

Shit. I had no clue.

I wasn't sure what Ben felt for me, but I knew we were close. If nothing else, we were friends and I was content with that. As for Justin… He was an enigma. He kept his emotions guarded and I felt as though he merely wanted to use my body when it was convenient for him. Not that I minded. I was enjoying that part. Of course, that had me thinking about Ben again. Ben was Justin's submissive. Did that mean that Ben took orders from Justin even when he was the dominant one? Was he only with me because Justin instructed him to be?

And Landon… I felt something deeper with him. I'd spent enough time with him to know that we had connected on an emotional level. Except he didn't seem to be fighting for me.

Then I realized that I didn't have all the tools necessary to make a decision. If these men wanted me to make a choice, it only seemed fair that they had to be held responsible for their actions, too. I certainly wasn't going to make it easy on them. They had specifically stated that they couldn't make contact with me, but if I initiated it…

Grabbing my phone, I pulled up Landon's—yes, I was back to calling him Landon because right now he didn't deserve to be called Sir—number. I would text him my instructions since he seemed to be the one trying to bring this to a close.

Luci: *In order for me to make an informed decision, I need to make a request.*

Landon: *Anything, sweet girl. Just name it.*

My heart once again did a slow flip in my chest at his pet name for me. I liked that he used it. In fact, I liked that they all had a different one for me.

Luci: *I'd like for each of you to write me a letter. Doesn't have to be lengthy, but I'd like you to write me a letter telling me what these past few months have meant to you. Once all four letters have been written, seal them in an envelope and give them to Jordan. I'll arrange to get them from him.*

Landon: *I'll let the others know and we'll have them to Jordan first thing tomorrow morning.*

Luci: *Thank you.*

Rather than go into a detailed explanation of why I felt this was necessary, I put my phone down. I didn't want to chat with Landon and disobey the rules. However, I knew better than to email them at their work addresses because this was not technically company business. Although we had an arrangement, I wanted this to be separate.

•

I received a text message from Jordan at 5:40 p.m.

Jordan: *Dale and I would be honored if you'd join us for dinner tonight. Would six thirty work for you? I'm not sure how long it'll take you to get here.*

He followed the first text with his address, which I learned—thanks to Google Maps—that he was about three blocks from the office. I texted him back to let him know six thirty would be great. Knowing I looked like a bum, I quickly changed into jeans and a nice sweater, pulled my hair back in a ponytail, and touched up my makeup before hopping in my car and heading back downtown.

It didn't take long to locate Jordan's apartment. When I knocked, I was instantly met by Dale, who gave me a huge grin as he pulled me inside.

"You made it," he said in a huff. "I think my Knight's going a little crazy worrying about you."

I smiled, loving how he referred to Jordan as his Knight, even in such a casual environment.

"Well, he has no need to worry. I'm perfectly fine."

Dale lifted one dark eyebrow. "Fine? Honey, you're not fine until you've had a couple glasses of wine and you share all the deets of what's going on. J won't tell me anything and if I don't get something soon, I'm going to lose my mind."

I laughed. I liked that Dale was as eccentric as Jordan. I hadn't expected it, honestly.

"Where is she?" Jordan yelled seconds before he appeared in the small entryway. "Get your little butt in here, woman."

I let Dale lead me into the kitchen, where Jordan set a glass of wine on the breakfast bar and pulled out a stool for me.

"Sit. Drink. Dish."

I couldn't help but laugh. I was so glad I'd decided to come over. Truthfully, after what had happened earlier, I wasn't sure I was going to be smiling, much less laughing for quite some time.

"What are we having?" I asked, mostly in an attempt to put off the inevitable, but also because it smelled delicious.

"Homemade beef stroganoff," Jordan informed me. "My boy knows how to cook."

I glanced over at Dale, enjoying the way he blushed when Jordan said such sweet things about him.

"Is there a reason you call him my Knight?" I just had to know.

Dale blushed again, but Jordan was the one who spoke up.

"We met at a club one night and my boy here was with another Dom." He waved a hand dismissively. "A pretentious asshole who called himself a Dom."

"Don't get him started," Dale warned with a chuckle.

"Anyway, I saw them arguing and I didn't like the way the man was talking to him, so I intervened. The rest is history."

"And because he came riding in on his white horse, I call him my Knight."

I lifted my wineglass in a mock toast. "Well, that makes perfect sense. Plus, it's a romantic story."

"But enough about that," Jordan said as he laid the plates out before me. "Either you start talking or I hide the food."

Taking a sip of wine, I narrowed my eyes at Jordan. "You wouldn't dare."

"Try me, little girl. Remember who the Dom is here."

"About that," I said, pointing toward him with my glass. "How did I work with you for nearly three months and not find out that you were into the lifestyle until you showed up out of the blue on the island? Hmm? I can't quite figure that one out."

Jordan grinned over at Dale. "I told you that was the first thing she was going to ask."

Dale nodded. "It's true. That's exactly what he said."

"Well? I deserve answers."

"You'll get them," Jordan assured me. "Just as long as you promise to talk to me."

I sobered, my smile somewhat sad. "I promise, I'll talk."

"Good." He sighed, then took a long sip of his wine. "And the fact that I'm a Dom and I have a full-time submissive is not something I share with many people. Not because I'm embarrassed but because it typically doesn't come up in conversation. I'm not sure when the appropriate time to tell you that I had a man at home who called me his Knight and allowed me to tie him up and do wicked, dirty things to him would've been."

Again, I glanced at Dale, who was now blushing profusely.

"Okay, fine. You've got me there." It was true. It had never come up in conversation.

"But I could say the same to you," Jordan continued. "When were you going to tell me that you had four masters?"

I sighed. "I don't have four masters." That much was true. At the moment, I didn't feel like I had any. I wasn't sure what I was going to do come Thursday.

Jordan came around and took the seat beside me, his hand resting on my forearm. "Talk to me, sweetie. Dale and I won't judge you and maybe we'll help you figure out what your next steps are."

I smiled, willing the tears not to fall. And two seconds later, I found myself telling Jordan and Dale everything that had happened from the moment we left the island until this afternoon when I'd been told to go home and think about my options.

Needless to say, we had needed the two bottles of wine.

TWENTY-ONE

ON WEDNESDAY MORNING, I ARRANGED to meet Jordan in the office at eight thirty in order to get the letters. When I texted him at seven forty-five, he assured me the boss fairies had come through for me and there was an envelope locked in his desk for safe keeping.

When I arrived, his eyes were as round as saucers when he took in my bedraggled appearance. I hadn't bothered to shower yet, so my hair was loosely knotted on top of my head, I had no makeup on, and I was wearing my favorite yoga pants and an oversized sweatshirt. I was a hot mess, I wouldn't lie. Even after last night, after spending time with Jordan and Dale, laughing and talking and drinking wine, I still couldn't sleep for shit. My bosses' request was weighing heavily on me.

"Okay, so this is not how I expected you to look after our talk last night," he stated as he hesitantly passed over the envelope, still checking me out.

I peered down at myself. "Oh, this old thing? I was going for shabby chic. Too much?"

He smiled, but I could tell he wasn't completely taken by my charm. "Are you sure you're okay?"

I hugged him, wanting to reassure him. "I'm fine. I just have a lot of things to think about, but I promise I'll be back in the morning."

"I'm holding you to that. Have you talked to Kristen yet?"

Last night, I had talked to Jordan a little about Kristen, telling him all about how she had also kept her kinky life a secret all this time, plus how she was the one who had connected me with the job opportunity. After a little too much wine, I had also conveyed that she was personally responsible for setting things in motion with my bosses. He hadn't found that amusing in the least. I informed him I was scared to bring it up to her because I wasn't sure I could keep my anger in check after what she did to me. The fact that she pimped me out to my four bosses still bothered me more than anything.

"I have not. But I will. I plan to see her at yoga tonight."

"You need to talk to her. I think you'll feel better once you do."

"I know."

Not wanting to risk the chance of running into Ben, who would likely arrive any minute, I told Jordan I had to go, then darted back down to my car, which was being held at the front. Ideally, I wouldn't have had to deal with rush-hour traffic on my day off, but I knew there was no other way to get the letters because my bosses hadn't given them to him before he left last night.

The drive home took a little less time, but it felt like an eternity with the envelope practically calling my name from the passenger seat. Rather than go back to my apartment, I decided I would stop at Starbucks. Not only did I want coffee but I was hoping that by being in public, I wouldn't get too emotional about whatever they had to say in those letters.

After ordering a croissant and a grande caramel macchiato, I took a seat in the corner and flipped the envelope over and over in my hand.

I was terrified to open the damn thing, freaked out about what they might've said after they had some time to think about what was going on. But I knew I had to. I just wasn't ready yet. So, I managed to procrastinate a little longer by eating my croissant and watching the other patrons milling about.

There were several people setting up laptops alongside their coffee, some looking to be settling in for the long haul. I briefly wondered if any of them were my bosses' team members. It was possible, right? Since they were all remote, they might enjoy working in a Starbucks while they had their morning coffee. A change of scenery perhaps.

Or maybe one of them was one of Landon's or Langston's authors, writing their next bestseller.

That thought pleased me. I liked the idea of an author sneaking away from their normal writing spot to watch the world move around them. I glanced around, trying to figure who might be an author. I decided the young lady who looked a lot like me with her messy ponytail and lack of makeup. Her sweat pants were stylish, so at least she'd made a little effort.

It wasn't until I'd finished my croissant and my coffee that I realized I was putting off the inevitable. I had to open the letters, had to know what their true feelings were so I could make a decision and get on with my life.

Because that was what it all boiled down to. After three months of playing around, my bosses were asking me to make a choice. I seriously doubted it was for my benefit either, because, until yesterday, I'd been perfectly content with the way things were going.

Okay, maybe not perfectly. But I couldn't very well make any of my bosses fall in love with me and want a happily ever after, so one day at a time was all I had.

"Excuse me."

I looked up when I heard a woman's voice.

"Is this chair taken?"

I looked at the empty chair at my table, then around the space again. I hadn't realized how crowded it had gotten and I suddenly felt overwhelmed by all the people.

"Actually," I told her, getting to my feet and grabbing my trash, along with my envelope, "I was just leaving."

"Thanks."

With a quick nod, I headed out to my car, trying to think of a place to go where I could have some privacy but not be completely alone. I still didn't want to go back to my apartment. Truth was, I was dreading what the letters would say and crawling into my bed and crying for the remainder of the day wasn't something I looked forward to.

As I pulled out of the lot, I saw a sign for the lake and decided that was the perfect place to go.

Twenty minutes later, I was sitting on a secluded park bench watching joggers and walkers get in their morning exercise while the waves gently lapped at the shore.

"Now or never," I muttered to myself, holding the envelope up and staring at my name scrolled across the front. It looked a lot like Landon's neat, bold lettering. Or maybe Jordan's.

My shoulders tensed as I carefully opened the seal, then pulled out four sheets of paper. They didn't have names on them, so I wasn't sure whose letter was whose. I figured that was a good thing. I would read whichever one I opened first. No bias.

I slowly unfolded the first paper, my eyes dropping to the bottom of the page to the signature.

I smiled because I'd opened Justin's first. It seemed fitting since he was the first of my four bosses I'd actually spoken to on the day I showed up for my interview. I could still see his startled gaze when he looked at me.

Swallowing hard, I took a deep breath and started reading.

Princess,

I have to admit, when Landon informed me of your request for a heartfelt response, I was a bit surprised. Then, I was worried. I must tell you, I haven't written a letter like this since high school. Back when I thought I was in love with Suzy something or other. I wasn't, by the way. In love with her. Nor was she in love with me. It was merely young lust, but I have to give Suzy Whatsit some credit because she actually introduced me to this lifestyle. Or rather, her mother did. But I digress. And because you requested it, I'm going to give it my all.

Since you want to know what these past few months have meant to me, I need to start at the beginning. The day I stepped off the elevator and saw you standing in the office, waiting for your interview, I felt as though my life had been changed. There before me stood the most beautiful woman I'd ever laid eyes on. Sure, that probably sounds corny. For a man like me to be captivated by little more than a pleasant smile and a nicely put together face seems all kinds of wrong, but it's true. The moment I laid eyes on you, I knew you were going to play an important role in my life.

And since that day, my outlook on a lot of things has changed. Before you, I'd gotten myself into a rut, spending the majority of my time working and thinking of little else. Since you arrived, I've found myself looking forward to more. More time with you, more time with Ben. Hell, more time with the less rigid side of myself.

Now, I'm not the greatest at expressing how I feel, so I'm sure you're staring at this page with wide eyes, trying to tie it all back to the man you know me to be. However, I assure you, it's true.

No matter the decision you make, princess, I want you to know that I've enjoyed our time together. I'm hoping for more, but if the time I've had is all I get, I'm a better man for it.

Justin

I had to read the letter twice before I could move on, but even then, I had tears pooling in my eyes. Justin Parker wasn't a cold-hearted Dominant. He was a man with feelings and desires. However, what he said was true. I was having a hard time tying back his words with the man that I knew. And I couldn't help but think that meant I hadn't spent nearly enough time getting to know him.

This wasn't going to be an easy decision.

With a heavy sigh, I folded the letter and placed it back in the envelope before opening the next one. I instantly glanced at the signature. My heart pounded in my chest when I saw that it was from Langston. I immediately folded it back and put it at the bottom of the pile. Although I was trying not to be biased, I knew I couldn't avoid it. That man had the power to break me and I wanted to hear what the others said first.

I opened the next letter. It was from Ben.

Gumdrop,

If it all seems chaotic right now, I want to assure you that it will pass. Like all the complications we encounter in this life, things will get better. I know that's not what you want to hear from me, but it's the wisdom I wish to bestow. I'm a firm believer that our lives are mapped out for us and on every path we find ourselves on, we are meant to make a decision before moving forward. You're now at that crossroad.

I could go on and on about how I've enjoyed our time together and how I want to spend more time with you, but it would all be noise at this point. Follow your heart and we will all end up on the path we're supposed to be on.

Ben

I sniffled, willing myself not to cry. Ben was one of the kindest men I'd ever met. He had such a good heart. I smiled as I reread the short but sweet letter. I should've expected as much from Ben. He had always been there to give me advice, to steer me in the right direction. And yes, we'd had some great times together. I had enjoyed that man more than I could express. However, I also knew that he was devoted to Justin. They had something that no one could impinge upon. He might've shared a small piece of himself with me, but I knew where his heart belonged and I couldn't blame him.

Needless to say, his letter didn't help me to make a decision; however, it did make me feel better.

Quickly flipping the third letter open, I took a deep breath and jumped right in.

Sweet girl,

If I had all day, I couldn't tell you how I feel. I've never been the type who could express it in words. I'm more a hands-on kind of guy. And by my saying that, you should know that my feelings for you run deep. Far deeper than I anticipated. Although we've shared some intimate encounters, I feel as though I haven't had enough time with you and I'm not ready to give that up. I'm not.

You may have figured out that my brother and I do a lot of sharing. It's true. And above all else, it's what I want. Unfortunately, we don't always get what we want.

In order to get to that perfect point, I feel it's necessary to have you to myself, to get to know you on a different level. If we didn't have that opportunity and you were to always look to Langston for guidance and control, I'd be doing a serious disservice to you.

Regardless of your decision, I will respect it.

Landon

My eyes teared up again as I read the letter. Landon wasn't the type to mince words, and I could practically feel his emotions on the page. I was right in thinking that Landon and I had a connection, because I felt the same way about him. I wasn't ready to let him go. Not yet. Maybe not ever.

Staring at the final letter, I prayed that Langston would say something that would help me make a sound decision.

Little one,

I saw the pain I caused you when I laid out the truth, and I will admit that it hurt on a level I've never experienced before. However, in that same regard, what I said was true. In fact, everything I've said to you is true. Such as how I knew you were mine the first day that I saw you.

However, when I say that, I'm not sure you can completely understand what I mean. My brother and I are two halves of a whole, always have been, always will be. That means that if you're mine, you're his also. Unfortunately, I don't think I've been good at making that clear, or even figuring out the right way to pursue this that won't confuse you more.

As far as I'm concerned, you belong to both of us, pet. However, I don't think you've had time to truly understand what that means. Which is the very reason I forced my hand and insisted you make a choice that I hoped you wouldn't be able to make. I don't want you to choose me. Not just me. And that's why I said what I said.

No matter what your decision, I know that there is more in store for you and me and Landon. The question is, how long will it take before it's realized? Unfortunately, no one has the answer to that right now.

Master

Tears dripped down my cheeks as I read and reread Langston's letter. However, they weren't tears of sadness, they were tears of anger. It pissed me off that he could be so stubborn, that he could seemingly play God in so many lives. More so that he couldn't simply tell me what he was feeling. I didn't want only him. I wanted them both equally. Had he simply asked me, he would've known that.

But Langston had been in control since the beginning. He was the one who had switched the gears, veering off the track that we had been going down. And Landon was right. I did look to Langston for guidance and control because of the way he had handled things. It wasn't fair to the others, nor was it fair to me.

Especially since he wasn't willing to move this thing we shared any further. I even had to wonder whether he was holding Landon back as well.

Not that I hadn't expected it from him. Langston hadn't opened up to me. Not with his feelings. I could tell he wanted something from me. And fine, maybe he didn't know how he truly felt, but I did. I saw it when he looked at me, when he made love to me. It was there.

But he didn't want to accept it.

And because of that...

I sighed as I stared out at the water.

Because of that, I knew exactly what I had to do.

But first, I had to confront my friend.

TWENTY-TWO

AT A FEW MINUTES AFTER five, I forced myself up off my couch and headed to the bathroom to get ready. I had texted Kristen earlier, letting her know that it was important that I talk to her. She assured me she would be at the six o'clock yoga class. Which meant, if I wanted to be there on time, I would have to hurry.

Not only did I intend to call my friend out tonight but I was also looking forward to yoga. It would help to clear my mind. And when it was over, I would get a chance to confront Kristen. If nothing else, she had a whole lot to explain. After all, she was the one who had pimped me out to the men who were now making my life difficult.

Then, if she was still my friend when it was all said and done, I was hoping she could give me some advice about how to proceed. I knew what I wanted; now I just had to figure out how I was going to make it happen.

•

"Well, hello there, stranger," Kristen greeted when I walked into the yoga studio a few minutes before the class was to start. "You've still got the beach glow going on. Or maybe that's just what being in love looks like on you."

"Nobody said anything about love," I countered with a grin.

Kristen frowned, her eyes studying my face as though the answers to all her questions were etched into my skin. "Uh-oh. Trouble in paradise?"

"Something like that."

I think she knew where I was heading. I was trying to keep my tone even, but it was difficult. I was upset with her, but it wasn't fair to her because I had yet to explain it.

Although I didn't know every intimate detail of Kristen's life—such as she was a member of a BDSM club—I'd thought I knew her better than I did. I mean, I knew that she turned thirty last year, lived with her long-time boyfriend, worked as a sous chef for one of the upscale restaurants nearby, wasn't a big fan of sushi, and drank red wine like Kool-Aid. Those were important things to know about a person.

The fact that she had obviously helped get me a job had made me believe we were good friends. The point was, I'd trusted her.

Only to find out she was a Domme, her boyfriend her submissive, and she had purposely put me in the path of my four bosses for reasons that weren't altruistic—to use Justin's word.

Kristen narrowed her eyes. "I guess I have some explaining to do."

I nodded. "That would be nice."

She hugged me again. "Let's grab a bite after class and I'll tell you everything. Just don't be mad at me, okay? It's bad for your chi."

I chuckled. Although I felt slightly set up, I wasn't really mad. I wanted to be, sure. But there was so much upheaval, right now I just wanted a friend who wouldn't abandon me. I had Jordan, but I couldn't deny that Kristen and I had once been close. I still needed her more than I was willing to admit.

I smiled. "Food would be good."

"Perfect."

With that on the agenda, we both settled in for class.

•

"So, first off, tell me about the job. Is it going okay?" Kristen prompted when we sat down for a light dinner an hour and a half later.

"For the most part, yes. The actual work is fantastic. They're trusting me with more and more every day. And I really enjoy it." Since she wanted to keep this superficial to start, I turned the table on her. "How about you? How's the restaurant business?"

Kristen beamed back at me. "It's fantastic. A couple of weeks ago, the head chef decided to add one of my recipes to the menu."

I clapped with excitement. "That's fantastic! I knew you were hoping for that someday."

"I know, it's great."

It felt just like old times. It was almost a shame that I was going to ruin everything by confronting her.

We studied our menus momentarily, neither of us saying anything. The pleasantries were out of the way and the only thing left to discuss was the elephant in the room. I looked up to see Kristen smiling at me.

"What?"

"I was just wondering when you were going to tell me about…your newfound fetishes."

I couldn't keep from laughing. "Oh, you know me. Fetishes, smetishes. Nothing to really brag about. How's Tim? Everything good?"

That question wasn't easy to ask at this point in our relationship. After all, the guy's tongue had been in my pussy. It kind of changed everything between us.

"Peachy. We're still truckin' along."

"That's good to hear."

She put her chin on her hand. "But I really want to know more about the job."

"It's fine," I finally said. "The work's great."

"But the relationships are a little…different, huh?"

Obviously, she knew what Landon and Langston were into because she knew them. But that didn't mean I was ready to give up everything. I was still a little perturbed by the way things had all played out. I leaned forward and kept my voice low. "Why didn't you tell me you belonged to a BDSM club?"

Kristen's eyes widened and she looked around, probably to make sure no one had heard me. I had made sure no one was within earshot, so she was safe.

"It's not something that usually comes up in conversation." She sounded just like Jordan.

"But you sent me for an interview with a bunch of Doms, Kristen. Don't you think I should've at least had an idea of what I was walking into?"

She smiled sadly. "Are you really upset with me?"

Dropping my hands into my lap, I sat up straight. "Yes. No. Crap. I don't know. I want to be, but no. I'm not. I just feel a little betrayed, that's all. I feel like you pimped me out. Not like you thought I'd be good for the company, more so for them specifically."

"That's not…" Kristen frowned. "I swear, that wasn't my intention, Luce. I really did think you'd be great at the job. Which you are. But I can understand why you feel that way. I don't blame you either. Looking back on it now, I could've handled it better. But honestly, I did it because I thought…" Kristen sighed. "I thought it would be good for you."

"You thought it would be good for me to submit to four men?"

Her eyes widened.

Okay, so maybe I shouldn't have told her that much.

The waitress chose that moment to saunter up, cheerfully asking for our food and drink order. We quickly rattled it off and when she was out of earshot, Kristen leaned in again.

"I did *not* know that all four of them would want to dominate you."

"Well, they did."

"And…?"

I shrugged. "And you were on the island. You can pretty much figure it out, right?"

"No. Hold on a minute. On the island and at TJ's, I saw you with Landon and Langston. I didn't know the five of you were playing together."

"Well, technically, we're not. We're at an impasse at the moment."

"What does that mean?"

"It means something happened and none of them seem to be happy about it. Ben and Justin are keeping themselves closed off. Landon's being Landon, which I can't figure out. And Langston…well, he's the most forthcoming, but not in a good way. He seems to have taken charge, only to have backed off."

The slow smile that pulled at Kristen's mouth caught me off guard. "I probably should've known Langston would do that." Her expression turned thoughtful. "Then again, I figured Landon would give him a run for his money. They usually co-top."

"Yeah, well." I dropped my gaze to my napkin in my lap. "It's gotten complicated."

"That doesn't surprise me."

Before I could process the words coming out of my mouth, I blurted, "What part do you play in this whole BDSM thing, anyway? If you're a member of a club, then you're into the lifestyle. And I saw you playing with your boyfriend. I assume this is a big part of your life?"

Kristen's eyes slowly lifted to my face as though she was guarding her expression. "It is." She seemed to consider me for a moment before she sat up straight. "Okay, yes. I'll admit it. I'm into the lifestyle, probably more now than I used to be."

"Do you know how much easier this would've been on me if you'd just told me that up front? I could have bombarded you with questions instead of fumbling around blindly trying to find my way."

"I'm sorry, Luci. I really am. But if it's any consolation, you were in good hands. I completely trust Landon and Langston."

I did, too. Now.

Or I had.

Until yesterday afternoon.

But I wasn't ready to think about that just yet. "I've read that some people only do this in the bedroom. Others live the lifestyle twenty-four seven. Which corner are you in?"

"They do. It varies, depending on the individuals. Tim and I don't have a twenty-four-seven D/s relationship. However, we do actively engage in the community."

From what I had gathered, Landon and Langston were looking for a full-time relationship on that level. I liked the idea because it offered me a sense of comfort that I hadn't realized I'd been lacking in my life until they introduced me to it. Then again, Langston had been very up-front about the fact that he wasn't looking for anything permanent with me. Landon, not so much.

"So, tell me why things are complicated. Aside from a little alpha posturing. Are you confused about what you want?"

I swallowed hard, considering what I should say. "I'm not confused," I admitted. "But they seem to be. Because things have gone off track, they've given me three options."

"And those are?"

"Take things back to the way they were in the beginning when we were just playing. The whole no-strings-attached thing. Or move in a new direction where I get to spend more time with each of them, as their part-time, temporary submissive."

"And the last option?"

I couldn't look at her. "Langston offered to be my master, but only temporary. Nothing serious. He specifically said he isn't interested in collaring me. And he was finally forthcoming when he told me he was hoping I would reject that option." I didn't bother to tell her the last part came in a letter.

"What about Landon?"

I shrugged. That was the part that confused me the most.

Kristen took a sip of her water when the waitress delivered it. "Let me ask you this. Being a submissive…is it something you want? On a permanent basis?"

Before I could answer, the waitress delivered our salads. I took a moment to consider my answer while we both started eating. I could feel Kristen watching me, knew she was waiting for my response.

"Okay, fine," I huffed, putting my fork down and looking her in the eyes. "Yes. It's what I want. I've spent the past couple of months getting my feet wet, learning from them. It appeals to me on a fundamental level. Until recently, I hadn't even known that type of…relationship, I guess you could call it…even existed."

"First and foremost, do you understand the terms safe, sane, and consensual?"

I felt it was a little late for her to be asking that now, but I answered with a resounding yes, anyway.

"I know I thrust you into this world and it probably caught you a little off guard. I just want to make sure you're going into this with your eyes wide open."

I nodded. "I am. They're not moving fast by any means. Not where play is concerned. I've even filled out a limits list. It took a while and Langston actually made me go over it twice. I had several options for each and I even asked for more information."

"That sounds like a very good start."

"Oh, there's definitely no pressure. Not from them, anyway. I'm putting on myself more than anything. What progress I've made has been by my own choice. And what I've been hesitant to ask them, I've searched on the Internet." I widened my eyes. "Did you know there's a wealth of information regarding the various kinks involved?"

Kristen chuckled. "I did know that. And I'm glad to see you've done some research. I commend you for that, but I wish you would've called me. At the very least answered my calls."

"I was too embarrassed. I didn't want you to judge me." My eyebrows darted down. "And in case you don't recall, I wasn't even aware that you were into the lifestyle until I saw you on the freaking island."

I could tell Kristen truly felt bad for the way things were handled. And honestly, I wasn't going to hold it against her. In fact, now that I knew, I could bounce questions off her.

"I'm gonna sound like a real buzzkill right now," Kristen said, her expression serious. "However, it's important to know that you have to protect yourself first. No matter how much fun you're having, if you're ever in a situation that doesn't feel comfortable to you, remove yourself."

"I have a safeword," I admitted.

"Good. But that's only helpful when you have a Dom who will concede should you use it. Landon and Langston are good guys. I trust them. But…should you end up playing with someone else, you have to think about your own safety. If you ever have any questions, I want you to call me, Luci. I'll help you as much as I can. And if you ever simply want to talk, I'm here, too." She smiled. "Plus, I'd be more than happy to introduce you to a few more people. Good people like Landon and Langston, who are also into the lifestyle."

I reached over and squeezed her arm. "Thank you so much. I really appreciate that, but it's not necessary. I'm still trying to find my footing, but it's been a great experience so far."

Maybe not always rainbows and unicorns, but at the very least, it was an experience I knew I would never forget.

"However…" I offered a sinister grin. "I do have something that I need your help with."

TWENTY-THREE

I WOKE UP EARLIER THAN usual on Thursday morning. I spent a little more time on my appearance, curling my hair and paying extra careful attention to my makeup. I donned a few pieces of my favorite jewelry, then put on the exact same outfit I'd worn on the first day they had introduced me to this new world of what I'd come to refer to as office intrigue. The off-white skirt, chocolate-brown sweater, and cowboy boots made me feel bold and I needed that today.

On the way into the office, I stopped at Starbucks and ordered coffee for myself and Jordan, then paid for the person behind me, wanting to give a little back today. Even with the detour, I arrived at the office at seven twenty. I went through and turned on all the lights, then unlocked all the doors after setting Jordan's coffee on his desk. I grabbed a pen and drew a smiley face on a napkin and placed it beneath the cup. I wanted it to be there for him when he arrived.

I didn't linger in the lobby. Instead, I went to my desk, got the coffee prepared to brew, but I didn't start it. I figured I could do that as soon as Ben arrived so that it would be fresh for him. I then pulled up the calendar to see what was on the agenda for the day. I was surprised to see that all of the day's meetings had been canceled. All except for one, the one scheduled for nine o'clock with all four of my bosses and me.

I felt better knowing that they were waiting for my decision.

Not wanting to dwell on it, I pulled up my email and started working from the bottom up. I had a lot more than usual because of my absence yesterday. There were a couple from various managers asking about the next quarterly meeting and wondering if it was possible to hold it somewhere other than the home office. I thought that was a great idea. It would give people a chance to mingle in a different city and for my bosses to visit the teams on their turf.

I jotted down a note to discuss it at the next Monday meeting.

When I finally got to a stopping point, I looked up to see that it was eight forty-five and no one had arrived. I tried not to let that bother me, deciding it was actually an opportunity. With that in mind, I chose to get the back conference room set up and ready for their arrival. Before I did that, I quickly called Jordan and informed him that we would all be in a meeting and to hold all the calls. I then grabbed the items I'd stashed in my purse, along with the items that were in my desk, shored up my nerve, and headed down the hall.

I knew this was a long shot, but I had to do it. For my peace of mind, if nothing else. No matter the outcome, I had decided that I wanted this to be on my terms. They'd placed the decision squarely in my hands and I knew exactly how I wanted this to go. Now I merely had to relay that to them in terms they would understand.

I quickly removed my clothes, placing them on the coffee counter, took the items I needed, and knelt on the floor near the small table, facing the door, paying close attention to positioning myself the way Kristen had helped me to perfect. My friend had been more than willing to give me a quick lesson in submission. Granted, her version of quick had taken three hours, but I was grateful for the wisdom she'd bestowed upon me. It allowed me to take this giant step forward with the confidence I needed.

Now, I just had to be patient.

•

When the conference room door opened a short time later, I didn't budge from my position. I kept my eyes on the floor and waited patiently as the footsteps neared me.

Kristen had informed me that there was a certain protocol that would be adhered to by any Dominant who was willing to accept me. I hadn't told her what my final decision was, so I wasn't sure this would go exactly as planned, but I held out hope.

A few seconds later, Master's shoes appeared in front of me. I felt his hand gently rest on the top of my head. I didn't move, knowing that by remaining in position, I was not accepting his acknowledgement.

I was, but not entirely.

Silence surrounded me as I continued to kneel, my breath lodged painfully in my chest as I held my breath and waited.

Then it happened.

More shoes appeared and another hand touched my head, then another, and another. It wasn't until all four were there that I breathed a sigh of relief. When they moved their hands, I grabbed the four items I'd brought with me and got to my feet. All four had accepted that I was their submissive. It wasn't a formal process by any means; however, I knew that it meant something. For me to kneel and to wait for my Dom to acknowledge me would mean something to them, too.

I looked at each one of them, holding the items they had adorned me with originally. I turned to Ben first. "Master Snowden, I'm offering you these as your submissive." I handed over the nipple clamps.

He took them, lightly brushing my fingers as he did. "Thank you, gumdrop."

I turned to Landon. "Sir, I'm offering you this as your submissive." I held out the butt plug. He took it from my hand, then leaned in and kissed me gently on the lips.

When he pulled back, he whispered, "Thank you, sweet girl."

Justin was next. "Master Parker, I'm offering you this as your submissive." I couldn't help but smile as I looked into his eyes. "For the record, I absolutely despise the toy, but...for you, I'd do just about anything."

Justin took the ball gag from my hand, rubbing the inside of my wrist with his thumb before pulling back. "Thank you, princess."

I cupped the Venus Butterfly in my hand and held it out. This was the hardest one for me. Knowing that I was giving myself to a man who wasn't willing to take all of me was difficult. "Master, I am offering you this as your submissive."

His hands curled over and under mine, and for a second, I thought he was going to refuse me. My heart skipped a beat as I waited, silently praying he wouldn't deny me. I wasn't sure I was strong enough to handle his rejection.

"Thank you, pet," he said softly, his voice raspy.

When he took the item from me, I stood up straight, placed my hands behind my back, then lowered my head. "I'm offering myself up to the four of you. Not only my body but also my trust, my will, and my submission." I had opted to keep the L word out of it. Although, whether they wanted it or not, they also had my love.

I hadn't come to the decision lightly and I think they knew that. I wasn't looking for one of them to collar me as his own. This was still a new world for me, one that I wanted to explore in depth with each of them. By offering the gifts they'd bestowed upon me, I was giving that part of me back to them.

Kristen had assured me that, should they truly accept what I was offering, they would place the items on me. Something about a Dom knowing what their submissive needed. It wasn't a guarantee, but I needed to know that they understood me the way I understood them. Submission was a precarious balance of give and take.

I waited, slightly awed by my own patience. In the coming weeks, I knew these men would teach me everything I needed to know about myself and that was what I was looking forward to most. Getting to know them and getting to know me.

If they accepted me, that was.

Several seconds later, Ben stepped forward, nipple clamps in his hands. He reached out and brushed my nipple with his finger. "I accept, gumdrop."

I remained still while he teased my nipples into hard points, then prepared to place the clamps on. The brief fondling was more than enough to spike my arousal. The air rushed from my lungs, pain shooting through all nerve endings as he placed the clamps, then tightened them. Master Snowden then leaned in and kissed me. His lips were soft and warm, gentle yet demanding.

I waited until his hands fell to his sides before saying, "Thank you, Master Snowden."

Ben then stepped back and moved to his chair.

Master was the next to step forward, his hand curling behind my neck as he pulled me in for a kiss. I sighed against his mouth, welcoming his demanding tongue as he showed me with his lips and tongue how much he wanted me. While he positioned the butterfly vibrator over my clit and attached the straps, I focused on breathing.

"I accept, pet."

"Thank you, Master."

I inwardly smiled as Master took his seat.

Landon then stepped forward. I looked into his eyes as he brushed the backs of his fingers over my cheek. "I accept, sweet girl." He leaned in, his mouth close to my ear. "And thank you."

I swallowed hard. "It's my pleasure, Sir."

He took a step back and motioned for me to turn around. "Bend over and place your hands on the table. Spread your legs wide."

Feeling extremely vulnerable and more than a little exposed, I did as he instructed.

"Lean all the way down. Put your forearms on the table."

I'd never been more grateful for yoga than in that moment. I managed to put my elbows on the table, bending my body in half while keeping my legs straight, feet far apart. I was shocked when I felt his finger brush my anus, something cool sliding over my sensitive skin. He'd obviously come prepared with lube. I wondered whether he always had some. It wouldn't surprise me, considering his penchant for fucking my ass.

With one hand on my back, Landon teased me for a few minutes before pushing the thin plug in deep. I groaned, surprised by the pleasure I felt. It seemed I was getting used to this. Or maybe I was just that eager. Either way, my body accepted the plug.

"Very pretty, sweet girl."

I stood and faced him. "Thank you, Sir."

Rather than take a seat, Landon moved over to the sink, washing his hands.

Justin took his place in front of me. I lifted my head to stare into his eyes. He watched me for long seconds, his eyes caressing my face.

"It's my pleasure to accept, princess."

"Thank you, Master Parker."

Before he placed the ball gag in my mouth, Master Parker leaned in and kissed me. It was rough and I loved every second of it. Then he was securing the gag in my mouth, the strap around my head.

I waited until they were all four seated, then I laid myself out on the table, placing my feet near the leg restraints still connected to the table, and my arms over my head near the arm restraints. I paid close attention to the position of my body, showing them my intent to please them by offering myself up gracefully.

They seemed to know exactly what they were to do, because they all leaned forward at the same time and cuffed me to the table with the restraint nearest them.

When I was secured, my four masters staring down at me, it was in that moment that I knew everything was right in my world.

This was the path I was meant to be on.

And I was looking forward to the rest of my journey.

•

"I think our plaything deserves to be rewarded for her courage," Justin said, speaking to the others. "And once we've made her come at least a dozen times, we'll let her get back to work and discuss how we want this to play out."

My body trembled as I envisioned myself coming for them. I doubted it would take much at this point.

"Agreed," Master said.

As he said the word, the vibrator on my clit came to life, making my body twitch. I moaned against the gag in my mouth, my pussy clenching tightly as the sensations assaulted me. Ben's big hands then gripped my tits, squeezing roughly while Justin tugged on the chain dangling from the nipple clamps. They teased me for long moments, but when Landon thrust two fingers into my pussy, I cried out, my voice muffled by the gag.

"Oh, yes. She's coming nicely," Landon said, his tone ringing with approval.

It was true. In my defense, I'd been primed and ready since the moment I woke up.

I watched as Master leaned over and I only had a moment to wonder what he was going to do. Then I felt more fingers stretching my already filled pussy. The twins began fucking my pussy in unison, filling me with four fingers. The pain was intense, but it made me hyperaware of everything that was going on. The dull throb in my nipples, the plug filling my ass…it coalesced into a wondrous rush of awareness that had me coming again, my body bowing off the table as my climax rocketed through me.

They tormented me for what felt like forever, drawing two more orgasms from me before my wrists and ankles were released from the restraints.

Landon lifted me to my feet, then turned me around, my palms flat on the table once more.

"Hold on tight, sweet girl. I'm gonna fuck you until you scream."

He impaled me with his cock, fucking me roughly while his hands gripped my hips, holding me still. I didn't stand a chance with the vibrator still buzzing against my clit. I came within a minute and he pulled out. He did not come, I noticed.

Before I could come down from my sensual high, Ben was behind me, thrusting into my pussy roughly. He fucked me hard, my body jerking with every punishing thrust. I cried out his name as I came a short time later, but the ball gag made it impossible to make out my words.

Like Landon, Ben pulled out before he came. Then Justin was next and he wasn't gentle. Not that I wanted gentle. I wanted them all to use me, to claim me in a way I'd never experienced before. He reached beneath me and held the vibrator directly on my clit. Another climax rocked me, making me sway on my feet.

And when Master took me, he fucked me for long minutes, keeping a steady rhythm as his hips slammed into my ass over and over. I held on, riding out the sensations until he reached around and tugged on the nipple clamps. The sudden, shocking pain had me coming again.

By the time they were finished, I wasn't sure I could stand.

But I wouldn't have traded that for the world.

I had officially been claimed.

And this time, it was on my terms.

TWENTY-FOUR

BOSS MEETING

LANGSTON

HONESTLY, I WAS RATHER IMPRESSED with Luci's scene. The way she had presented herself to all four of us was quite a treat. Something I truly hadn't expected.

Nonetheless, I was content with the outcome.

Sure, I had secretly hoped she would've come up with a different conclusion, perhaps selecting me and Landon as her own. However, she had done the right thing by following the rules laid out for her. I had known she would because that was the way Luci operated. It was what made her such a phenomenal submissive.

"She's made her choice," Landon told Justin. "What do you suggest we do now?"

Justin seemed a little surprised by Luci's decision. I wasn't sure what he'd expected her to do, but selecting time with all of us obviously wasn't it. It took him several moments to come up with the next steps.

"I'd like to assign her a Dom for two weeks."

"And by assign, you mean...?" I didn't like the way it sounded.

Justin glared at me. "I have every intention of being fair."

"Do you?" I couldn't help it, I was still pissed at him for pulling this shit in the first place. He'd thrown a wrench into the works just when things were starting to go in the right direction.

Then again, I'd thrown my own wrench by backing off when I should've been taking the reins and claiming Luci as our submissive. However, I had my reasons and they all revolved around ensuring Luci got what she needed.

I could admit that I was a hard-ass. The Dominant in me was my most prominent part. And I liked it that way. I knew from the beginning that I was being hard on Luci. However, I was serious when I said I knew she'd be mine. More accurately, mine and Landon's. Unfortunately, I'd played my cards wrong and confused the situation.

Hence the reason I was backing off. I needed her to figure out on her own exactly what she wanted.

"What are you doing?" Landon asked Justin as the man was folding small sheets of paper.

"The person who picks the lowest number will be Luci's Dom for the first two weeks, and so on."

I glanced at my brother. He nodded his head, so I figured what the hell. We could play it this way.

Each of us selected a sheet of paper. Unfolding mine, I noticed I had the number three. I assumed that meant I would go third.

"I've got one," Landon said, although he didn't sound at all excited about the prospect.

"There a problem with that?" I asked, confused.

"No. No problem. I was just hoping for a little time."

"Time for what?"

"Never mind. It's not important. Let's go over the rules so I can lay them out for Luci. I'll take it from there and we'll figure it out as we go along."

And with that, we quickly mapped out what I hoped would be the beginning of how it all worked itself out.

Admittedly, I was a bit skeptical. Then again, that was another prominent trait of mine.

TWENTY-FIVE

THAT AFTERNOON, I OPTED TO go to lunch with Jordan. I knew he was worried about how things would play out and I wanted to reassure him that it would all be fine. I had decided not to share all the details. For a little while, I wanted this experience to be my own. It wasn't that I didn't trust him, because I did. I was merely being selfish.

After I shared as much as I was willing—which honestly wasn't much at all—Jordan said he understood, hugging me tightly and telling me he only wanted me to be happy. I was grateful for his acceptance and understanding and vowed that one day I would give him the entire story on how I officially became the play toy of my four bosses.

When I returned to my desk, there was an envelope sitting on the top, partially tucked beneath my keyboard. It had my name scrolled across the front. My heart leapt in my chest as I thought about what this meant.

Without haste, I sat down at my desk and opened the letter.

In the months to come, you will be introduced to a world you didn't even know existed until recently. Consider it training if you will. During that time, you will experience things you've only read about, some you've never thought possible. There will be rules to follow. Please review carefully.

1. You will be under the care of one Dom. We will alternate every two weeks, exposing you to endless possibilities during your time with us.

2. You will willingly submit to your Dom, giving him your undivided attention and devotion.

3. You will reside with your Dom during your time in his care.

4. You will do everything your Dom asks of you. Should you have questions or concerns, you will seek only his input, follow only his instructions.

5. You will have a safeword to use, and it will be abided by without failure.

If you agree to these rules, open the letter attached.

Feeling a measure of relief, I folded the letter and grabbed the attachment. Unable to hide my smile, I slowly unfolded it, my heart rate spiking when I saw Landon's signature.

Sweet girl,

I'm honored that you have accepted and I look forward to our time together. To show me your acceptance, I ask that you go to my office at five thirty. At that point, you will strip and kneel by the door, waiting for my arrival.

Landon

There was no way that five thirty would come fast enough for me. My excitement was palpable and I was ready for what was in store.

More than ready, in fact.

And to think, I got to start by spending more time with Landon.

Needless to say, I was one happy submissive-in-training.

•

At exactly five thirty, I went to Sir's office. After removing my clothes and neatly piling them on the chair near his desk, I went to the door and knelt in front of it, maintaining the stance both Master and Kristen had shown me.

Sir did not keep me waiting. I hadn't been on my knees but a few minutes when the door opened and he stepped inside.

"Very pretty, sweet girl." He placed his hand on my head. "Now stand and greet your Master."

I got to my feet, my belly fluttering with my eagerness. I couldn't hide the smile from my face and I was grateful when he smiled back at me.

"Despite what may happen over the next two weeks, I want you to know that your gift of submission will not be taken for granted. You may feel otherwise as you'll experience a broad range of emotion during this time. It's expected."

I nodded. "I'm eager to please you, Sir."

He nodded. "Going forward, you will refer to me only as Sir. No matter where we are or who we're around. This is important, sweet girl."

I did not have a problem with that. "Yes, Sir."

With his hand cupping the back of my neck, Sir leaned down and kissed me. His tongue leisurely dipped into my mouth, slow and gentle. He explored me only with his mouth. By the time he ended the kiss, my head was spinning.

"Are you ready to go home?"

"I definitely am."

"We'll stop by your apartment and get your things. You should not expect to go back there for two weeks, so be sure you get everything you need."

"Yes, Sir."

He smiled. "As much as I'd like to parade you around naked, unfortunately, it wouldn't be appropriate. You may get dressed."

With a giggle, I hurriedly dressed while Sir gathered his laptop and his keys.

"For now, we'll keep your car here at the office. Should we need it, I'll have it brought to you. However, don't expect to need it. For the next two weeks, you are under my supervision. I will care for you the way I choose."

"I understand."

"I will not hide the fact that you belong to me either. I expect there will be times that people who know you will notice that we're together. Do you have a problem with that?"

I gave that some thought. It meant that Jordan would eventually find out what was going on. He would likely see me with each of my bosses, letting him know that I belonged to no one specifically. Well, at least if my other bosses opted to act the same way. I wasn't sure what he would think of me once he saw me with more than one of them, but I couldn't bring myself to care.

"No, Sir. I don't have a problem with it."

"Good."

Sir took my hand, linking our fingers as he led me out of the office. I stopped at my desk and grabbed my purse before we headed down to the main lobby. When we arrived at the front doors, there was a truck waiting for us. With his hand still holding mine, Sir led me to the passenger door, then opened it and waited until I got inside.

"Buckle up."

He closed the door while I adjusted the seat belt.

"Do you have any questions?" he prompted as he pulled out on the street.

"A million," I confessed, giggling. "But nothing that can't wait."

"I'm sure many of them won't be necessary. But feel free to ask me anything at any time. That doesn't mean I'll always answer, depending on the nature of the question, but you can ask me anything."

It wasn't easy, but I managed to keep all my questions to myself as we drove to my apartment.

"First rule. You will not open your door yourself. Not getting in or getting out of the vehicle. Understood?"

"Yes."

"Wait there, sweetness," Sir said when he opened his door.

I watched as he walked around to my side of the truck and opened the door. He helped me out, then took my hand in his, linking our fingers the way he had at the office. We made it to my floor and into my apartment without encountering anyone.

"Where's your suitcase?"

"I put it back in my closet."

He smiled. "Then let's get this show on the road."

I led the way and was surprised when Sir started selecting my clothing for me. It wasn't like I had a lot to choose from and most of what I did have, he'd seen me in numerous times over the past few months. Still, he diligently pulled out what he wanted, handing each piece over to me so that I could pack it.

He then moved to my dresser, doing the same with my panties and bras. Not wanting to feel useless, I packed up my makeup and other bathroom necessities while he rummaged through my unmentionables. Since I would be staying with him, I made sure to take everything I used.

Once I was finished packing, I joined Sir in the living room.

"Do you have any medications you need to pack?"

I held up a small bag. "Just my birth control pills."

"Very good. You'll need to contact your doctor, see if it's all right if you skip the sugar pills."

"So that I skip my period?"

"Exactly."

Well, I definitely liked that idea. I'd actually talked to my doctor about it before. Back when I took a cruise a few years ago. In an effort to avoid the inconvenience of a period, she had advised that it wouldn't be a problem. I shared that information with Sir and he seemed pleased.

"Have everything?"

"Yes, Sir."

"Good. Let's go home."

I wasn't sure why, but the sound of that was music to my ears. Sir grabbed two large bags and I grabbed a couple of smaller ones. I then locked up my apartment and we headed back down to his truck.

•

"You have horses!" I exclaimed, looking out the back window of the huge ranch house that Sir had taken me to. The place was enormous and the second I walked in the door, I felt as though I was at home. In every square inch of the place, I saw bits and pieces of Master and Sir. It was open and airy yet warm and comfortable. I couldn't wait until I could take a full tour.

Sir chuckled softly, peering over at me. "We do. Have you ever ridden a horse?"

"No. But I've always wanted to."

"Good to know." He moved to stand behind me. "Tonight, I want you to get settled in. Check everything out, make yourself at home."

He seemed so casual while I was tied up in knots. Perhaps he knew that and he was attempting to put me at ease.

"Give yourself a tour of the house while I throw something together for dinner," he instructed. "You can unpack your things in my bedroom."

He pointed toward a room on the far side of the living room. "There are two master bedrooms. Downstairs is mine, upstairs is Langston's."

Giddy about the opportunity to explore, I wasted no time at all. I hurriedly unpacked my things, placing them in a small section of the large walk-in closet inside the enormous bathroom.

The space reminded me a lot of Sir's office. Very rustic in design yet comfortable.

After I had everything stashed in its place, I ventured into the living room, then toward the front of the house.

There was a dining room with a huge table that sat at least ten people. A matching dark wood hutch held glass dishes embossed with a barbed wire pattern. Across the open foyer was another room. I assumed it was originally a formal living room, but it had been converted into an office. I could imagine Sir and Master working in there when they were home.

"Come eat, sweet girl," Sir called from the kitchen.

I hadn't had the opportunity to make it upstairs, but I figured there was plenty of time for that, so I made my way to the kitchen.

"You have a lovely home, Sir," I said as I took the seat he was holding out for me.

"Thank you. We enjoy it."

"Have you always lived with…Langston?" I wasn't sure how to refer to him. I'd been thinking of him as Master for so long, but I wasn't sure what the protocol was when I was with another Dominant, so I opted for casual.

"I have. It's never been something we've discussed; it simply happened."

"The two of you are close." It wasn't a question because it was obvious.

"Yes."

"I remember growing up," I told him, "I always wanted a brother or sister. My mother informed me right away that she was never having any more children. She said my father was the one who wanted kids, not her."

Sir frowned.

I chuckled, although there was no humor behind it. "It's been obvious my entire life that my mother felt as though I was a burden. Looking back now, I think she was angry that my father died, leaving me with her. Thankfully, she met Jim not long after. My stepfather attended school functions when he could. Being a firefighter, it worked into his schedule fairly well. My mother, on the other hand, didn't attend, even if she was home."

Sir smiled, but I could tell it was forced. "As you can imagine, our mother attended every function for all three of us. Even when we didn't want her to. And yes, King was also a big presence in our lives. He was there for meet the teacher, our school plays, most of our football and baseball games. Everyone knew who he was. The other mothers fawned all over him and my mother took pride in the fact that he was hers."

I giggled because I could imagine that.

"Your mom mentioned that your sister wasn't fond of their relationship?"

Sir shook his head. "Not so much, no. She pretended they didn't exist for the most part. As much as my mother would allow it, anyway. Laura ended up marrying her high school sweetheart, then moved to Kentucky with him for college. She settled down there and rarely comes back."

"Do your parents see her often?" I remembered they were heading there for Christmas.

"Oh, yes. My mother insists. They go to Kentucky at least six times a year. My sister claims she hates it, but I know she doesn't. My nieces and nephews adore their grandparents."

It was nice to hear about parents who went to the effort of making the relationship work. It was obvious their sister would've kept her distance if they'd allowed it.

We finished eating in silence. Surprisingly it wasn't awkward although I was sure I'd dampened the mood by talking about my mother. I certainly hadn't meant to.

TWENTY-SIX

I GOT A LITTLE GLIMPSE of Sir's routine the next morning. He was up at five, so I was, too. While I headed for the shower, he went upstairs for a long time. I had no clue what he was doing, nor did I try to find out. I went through my ritual of getting ready for work. Although I was with Sir, I didn't want anything to interfere with work. I was ready and waiting for him by six thirty. He was showered and dressed a short while later.

We arrived at the office right at seven thirty and went right for our respective desks. In fact, the entire day went by as normal. And not once did anyone suggest I work naked.

•

"Are you hungry?" Sir asked when we walked in the door that evening.

"Starving." It was true. My stomach was growling. I'd had a sandwich for lunch, which had been delivered to me at one o'clock by Jordan, who informed me that someone (Sir) had placed the order for the two of us. Jordan and I had shared our meal in the break room shortly thereafter. I couldn't deny that Sir's thoughtfulness had gotten me a little misty-eyed.

Sir leaned down and kissed my neck. "Do you cook?"

I shrugged. "A little."

"Why do I get the impression you're downplaying that?"

I laughed. "Since it's just me, I don't often have the chance to cook. But I do enjoy it."

"Is it edible? Because my brother says he's capable of cooking, but most of the time, it's not all that edible."

Still laughing, I turned to face him. "Of course it's edible."

"Good." He nodded. "The kitchen's that way. You'll find all you need to make pretty much anything you want."

I stared up into his eyes. "Is there anything you don't like, Sir?"

"I'm relatively flexible when it comes to food."

Turning, I headed toward the kitchen. Before I got two steps away, Sir smacked me on the ass.

"You have thirty minutes. That's all. Impress me, sweet girl."

A thrill shot through me as I skipped to the kitchen, eager to do as he requested. I spent a couple of minutes reviewing all the ingredients he had. Being considerate of the time I'd been allotted, I pulled out the items I would need to make beef liver and onions, as well as mashed potatoes and peas.

I didn't know where Sir wandered off to, but I focused on my task, wanting to ensure I got this right. Admittedly, I sought the instructions on how to make beef liver on the Internet. I liked the idea of cooking for my master. It seemed so domestic.

Almost exactly thirty minutes later, Sir returned to the kitchen, just as I was putting everything on the table.

"What would you like to drink, Sir?"

"Iced tea would be great."

"Sweet or unsweet?" See, my time as a waitress hadn't been pointless.

"Sweet."

I quickly made two glasses of sweet tea and joined him at the table. We ate in silence, but it wasn't uncomfortable. For some reason, I didn't feel the need to fill the void with words. Instead, I enjoyed looking around the space and out the windows at the barn and stables I could see in the distance.

When we were finished, Sir instructed me to clean up, then join him in the living room.

I loaded the dishes into the dishwasher, then set it to start. Once I'd wiped all of the counters and the table, I lit a candle to get rid of the liver smell that overpowered the space, leaving it on the island where it would be safe.

I found Sir sitting on the sofa, his shirt off, his feet propped up on the table. He was watching television and when he glanced my way, I noticed he wasn't wearing his glasses. Admittedly, I liked seeing him without his glasses. Sure, those specs were quite appealing, making him even hotter, but it felt as though he was letting down his guard a little when he wasn't wearing them.

"Something wrong?" he asked, frowning.

"You're not wearing your glasses."

He smiled. "I usually only wear them in the office or when we're around a lot of people. Too many times people confuse me and my brother, so it's easier that way. However, I prefer contacts."

Ahh. Now I understood. Without the glasses, they were identical, aside from that small scar on his left eyebrow. Granted, their demeanors were quite different and I was fairly certain I'd be able to tell them apart regardless.

Hopefully.

"Come here, sweetness," Sir instructed, patting the spot beside him. "Strip and join me."

I'd gotten used to stripping on command, so it didn't bother me anymore. Plus, the chances of him making me come seemed greater if my clothing was removed. At home, I would've discarded my clothes on the floor, which was the reason I was always conscious of making sure I was neat and tidy when I removed them. I stacked them on the end table, then sat down beside Sir.

"Lean back against the armrest," he said, pointing toward the other end. "Put your feet in my lap."

I leaned against the arm, propped my head on a cushion, and placed my feet in his lap. Sir rubbed my feet while we watched a movie.

Well, technically, he watched the movie while I spent most of my time watching him.

"Is this what you like to do on the weekends, Sir?" I asked when there was a commercial.

"Only on Friday. Saturdays I tend to go to the club. But Fridays are my night off. I like to chill. Relax."

"I like this, Sir."

His gaze traveled the length of my body before turning back to the television. While we watched some gangster movie, Sir massaged my feet, his hands slowly drifting up my legs until he was absently petting my pussy. The feeling was remarkably relaxing. The way his hands gently glided over my skin, drifting between my lips to find my clit. He didn't seem to be paying any attention to me, although I couldn't say the same about me. I was hyperaware of every touch.

Sir eventually lifted my left foot from his lap. "Put your foot on the back of the couch."

I propped my leg up, which opened me up to his roaming fingers.

"Other foot on the coffee table."

I was splayed open for him, but Sir continued to watch the movie, still teasing me with his fingers. I was panting, doing my best not to move, although I was silently willing him to put me out of my misery.

He looked over at me.

"You have a pretty pussy, sweet girl."

I blushed at the compliment. "Thank you, Sir."

Once again, he focused on the television, but this time he inserted one finger inside me, curling it at the perfect angle to brush my G-spot. I moaned as I watched what he was doing to me.

"Do you not like the movie?" he asked.

"I…" I hissed when he inserted two fingers. "I do like it…Sir… Oh, God!" He thrust both fingers in, then retreated slowly before repeating the action.

"Then why aren't you watching it?"

"Because…" My hips bucked under his sensual onslaught. "Because I like…oh, God…what you're doing to me…more."

"Do you want to come, pet?"

I swallowed hard. "Only if it pleases you, Sir."

"Good girl. But not yet. I'm not done playin'."

I swallowed a groan, glad when he pulled his fingers out of me and continued to pet me. His wet fingers caressed the smooth skin of my mound. It wasn't long before he was once again testing my restraint by finger-fucking me.

"Don't come for me, pet. Not yet. I want to be inside you when you do."

"Please, Sir," I begged. "I want you inside me."

His attention was once again on the television, but I knew he wasn't focused on it. I could see the hard ridge of his erection behind the zipper of his jeans. I wanted him to fuck me.

I was on the verge of explosion when his fingers slipped out of me once again.

"Come here, sweet girl."

Sir unbuttoned his jeans and pushed them down his hips before reclining into the cushions once more. My eyes locked on the way his abs flexed when he shifted. The man's stomach was what I'd refer to as an eye-gasm. Seriously. I would never get enough.

"Kneel right here," he said, patting the cushion beside him. "Take me in your mouth, but don't make me come."

I scrambled onto my hands and knees, pleased to finally get to tend to him.

"Bring your chest down to your knees and spread your legs wider," he instructed, smacking my ass as he reached around behind me.

When I adjusted my position, he extended his arm over me, his fingers finding my wet entrance, and he was once again fingering me while I focused all my attention on his cock. I laved him, sucking, licking, but careful not to push him over the edge.

"Take all of me," he whispered. "All the way in your throat."

I'd gotten better at deep-throating, although I wouldn't consider myself a pro by any means. I focused on opening my mouth around him, then lowering my head and taking him as deep as I could. When the swollen head caressed the back of my throat, I eased down a little more.

"Just like that," he praised. "A little more."

I couldn't breathe, but I didn't care. I lowered my head until I felt the wide tip of his cock in my throat. I swallowed twice, then instantly pulled back. Sir's free hand went to my hair and he guided me back down. He didn't rush me, slowly pushing until he was once again deep in my throat. When I tried to pull back, he halted me, pushing me down a little more.

"You can do this, sweet girl. I know you can. Relax your throat."

I did, breathing in through my nose and fighting my gag reflex.

Sir tugged on my hair and I released him from my mouth.

"Two more times, pet. Then I want you to climb up on my dick and ride me until we both come."

Knowing there was an end in sight made it easier. Knowing he was going to fuck me was even better. I pressed my head down until my nose was against his neatly groomed pubic hair. I swallowed several times, waiting until he groaned. Only then did I lift my head, taking a deep breath before going down on him again.

"Aww, fuck, baby. That's so fucking good."

Sir wasn't the type to swear, but for some reason, his foul words fueled the fire burning inside me.

He finally pulled my head up, his breaths coming rapidly. "Good girl. Now climb up here. Let me feel that sweet pussy on my dick."

Sir helped me onto his lap, his arm banding around me as he used his other hand to pull my mouth down to his. Our lips crashed together as I guided him inside me, sinking down on his cock. I groaned, loving how deep he went, how much he stretched me.

I began rocking on him as we kissed.

"Sit up, pet. Let me watch while you fuck me."

I sat up straight, placing my hands on his chest.

"Lean back," he instructed.

Repositioning my hands behind me, gripping his thighs, I tipped my body back while he held my hips.

"Now watch as my cock disappears inside your warm, wet cunt."

I did and it was hot to watch as he fucked me.

The man had a tremendous amount of stamina, because we remained like that for long minutes. Me impaled on his cock, sliding my pussy up and down his shaft.

When his eyes lifted to mine, I met his gaze.

"I don't want you to come yet."

I nodded.

His thumb circled my clit and I cried out, increasing the pace as I lifted and lowered on him.

"That's it, sweet girl. I love watching you fuck me."

I was moaning, desperately holding on, waiting for him to give me permission to come.

"Ask nicely, pet."

"Please, Sir. Please let me come on your cock."

"You may."

He started jerking my hips harder, pulling me onto him. Within seconds, I felt my orgasm barreling down on me.

"Scream for me, pet."

Sir slammed his hips upward, driving into me hard and deep. I screamed, giving in to the intensity as my climax stole my breath.

"That a girl," he said. "Come all over my cock."

His words caused another tremor to race through me.

When my muscles relaxed, I leaned forward, but Sir didn't stop fucking me.

"Hold on and press your hips down."

I wrapped my arms around his neck, molding my body to his as I kept my hips pointed down. He thrust up into me again and again, over and over until he was breathing as hard as I was, sweat slicking our bodies.

Sir pressed his face against my neck, then jerked me down onto him. His teeth latched on to my neck, and when he bit down, I came again, crying out as the pleasure overwhelmed. The man knew just what to do to make me lose my mind.

"Mine," he growled roughly, his hips stilling, his cock pulsing deep inside me.

I didn't let go, holding him as tightly as I could, knowing that at the end of this two weeks, this man was going to ruin me.

And I looked forward to every single second until then.

TWENTY-SEVEN

THE NEXT MORNING, I WOKE up alone in Sir's bed. I stretched, feeling the familiar ache in my body from Sir's ministrations last night. After we had fucked on the sofa, we had retired to his bed, where he worked me into a frenzy with his mouth, making me come loudly before he flipped me over and fucked my ass.

The man knew exactly how to use my body and I found I had been hoping for a little more play time this morning. I fought off the disappointment, remembering that Sir had a regular routine and he shouldn't change it because of me.

Eventually, I got out of bed, used the restroom, then brushed my teeth. I contemplated taking a shower, but wondered if I should find Sir first. I didn't want to do anything if he had other plans. Then again, after last night...

Yeah. I decided a shower was in order.

I tried to hurry, eager to find Sir, to see what his plans were for the day. Still, it took roughly thirty minutes to go through my routine, then another twenty to dry my hair. I opted to forego makeup for the time being. If he planned to go out tonight, I would have to redo it anyway.

After wandering through the giant house, I finally found him upstairs in what appeared to be a state-of-the-art gym. You could've fit two of my apartments in the room. Maybe three. And it held every piece of equipment that a normal gym held, from weight machines to treadmills to a section that held large ropes and some sort of contraption decorated with various ropes and straps.

"Mornin'," he greeted, grabbing a towel and wiping off his face.

I leaned against the doorjamb and smiled at him, admiring his lean, muscular form. "Good morning."

"I was startin' to think you were gonna sleep all day."

"I could have," I admitted. "But I missed you."

He quickly looked away and I wondered if my statement bothered him. Honestly, it had slipped out. I hadn't meant anything by it, but I could tell he didn't want to hear things like that. I decided not to think too much on it, mentally warning myself not to do it again.

I plastered a smile on my face and changed the subject. "So, what's on the agenda for today?"

"Well, I have a conference call in half an hour. I thought I'd shower while you make breakfast. Then tonight, we're going to the club."

"Is it a dance club, Sir?" I already knew it wasn't, but I was trying to get his mind off my blunder.

He peered over at me with a wicked grin on his face. "No, pet. Definitely not a dance club."

"Oh."

"I promise, you'll enjoy it." He moved toward me, carrying the towel with him. "While I shower, please throw something together for breakfast. Nothing fancy. I don't eat much in the mornin'."

Before he passed, he leaned over and kissed me on the lips.

I sighed to myself when he disappeared around the corner.

This was going to be interesting for sure.

I made oatmeal and fruit for breakfast. I wasn't sure what Sir liked, but I figured that was a safe bet since he had both in the house.

I had the table set, including a cup of coffee, when he returned. Like last night, he was wearing a pair of jeans with no shirt or shoes or glasses and the man stole my breath.

"I hope you like oatmeal," I said, motioning toward the table.

His smile seemed somewhat forced. "It'll do." He nodded toward the chair opposite him. "Sit."

I sat while he opened his laptop and sipped his coffee. I ate in silence, watching him as he typed. When his gaze lifted to mine, he seemed to be checking to see if I was eating.

"Are you finished?"

I nodded, pushing the remainder of my oatmeal away. I rarely ate breakfast and the only reason I had was because I hated to see all of it go to waste. It was evident Sir was not going to eat. I had no idea why he even bothered having me make anything.

"Good." He picked up his phone. "I need to take this call."

I started to get up. "I'll just go watch TV or something."

Sir shook his head, then motioned for me to come toward him.

"I'd actually like to feel that sweet mouth on my dick while I'm on my call."

Heat infused me at his words.

"Crawl under the table, sweetness. Work me over with your mouth, but if you make me come, you will be punished."

The thought of punishment still terrified me. After what Master had done…

"Don't make me ask twice."

Realizing I'd frozen, I shook off the thought and dropped to my knees, crawling beneath the table. Sir did the honors of freeing his cock before taking a seat in the chair.

"Yes, this is Landon Moore."

Deciding to treat this as the honor that it was, I started teasing Sir's cock with my tongue, taking my time tasting him while he spoke above me. I couldn't make out every word, but I wasn't trying to either. I got lost in the taste of him, using my hand to stroke him while licking and sucking his cock and balls. I had no idea how much time had passed when Sir pushed back his chair, stealing his cock right out of my mouth.

"Come here, pet," he ordered.

I crawled out from under the table and got to my feet. I had barely managed to stand tall when he physically lifted me and carried me over to the island, setting my butt on the cold granite.

"Lie back." His tone was rough, commanding.

I lay back and he pushed my thighs apart, driving my knees toward my chest, then fused his mouth to my pussy. It didn't take long before I was writhing and moaning while his tongue worked me over, sending me spiraling dangerously close to orgasm.

He hadn't told me that I couldn't come, but he hadn't given me permission either, so I was torn, not sure what I was allowed to do.

Sir must've realized my indecision because he lifted his head briefly.

"Come in my mouth, pet." It was a growled command.

When he suckled my clit, flicking his tongue over the sensitive bundle of nerves, my body soared once more until I was panting. I tipped right over the edge within seconds, flying high on the sensual storm that assaulted me.

"Sir! Oh, God! I'm coming!"

As my release made my body jerk, Sir continued to eat me, driving me right to the precipice again. When he thrust two fingers in my pussy, I contracted around the intrusion, coming again.

I was limp and sated, but clearly Sir wasn't finished. He stood, jerking my hips toward him. With my ass resting on the very edge of the counter, he impaled me, fucking me roughly, slamming into me again and again. He didn't stop until my pussy once more squeezed him as another orgasm had my heartrate spiking and my senses going numb.

He came with a roar, stilling inside me as his cock jerked and twitched.

I lay there with a smile on my face, wondering what had brought that on. I had never expected him to lose control like that. When I looked up to ask him, I noticed Sir staring down at me. He didn't look at all happy and I felt an invisible fist clutch my heart, squeezing tightly.

"Sir? Is something wrong?"

He helped me to my feet.

"Go take a shower, pet."

"But I already—"

"Go," he growled roughly. "Shower. Now."

I stared at him.

His tone was downright cruel when he added, "Don't make me tell you again."

Confused, I forced my feet to carry me out of the room. I waited until I was in the living room before I took off at a run, tears flooding my eyes.

I had no idea what I'd done, but obviously, Sir wasn't pleased.

And once again, I was left feeling as though I had failed him.

It was a feeling I didn't care for at all.

•

I hiccupped as another sob ripped through me. I was trying to hide my tears beneath the shower spray, not wanting Sir to know that I was crying. I felt stupid, because try as I might, I couldn't figure out what I'd done wrong. I had been under the table, following his instructions to the letter, when he practically dragged me out before ravishing me.

Still, I knew it had to have been something I did that would make him look at me that way.

Another hiccup echoed against the tile.

The sound of the glass door closing had me spinning around.

Sir moved toward me, completely naked. His eyes scanned my face and he frowned as I took a step back. I didn't know what to expect and retreating was my natural instinct kicking in.

"Come here." His words were soft and gentle, the complete opposite of a few minutes ago.

He held open his arms and I walked into his embrace while the warm water poured down on us both.

"I'm sorry, pet," he whispered in my ear, his hand sliding over my wet hair.

"I don't know what I did," I managed, the words broken from the sobs I tried to hold back.

"You didn't do anything wrong, sweet girl."

Sir pulled back and cupped my face, forcing me to look at him.

"But…"

"That was all me," he said, his tone laced with something I didn't recognize. "You test my control and I don't like it."

That didn't sound good at all.

He tilted my head back more, locking his eyes with mine.

"I'm not allowed to lose control. It's my job to take care of you. And a Dom who can't maintain his self-control is worthless."

I didn't understand. Well, I did, but I didn't.

"I promise it won't happen again," he said, as though I needed to hear it.

Rather than arguing with him, I wrapped my arms around him and buried my face in his chest. I breathed him in and relaxed, the tears finally stopping. He palmed my head, holding me against him while his other hand caressed my back.

"If I'm bein' honest," he said softly, his words rumbling against my ear. "You shouldn't be here right now."

I jerked as though he'd slapped me. When I tried to pull away, he tightened his hold, keeping me close.

"I've been fueled by emotion, sweet girl. The time we've spent together...I want more. But, Langston..." He sighed heavily. "I should've let Ben or Justin take the first turn. I would've been in a better position to handle things if I'd had a little time."

I didn't want him to be in a better position. I liked him just the way he was.

Pulling back, I looked up at him. "Sir, I don't want to be with anyone else but you right now."

I knew I couldn't say too much because he wouldn't want to hear that either. I'd already made that mistake that morning. I had no intention of pushing him away, making him think I wanted more than he was willing to give.

Which meant I had to tread lightly.

"I don't want you to either," he said, curling his fingers behind my neck as he leaned down and pressed his lips to mine. "Come on. Let's finish in here and we'll go for a ride. It helps to clear the mind."

"Horses?" I asked, my eyes wide.

Sir chuckled, turning me to face the water and swatting my butt. "Yes. Horses. Now hurry up."

"Yes, Sir!" I definitely wasn't going to argue with that.

TWENTY-EIGHT

"SIR, ARE THERE RULES THAT I should know about?" I asked when we left the house to go to the club later that night. It had been a relatively normal day, with the exception of the fact that I'd been battling anxiety over going to this club every single second.

"Yes, there are rules."

"Will I be allowed to speak? Or look people in the eye?"

Sir's gaze darted over to me and he grinned. "Yes. For the most part."

I frowned. "What does that mean?"

"It means, you're there with me tonight. Should another Dom try to engage you in play, I expect you to politely excuse yourself and find your way back to me. You must show respect for any Dom you encounter."

"We're going to be separated?" I didn't like the idea of that.

"If it happens, it'll only be for a few minutes."

I nodded, then forced my gaze out the window. I wasn't sure why disappointment flooded me, but the idea of Sir taking me to a club and then abandoning me wasn't appealing at all. Certainly not at a BDSM club where another Dom might want to…do whatever.

"If you're watching a scene, you need to be silent. Do not interrupt or draw attention to yourself."

"Yes, Sir," I mumbled.

"And when we scene together tonight, you know your safeword, right?"

I had to look at him then. "I don't know what it means to scene, Sir."

He smiled, his eyes on the road. "I've got something in mind for you, pet. You'll enjoy it, I promise."

"Will I be naked in front of people?"

"Yes."

I swallowed hard. I'd gotten used to it in front of my bosses, even managed at the island, but the idea of being in a club full of people I didn't know…it kind of freaked me out. It would be like on the island, only I would have more time to fret about it. I didn't do well with all that time to think.

Then again, it wasn't like the outfit I had on covered much anyway. The ruby-red corset was definitely sexy and the indecently short miniskirt flared out when I moved, which, I knew, exposed me to any curious eyes. After all, Sir hadn't allowed me to wear panties tonight.

My favorite part of my wardrobe was the boots though. I had been surprised when Sir asked me to wear them. They were black leather, high-heeled, and went over my knees. I never considered them something a submissive might wear, but I definitely didn't tell Sir that.

In my opinion, I looked hot. If it were up to me, I'd like to keep the clothes on, but it wasn't my decision and I was cognizant of my role tonight, despite my reservations.

"I expect Langston, Ben, and Justin to be there, so you'll be protected."

"Protected from what?"

"Since you aren't collared, the other Doms won't know that you're spoken for."

"Oh." I looked out the window again. This whole collar thing kind of pissed me off.

"Word will get out quickly that you're there with me, so you won't have to worry about it."

I wasn't worried about that, but I didn't feel like elaborating, so I kept my trap shut.

"I'm bringing you here tonight to introduce you to the club scene. I want you to get a taste of what it's all about. While I know you've done your research online, and you've had a small taste, I don't think you truly grasp it yet. And that's understandable. You can read every book and every blog out there, but you won't really understand until you're in the middle of it."

I nodded.

"You will call me Sir. At no point will you use my name. If you speak to Langston, you will refer to him as Master."

A chill raced down my spine at the thought of seeing Master while I was with Sir. Even more appealing was the idea of being with them both at the same time. Okay, so maybe this club thing wouldn't be as bad as I thought.

"And should you speak to Ben or Justin, you'll refer to them as Master Snowden and Master Parker."

"Okay."

"However, you do not speak to them unless spoken to."

I sighed. It sounded so complicated.

Looking out the window, I noticed we'd returned to downtown; however, we weren't going to the building the firm was located in. We went deeper in, to a section I probably wouldn't have gone to by myself.

"Sir, what's the name of the club?"

"Dichotomy," he answered easily. "It's owned by a friend of mine. He opened one up in Texas not too long ago, and due to the overwhelming response, he decided to open one here."

Never heard of it. "Do you go there often?"

"I do."

"Do you scene with a lot of submissives there?"

"I have."

I looked at him again, a feeling of dread filling my belly. "Will you be…spending time with any of them tonight?"

His eyes narrowed and I realized instantly that I had offended him.

"When I'm with you, I'm only with you, Luciana."

The fact that he used my full name confirmed that I'd struck a nerve.

"I'm sorry, Sir. I didn't mean…" I sighed and decided to tell him the truth. "I just know that if I saw you with another submissive, I'd be jealous."

"Thank you for being honest with me, pet. However, don't disrespect me again by assuming the worst."

Feeling appropriately chastised, I nodded. "Yes, Sir."

We pulled into an underground garage. Sir found a spot and parked, then ordered me to stay in the truck. He came around to my side and opened the door.

He stopped me before we started toward the street.

"We're here to have fun tonight." He placed his thumb under my chin and forced my head back. "I fully intend to enjoy you while we're here. I need you to trust me to know what your limits are." He cocked an eyebrow. "And yes, I've seen your limits list. Langston shared it with us. So, you have to trust me."

"I do trust you, Sir," I whispered. It was true. I did trust him. Completely.

He gently kissed my lips.

"What's your safeword, pet?"

"Red."

He nodded. "This club has rules that must be followed. It's imperative that you don't break them. And red also happens to be the club safeword as well, so should you use it, a monitor will come over. You want that anytime you're playing. It's for your safety."

I nodded.

"Should you break a rule and another Dom witnesses it and I don't, you will be punished. By that Dom."

I frowned. I didn't like that idea at all.

Sir grinned. "So don't break the rules, okay?"

"Easier said than done, Sir."

He laughed. "I like you, pet. A lot."

His admission made my heart swell.

"Come on. Let's go enjoy ourselves."

Sir linked our fingers together and led me out of the parking garage and onto the sidewalk. We stopped in front of a red door. There were no signs directing people to the club and I assumed that had been done on purpose.

"Members only," Sir said, answering my silent question.

We stepped inside a small room that held nothing more than a desk and a scantily clad woman. "Welcome back, Master Moore," the woman greeted.

"Jessica," Sir acknowledged. "I'd like to introduce you to my submissive, Luci."

I smiled. "Nice to meet you, Jessica."

"You, too," she said sweetly, then glanced up at Sir. "You'll just need to sign her in for tonight. If you'd like to borrow a protection collar, we have some."

"It won't be necessary," Sir said. "Have you seen my brother tonight?"

"No, Master Moore."

"Is Master Ramsey here?"

"He is."

Sir nodded, then scribbled some information on the sheet of paper before he handed over what appeared to be a membership card. Jessica perused it, then slid it through a scanner on the desk. She handed it back with a smile. "Have a good evening, Master Moore."

Sir placed his hand on the back of my neck and guided me into another room. There was a giant man standing there, waiting for us.

"Master Moore, it's good to see you again," the man said.

Sir nodded, then waited while the man waved a wand over him from head to toe.

"Any cell phones or cameras?"

"Of course not," Sir told him, sounding displeased that he'd been asked.

"Just have to ask," the man said, looking slightly sheepish.

"Understood."

"Do I have your permission to check your submissive, Sir?"

"You do."

The man then took the wand and ran it over me from head to toe. It was very clinical, but felt strange considering the setting. I definitely liked the idea of not allowing cameras or cell phones into a place like this. The thought of having videos or pictures of me out there on the web was terrifying. I seriously doubted my mother would understand if she happened to stumble across a picture of me naked, being whipped with a flogger.

"You're both good to go, Sir."

Once again, Sir placed his hand on the back of my neck, this time beneath my hair. It was warm and comforting, a subtle reminder that I was here with him.

When the door opened and we stepped into the main club, my senses were assaulted by the bright lights and the boom of bass bouncing off the walls. I couldn't resist checking it all out. It looked a lot like a regular club, with the exception of the nearly naked submissives wandering about. There were various seating areas as well as a bar that ran the length of one wall, and the music thumped through the speakers in the ceiling.

"They do not serve alcohol here," Sir informed me. "It's the owner's preference. He'd prefer not to risk the chance of something going awry due to overindulging."

"Such as?"

"Alcohol impairs consent," he stated. "And in this realm, consent is the foundation we're built upon."

"Wow. I didn't think about it that way."

Although Sir was absolutely right. Alcohol impaired judgment; therefore, it impaired consent. That made complete sense to me. I was thinking along simpler lines. Such as, it seemed safer to have a level head when using implements of torture.

"What're you smiling at, pet?"

"Just thinking about how it wouldn't be wise to mix alcohol and a flogger."

He chuckled. "Not always, no."

Sir steered me across the room, stopping a couple of times to greet the people we came in contact with. Unlike the party I attended with Master, the people here were friendly enough and Sir always introduced me, using my first name. I caught curious glances being shot my way from everywhere. I wasn't sure if they were surprised that Sir had a submissive with him or if they were looking at me specifically.

I did my best to be respectful, not looking anyone in the eye for fear I would offend them. It wasn't until I heard someone say Trent Ramsey that my interest was piqued. In case you didn't know, Trent Ramsey was only one of the absolute hottest men in Hollywood.

"Master Ramsey," Sir greeted. "Good to see you."

I couldn't help it, I openly stared at the man approaching us. It was none other than *the* Trent Ramsey. In the flesh. Standing less than two feet away. The guy was a god among men and I knew my mouth was hanging open, but I couldn't help it.

"Master Moore. It's been a while, huh?"

"Not that long," Sir answered, squeezing the back of my neck gently. "I'd like to introduce you to Luci. She's my submissive for the evening."

Trent Ramsey held out his hand and I didn't move.

The chuckle that came from the larger-than-life man standing before me shocked me into reality.

"I'm so sorry, Master Ramsey," I apologized, holding out my hand.

"A little star-struck," Sir explained.

A little? I could hardly breathe.

"I get it all the time," Master Ramsey said. "If you get a minute later, I'd like to chat."

"Absolutely. Let me get her settled in and I'll find you."

Master Ramsey patted Sir's back, then moved on to speak to someone else.

Sir turned to face me. "Close call, pet."

"I know. I'm sorry, Sir."

"Turn around," he instructed.

I pivoted, facing away from him.

When I felt the laces on my corset loosen, I knew exactly what he was doing. Heat infused my face when he relieved me of the garment, exposing my breasts to everyone in the room. Granted, no one seemed to be paying me any attention, but that didn't ease any of my humiliation.

"Very pretty," Sir said when he turned me back around.

He caressed my nipples with the backs of his hands and they instantly pebbled, betraying me. Sir leaned in close, his lips brushing my ear. "Be respectful, or the next thing to go will be the skirt."

Shit.

I wasn't sure that I was ready for that.

However, I also wasn't sure I could be as respectful as they expected.

I feared I was doomed to fail because I was totally out of my element.

TWENTY-NINE

SIR SPENT THE NEXT HALF hour escorting me through the club. He showed me the dungeon, which, as it turned out, really looked like a dungeon. At least this one did, anyway. From the stone walls and dark concrete floors to the intimate lanterns mounted on the wall, it held a dark appeal that called to me. I'd never seen anything like it. The scene outlined before us was kinky and sexy and...I didn't want to ever leave.

Once at the bottom of the stairs, Sir led me around, continuing to keep his hand on the back of my neck. We stopped while he talked to several people, and a couple of times to admire a scene. I was mesmerized when I noticed a stunning woman wearing black latex using fire on her submissive. It was an interesting trick for sure. The guy's erection was impossible to miss, so I could only assume that he enjoyed what she was doing to him.

Personally, I wasn't sure I wanted the flame anywhere near me. But in the same sense, the woman—a Domme—appeared to be enjoying herself, her pleasure recognizable on her pretty face. I figured it was as gratifying for her submissive, simply knowing how much it pleased his Mistress.

It was true that in the past few months, I had learned a lot about this lifestyle. Not simply by reading, but also by experiencing it. Every single interaction I'd had with my bosses had taught me a lesson. I felt as though I wasn't quite as "wild" as King had initially accused me of being.

I discreetly scanned the room, looking to see if I recognized anyone. I figured some of the people I'd been introduced to at the island were also members. I knew that Kristen was for sure, as was Jordan, which meant it was possible they were here, too. Of course, I was secretly looking for my other bosses, hoping they'd make an appearance.

"I need to speak with Master Ramsey," Sir informed me when we stopped in front of a naked woman tied to a pole while a large man used a whip—a real one, with a wickedly long tail—on her back. She was writhing and moaning, pleading for more. Inside, I was cringing, wondering exactly how these people could tolerate being physically hurt for the pleasure of others.

"I want you to stay right here," Sir instructed. "Don't make eye contact and if another Dom approaches you, be polite."

"Yes, Sir." Although I outwardly agreed, I was terrified that some unknown man was going to come over and insist that I do something for him. I knew how to be respectful, but what if the guy didn't take it that way? Would he punish me?

Sir leaned down and pressed his lips to mine at the same time he tweaked my right nipple.

I squeaked into his mouth, which made him chuckle.

"You'll be fine, sweet girl. Do not leave this spot for any reason."

Remembering how upset Master had gotten when I wasn't kneeling by his desk when he returned that day had me planting my feet firmly. I had absolutely no intention of moving, no matter what. I would not disappoint Sir in that way.

When Sir left, his comforting touch went with him and I felt a strange chill dance down my spine. I did my best to focus on the big guy swinging the nasty-looking whip, snapping it against the woman's back, leaving crisscrosses of red welts in its wake. She moaned every time the leather came in contact with her skin.

Across the room, I heard a woman scream. My head instantly jerked in that direction. I found the source of the sound on the floor, kneeling. She was attached to what appeared to be a leash and the man standing over her was wielding a belt. He reared back and slapped her ass, the leather echoing with a loud crack. The woman screamed again.

"No, please, Master. Don't! I promise I'll be good."

He leaned down, his hand grabbing her around the neck. He held her tightly, their eyes locked. She looked terrified.

I kept my feet rooted in place, refusing to leave my position. That didn't stop me from watching. I was scared something was wrong, that this woman was being beaten and she didn't want it. However, she wasn't using her safeword, so that meant she was okay. Or that's what I'd been led to believe. My heart raced with fear for her safety as the man once more spanked her with the belt, his hand still tightly around her neck.

"She's fine, pet," a deep rumbling voice sounded in my ear.

I froze in place. I knew that voice. It was the same as Sir's only slightly deeper, a tad raspier. My body instantly heated as he moved closer.

"He's a regular here," Master explained. "And they're role playing right now."

"How do you know?" My voice came out raspy.

"Because I know him well."

"But he's choking her," I insisted.

"He's a Primal," Master explained, although I had no clue what that meant. "And she's primal prey."

I frowned.

"There are certain aspects of their play that's allowed here, although they're closely monitored," Master continued. "The man over there…"

I glanced in the direction of his gaze.

"He's a dungeon monitor assigned specifically to watch them. Due to the brutality of their play, Master Ramsey insists on close observation."

Okay, now that sounded terrifying.

Daring to turn, I slowly pivoted so that I could look up into the handsome face that was eerily similar to Sir's. They really were identical when Sir wasn't wearing his glasses; however, they carried themselves differently. Most people probably wouldn't notice the disparity right off, but I'd been around them long enough to have detected the nuance.

"Where's Landon?" Master asked.

"He said he had to take care of something."

Master glanced around the room as though searching for him. "Good, then that'll leave us a few minutes alone together."

When Master started to urge me to move, I held my ground. "I'm sorry, Master," I said quickly. "Sir told me not to move."

I could see what looked to be a smirk, but it dropped instantly. I wasn't sure what that meant or if I should be worried.

"Did he tell you why?" Master probed, his eyes scanning my face.

"No."

"Did you ask?"

"No."

"Why not?"

I frowned. "Because it isn't my place to question his instruction."

This time, Master did smile, and a second later, Sir joined him, also wearing a grin.

Sir put his hand on the back of my neck and pulled me to him. When his mouth met mine, he thrust his tongue past my lips and kissed me roughly. I sighed against him, grateful for his return.

"I'm proud of you, sweet girl," Sir whispered as he stared down into my eyes.

I studied his face momentarily, trying to read his mind. I could tell he approved of my reaction and then I realized why.

"That was a test, wasn't it?" I asked, feeling as though I'd been played.

"It was. And you passed."

His answer didn't make me feel any better.

"Why the frown, pet?" Master asked, moving to stand beside Sir.

"I don't like to be tested," I admitted truthfully.

"Well, then you're not gonna like a lot of things," Sir said, chuckling. "Come on. I've got something in mind for you."

Swallowing hard, I glanced between both men, slightly wary of what they intended to do to me. Then again, I think I was more intrigued than anything else.

Not that I was going to let *them* know that.

•

Sir led me upstairs to the main floor, but we didn't stop. We continued up another flight of stairs to the second floor. This one was the exact opposite of the dungeon, despite it still being dark. The blue lights cast an eerie glow over the faces of those wandering around, giving it an erotic ambience. Well, that mixed with the people in various stages of undress.

"Come here, sweet girl," Sir said, directing me over to an empty corner.

I instantly noticed the restraints dangling from the ceiling and more on the floor. A tremor vibrated through my body at the thought of being restrained here, in front of all these people.

"Remove your skirt and boots, pet," Sir instructed.

I inhaled sharply, my nervousness causing me to pause.

Sir turned to face me. "Are you defying me already?"

My eyes darted up to his face. "No, Sir."

"Good. Then do as I asked."

Swallowing hard, I decided to ignore the fact that there were people everywhere, a few of them having already started moving toward us, gathering in a semicircle around us.

I reached for the zipper on my skirt but paused.

Sir came over, tilting my head back so that I was staring into his hazel eyes.

"Who is your master?"

"You are, Sir."

"Who do you wish to please?"

"Only you, Sir."

"What's your safeword?"

"Red, Sir."

"So, you're aware you can use it any time you feel you need to?"

"Yes, Sir."

His voice was hard, his eyes penetrating straight through me. "Unless you intend to use it, I expect you to strip. Now."

I nodded, my hands trembling.

"Your only focus should be on me. I am the only person who matters in this entire building. *Only* me."

My head jerked in an understanding nod; still, I was frozen.

"You have to trust me, pet. That's all I ask of you."

I did trust him. It was myself I didn't trust. The thought of all these strangers watching me come...it was terrifying. It made me feel incredibly vulnerable. *Too* vulnerable.

"I'll give you two more seconds. If you don't do as I asked, I *will* punish you, and I promise, that will be far worse than anything I intend to do to you here."

That spurred me into gear and I instantly leaned down and removed my left boot, then my right before unzipping my skirt and removing it. I handed my clothes to Sir and he placed them on a small table near the wall. I fought the urge to cover myself, knowing Sir wouldn't like that.

When he returned to my side, he kissed me sweetly. It melted my insides, and for a brief moment, I forgot that I was standing naked in the middle of a BDSM club while people watched.

Someone cleared their throat.

Okay, so maybe I didn't completely forget. But I did maintain my focus, looking only at Sir, willing everyone else to fade away.

The next thing I knew, Sir was tugging me toward the restraints that hung from chains hooked to large beams in the ceiling.

"Turn around," he stated firmly.

I did, and once again, I was facing the crowd, my naked body on full display.

Sir went to work hooking my wrists to the cuffs above me, then my ankles to the ones in the floor. The position had my body in the shape of an X and I scanned the crowd, wondering what they saw when they looked at me. Did they find the sight of my nakedness a turn-on? Or were they focusing on my every flaw?

Those were questions that continued to flood my mind, making me nervous, on the verge of panic. I could hear them murmuring to one another and I couldn't help thinking they were talking about me.

My eyes were drawn to a man moving toward us and I realized Master was returning, this time carrying a large black bag. He slipped out of my line of sight and I fought the urge to twist, curious as to what he had in that bag. More importantly, what he was going to do with whatever he had in that bag.

"I like you just like this," Sir said softly. "Restrained and naked for my pleasure."

My eyes shot up to his and I held his stare, wondering if he could see my fear.

He brushed the backs of his fingers over my cheek. "I'm going to have fun with you."

His words made me tremble.

Master appeared in front of me, holding something out to Sir. I watched them exchange what appeared to be a small black case as well as several long cotton swabs. The kind you see in a doctor's office.

"This is what is known as sensation play, sweet girl," Sir explained, opening the case. There were several small canisters, each with a lid. They looked almost like lip gloss containers. Sir retrieved one, then handed the case back to Master.

"Bring the blindfold," Sir directed Master.

My heart slammed against my chest as I thought about being blindfolded. Taking away my sight meant I would not be able to see who was around me, who was touching me. I wouldn't know what they were doing.

Then again, I realized that was the point. I was to put my trust in Sir.

"Breathe, little one," Master crooned softly in my ear as he pulled my hair back and secured it before placing the blindfold over my eyes, effectively blocking everything out. "I want you to focus on our touch." His hand caressed my cheek. "On the way it makes you feel."

I exhaled slowly, trying to relax as his skin brushed mine before he secured the blindfold behind my head, making sure it was fixed in place. I could see nothing, not even light coming through.

My other senses were instantly heightened. I could hear the drone of conversation taking place around us, the clink of the chains above me when I shifted. The scent of sex and a variety of cologne and perfume permeated the air.

Something cool touched my left nipple. I could tell it was the cotton swab. It was dragged over my nipple, coating it with liquid. My other nipple was soon covered and I focused on breathing. The touch had barely disappeared when my nipples contracted from the intense chill consuming them. It had to be whatever Sir put on me. I inhaled sharply, my entire body feeling the overwhelming cold from whatever it was.

"You're safe, pet," Sir assured me. "I would never do anything to harm you. What I'm using will not damage your skin, only heighten your senses."

I jerked when something brushed over my clit. It was too hard to be a finger, so I assumed it was the cotton swab. I listened intently, trying to determine what was being done to me. The only thing I heard was the steady thump of my heartbeat.

A second later, a soft puff of air blew between my legs and heat swamped me. Unlike the stuff on my nipples, this was warm, growing hotter by the second. I moaned as heat infused my clit.

"Very pretty," Sir whispered. "Tell me what it feels like. How are your nipples?"

"Cold," I whimpered.

"And your clit?"

"Hot."

"What's your color?"

"Green."

"Very good."

It took a moment for me to realize I was panting as the sensations warred. The cold on my nipples and the heat on my clit…it brought me to a new level of awareness.

Something soft brushed down between my shoulder blades. It felt almost like…a feather. I tried to relax, allowing the gentle teasing to block out the other sensations. Then something soft outlined my breasts, teasing over them, then under, before sliding down my belly.

A moan built as the pleasure intensified. Whatever they were doing, it was engulfing me, stealing my thoughts, leaving me unable to formulate words as the sensations overtook my body.

"Be very still, pet," Master instructed, his voice gruff in my ear.

I tried to keep my muscles from twitching, but the sensations were too much. The feather—or whatever it was—glided over every inch of my skin from my neck to my toes, on the front and back of my body. The instant I would relax, my skin would be tickled in another spot, bringing attention to the chill on my nipples and the heat between my legs.

I swallowed another moan, remembering there were people watching.

A smack landed on my ass and I shrieked from the instant sting.

"We want to hear you," Sir growled. "I want the whole building to know what you're feeling. Understand?"

"Yes, Sir," I said on a breathless moan.

The feathers continued to tease for what felt like forever, and I found myself drifting on that same sensual haze I'd felt when Master had flogged me. It was a feeling I remembered well, a state of bliss I found myself looking forward to. It allowed all thought to dissipate, leaving me suspended between time and space.

When something sharp touched my chest, I jerked, instantly pulled back to reality.

"Don't move," both men said firmly.

I swallowed hard, my mind once again focused on the sensations. The soft stroke of the feather, the heat on my clit, the icy chill on my nipples, and now the pinprick on my chest. It was the same feeling as when they'd teased me on the island. I had no idea what it was.

I cried out when something touched my back. It was sharp, too.

"Color?"

"Green."

The feathers began moving and the pinpricks slowly rolled down my body. I couldn't focus on one over the other because they moved at the same time. One feather slid up the insides of my thighs, the other over my mound while the slight sting on my chest and back gradually progressed downward.

Everything started to morph into one and I found myself floating again, unable to focus on just one sensation at a time. My clit throbbed from the heat, my breasts were severely sensitive, and my arousal spiked. When the pinpricks moved to my legs, I trembled as a wave of heat traveled through me. Electricity sparked in my core and I realized I was going to come.

"Oh, God," I moaned, giving myself over to the sensation. The pinpricks trailed down my legs, the front of my right leg, the back of my left, while the feathers teased my chest and back. My heart rate spiked as the electricity inside me grew stronger.

It was then that I noticed the music, the bass pulsing in the air around me. It was industrial, sexy, and it caused everything to coalesce, transforming as my adrenaline spiked, my body no longer my own. I was soaring, my brain fuzzy, my body warm from the sensations, my insides trembling as electrical sparks ignited in my core.

I didn't want to come, didn't want the people watching to see me orgasm. I preferred to save the climax for when Sir and I were alone.

I cried out, unable to hold back as my insides tightened, the pleasure so great it bordered on pain.

"Tell me when you come," Sir said, his voice coming from somewhere in front of me. "I want to hear you scream, sweet girl."

I whimpered, trying to hold on, desperate to hold back. But it was too much, overwhelming with its power. It was a sensation unlike anything I'd ever felt, overtaking my mind, leaving me gasping and panting, both anxious and dreading what was going to happen. I began panting in earnest, trying to hold back as my body trembled from head to toe.

As the various sensations moved upward, returning to my chest and back, I knew I couldn't hold on much longer. I felt warm breath on my shoulders and I could hear Sir and Master breathing. The feathers never stopped their relentless teasing, nor did the little nips of pain from the points rolling over my skin.

Warm lips caressed my shoulders on both sides of my head, then trailed to the junctures where my neck met my shoulders. I panted, my chest heaving as my clit pulsed and my pussy clenched.

And then it happened.

Teeth bit into me on each side, a sharp, delicious sting, detonating my orgasm as I screamed out, pleasure slamming through every inch of my being, drowning out everything else.

My entire world centered on the climax that stole my breath.

THIRTY

AT SOME POINT, MY MIND must've drifted. That or I passed out, because I came to in Sir's arms, wrapped in a blanket. I forced my eyes open, trying to put all the puzzle pieces back together. We appeared to be in a small room with windows facing the play area. I could see the section we'd been in, noticed Master doing something.

Sir was brushing his hand down my hair. I peered up into his eyes. Although his face was expressionless, I could see a smile in the hazel depths.

"Welcome back, sweetness."

I took stock of myself, noticing that my nipples were no longer chilled and the heat between my legs was gone. Although I shivered, I wasn't cold. I was weak, tired, but felt an overwhelming sense of calm.

"I have to say, watching you come was a treat for many people."

Heat infused my face as embarrassment drove out every other feeling. I had come in front of all those strangers. On the island it had been slightly different because I felt I knew the people who'd been there. Most of them, anyway.

God, I could only hope that Trent Ramsey hadn't been there to witness it. Talk about embarrassing.

"You were beautiful, pet," Sir praised.

His words shifted something inside me. He sounded pleased, as though simply allowing him to make me come gave him great pride. Surprisingly, I wasn't bothered by it as much as I thought I would be. Instead, a new feeling infused me. A sense of peace.

Master appeared, holding a bottle of water.

"I got everything cleaned," he told Sir as he peered down at me. He smiled and the sight warmed the remaining cold places inside. "Glad to see you made it back to us."

To us.

His words had a strong emotion building in my chest. It was strange but not unwelcome. I found that being with both of them gave me a pleasure I'd never experienced before them. Although I had enjoyed being with both of them separately, I'd never felt anything as good as being with them at the same time.

I sat up on Sir's lap, curling close to him as I buried my face in his neck. "Thank you, Sir," I whispered softly.

"My pleasure, pet."

The bottle of water appeared before me and I was ordered to drink. I took a few sips as my limbs gained more strength. When I tried to get up, Sir merely pulled me back to him.

"A few more minutes, then we'll go."

I studied his face. "We're leaving?"

"Don't want to overload your circuits on your first night."

I smiled to myself. They'd already done that, but I figured he already knew, so I focused on my surroundings, my strength returning quickly.

"If you're finished with me..." Master said, speaking to Sir.

"For now," Sir told him. "Are you coming back to the house tonight?"

Master shook his head. "I'm staying at the apartment."

I made sure not to move, not wanting them to see my disappointment. For a brief moment, I had hoped that Master would come back to the house with us. The thought of spending the night with both of them almost made me giddy.

"Okay," Sir replied, his tone not hinting at what he thought about that. "I'm gonna take her home shortly."

Master's hand trailed over my cheek and I turned my attention to him. He was watching me closely, a wealth of emotion whirling in his hazel eyes.

"Thank you, little one." His lips lowered to mine briefly.

I wasn't sure what he was thanking me for, but I smiled. "Thank *you*, Master."

With my arms around Sir, I watched as Master walked away, coming to a halt almost immediately when a woman moved into his path. She instantly dropped to her knees and bowed at his feet.

"Master Moore, it would be my pleasure to serve you."

I could actually feel the ache in my chest as I watched another submissive present herself to Master. I knew I didn't have any claim on him, but the thought of him taking his pleasure from her made my stomach knot.

A strong hand circled my arm and I realized I'd gripped Sir tightly. He soothed me by brushing his hand down my arm, his eyes focused on my face. I couldn't look away as Master instructed the woman to get to her feet before he led her toward the stairs. When they disappeared from sight, I choked back a sob.

I didn't have the right to be upset. Not to mention, I was with Sir and I wanted him with a passion that rivaled all. Had that submissive presented herself to Sir, I would've felt the same pain that I felt now.

Knowing he had sensed my discomfort, I looked at Sir, meeting and holding his gaze. I wanted him to see the true extent of my feelings for him. Like Master, I knew Sir didn't want me for himself. I had learned that based on his response to me that morning at his house. Sure, they wanted to play and to enjoy whatever pleasure they could take from me, but they didn't want me. Not the way that I wanted to be wanted.

It hurt to acknowledge, so I forced the thoughts away, grabbing the water bottle and chugging half of it down.

When I moved to get up, Sir didn't stop me this time. He got to his feet and pointed at my clothes, which were sitting on the floor beside us.

"Get dressed."

His words were clipped and I knew I had hurt him. Then again, they had hurt me and I couldn't bring myself to feel sorry for him. Or for myself. I'd gone into this with my eyes wide open and it wasn't fair for me to want something they weren't willing to give.

Didn't mean my heart wasn't breaking.

•

The rest of the weekend was uneventful.

I spent Sunday at Sir's. While he worked out in his gym, I meditated in the bedroom. And when he came to take a shower, he instructed that I spend at least thirty minutes walking on the treadmill. I did as he requested, then made lunch. We ate in silence, neither of us having anything to say.

That afternoon, he said he had some errands to run and left me alone. I continued reading the manuscript Master had given me a while back and lost track of time. Admittedly, I felt slightly better, getting lost in fiction, despite the fact that I was trying to figure out which scenes the author was worried about, then trying to visualize myself in those scenes, acting them out. I wasn't sure Master still intended to do that, considering all that had changed between us, but I felt the need to fulfill his wish anyway, in the event he asked me to.

It was dark when Sir returned. I then made us dinner, cleaned the dishes, then went to bed with him. Surprisingly, he didn't make love to me, nor did he tease me in any way. It seemed I'd hurt him with my reactions on Saturday night. Since I felt betrayed by Master, I couldn't even bring myself to care.

This morning had gone off without a hitch, though, and I was sitting at my desk when a reminder popped up on my computer screen. It was time for the Monday meeting, so I got to my feet and wandered down the hall. I got the coffee started, then took a seat and waited for my bosses to join me. I had a notepad and pen at the ready, wanting to at least show them I was ready to work.

When Ben arrived, he smiled at me, but it didn't last long. His eyes scanned me quickly before he headed to the coffeepot. Justin wasn't far behind him and I got the same reaction from him. I wasn't sure what they saw when they looked at me, but whatever it was obviously concerned them.

Landon and Langston arrived at the same time and I couldn't help admiring the two of them as they strolled in. I didn't want to admire them, but it happened anyway. I was still angry, still hurt by what Langston had done. And no, I was no longer thinking of him as Master. As far as I was concerned, he no longer deserved the title. He had abandoned me for another woman.

They were talking, their voices hushed as they went to the coffeepot. Neither man acknowledged me and the pain in my chest intensified.

Apparently I wasn't the only one who was angry.

I had fucked up by reacting the way that I had and I was being punished for it. Rather than feel guilty, I wanted to lash out. A sense of defiance consumed me, and for the first time, I understood how that bratty sub had felt. The need to get their attention was great.

When everyone was seated, Sir cleared his throat and locked eyes with me when I looked his way. I knew I appeared aloof because I was. I was angry and hurt because he hadn't bothered to talk to me, to share how he felt. Not that I had asked.

He pointed at the floor beside him and said, "Kneel at my feet."

I was tempted to tell him no, but my underlying need to submit was too great. I placed my notepad down on the table, then moved over to the spot he had directed me to. I knelt beside him, facing the others, a physical act of defiance.

"Face me," he barked.

I snapped around to face him, noticing the anger etched on his features. It shocked me. I'd never seen Sir upset. He was always so passive, sometimes a little tense, but never angry.

"It seems you're confused about who you belong to." His words were spoken with disdain, and I could tell he was at his tipping point.

My eyes widened at the harsh tone of his voice. I shook my head. "I'm not confused." Pissed, yes. Confused, no.

"No?" His skepticism was like a blade to my heart.

"I belong to you…Sir."

"You have a funny way of showing it."

All the insolence and rebelliousness drained from me. I wasn't sure what I was supposed to do. Aside from telling me to kneel at his feet just now, Sir hadn't instructed me to do anything, so I wasn't sure what he wanted or how I could possibly make this right.

Knowing he was waiting for some sort of response, I did my best to explain. "I've done everything you've asked, Sir." Which was nothing at all. I kept that part to myself though.

"Is that what you expect? For me to direct your every move?" A deep groove marred his forehead as though he couldn't fathom the notion of him giving me direction.

I shrugged, suddenly feeling as though that wasn't the right answer. "I thought that was what you wanted."

His lips thinned and I could tell he was growing more frustrated with every passing second. I racked my brain, trying to figure out what I'd done wrong aside from the other night at the club when I'd gotten upset that Master left with another sub.

"Langston, please inform Luci what happened Saturday night at the club with that submissive."

I didn't look away from Sir, even when Langston spoke.

His tone was flat as he explained. "I escorted her to the submissive holding area, then informed Master Ramsey of her infraction. When she dropped to her knees, she broke protocol. I hadn't approached her, nor had I shown any interest in what she had to offer."

My gaze snapped over to his.

"She was suitably punished for her misconduct. I did not touch her."

I looked back at Sir. I could see his disappointment, which made me feel lower than low.

Sir didn't say anything and I felt all eyes on us, but I didn't look away. My heart pounded against my ribs and my chest felt as though it would explode from the pressure. I watched him breathe in and out, taking long, deep breaths. He was obviously keeping his emotions reined in, holding on to his control.

When he finally spoke, his tone was harsher than I'd ever heard it. "In this role, as my submissive, your objective is to please me. No one but me. A D/s relationship isn't... You know what, I can't explain this to you right now. I need you to go to my office, strip, and kneel beside my desk. Do not move until I come for you."

"Yes, Sir," I whispered, my voice rough with emotion as I stumbled to my feet.

"I want you to think about these past two days, Luci. I expect you to explain to me why I'm disappointed."

I choked on a sob as I nodded, my heart breaking at the thought of upsetting him. Without another word, I ran from the room, heading straight for his office. I quickly stripped off my clothes and knelt beside his desk, tears streaming from my eyes as I tried to figure out what he had expected from me and what I hadn't given in return.

Since the moment we left the office on Friday night, I had done everything he asked of me. I cooked, I cleaned, I let him tease me, fuck me. We went to the club and I allowed him to put me on display and torture me until I orgasmed. I'd done every single thing he asked. On Sunday, I did my best to stay out of his way, waiting until he told me what he needed from me.

And then it hit me.

My chest expanded and a sob nearly ripped me open.

I had abandoned Sir by only being physically available to him. I hadn't anticipated his needs, I hadn't tried to take care of him, I had merely followed instructions as though that was my one and only duty. I recalled plenty of things that I'd read, conversations I'd witnessed in the online groups. Submission wasn't about becoming a doormat.

I had offered him my trust and my submission, but since he'd taken me as his submissive, it was my responsibility to take care of him in return. Not only physically but emotionally.

While I sat there, I allowed the tears to stream down my face. I didn't even try to wipe them away. My thoughts drifted back to Saturday night after our scene at the club. Sir had taken care of me and then he had witnessed my disappointment when Master left with another submissive. At that point, I had abandoned him. I hadn't told him how I felt about him, about what he'd given me.

I felt lower than low and I fully expected, if and when Sir returned, he would release me as his submissive.

And that was the moment my heart truly broke. Right in two.

THIRTY-ONE

BOSS MEETING

LANDON

"WHAT THE FUCK HAPPENED?" JUSTIN growled when Luci ran from the room.

It was a fair question. One I didn't care to answer, but fair, nonetheless.

"She misunderstood something that took place on Saturday night," Langston explained.

"Well, obviously." Justin glared at me. "So, why didn't you set her straight? Talk it out?"

Another good question.

"I think this is something they need to work out between them," Langston offered. "It was a misunderstanding. Now that she understands, I'm sure it will blow over."

"Blow over?" Justin snapped. "You let this shit fester since Saturday night? How the hell is it going to blow over?"

"It's not," I hissed. "I'll take care of it."

"You could've fool—"

"Shut up!" I growled his way. "This is my business. I'll take care of it how I see fit. Sometimes I think you forget we're not all your submissives."

Justin sat back, his eyes wide.

I hadn't meant to go off on him, but this thing between me and Luci had gotten out of control. It was my own damn fault. I'd witnessed her reaction, knew she'd been upset by the submissive who had dropped to her knees in front of Langston. I could've very easily cleared it up at the time, but instead, I let my fucking emotions get the best of me. Rather than set her straight, I'd let my fucking jealousy eat a hole in my stomach.

"You're right," Justin finally said, his tone once again normal. "I apologize. I have no right to interfere. This is the agreement. She belongs to you right now."

He sounded genuine, so I offered a nod. "Can I have a few minutes alone with my brother?"

"Of course." Justin got to his feet, straightened his tie, then nodded for Ben to follow him.

When the door closed behind them, I turned to face Langston. "This isn't how I imagined this going."

It appeared Langston had a difficult time looking me in the eye. "I know."

"No," I snarled. "You don't know. I'm not willin' to give her up. I've made myself clear. However, this is not how I want things. I want you involved. That's the way we've always planned it. Sure, I want to dominate her, but I need to know that we're on the same page. That we have the same goal in mind."

"We do." He looked torn, his eyes hooded. "I want the same thing you do. But right now isn't the time. You need to spend time with her. Establish your role. She's looking too much to me for dominance." He sighed. "That's my own damn fault. I get it. But this is the only way I know to fix things."

"It's a fucking mess," I admitted. "You should've seen her face. She was devastated. And I knew exactly what she thought and I didn't bother to correct her because I'm so fucking angry with you."

Langston nodded. "You have every right to be."

"This isn't a game for me." That was the problem. I didn't want to play this way anymore. I wanted Justin and Ben out of the picture. I wanted Luci to belong to me and Langston. Enough of the office bullshit. I was tired of it. The closer I got to her, the harder it was to think about her with the two of them anymore. It made me see red to think about sharing her with them, or anyone for that matter.

"Address this issue with her," Langston stated, his tone calm. "Punish her so she understands that you make the rules. She can't walk all over either one of us. She certainly can't top from the bottom, which is what she's doing."

"I know that." And I did. But I had let her get away with it. That was my fault.

Langston leaned forward. "If I didn't think this was what she needed, I would've been there on Saturday night. No one seems to see how much she wants to be dominated. She doesn't want to make the rules. Hell, I even noticed how lost she looked this morning."

She'd looked lost since we left the club. I saw it, and again, I'd done nothing about it.

"I'm tired of the fucking games," I told him, locking eyes with my twin. "I'm in love with her, Langston. Don't you get that?"

"Of course I do." He immediately looked away. "I know exactly how you feel. Which is the very reason this has to happen. Once you address it with her, come talk to me. We'll figure out what our next steps are."

"I don't want her to belong to Justin." I hated admitting it, but I had to get it out there.

"I don't either."

"Yet that's exactly what's going to happen when my two weeks with her is up."

Langston got to his feet, righting his jacket and buttoning it. "Give it some time. Luci knows what she wants. We have to trust her to make the right decision."

I sighed, staring out the window as my brother left the room.

He was right about one thing. I did have to punish Luci for what she'd done. I couldn't go on with her thinking that she could act out in an effort to get the attention she wanted. I needed to talk to her, find out what she was thinking.

Unfortunately, right now, the only thing I wanted to do was punish her, to make her see that she had hurt me with her actions.

The more I thought about it, the angrier I got. Not necessarily at her but at the situation. At myself for allowing this to happen.

More importantly, I needed her to tell me that she cared for me as much as she cared for Langston. Deep down, I knew it was true. However, I'd been far too passive over these past couple of months. I had allowed her to believe that I wasn't capable of dominating her the way she needed. And my brother was right about that, too.

Luci was nothing if not submissive.

And now it was time I showed her who her master really was.

THIRTY-TWO

I HAD NO IDEA HOW long I knelt beside Sir's desk, but I knew it had been a while. My tears had long ago stopped and my entire body was numb. I heard Justin and Ben return from the meeting. At one point, I thought I heard Langston's office door close, but I couldn't be sure. Still, I remained where I was, not willing to get up until Sir instructed me. I needed to apologize, to tell him how I felt, to beg him to keep me.

I played out what I wanted to say to him over and over in my mind until finally the door opened and Sir came inside. He closed the door. I didn't look up, not wanting to disappoint him further.

When he approached, Sir placed his hand on my head. "Stand and greet your master."

I slowly got to my feet, then turned to face him before lifting my head. I met his gaze head on. I knew he could see the tear streaks on my face, but I didn't move to wipe them away. I wanted him to see my shame, to know that I recognized the pain I'd caused him, and more importantly to see that I was sincerely sorry for my actions.

"Tell me what you did wrong, Luci."

I hate that he used my name rather than one of the pet names for me, but I understood, so I mentally shrugged it off.

"I didn't anticipate your needs, Sir," I explained. "I was selfish, expecting you to tell me what you needed from me."

His eyes studied my face as he stared down at me.

"I'm sorry, Sir," I said, another sob contracting my chest. "I'm so very sorry." I couldn't stop the tears. "Please don't let me go, Sir. I promise, I'll do better in the future. You deserve more from me." I rambled on as I cried, praying that he wouldn't discard me. I wasn't sure I could handle the rejection.

"I'm not letting you go, Luci. That's not even an option for me. However, we will address this."

When Sir's warm hands cupped my face and he kissed my forehead, I cried even harder. I hated knowing that I had been so selfish, that I hadn't seen what was right in front of me. It bothered me that I could do that to someone. Especially Sir.

He placed one of his hands over my heart and I knew he could feel the way it pounded in my chest. I was terrified of what his decision would be.

"What do you think your punishment should be, pet?"

"I haven't given it any thought, Sir."

He nodded. "Then kneel beside my desk until I acknowledge you."

Sir pulled one of the pillows from the sofa and dropped it to the floor.

Once more, I dropped to my knees and lowered my gaze. Sir moved to his desk and took a seat.

As much as I hated the idea of him punishing me, I knew I had to come up with something.

•

After an hour of kneeling, Sir asked me to get to my feet. I did, although he remained where he was at his desk. He then ordered me to turn away from him. He left me in that position for a long time, but I had no way of telling the time. It could've been an hour, or three, I wasn't sure. However, when he finally acknowledged me again, my back was hurting and my legs ached. Plus, I had to go to the bathroom badly.

I tried not to dance around, but I couldn't help it and I suspected he noticed, which, I figured, was the reason he spoke to me.

"Is there something you need, pet?" Sir asked.

"I need to use the restroom," I admitted.

"Is this something you can handle on your own?" He sounded skeptical.

"Yes, Sir," I blurted, crossing my legs.

"If you can't handle taking care of *my* needs, how can I expect you to take care of your own?"

"I'm sorry, Sir." The urge to pee was so great I feared I was going to have an accident.

"Go to the restroom," he stated. "But leave the door open."

My gaze shot to the bathroom in his office and I noticed I could see the toilet from where I stood. Which meant Sir could see it as well. The thought of peeing in front of him was terrifying. I tried to fight back the urge.

"Suit yourself," Sir said, the keys on his keyboard once again clacking. "When you have to go, you have permission. But you must keep the door open."

I swallowed hard, staring at the toilet. With every passing second, the urge was getting greater. If I didn't give in, I was going to pee on myself, which, honestly, would've been more embarrassing than using the bathroom in front of him.

Several minutes later, I lost the battle and ran to the bathroom. I kept my eyes down as I sat on the toilet. I didn't look up, but I could feel Sir watching me. I knew he was doing it because it made me uncomfortable. My shy bladder finally released and I sighed heavily as the relief swarmed me.

Once I was finished relieving myself, I wiped, flushed, then went to the sink to wash my hands. I knew my face was red because my ears felt hot. I wasn't sure I would ever forget that he'd made me pee in front of him.

"Return to your spot," Sir commanded.

I took a deep breath and walked back over to him. This time, he swiveled his chair, leaning back and regarding me intently.

"Have you given some thought to your punishment?"

Personally, I thought having to pee in front of him was enough. Obviously, we weren't on the same page.

"I haven't come up with anything, Sir."

"Well, spankings are out," he said blandly. "And I'm not ready for serious orgasm denial just yet. However, I think I have an idea of what you *don't* want." His gaze shot to the bathroom.

I swallowed hard, refusing to look away from him.

"For the next twenty-four hours, you will ask my permission before you do anything. Whether it's to get a cup of coffee, to use the restroom, to eat, to drink, to sleep, to read, to call someone. Every single one of your needs must be approved by me."

Although the thought was not appealing, it seemed fitting. After all, I had disregarded all of his needs. Then again, the idea of asking him seemed as though it would be a tremendous burden on him. He was already dealing with his own life, plus being my master.

Damn, I'd made a terrible mess of this.

"Yes, Sir," I agreed humbly. "I will ask your permission."

"Good." He went back to his computer.

I turned to head out of the office, but he cleared his throat. I realized I hadn't asked permission and I instantly knew this was going to be far more difficult than I originally thought.

"Sir, may I return to my desk and work?"

"You may."

"May I get dressed?"

"No, you may not."

I nodded, then headed for the door.

"You need to thank your Master, pet. It's a privilege to be allowed to do anything at all."

I turned to face him, wanting to show him the respect he deserved. "Thank you, Sir."

He nodded and I took that as my dismissal. I hurried out of his office and went right to my desk. I called Jordan to let him know he could send any calls to me. When he tried to see if I was all right, I told him I couldn't talk. No way was I going to go into detail about this.

And for now, I was going to take full advantage of being able to catch up on my job duties.

•

When five thirty rolled around, I hadn't seen Sir. He was still in his office. The only person who'd talked to him was Langston, but even he had left half an hour ago. I was still naked, and in order to get dressed, I would have to go into Sir's office to get my clothes.

I felt bad for interrupting since I'd done so at least a dozen times already since he'd allowed me to go back to work, but I was supposed to leave at five thirty. Anything after that would be overtime and they hadn't approved for me to work additional time. So, I forced myself to my feet and went to Sir's office door. I knocked and listened for him to invite me in. A second later he called out.

I opened the door. "Sir, I'm finished for the day."

"Please, come in." He didn't look up from his computer. "Have a seat."

Before I could put my butt in the chair, Sir reached into his desk, then held out his hand to me. I instantly recognized the small bullet vibrator. Knowing what he wanted, I reached over and took it from his hand. When my fingers brushed his palm, electricity shot up my arm. I missed his touch.

"I want to watch," he informed me. "I need thirty minutes or so before I'll be ready to leave. While I work, I want you to tease yourself."

I realized he didn't say that I couldn't come; however, I knew that would be something I would have to ask permission for.

"Thank you, Sir," I said, repositioning myself in the chair so that he could see between my legs.

I couldn't deny that my body instantly warmed at the thought of Sir watching me masturbate. Although I should've been embarrassed, I found that I wasn't. I was eager to get close to Sir again and I hoped that this was a step in the right direction.

I turned on the vibrator, then eased it between my legs, hovering over my clit so that the vibration was a light caress. I continued like that for several minutes, teasing my labia, my clit, my entrance. I continued to watch Sir, but he didn't look up at me one time, much to my disappointment.

It didn't take long before I was panting, my body fully engulfed by my arousal. I held the vibrator against my clit, applying enough pressure so that the stirrings of my orgasm were present. I backed off a little, inhaling deeply.

Sir's gaze darted over briefly before returning to his screen. His expression never changed and I wondered if he was intrigued or merely checking to see that I was doing what I was told.

"Spread your legs wider," Sir instructed.

His direction brought me out of my sensual haze and I repositioned so that my legs were farther apart. It wasn't a comfortable position, but I was so close to orgasm I didn't care. I continued teasing myself, my eyes drifting closed as the heat inside me built to a crescendo.

A moan slipped past my lips, but I didn't stop. I was so close.

The creak of Sir's chair had me opening my eyes. He had moved around the desk and was sitting in front of me. His posture said he was merely observing, but he couldn't deny the erection tenting his slacks. The sight of it only spurred me on, intensifying my pleasure.

"Sir…" I moaned loudly. "Oh…Sir…may I come? Please?"

"You may come," he replied, his voice gruff.

I didn't hesitate, giving in to the electric storm that erupted in my womb. It spiraled out of control as I held the vibrator securely on my clit. I could feel the gentle pulses as I came, the warmth radiating out from my center.

When I opened my eyes, Sir was still watching me, his eyes locked on my face. I couldn't tell what he was thinking. It took a moment for my breathing to get under control, and when it did, Sir instructed me to get up.

"Please me, sweet girl." His voice was rough.

I didn't want to make any assumptions about what he wanted, so I whispered, "What's your pleasure, Sir?"

"You," he answered simply. "You are my greatest pleasure, pet."

My heart soared as his words hit somewhere in the center of my chest.

"May I suck your cock, Sir?"

"You may."

I slowly moved closer, then went to my knees before him. I reached for the buckle on his belt, then worked his slacks open, freeing his cock. I maintained eye contact while I slowly stroked him, gauging his reaction. I didn't want him to tell me what he wanted, but I intended to use his expression to guide me.

Leaning in, I licked the head of his cock and he moaned. I did it again, remembering how he had instructed me on Friday night. The way he had urged me to take him deep into my throat. I knew he had enjoyed that, so I focused on pleasuring him that way.

"Ahh, sweet girl," he groaned, his hands sliding into my hair. "I do love your mouth. Take more of me. All the way."

It took me a few minutes to get it right, but I managed to take his thick cock deep into my throat without gagging. When he held my head down, I swallowed, shifting my head so that his cock worked deeper. I finally pulled back as I fought for breath.

Before I could go back down on him one more time, Sir surged to his feet, bringing me with him. He spun me around, forcing me over his desk.

"I'm going to plow this little pussy. Feel free to come as many times as you'd like, but you must ask my permission each time."

I moaned as he thrust inside me without warning. I was still wet from my orgasm, but also from the blow job. It didn't take much for this man to turn me on and I was desperate and aching for him.

Sir held my hips and fucked me, the desk creaking beneath me. I grabbed the edge, forcing myself back so that I met every punishing thrust.

"Sir! Oh, God...may I come, Sir? Please?"

"You may," he growled as he slammed into me again and again.

My body tensed, my pussy clamping down on him as my orgasm had every muscle in my body locking up. The intensity of it had my mind spinning. I hadn't expected that.

Sir didn't stop fucking me. He thrust into me again and again, impaling me harder, faster, deeper until I was once again crying out his name, begging for permission seconds before I came again.

His stamina awed me and it wasn't until I could hardly move, my body wrung out from the sheer number of orgasms he drew out of me, that he gave in to his release, coming with a roar.

•

After cleaning us both, Sir got dressed and I waited for his instruction. It didn't come and I realized he was waiting for me to ask permission, as per my punishment.

"Sir, may I get dressed?"

"Yes."

I hurried to dress while he waited by the door. It bothered me that he was waiting. I felt as though I'd failed him again. We walked out of the building, me following several feet behind him. His truck was waiting at the front doors and he opened the passenger side and waited for me to get inside.

Feeling slightly embarrassed, I waited until he climbed inside before I asked if I could buckle my seat belt. He gave me permission.

A short time later, we arrived at his house. Remembering his rule, I waited until he opened my door for me before I exited the vehicle.

"Are you hungry, Sir?" I asked when we stepped inside.

"Yes."

"Would you like me to make dinner?"

Sir turned to face me. "That would be nice. Something fast. But remove your clothes first."

I nodded, then in a flurry of movement, I did as he requested, placing my clothing in a pile on the counter. Once I was naked, I headed for the kitchen. He left me there and I glanced through the ingredients. My first choice was baked potatoes with broccoli, cheddar cheese, and ham. Before I started preparing it, I went in search of Sir. He was in the bedroom, changing into jeans.

My breath halted in my lungs as I stared at his nearly naked form. His muscular calves, his thick thighs, his perfectly curved butt, the sexy taper of his waist and the breadth of his shoulders made my mouth water. The man was inherently male and the sight of him called to me on so many levels.

Although he was definitely sexy, I wasn't in here to ogle him, so I shook off the thought and told him what my thoughts were on dinner and asked if he was okay with that. He answered with a simple yes.

It felt strange asking him so many questions, but I was trying to abide by the rules. I realized it was inconvenient for both of us; however, it was better than what had happened after our incident at the club. I had practically ignored him, which I now realized was both selfish and childish. The fact that he hadn't let me go told me he held out hope for me, and I wanted to prove to him that I was worth the effort.

When dinner was ready, I found him in the living room reading something on his iPad. He joined me at the dining table. We ate in silence until I decided to broach the subject of the club.

"Sir, would you mind if I ask you questions about what happened on Saturday night?"

His eyes lifted to mine. "You can ask me anything. I've already told you that."

I took a sip of sweet tea. "Do you usually scene with Master?"

"Not always, but a majority of the time, yes."

I felt myself blush as I thought of my next question. It took me a second, but I finally blurted it out. "The scene we did…you called it sensation play. Do a lot of subs enjoy that?"

His dark eyebrows lifted. "Did *you* enjoy it?"

"Yes, Sir. I did. Very much." I took a deep breath. "I was hesitant at first, but I trusted you to know how far to push me. The thought of orgasming in front of other people frightened me the most. It'd been somewhat different on the island, but at the club…it was terrifying."

"I noticed that."

I wasn't sure how he could read me so well, but I figured it had to do with his experience.

"What was the prickly thing that you used?"

"It's called a Wartenburg wheel." He leaned back, seemingly more comfortable with my line of questioning.

"It scared me at first, but I enjoyed it. The opposing sensations were overwhelming." I glanced down at the table, then back up to look in his eyes. "I know that there were two of you. Is it the same without so much sensation?"

"It depends on the sub." He narrowed his eyes. "I know what you want, Luci. I'm not oblivious to it. I can see the attraction you have for my brother." His eyes went back to his plate. "You know what? I'm done with dinner. Why don't you finish eating, then clean up? We can continue this conversation in the living room."

My heart ached at the way he said it. As though I felt more for Master than I did for him. I knew he had purposely changed the subject and I couldn't blame him. Based on the way I reacted Saturday night, he had no idea how I truly felt.

"Yes, Sir."

I watched as he left the room before I got up and cleared the table. I hand washed the dishes since there weren't that many, then wiped down the counters and table. When I was finished, I shored up my nerve and went to the living room.

He was sitting on the sofa, but the television wasn't on and he wasn't reading.

I knew what I had to do.

"Sir, may I kneel at your feet?"

His eyes slowly lifted to mine. "Yes."

I walked over to him, then eased down onto my knees in front of him. I sat close enough that I could touch his leg, wanting to be near him.

"Can I be honest with you, Sir?"

"I expect nothing less."

Knowing that he didn't feel the same for me that I felt for him, I decided I would tell him exactly what was taking place inside my heart, no matter how he reacted to it.

"This is all new for me. Before I came to work for the firm, I had very little experience when it came to…sex. Much less when it came to my own desires. I've been surprised by what I'm discovering about myself. And I'll admit, I'm led by my emotions. It's who I am. Things have been moving quickly and it wasn't until I was asked to make a choice that I had time to step back and look at it all rationally. I'm glad I did, and believe it or not, the decision was easier than I thought it would be."

I paused, gathering my thoughts. Part of me expected him to say something, but he remained silent.

"I didn't choose option one because I didn't want this to be superficial. I'm not the type to go back to the beginning because it seems pointless. And no, I'm not expecting anything from any of you. I know you're not offering anything more than to train me and to teach me more about this lifestyle. For that, I'm grateful."

He looked as though he wanted to say something, but he held back, so I continued.

"I didn't choose option three for two reasons. First, I know Master doesn't want me. Not the way that I want to be wanted. But that wasn't my main reason for discarding that option."

Sir's eyes narrowed on my face, as though he was hanging on my every word.

My words came out raspy with emotion when I admitted my true reason for not choosing that option. "I decided to go with option two because…" I held his stare, feeling my heart race. "Because I wanted more time with you." I shook my head. "I know that sounds like I'm professing my love, but I'm not. I understand what this is. But that hasn't stopped me from developing feelings. And I have. For both you and…Langston. Maybe it's wrong, but I want both of you. Not one without the other. I don't have any expectations, so please don't think that. I just thought you deserved to know the truth."

The silence nearly choked me, but Sir didn't speak and I didn't feel the need to fill the void. He now knew how I felt and it was up to him to do whatever he thought was necessary with that information.

Time seemed to stand still and I let my gaze drop, my heart pounding against my ribs. I felt something for this man. I couldn't deny that. I also felt something for Master. I knew going into this that my time with either of them was going to be the most difficult. Although I looked forward to spending time with Ben and Justin, I knew that I wouldn't develop the level of feelings for them that I had for Master and Sir.

When Sir's hand curved over my head and he pulled me closer, I rested my cheek on his thigh. He brushed my hair back from my face, but he didn't say anything. We sat like that for what felt like a really long time.

"Thank you for sharing that with me, pet," he said roughly. "It means more than you know."

"You're welcome, Sir," I whispered, not moving.

I was content to remain right there, just like we were, for as long as he would have me.

THIRTY-THREE

AFTER CONFESSING MY FEELINGS TO Sir and getting through the twenty-four hours in which I was required to ask for every single thing I needed, it seemed as though we developed a rather comfortable routine with one another.

And by comfortable, I meant that Sir took his role as my master very seriously. To the point I looked forward to every single interaction I had with him. Each morning, he gave me a list of things he wanted me to do that day. Not a long list, mind you, but his ideas were extremely creative.

Hence the reason I was currently vacuuming naked while he sat on the sofa and watched me. I probably should've been self-conscious, but I wasn't. Or I hadn't been, right up until the moment that Master walked in the door with a man I didn't recognize, although he looked vaguely familiar. The woman standing beside him looked familiar, too, but I couldn't place either of them.

"Don't stop until you're finished," Sir instructed when I paused what I was doing.

I did my best to focus on my task while Master and the newcomers took their seats in the living room. It wasn't easy while everyone seemed to be watching me intently. They were all dressed; I was not. However, I did notice that the woman was wearing a collar, so I took that to mean she was a submissive. Perhaps that was the only reason I managed to complete my task without having an anxiety attack.

After I put the vacuum back in the closet by the stairs, I rejoined Sir in the living room, kneeling at his feet without being instructed.

"Thank you, pet."

"My pleasure, Sir."

"Thank you for joining us," Sir told them. "Luci, this is Master Harris and his wife, Bethany. Greet them, pet."

I lifted my head and smiled. "It's very nice to meet you."

"Likewise," Master Harris stated. "I have to admit, my wife has been eager to meet you. You might say she has an overactive imagination, and in an effort to quell it, she tends to jump on new experiences. Don't be surprised if she asks a million questions."

I had absolutely no clue what he was talking about.

"Master Harris's submissive is the author whose manuscript I asked you to read," Master clarified.

My eyes widened as it all made sense. I couldn't help but blush, remembering that Master said he wanted me to act out a couple of scenes in the book so he could relay the information to the author. We'd never actually gotten around to doing that, although I had recently finished the book.

"I think she figured it out," Master said, chuckling.

Sir placed his hand beneath my chin and tilted my head up so I was looking at him. "I invited Master Harris and his submissive here so they could watch us act out one of the scenes. Thought it would be beneficial for both you and her."

I was confused. How was this supposed to benefit me?

"She's an exhibitionist," Sir explained to Master Harris. "It will only heighten her pleasure to know that you're watching."

Oh, crap.

My face flamed with embarrassment. He was right. I was an exhibitionist. He was also right, it would turn me on immensely to know that they were watching. Even more so because I would get to be with both Master and Sir.

"So, which scene were you wanting to confirm, love?" Master Harris asked his wife.

She pulled a book from her bag and handed it over. I could tell there were two sections with tabs, so I assumed it was one of those two that I'd be acting out. Admittedly, there had been quite a few scenes in that particular book that had been appealing to me. However, one of them involved three men, and another involved a paddle.

Master Harris opened the book and skimmed the page. When he handed it over to Master, he was grinning. Surprisingly, Master didn't even look, he simply passed the book over to Sir. I waited patiently along with everyone else while Sir read a couple of pages, then turned to the other tabbed section. When he looked up, he nodded.

"The first one should prove to be interesting. Although my pet is quite small and rather limber, I'm not sure how we'll fare, but we'll certainly give it a shot. If you'll excuse me for a moment, I need to get a couple of items." Sir turned to me. "We'll be doing the scene here in the living room."

Master helped me to my feet, then pulled me onto his lap while Sir disappeared into the bedroom. I couldn't help peeking over my shoulder, wondering what he was going to get. I could feel my body preparing for the scene, even as I sat there and tried to recall which of them took place in the living room. I recalled one, but it involved some interesting uses of vegetables, something I truly hoped wouldn't be used on me.

Sir returned a minute later carrying some rope as well as a relatively large anal plug.

"While you seem to have a penchant for vegetables," Sir said to Beth, "I'm going to improvise and use this instead."

Beth blushed. "I completely understand."

Thank God.

However, I now knew exactly what he had in store for me. And truthfully, I was quite curious to see how this would work. I'd questioned the position myself.

"Would you care to set the scene, love?" Master Harris asked Beth.

"Master Langston, if you'll please disrobe and then have a seat until Master Landon is ready." Beth and Master Harris stood, then moved around to the other side of the room.

"I think it's only fair, love, that you undress as well, since you're asking everyone else to do so."

"Yes, Master." Beth didn't hesitate before she began stripping her clothes off. She was a beautiful woman and obviously quite comfortable in her own skin.

Master moved me to the cushion beside him, then began removing his clothing while I watched him.

"And Master Landon, you can start by restraining her arms behind her back. My Master can assist with the ropes, if needed."

"Not necessary," Sir said, nodding for me to come stand in front of him. "I've got quite a bit of experience with jute."

While he unwound the rope, I moved to stand in front of him, turning to face Master.

Sir brushed his mouth against my ear. "What's your safeword, pet?"

"Red, Sir."

"If at any time you wish to stop, use your safeword."

I nodded.

Within minutes, my arms were restrained behind my back, the rope twined from my shoulders to my wrists. I was unable to move them at all, but it didn't bother me. I had come to enjoy being restrained by my masters.

"What's your color, pet?"

"Green, Sir."

More so now that Master was sitting on the sofa, stroking his cock as he watched me.

"On your knees, sweet girl."

I went to my knees directly in front of Master.

"While I tie your legs, you may use your mouth to pleasure Langston."

Leaning forward, I licked the head of Master's cock, not even remotely concerned that there were two other people standing there watching as I did. Master twined his fingers in my hair and controlled the pace, guiding me down, then up as I sucked him as deep as I could.

"I love watching those lips wrap around my dick," Master breathed out roughly.

I focused my attention on Master as best I could. It wasn't easy when Sir tipped me forward as he secured my ankles to my thighs. It was an odd position, leaving me on my knees without any balance of my own. My torso rested on the cushion between Master's thighs, but it wasn't much support.

"We won't let you fall, little one," Master assured me, still guiding me up and down on his cock.

Once Sir was finished, I felt him move away from me, then I heard the rustle of clothing as he undressed. Warm hands were then on my shoulders.

"Ease her down for a minute," Sir instructed.

Master pulled his cock from my mouth, then shifted me as he settled me onto the carpeted floor. My arms were behind my back, my ankles strapped to my thighs, which left me completely trussed up, unable to move even an inch. I could touch my calves with my fingertips, but that was about it. Although I was grateful for yoga, I was beginning to feel panic set in.

"Color, pet?" Sir asked as something cool dribbled down the crack of my ass.

"Yellow, Sir."

In an instant, he was kneeling behind me, leaning over me with his mouth against my ear. "Breathe for me, sweetness. You're safe with us, I promise you that. We won't let anything happen to you."

"I know that, Sir." My anxiety was merely getting the best of me. I enjoyed being restrained, but this was a little more than I'd anticipated.

"Luci, if you need to stop, I completely understand," Beth said softly.

"I'm okay," I assured them all.

Sir's finger dipped down between my ass cheeks, teasing me. It was enough to get my mind off the restraints and back where it needed to be.

"I wish I was fucking this ass," Sir admitted, his voice just barely above a whisper. "Unfortunately, you're gonna have to deal with an imposter."

The blunt end of the plug pressed against my asshole and I moaned, wiggling back against the intrusion. I wanted it more than I cared to admit.

"Fuck, that's pretty," Master said, his voice coming from somewhere above me. "Watching that toy slide into your ass…"

Yep, his dirty words were turning me on even more.

Several minutes later, I was panting as the plug stretched my ass and Sir fingered my pussy. I was still on the floor, unable to move, but I didn't care. He was pushing me closer and closer to the breaking point.

"Come all over my fingers, sweet girl. Then I'm going to fuck you until you scream my name."

He plunged his fingers deep in my pussy while he pushed the plug into my ass. It didn't take long before I was shaking, my breaths racing in and out of my lungs as that sweet electric current started in my womb, then radiated out through my fingertips.

"Oh, God! I'm coming!" I didn't even care who was there, I couldn't keep the words in. It felt so good, even being tied up like I was.

They allowed me to catch my breath.

"Are you ready?" Master Harris asked. "I'll assist in getting her into position. I'm not even sure it's possible without three people."

"Agreed," Sir said, and then I was lifted off the floor completely. I realized then that Sir and Master Harris were holding me while Master shifted to the floor beneath me, his cock moving into my line of sight. Technically, we were in a sixty-nine position, only I wasn't on top of him, I was suspended above him.

"All right. This is where it gets complicated," Beth said. "Master Langston, you'll need to hold her upper body while Master Landon holds her legs. She'll be positioned at an angle and, Master Landon, you'll have to stand above Master Langston."

Okay, this was definitely strange. I wondered how odd it was for Master since he was the one on the floor.

His arms came up and gripped my rib cage while Sir kept his hands on my hips, his arms wrapped under my thighs, bearing the brunt of my weight. I was leaning forward, feeling as though I would tip over at any moment.

"Now," Beth guided us, "Master Landon, you'll fuck her pussy while Luci, you'll be sucking Master Langston's cock."

Yeah. Well.

I leaned forward as Master inched me lower and I attempted to take his cock in my mouth. Unfortunately, I had absolutely no use of my hands to guide me so I was relying on Master's strength. And because he had to hold me, there was no way for him to assist.

"You're testing me, aren't you, Beth?" Master grunted. "Checking to see if I've been working out."

I could see his arms, noticing the way his biceps flexed as he held my weight above him.

"As eager as I am to make this work," Sir said, "I don't think it's feasible. No one is going to get much pleasure when we're working so hard to keep her from falling."

"Dang it," Beth said with a giggle. "I was hoping it would work."

"Unfortunately, that's not gonna happen," Master said, "but I think I know what will."

Master Harris once again moved over and wrapped his arms around my torso, then lifted me up. I felt almost like a circus act, being shifted and moved in so many directions. It was certainly having an impact on my arousal, to say the least. And not in a good way.

"Lay her on her back on the couch," Master instructed.

Thanks to the restraints, my back bowed, thrusting my chest out and making my knees ache from the odd angle. The next thing I knew, Master had fused his mouth to my pussy, licking me like a lollipop. The position I was in was uncomfortable, putting a tremendous strain on my thighs, but it didn't matter. The way his mouth worked me into a frenzy trumped everything else.

"Master...oh, God..."

Before my climax could erupt, he stopped what he was doing, picked me up, and turned me over so that my ribs were resting on the cushioned armrest of the sofa. Warm hands gripped my hips, keeping my knees off the floor.

Master then positioned himself in front of me, his cock right at my mouth.

"Take me in your mouth, little one."

As I was leaning forward, I felt Sir shift, and a second later, he was impaling me from behind. I cried out as he filled me. Between his thick cock and the enormous plug in my ass, I felt stuffed to overflowing.

"Color, Luci?" Sir questioned as he held himself still.

"Green, Sir. So very green."

Master guided his cock to my lips and I sucked him inside. He was sitting up, trying to take the strain off my shoulders, but I still had enough room to bob up and down on him. It wasn't long before I was so focused on what they were doing that I didn't even notice the strange position.

"Aww, fuck, little one. Keep that up and I'm gonna come down your throat."

I wanted that so badly.

They both continued to use me, Sir fucking me from behind while shifting the plug in my ass and Master pushing his cock deep into my throat. I moaned and whimpered as my orgasm was once again just out of reach.

Master's hands moved, his fingers finding my nipples. He pinched and tugged until I couldn't take any more. I let his cock fall from my mouth as I cried out, coming without an ounce of shame.

"Fuck…" Sir groaned as he came, triggering a delicious aftershock.

"Release her legs," Master instructed Sir.

It wasn't long before the rope was removed from my legs and Sir was massaging my muscles as I moaned softly.

"Come sit on my cock," Master ordered.

With Sir's help, I managed to straddle Master's hips while he laid back on the sofa. My arms were still tied behind my back, but with my legs free, I had so much more freedom. I lifted and lowered on his cock, loving the way he squeezed my breasts, pinching my nipples.

"Sir," I whimpered, trying to look over my shoulder to see where he was. I wanted him right there with us.

"I'm right here, sweet girl."

His fingers twined in my hair and he turned my head, feeding his cock to me. I then bounced on Master's dick while Sir stood beside the sofa and fucked my mouth.

"Squeeze my cock," Master commanded. "Oh, fuck, yes."

He roared as he came, his orgasm triggering mine.

"Don't stop," Sir insisted, holding my head as he fucked my mouth. I knew he'd come only a few minutes before, so I didn't think he would come again. He proved me wrong seconds later when his cock twitched in my mouth.

When he pulled back, I fell forward, completely exhausted.

"I think it's safe to say you're gonna have to make some changes to that scene, love," Master Harris told Beth.

"I agree. And I now know exactly what I'm going to change it to."

THIRTY-FOUR

ON FRIDAY AFTERNOON, I WAS finishing up some filing when I turned to see Sir coming out of his office. It wasn't time to leave just yet, but I could tell he wanted something.

He cleared his throat and waited until I peeked at him over my shoulder. "Are you finished?"

"Only a few more to go." My mouth was curling into a smile at the same time I noticed the wicked gleam in his eyes.

My Sir was thinking of doing something extremely naughty and I got the feeling he was planning to turn all those dirty thoughts directly on me.

"Put the papers down," he ordered, his tone rough.

I placed the papers on the top of the filing cabinet, then turned to face him.

He glanced over at my desk, then nodded in that direction. "Move over there." His voice was rough, as though he was trying to maintain his control and not quite succeeding.

Not sure what he had in mind, I walked over to my desk. Before I could turn around, he was behind me, pushing me face down on the desk. He wasn't rough, but he wasn't gentle either. All my girly parts started to sing.

His body pressed down on me, his lips brushing my neck. "I need you, Luci."

His words warmed me as they always did. "I'm yours, Sir. Any way that you want me."

It was nothing less than the truth. I would give anything to this man.

Warm hands brushed over the backs of my thighs as he pushed my skirt up, baring my ass.

"Such a beautiful ass." His words rumbled in my ear as he palmed my butt cheeks, squeezing firmly. "Who does this ass belong to?"

"You, Sir."

His hands dipped between my legs, his fingers slipping between my pussy lips.

"And who does your pussy belong to?"

"You, Sir." I was panting at this point, eager for him to take me right here on my desk. I didn't even care that all my bosses were in their offices, or that Jordan was at the front.

His weight disappeared, but his hands did not. He once again palmed both of my butt cheeks, kneading them with his fingers. His breaths were coming in as fast as mine.

"Spread your legs wide for me," he insisted.

I did as he instructed, widening my stance while I remained bent over my desk. I felt his shirt brush the backs of my thighs as he knelt behind me.

"You're wet, sweet girl."

"Yes, Sir." I was definitely wet. I hadn't expected this from him and quite frankly, I liked the rough treatment, the way he dominated me, taking what he wanted.

His fingers separated my pussy lips and then his tongue was teasing me, pushing inside me as he groaned. When he turned his attention to my clit, I pressed my hips back, enjoying everything he was giving me.

He swatted my ass, making me yelp.

"Do not move."

My body was trembling, but I fought the urge to press back against him when his tongue resumed its feast. He lapped at me, his hands still roaming over my ass, squeezing my flesh as though he was trying to hold himself back.

When he finally stood, I was panting and moaning, urging him to take me.

"Stay just like that," he commanded.

I did.

I heard him moving behind me, but I wasn't sure what he was doing. A minute or two later, he was lubing my ass with his fingers, pushing in, retreating. It felt so good for him to take me like this. I hadn't expected it and I figured that was what made it even more erotic.

Ben's door opened just as I felt the head of Sir's cock press against my asshole. Okay. So that was how he wanted to play it.

"I need your ass," he growled as he pushed his hips forward. "Relax for me, pet. Let me fuck this little ass."

"Please, Sir. Please fuck my ass." The words just came out. I didn't necessarily mean to speak them aloud, but I couldn't help myself. I was so caught up in the moment, in his demanding tone.

Another door opened and then another. I knew Ben, Justin, and Master were all watching Sir fuck my ass while I was laid out over my desk, my skirt hiked up. Even thinking about it made me hot.

He smacked my left butt cheek, making me groan as pleasure darted up my spine. His hand landed on my right cheek.

"Oh, God, Sir…please…"

"Squeeze my dick, sweet girl. Make your master come in your ass."

His words spurred me on, driving me closer to the edge. I'd never come from being fucked like this before. Not only like this, anyway. Usually it was double penetration or after he'd worked me into a frenzy, so I was surprised that I was racing to the edge, my body trembling as the fire ignited in my veins.

Sir slammed into me, taking me harder than he'd ever taken me before. I knew without a doubt that I'd be sore when he was finished, but I didn't care. I wanted this. I wanted him to stake his claim, to take me like a man who needed nothing more than me.

"Oh, Luci…fuck, sweetness. Your ass is so damn tight. Fuck, yes…"

Sir didn't let up, pounding me like a man who'd been starved and finally found nourishment. I had to grip the edge of the desk to hold on, doing my best to push back against him.

"Tell me who you belong to," Sir demanded.

"You! I belong to you, Sir!"

"Fuck yes, you do."

His words triggered my orgasm and a few seconds later, he followed me over.

•

"When we get home, I want you to shower and change," Sir said as he steered the truck onto the main road.

"Of course, Sir. Are we going somewhere?"

"I want to take you out to dinner tonight."

I smiled to myself as I stared out the window. The idea of a night out on the town with him made my heart sing.

Sir was quiet for several minutes, and I tried not to fill the void with unnecessary chatter. So, when he finally spoke up, I was startled.

"Did I hurt you this afternoon, Luci?"

My smile disappeared at the concern I heard in his tone. "No, Sir. You didn't hurt me."

He didn't say anything, keeping his eyes on the road.

"I enjoyed what you did," I told him, wanting to be sure he understood. "It was hot."

"Was it?" His eyes cut over to me briefly.

"Absolutely." I decided to be honest. "I actually love moments like that. When you can't seem to hold back. Then you command my submission... I live for those moments." And that was true. I honestly craved when Master and Sir turned their dominance on me.

Sir reached over and took my hand, twining our fingers together. I was surprised by his vulnerability, although I wasn't sure why that was. He was a man, like any other. Just because he was a Dominant didn't mean he wasn't worried about the same things most men worried about.

I gave his hand a gentle squeeze and settled into my seat, enjoying the moment.

As soon as we arrived at his house, I hurried to take a shower. Since I had no idea where he was taking me, I wrapped myself in a towel while I did my makeup and dried my hair. When I was finished, I went in search of him.

Sir was sitting in the living room with his phone to his ear, one ankle crossed over the opposite knee. He looked relaxed, sexy. The second he saw me, he motioned me over, then pointed toward the table in front of the sofa.

I sat down facing him, waiting patiently.

Rather than get off the phone, Sir leaned forward, then unhooked the towel that had been fastened over my breasts.

He smiled when it fell away, leaving me naked before him.

"Yes, I'm taking her out to dinner."

I don't think Sir knew how happy it made me that he was taking me out on a date. Although we spent a lot of time together and we had been out on a date before, it felt different this time.

"No can do. Tonight she's all mine."

That made me feel even better.

"A movie?" Sir met my gaze. "That's rather vanilla, don't you think?"

I watched him intently. I didn't mind vanilla one bit. Although, I got the feeling that Sir could easily turn a vanilla movie date into something rather erotic. It excited me to think about it.

"If her nipples are anything to go by, I'd say she likes that idea."

I glanced down. Sure enough, my nipples had pebbled.

"I'll leave that up to her. If she goes for it, I'll text you and let you know."

Now my curiosity was piqued and I wanted to know what devious idea Sir had come up with.

Unfortunately, the man liked to keep me waiting, because he hung up the phone, set it on the cushion beside him, then continued to look at me, his eyes heating as he took in my nakedness.

"This is a very nice look for you," he said absently, his gaze slowly traveling back up to my face.

I grinned. "I was actually coming to ask you what I should wear. I don't know where we're going, so I didn't want to assume anything."

"I'd like to see you in one of your long black skirts and the burgundy corset."

Hmm. I hadn't thought to pair up the fetish wear with anything else, but I liked the idea.

"You can wear your heeled black boots. No panties."

I already had the perfect skirt in mind, so I bounced up to my feet.

"Hold on, pet. I'm not ready for you to leave yet."

Before I turned away, I paused, standing directly in front of Sir.

He leaned forward and pressed his lips to my stomach, his hand sliding up the inside of my thigh.

"Are you wet?" He didn't seem to need an answer, choosing to check for himself.

His fingers were gentle as he probed me.

"You are."

"Yes, Sir," I said around a moan as he fingered me slowly, leisurely, as though we had all the time in the world.

"Is your pussy greedy for attention?"

Even more so when he said things like that.

"Yes, Sir." The words escaped on a breathless moan.

"Then you might enjoy what Langston has in mind for you."

"Only if it pleases you, Sir." Honestly, I didn't care what happened, as long as Sir was happy. This was my time with him, not Master. If he wanted the three of us to spend the evening together, I was all for it. If he wanted it to be just him and me, I was all for that, too.

Sir's fingers slipped from my body and he curled his hands around my hips, pressing his forehead to my belly. I glanced down, confused by the response. Unsure what to do, I put my hand on his head, holding him to me. His hair was silky and soft.

"The last thing I want to do is to confuse you, Luci."

When he pulled back and looked up at me, I went to my knees before him.

"You're not confusing me, Sir. I'm well aware of what you and Master want. I want the same thing."

Something passed in his eyes, but I wasn't sure what it was. It was slightly terrifying because I was pretty sure it didn't end with a happily ever after.

Not that I was expecting it. I knew what was going on here. This wasn't a promise of something more, it was an arrangement, one I fully intended to abide by. However, I couldn't deny that I'd fallen in love with Master and Sir. That didn't mean I couldn't enjoy the time we had together. I was one of those people who understood she couldn't always get everything she wanted.

I noticed the moment he masked his expression, but I forced a smile.

"I'll go get dressed, Sir." I got to my feet. "And you can surprise me with whatever you have planned."

"When you're finished, I'll shower and we'll go."

"Thank you, Sir."

He nodded, but he didn't stop me when I turned to go.

Although there was a slight amount of trepidation curling deep inside me, I vowed to enjoy the evening, regardless of what happened.

And I also promised myself that I wouldn't think about tomorrow.

Only tonight.

THIRTY-FIVE

I DON'T REMEMBER THE LAST time I went to a movie. It wasn't something I tended to indulge in, choosing rather to watch Netflix at home or rent movies through Apple or Amazon.

However, I was excited about the possibilities.

Sir had taken me to a very nice restaurant where we dined on seafood and wine. He shared some stories about him and Langston when they were rambunctious teenagers. I'd learned that they had become members of their first BDSM club at the ripe old age of twenty-two while they were still in college. That hadn't surprised me in the least, considering what I knew of their parents. Although not directly, they'd been introduced to the lifestyle at a young age. For two alpha men, exploring the BDSM world seemed the natural next step.

When I'd asked what had gotten them interested in public relations, Sir had informed me that it had been a fluke. A friend of theirs knew someone who knew someone else who was publishing a book. They were curious as to how to market that and, according to Sir, the rest was history. They'd helped that person get the word out about their book and their names began circulating, especially when that person hit the *New York Times* best-seller list. So I guess the rest really was history; they'd only gone up from there.

When we arrived at the theater, Sir retrieved our tickets from a woman standing behind a long counter at the front of the place. I instantly realized that this wasn't a normal movie theater. Rather than a popcorn stand, there was a bar. Instead of dozens of people standing around, kids running amok, there were pool tables and tall tables where adults sat enjoying drinks and laughing.

"I heard there was some riffraff in the place tonight," a deep, booming voice said, causing Sir to turn around.

There was an older man, probably in his mid-fifties, standing there, a wide smile on his face.

"That's because like attracts like, Bill," Sir said with a huge grin. "It's good to see you again."

"Likewise, kid." Bill's voice boomed through the room.

The men shared one of those bro-hugs that consisted of rough pats on the back before they pulled apart and Sir placed his arm around me, pulling me close.

"Bill, I'd like you to meet Luci."

Bill turned warm brown eyes on me and his smile widened even more.

"I've heard so much about you, young lady. Welcome to my establishment."

When I went to shake his hand, Bill pulled me in for a hug, making me giggle.

"I'm glad you could finally stop in, check the place out."

"Thanks for accommodating us tonight," Sir replied.

"My pleasure. Even if it is a Friday night." Bill chuckled. "Well, you kids have fun now. I've got to go say hello to some more riffraff."

Sir guided me away after saying good-bye to Bill. I turned my head up to look at him, hoping for a little more information on who that man was and how he knew him.

"Bill's a good friend of my father's," Sir explained. "He's also a member of the club."

Ahh. So he was *that* sort of friend. The Dom type. It made me wonder what Sir meant when he mentioned accommodating us tonight.

Sir kissed my temple and steered me toward the back. We ended up going into a theater and were required to climb a set of stairs. When I reached the top, I noticed rows of recliners that stairstepped down toward the big screen.

"We're back here," Sir informed me, tugging on my hand to keep me from walking too far down.

We took our seats near the top and a few seconds later a waiter came by, asking for our drink order. I opted for another glass of wine and Sir went with Glenlivet, which I was surprised to learn they did have.

Once the drinks were delivered, Sir whispered something to the waiter, then turned toward the front. Oddly enough, no one else came into the theater. More minutes passed and I was getting confused.

"Are we the only ones here?" And okay, maybe I hadn't heard of the movie Sir had suggested we see, but surely someone besides us was going to see it. Like Bill said, it was Friday night.

"Yes."

"No one else is coming?"

"No one else is coming," he echoed.

"Really?" That seemed strange.

"I rented out this particular screening."

Well.

I couldn't keep the smile from my face. I knew without a doubt that Sir had something planned if he had rented the entire place out.

A short time later, the lights dimmed and the screen came to life. While I thought we were going to watch a rom-com, I realized rather quickly that I was wrong. What appeared on the screen certainly wasn't a romantic comedy. In fact, it looked more like a XXX movie.

Holy shit.

It *was* a XXX movie.

"You rented out the theater to watch porn?" I giggled because I couldn't help it.

"Thought it would be something different."

That it was.

"You have an issue with porn?"

"No. Not at all." I was merely surprised he enjoyed it. I don't know why that was. Perhaps because his life resembled one. Only with normal people who merely enjoyed kink of all varieties.

"Remove your clothes, Luci," Sir instructed just as the movie started to heat up.

I tried to peer around, to ensure no one else was there, but Sir stopped me, placing his finger beneath my chin and turning my face toward his.

"Don't worry about anything else except what I tell you to do. You have to trust me, Luci. That's how this works. I'm responsible for taking care of you and you have to let me do that. Do you trust me?"

Swallowing hard, I nodded.

It wasn't that I was worried that someone would see me. Well, I was. However, not for the way Sir thought. I simply didn't want to go to jail for indecent exposure. We were in a public place, after all.

"Luci?"

I hesitated momentarily and the next thing I knew, Sir was pulling me over his lap.

Instinct had me trying to move away. "Sir? What are you doing?"

"I asked you to do something and you didn't. You didn't think you'd get away with it, did you?"

Actually, I hadn't realized I'd hesitated that long.

"How many do you think you've earned?" he asked as he pulled my skirt up to my waist, baring my ass.

"I...uh...I don't know."

"Twenty," he said quickly.

Crap.

The idea of Sir spanking me both terrified and thrilled me. I knew it wasn't the same as when Master had done it because Sir wasn't angry. Not the way Master had been.

"Are you ready, pet?"

I shook my head but said, "Yes, Sir."

"Good. And when I'm done punishing you, I want you to take off your clothes and kneel in front of me. You will suck my cock until I tell you to stop. Understood?"

"Yes, Sir."

Rather than count how many times Sir spanked me, I got lost in the sensation. It overtook my mind, my arousal spiking while my brain seemed to disconnect from my body, bringing a sense of peace to me. It wasn't nearly as painful as I'd thought it would be, although I'd be lying if I said it didn't hurt. It did. However, the sting was a good one. I felt as though I was flying, my body humming with my arousal.

"What did I instruct you to do?"

Realizing he was finished, I instantly got to my feet.

"Turn around. Let me help with the corset."

I turned so he could deal with the laces. When I was free from the binding, I immediately removed my boots, then my skirt before turning to face him. I dropped to my knees on the carpeted floor as Sir was freeing his cock. Just when I leaned forward to take him into my mouth, I noticed light streaming in, as though someone had opened a door. A few seconds later, Master appeared.

"Suck me," Sir grumbled. "Do not make me tell you again."

Anticipation rose inside of me, warring with the desire to please Sir. I could hear the movie playing, heard the woman moaning and grunting as the man on the screen did something to her. I hadn't been paying attention to what was going on, so I had no idea what was happening.

Not that I cared. I had my own XXX scene taking place in front of me and I was the star of this one.

Sir's cock twitched and grew in my mouth, spurring me on. I sucked him deep, relishing his moans and the way his fingers twined in my hair.

"Do you like when Langston watches you suck my cock?"

I nodded but didn't release Sir's dick from my mouth. I wanted to focus my attention on him because that was where it was supposed to be. I didn't belong to Master right now, I belonged to Sir. And it was important that I showed him that I understood that.

"Good." His eyes were locked with mine. "Because this is what we want, Luci. We want you. Between us."

I fought back the tears that threatened. It sounded an awful lot like he was offering me something more. I didn't want to think too hard on that because I doubted that was the case. We were here to enjoy ourselves. Sir was my Dom for two weeks, that was all. At that point, I would belong to someone else. And my time with him would be over for a while.

"God, I love your mouth," he groaned, pulling my hair and letting his cock fall from between my lips. "But it's a wicked mouth and I'm not ready to come just yet. Stand up."

As I was getting to my feet, Master moved around and took the seat I'd been in. The one right beside Sir.

"Now, I want you to lie across us, on your back. We want to watch the movie while we tease you." Sir pulled me forward so that my face was almost level with his. "However, there's one condition."

"Anything, Sir."

"You are not allowed to come."

I could tell by the way he said the words that he was going to do everything in his power to make me come. I could also tell that I was going to fail.

"If you come, I will punish you. Twenty licks for every orgasm."

Shit.

This was going to be a long night.

THIRTY-SIX

IT WAS HARD TO BELIEVE, but my two weeks with Sir was coming to an end. Tomorrow would be the last day I spent with him. Not only that but he was getting ready to go on a week-long trip, which meant I wouldn't see him for several days.

I had been informed that I would learn who my new master would be on Monday afternoon, once the four of them had time to talk. Honestly, I wasn't sure I was ready to belong to anyone else just yet. My time with Sir had been intense, and not always in a good way. I felt as though I needed some time to get my head on straight. Then again, I had the weekend, so there was that. Too much more time to think would likely make it worse. And although I wasn't necessarily looking forward to the change, I was trying not to concern myself with it at the moment. I was focused on spending as much time with Sir as I could before our time was up.

All this week, Sir had forced me to work naked. I didn't mind anymore. It was almost natural. Plus, I looked forward to what Sir had in store for me. While we'd spent the remainder of last week exploring my limits after our mutual meltdowns, it was good for both of us. The man had some wickedly creative ways to make me come and every day I looked forward to what he wanted from me.

And this week, he'd proven that he certainly hadn't run out of ideas. Sir had come up with some pretty incredible things that had honestly tested my limits in ways I hadn't expected.

On Monday, Sir had left me a note informing me that I was to go into Justin's office at exactly two o'clock. I did as he instructed and found Sir sitting on the couch. He then proceeded to watch as Justin teased me with his tongue and his fingers. According to Sir, intercourse wasn't allowed, but that hadn't stopped Justin from making me come at least half a dozen times. It had been quite the experience to have him simply touch me, gently coaxing one orgasm after another. But the best part had been the fact that Sir was there to watch.

Then, on Tuesday, Sir had called me into his office. I'd then been instructed to slip beneath his desk and pleasure him with my mouth while he tended to a conference call that took over an hour. I had to admit, the man's stamina was awe-inspiring. Try as I might, he hadn't come during the conversation. And when he hung up the phone, he had fucked my mouth ruthlessly, coming down my throat.

On Wednesday, Sir had insisted that I wear the butt plug and the Venus Butterfly for the entire day. I spent most of my time on edge because he had amused himself with the remote control. I wasn't allowed to come, which had frustrated me to no end. However, he had relieved all the pent-up pressure by fucking me against the windows overlooking the building next door while my other three bosses and a room full of accountants had watched.

Today had been relatively quiet. When Sir and I arrived this morning, I learned that Jordan had requested the day off to take care of some personal business. I spent most of the day dealing with the phones. During the rare times they weren't ringing, I focused my attention on seeking input for the next quarterly meeting that would take place in March. It was still a ways off, but I figured it was best to get started early. I liked the idea of having a larger project to work on.

I felt as though I'd proven myself in the months that I'd been there. And I wasn't referring to the extracurricular activities. I was far more than a sex toy for these men to enjoy. Not once since I had arrived had they made me feel as though I wasn't a contributing part of the company. Perhaps that was why I continued to enjoy working there. Well, that and the sex. I certainly enjoyed the sex.

However, I had to wonder what it would be like if we were no longer enjoying each other's company the way that we were. Would I still be able to look them in the eye? What would happen if they moved on to another submissive?

The thought made my stomach turn.

Thinking about Master and Sir with someone else made my stomach bottom out. As for Ben and Justin…no, I wouldn't like it per se, but I could get used to it. Although I cared about them immensely, I wasn't in love with them.

I stared at Sir's door, then over at Master's.

I was in love with my bosses.

No matter how hard I had tried to keep this on a sexual level, I had failed. It was more than sex for me. And now that I'd come to the realization, I couldn't simply drop it.

Oh, I could pretend with the best of them and I would. No way was I going to let Master and Sir know that my heart had gone and caused a huge mess of this. They didn't need to know that.

Hell, no one needed to know that.

Thankfully, the phone rang.

I needed the distraction in a bad, bad way.

•

That night, Sir cooked for me, and afterward, I cleaned the kitchen before joining him in the living room. I curled up next to him while we watched some gangster movie and he teased my naked body relentlessly. By the time the movie was over, I was on the verge of implosion and he seemed to notice.

"I'll be right back," he told me, then disappeared in the direction of his bedroom. I listened, trying to hear what he was doing, while my body trembled with excitement.

When he returned, he wasn't wearing a shirt and the button on his jeans had been unfastened.

He leaned over and kissed me gently, then pulled back and looked into my eyes. "You ready for our last night together?"

I smiled, holding back the emotions that filled me. The thought of it really being our last night together broke my heart. I wasn't ready to leave him, but I knew that was the agreement.

"No, Sir," I admitted softly. "However, I look forward to whatever you have in store for me."

His eyes softened and he brushed his knuckles over my cheek.

When he stood to his full height, he held out his hand to me. I followed him into the bedroom, noticing that there were several candles burning around the room. Plus, the restraints he had on his bed were lying on the mattress, practically calling my name.

"Not yet, pet," he said, leading me into the bathroom.

The bathtub was full, steam drifting up from the heated water. Sir helped me in, then stripped out of his jeans while I watched. The man was ridiculously sexy. I wanted to spend the rest of the night memorizing every inch of his delectable body.

When he joined me in the oversized tub, he eased in behind me, then pulled me down to him. He used a sponge to caress my breasts and my belly, wringing out the sponge over my nipples, the warmth and attention causing them to harden.

Neither of us spoke while he kissed my neck, breathing me in. I was lost to the romanticism of the act, wishing this night never had to end. But the water eventually cooled, and when I shivered, we got out and he dried us both.

"Tonight is all about you, pet," he whispered.

He said it as though every night hadn't been about me. Although he commanded me to do things, the pleasure this man brought me was something I would forever treasure.

Sir placed a blindfold over my eyes, tying it at the back of my head. As the darkness consumed me, I gave myself over to him, knowing that he would care for me tonight. I'd come to trust him during the time we'd spent together and I knew he wouldn't hurt me. Not physically, anyway. My heart was an entirely different story, but that wasn't his fault. It was mine. I'd fallen in love with this man in the short time I'd known him.

I knew I couldn't admit that to him, so I held it inside and let it build, bringing me pleasure only he was capable of providing.

I felt something go over my head, settling just above my ears. "I want you to only focus on your sense of touch tonight. I'm putting noise-canceling headphones on you."

I nodded, curious as to what this would be like.

"Before I do, I want you to tell me what your safeword is."

"Red, Sir."

"At any point, should you feel it necessary, use your safeword. I will stop. And should you need a moment to collect yourself, yellow is the word. I'll give you a break at that point."

"I understand, Sir."

I hadn't needed to use my safeword up to this point, but I was grateful for the reminder. I knew that Sir had to trust me to know my own limits.

After he placed the headphones over my ears, Sir took my hand and we started walking. I could hear nothing except for my own breathing. It was almost terrifying to be robbed of both sight and sound. It left me feeling incredibly vulnerable, proving to me that I had established a great deal of trust for this man.

We didn't go far, so I assumed we were still in his bedroom. When my thighs met the mattress, I knew I was right.

He turned me around and then urged me to sit down. With care, he laid me out on the bed, then restrained my arms and my legs. I could feel the caress of the air against my flesh, pushed down by the ceiling fan. The soft brush of his fingers over my skin made the fine hairs on my body stand on end. My anticipation grew rapidly. Without sight, sound, or the ability to move, I was completely at his mercy. He would do as he pleased and I wouldn't rush him.

Not that I wanted to.

Sir's finger moved in a circular motion over my breast. I focused on that, sure he was trying to tell me something. I had no idea what he was planning to do to me. I'd already experienced sensation play, so I assumed that was his intent.

What happened next shocked me and I sucked in air as heat splashed over the lower curve of my breast. It trickled down and seemed to stop. Then there was more, dripping onto my body in intervals. A little here, a little there. Warmth pooled, then quickly cooled on my skin. It continued over my belly, my breasts, and the juncture where my thigh met my hip. The temperature of the liquid changed. Sometimes warmer than others, but it was deliciously stimulating.

I could only assume he was using wax. As I waited for the next, I held my breath, attempting to anticipate where it would be. It never landed where I expected, heightening my sense of touch. I was riding a wave of ecstasy when it finally stopped. Several minutes passed and I assumed he was allowing the wax to cool, to harden on my skin.

When he started peeling away the wax, that was erotic in its own way. Something cool grazed my breasts and I realized he was wiping the rest away. He took his time cleaning every inch of me, teasing me with his gentle touch as he went.

His hands disappeared and then I felt warm breath between my thighs. Something brushed against my clit and I realized it was his tongue. I inhaled deeply, lifting my hips to meet the welcome sensation. Strong hands landed on my hips, urging me back down to the mattress. They remained there and I was focused solely on the tongue lapping at me and the thumbs brushing over my hip bones.

Then the cloth returned to my breasts and that was the moment I realized we were not alone. There were two men touching me, teasing me. The knowledge instantly spiked my arousal. I knew who it was without asking.

Sir.

Master.

They were both here.

My heart rate sped up, my breaths ramping up to match.

The mouth on my pussy moved, lips brushing over my skin as the bed shifted around me. Then there were two mouths on my breasts. The sudden sensation shocked me and my body jerked. Teeth nibbled on my skin, then latched on to my nipples, one mouth rough, one gentle. I felt as though I was being tossed in the waves, unable to predict what would happen next.

While they feasted on my breasts, hands moved between my legs.

I felt the pressure of two fingers push inside me. Then two more.

They were fingering me at the same time, filling me up. My pussy gushed with excitement. I moaned, but I could hardly hear my own voice thanks to the headphones covering my ears.

Then everything stopped.

I lay there panting, eager. I wanted more, but I didn't say as much. I wanted them to do what they wanted to my body, to take their own pleasure while giving in return. It was a heady feeling, one I could easily get addicted to.

My body twitched when a feather brushed over my nipple. Then the pinprick of the Wartenburg wheel ran over the bottom of my foot. My leg instinctively jerked, trying to get away from the sensation. A stinging slap landed on my pussy. It should've been painful, but it wasn't. It was erotic.

They tormented me for long minutes. The soft brush of the feather, the pinprick of the wheel, the warmth of mouths and hands. I was so close to coming, my brain obliterated by the overstimulation, so when the vibration brushed my clit, I screamed, my orgasm plowing through me, shattering all my senses.

I rode out the climax as every sensation slowly disappeared one at a time.

While I lay there panting, the restraints were removed from my ankles, then my wrists. Firm hands massaged my limbs. Then the earphones disappeared, followed by the blindfold.

It took a moment for my eyes to adjust to the dim light. I noticed Sir first. He was leaning over me, his eyes scanning my face, a small smile tilting his lips. I touched his face, feeling the gentle scrape of his stubble over my palm.

"Thank you, Sir," I whispered.

"My pleasure, pet."

When he moved back, I glanced over at Master. He was watching me intently, his hazel eyes hot enough to scorch me. Then he was on me, his mouth crushing to mine as he flipped me so that I was lying on top of him, his cock nestled against my pussy.

"We're gonna fuck you now," he warned.

I wanted that more than I wanted air.

"Are you ready?" Sir asked, his lips grazing my shoulder as he leaned over me.

I turned my head to meet his mouth, kissing him as roughly as he kissed me.

I felt his fingers tease my anus. They were lubed for easy entry and he didn't shy away. I continued to kiss him while he fingered my ass.

"Answer me," Sir commanded.

Right. His question. Was I ready?

"More than ready, Sir."

Master adjusted his hips, then forced his cock into my pussy while Sir pushed the head of his cock against my back hole. He didn't tease, he simply pushed in. The dual invasion had my breath escaping me in a rush. Pain quickly morphed into pleasure as they began rocking into me. Sir paused and something cool dribbled over my ass when he retreated. I realized he was adding more lube. Then he slammed into me, filling me completely.

Sir forced me forward, planting one hand in the center of my back, crushing me between them. Then they were fucking me roughly, not holding anything back, pounding my pussy and ass with the force of their thrusts.

Then I was flying. It was the only way to describe the out-of-body experience. The pleasure was fierce, overwhelming in its intensity. They weren't gentle, but they knew exactly what I needed. My orgasm raced through me and I didn't attempt to stop it, riding wave after wave of pure bliss.

They used my body for their own pleasure, sending me spiraling higher and higher with every passing minute until I thought I would pass out.

Only then did they both come inside me, groaning their releases in what felt like the most intimate of claimings.

It was then that I knew, no matter what happened in the future, right here—between them—was the only place I ever wanted to be.

In the same instance, I feared it was the one place I would never be again.

THIRTY-SEVEN

BOSS MEETING

JUSTIN

I HAD SPENT THE PAST two weeks watching as things changed between Luci and Landon. Also with Langston, too. I knew that man wasn't far away whenever Landon was with Luci. It was the way they operated. Much like Ben and me.

However, we had agreed that during the two weeks we had Luci to ourselves, we wouldn't seek input or keep anyone else informed, so I had no idea exactly what had transpired during their two weeks together. But I knew it was something.

Luci had changed.

Not that I was upset with her for it. Nor was I upset with Landon or Langston. I'd known going in that the cards would fall one way or the other. It appeared they'd fallen right at Landon's and Langston's feet.

But I was going to honor my commitment as best I could. As of Monday, I would be Luci's Dom for two weeks. I wasn't sure how it was going to go, but I wasn't going to back down now. Which was the reason I'd called this meeting.

Luci and Jordan had left for the weekend and I felt it was necessary to ensure we were all on the same page, so I'd asked Landon, Langston, and Ben to join me in my office.

Admittedly, there was less tension in the air this time. Perhaps that was because I wasn't blowing a gasket. I knew I'd been the one to heat things up in the office. I wasn't perfect, and yes, I'd held out hope that Luci would be the one for me and Ben. However, I accepted the fact that that was no longer the case. It disappointed me, but I would deal.

"I told her you would let her know who her new master was on Monday afternoon. Since I'll be out of the office next week, I'll leave that up to you on how you handle it."

"A week-long trip?" Landon hadn't done that in quite some time.

He nodded. "Yeah. It's...necessary."

I noticed Langston look at his twin with sympathy in his eyes. I realized then that Landon's trip had likely been planned and it probably wasn't necessary for work, more so because he didn't want to see Luci with me.

I decided to let it go, moving on. "How did things go with her?"

"As you know, it started out a little rocky. But..." He shrugged.

Yeah. I didn't really need him to fill me in. I knew what Luci wanted. I was actually anticipating her telling me that she couldn't go forward with this. Then again, Luci was nothing if not obedient. She would do as she promised, and I would have her to myself for two weeks.

"Just so we're clear," I said, addressing Landon directly, "are you planning to make any moves that will alter our agreement?"

He shook his head. "Not at this time, no."

It sounded to me as though he wanted the opposite; however, I could tell by the look on Langston's face that they'd come to this decision together.

Now, I just had to figure out what I needed to do to make my time with Luci beneficial for her. I knew she wouldn't ever belong to me and Ben, but in regards to her submission, there were a few tricks I had up my sleeve.

If nothing else, she would enjoy her time with me.

Well, with me and Ben.

Because there was one thing I knew with absolute certainty. I wasn't giving up the best damn thing that had ever happened to me. And I damn sure wasn't going to alienate him either.

THIRTY-EIGHT

WHEN MONDAY MORNING FINALLY ROLLED around, I was eager to get back to the office. Once I was there, I wondered why I'd been so excited.

Things were chaotic.

Ben was dealing with a major issue. One of the new product launches for his second biggest client had flopped. The details had been leaked prior to the official launch and he was busy putting out the fires. Then, of course, Sir had left town and Master was handling everything for both of them until Sir's plane landed in Florida.

It was as though everything had purposely exploded at the most inopportune time. Well, technically there wasn't ever a good time for things to go to shit.

Because of all the drama, I canceled the Monday meeting at Justin's request and did my absolute best to stay out of their way.

By the time lunch rolled around, I hadn't even had time for a break. Jordan's call was the only reminder I got that I needed to eat. After making a quick detour to the restroom—the first time that day—I met him at his desk and we headed down to the sandwich shop.

"So, you ready to spill the beans yet?" he probed when we were in line.

I blushed. "Maybe."

His stern look made me chuckle.

Jordan leaned in and lowered his voice. "Just so you know, if my submissive were to say that, he'd have a red ass for the rest of the day."

I laughed, unable to help myself. "Good thing I'm not your submissive then."

His smile was brilliant when he countered with, "Yeah, you're cute and all, but totally not my type."

I certainly felt more carefree with Jordan than I had originally. Simply knowing that he understood what I was going through made it easier to even look at him. So, when we took our seats at an empty table in the corner, I decided I would tell him anything he wanted to know.

"Ask away," I told him as I unwrapped my sandwich.

"Really? You're ready to share?"

I nodded. "I've been ready for a long time, but it's been…"

"Complicated," he filled in. "I know."

"Yes, that's a good word for it."

"It was quite obvious the dynamic on Christmas. Has this been going on for a while?"

I glanced around, making sure no one was close enough to hear. "I assume you're referring to me being with Landon and Langston." It was difficult not to refer to them as Sir and Master because it had become second nature.

Jordan nodded.

"No. It's actually been…complicated." I laughed. "Sorry, couldn't come up with a better word."

He lifted an eyebrow. "Tell me more."

I proceeded to tell him about the rules that were implemented when they laid out the "job requirements" after I'd been there for a month. I also told him about the upset that took place when Master took the reins and changed everything. How Sir had sort of backed off. How Justin had forced me to make a difficult decision on how things would progress after that. I left out the part about Master informing me that he wasn't interested in collaring me or taking me on permanently. I'd already come to terms with that and decided it was better left unspoken.

"I always suspected that Landon and Langston would end up with one submissive."

I stared at him closely, hoping he would elaborate.

"I'm a member of the club also, so I've seen their interactions. To be honest, they haven't been active in quite some time. Not until you came along anyway."

That news did make me feel good.

"What about the secretaries before me?" I liked that I could be straightforward about my interest.

"I told you about the last few," he said between bites of his sandwich. "It's an unconventional request, I know, but it's been their path for as long as I've worked for them. It wasn't until you that I noticed things started to change."

Because I had agreed to be their office play toy, I knew.

"And who's your master now?" he questioned.

"I don't know," I told him, keeping my voice down. "I'm supposed to find out this afternoon."

"Who do you want it to be?"

I wanted it to be Master, but only if I could spend more time with both him and Sir, but I didn't say that. I hated that my heart was now dedicated. So, just to shake things up, I told him I was hoping it would be Justin.

"Oh, I can guarantee you'll have fun with him."

"Why's that?"

"He's very much into role playing."

"Really?" That probably shouldn't have surprised me considering the encounter we set up on the beach the last night we were on the island. Justin had seemed to morph right into his role. However, if I hadn't experienced it for myself, I wouldn't have believed it.

"Just keep an open mind and you'll enjoy yourself."

I stared down at my sandwich, shifting the paper but not eating.

"All right, kiddo, cough it up. I can tell something's on your mind."

When I looked up, I could see the concern in his eyes. "I think I've done something terrible."

His eyes narrowed and his expression sobered.

I fidgeted with the paper until he put his hand over mine, stopping me.

Sighing, I decided I would tell him the truth. "I think I've fallen in love with Master and Sir."

"Landon and Langston, I presume?"

"Yes."

"That doesn't surprise me."

"It's just…I know they don't want that from me and I'm so worried that I'm going to mess up what we do have by wanting more. It's not fair to them, but I can't help how I feel."

"Have you talked to them about it?"

I frowned. "Of course not. That's not part of the deal."

Jordan chuckled. "What? Talking?"

"No," I said haughtily. "Falling in love."

"And just to play devil's advocate, how do you know that they aren't in love with you, too?"

I shook my head. I didn't have an answer to that. Well, I did, but it wasn't one I was ready to divulge.

"Rules are meant to be broken, gorgeous. It happens all the time. And just because some people set out to handle things a certain way doesn't mean it'll always work out. But one thing I know for a fact, without talking to them, nothing will get resolved."

"I know."

I did know.

Forcing a smile, I sighed heavily. "I'm going to spend the next two weeks with whomever I belong to and I'm going to give him my all. I'm not ready to admit my feelings for anyone, and I know without a doubt, none of them are ready to hear it."

"Or so you think."

"What does that mean?"

"It means, just because you believe something to be true doesn't mean something else won't happen. What happens if you fall in love with Justin? Or Ben? What then? Will you still be in love with Landon and Langston?"

I dropped my head into my hands. This seemed to be getting so complicated.

Jordan chuckled, then tucked his finger under my chin and forced me to look at him.

"Enjoy yourself. Go into this thing with your eyes wide open. And if your new master asks you questions, be honest. He may already know how you feel and it may not bother him. Or he could be trying to win you for himself. You never know until you talk it out."

Oddly enough, Jordan had become my best friend in the few short months I'd known him. I couldn't imagine my life without him.

A real smile formed on my lips. "You're so smart, you know that?"

Jordan sat up straight, lifting his chin high. "And don't you forget it."

•

When I made it back to my office, I found a beautiful bouquet of flowers sitting on my desk. The large vase was full of delicate white roses; the outer edges of the petals were a fascinating shade of blue. I'd never seen anything like it. In a word, they were stunning. The card tucked into them had my name scrolled on the front, so I quickly pulled it out and flipped it open.

Princess,

I'm looking forward to our time together. In the interest of showing your acceptance, please put your apartment key in my top desk drawer. You will find mine in your desk. At five thirty, I expect you to go straight to my apartment, strip, and wait by the door until I arrive.

Justin

Merely reading the note had me giddy about the prospect of being Justin's submissive for the next two weeks. I guess I needed to get used to calling him Master Parker for the time being. It would likely make things easier.

After opening my top drawer to find the key Master Parker had referred to, along with a tag with the number fifty-seven on it, I then took my apartment key and placed it in his top drawer. I was taking my seat at my desk when Ben returned from lunch. After asking if he needed me to make afternoon coffee and being told he was good, I got to work going through emails. My inbox was flooded with messages from team members answering questions about the next quarterly meeting. The main request I received was that the bosses include all the team members for at least one session, not only managers. It was a great idea, but I would have to consider the costs before I presented it to my bosses.

For some reason, I was rejuvenated now that I had something to focus on, which had me putting forth a little more effort in everything I did. Rather than passing the random questions over to one of my bosses, I started seeking answers on my own. Sure, some of them I couldn't answer, so I forwarded them to the appropriate person. However, I was able to field a lot more than usual, making calls to get more details and offering my assistance as needed.

•

At five thirty, I quickly packed up my things and headed up to Master Parker's apartment. Using the key he gave me, I let myself in. The second I stepped inside, I was overwhelmed with curiosity, wanting to know more about him by getting a peek into his private space.

Having to hold back that part of myself was far more difficult than I thought. I had to read and reread his note over and over again to keep from getting up from my kneeling position in front of the door. I wanted to traipse through his space, to know how he functioned, what he liked, what he ate. I had no idea why I was so overwhelmed with this need.

However, I was happy that I did manage to remain where I was, naked and kneeling by the door. When I heard the key in the lock, my heart skipped a beat or two. I managed to perfect my position when he stepped inside and breathed a sigh of relief when he placed his hand on my head and asked me to stand and greet him.

"Princess," he said, sliding his thumb over my lips. "I'm impressed."

It was as though he knew what was rattling around in my brain.

"Thank you, Master Parker."

He placed a suitcase down near the door. I glanced at it and it finally registered that it was my suitcase. I smiled to myself, realizing that was the reason he'd asked for my apartment key. The same key he passed over to me with a smirk on his face.

"Are you hungry?"

I nodded. "Would you like me to make something?"

Master Parker began undoing his tie as he walked toward the kitchen. "Unnecessary, but thank you for offering. However, you're welcome to join me while I cook."

Smiling, I followed him into the kitchen, trying not to be modest about my nakedness, although it wasn't easy.

"Wow," I said in awe. "This is…really nice."

The kitchen was state of the art with stainless steel appliances and granite countertops. The cabinets were dark cherry Shaker and modern in design. It was similar to the design of his office.

While he rolled up his sleeves, Master Parker peered into the refrigerator. I took a seat at the island bar, watching him intently.

"Any allergies?" he asked, glancing back at me over his shoulder.

"Nope."

"Good."

He proceeded to pull out several ingredients: chicken, broccoli, snap peas, baby corn, and a few other things I couldn't identify.

"So, tell me what you thought of your visit to the island," he prompted, glancing up at me every so often as he worked.

Wow. The island. That seemed like such a long time ago. However, it was still fresh in my mind, so I didn't mind discussing it.

"It was interesting. A little awkward at first. Meeting Master and Sir's parents and all."

Master Parker grinned. "Good people, though, huh?"

"Absolutely," I said with a matching smile. "They made me feel welcome. Have you met them?"

"Of course." He smiled. "Many times. They're also members of the club."

The same club Master and Sir were members of? That seemed like it could get a little awkward at times. Perhaps they exchanged schedules? Made sure they weren't there when their parents were? That was what I would've done anyway.

"And what about the festivities?" Master Parker continued. "What'd you think of those?"

"Very…educational."

Another smile tilted his perfect mouth.

"And the club? What were your thoughts on it?"

"I liked it. A little more intense than I think I'd expected."

"No, more like the island was more subdued," he clarified.

"There was certainly a stark difference in play," I admitted. "But I did enjoy the club. Hopefully I'll get the chance to go back there one day."

"So, you're going to pursue this submissive thing?"

I knew what he was saying without saying it. He meant, if I was no longer with the four of them, would I still be interested.

"Yes. It's something that makes me happy. I feel complete for the first time in my life."

He nodded, as though that was an acceptable response.

While he worked, tossing everything into a wok, the conversation continued. We chatted about everything from college to our first jobs, even a little about his relationship with Ben; however, I could tell he was holding back where that topic was concerned.

"We actually met at a club," he informed me. "It wasn't long after his divorce and he was following his desires, something his ex hadn't been interested in."

"Was he a Dominant when you met him?"

"He's always been a switch, but I'd never officially topped a man before him. Sure, I'd had some casual encounters with men, having accepted my bisexuality in my mid-twenties. But nothing in the D/s realm." Master Parker smiled. "He was my first and only."

Aww. That was so sweet.

"When did things get serious between you two?"

Master Parker paused what he was doing to look at me.

Figuring I'd overstepped by asking something so personal, I was about to apologize when he smiled. "It wasn't until recently that we began pursuing things on a more consistent level."

I waited, hoping he would continue. Unfortunately, he didn't.

"While I finish this up, why don't you put your clothes on and set the table."

Feeling as though he didn't want to continue sharing with me, my heart lurched, but I managed a pleasant, "Yes, Master Parker," before doing as he asked.

When I returned, he was finishing up with the meal, so I set the table as he'd requested. Several minutes later, we sat down at the table. We ate in comfortable silence, but I couldn't shake the feeling that I'd said something wrong.

After placing my fork down, I waited until he looked at me before I spoke. "I'm sorry if I offended you in some way."

Master Parker frowned. "You didn't offend me."

"I...I was just curious about your life with Ben. The two of you seem happy. I didn't mean to overstep."

He stared at me for a moment, then pointed at my plate. "Finish eating. Then we'll take a bath. It's getting late and we both have to be up early."

I still couldn't shake the feeling that he was trying to buy some time, but I grabbed my fork and did as he requested.

THIRTY-NINE

OKAY, SO MY TIME WITH Master Parker wasn't going quite the way I'd anticipated.

Last night, after we finished dinner, he sent me into the bathroom to start the bath. While I did that, he cleaned up the kitchen, then joined me. We soaked for what felt like hours, talking about very little. I was too hesitant to ask the real questions, so we kept things superficial, mostly about work. Any time I tried to venture down a more personal path—such as his parents or where he grew up—I was met with a stony resolve. Eventually I gave up.

After that, he took me to his bed, curled up around me, and we went to sleep.

That was it.

It was weird but somewhat comforting. I was used to Master Parker wanting sex from me during most of our interactions. I guess that was what threw me off balance. I wondered if it was strange since I'd spent the past two weeks with Sir. I didn't know, but it sort of made sense.

Of course, I knew I wasn't going to get any answers unless I asked questions; however, I was confused. It wasn't that I only wanted him for sex, anyway. I simply thought that was what the arrangement was.

If I was being honest, I did crave his friendship. I wanted to know more about him, what he enjoyed doing, his favorite foods, movies. The typical things one friend wants to know about the other. However, it appeared that we weren't going to go that route and I wasn't sure how to change the direction we were headed.

This morning, I woke up alone in his bed. There was a note letting me know he had an early meeting and he would see me in the office later. There were no instructions, so I had no idea what to expect. I showered, then got ready and made my way down to the office at seven fifteen. Jordan hadn't arrived yet, so I went to my desk and got to work.

Part of me was hesitant to face Master Parker. The other part was anxious for some sort of sign.

•

The day went by quickly. It seemed as though the workload was doubled for everyone in the office with Sir gone. The other three were bouncing from one meeting to the next, conference call after conference call, while Ben still tried to clean up the mess with his client.

They were in and out throughout the day and I found myself adding more and more meetings to their calendars as people began demanding their time. Not that I could complain. It was a good thing for the company that we were busy, and bringing on new clients was the name of the game.

It was during my interactions with some of the team members that I learned there were satellite offices across the world. I'd realized there were team members, but I hadn't understood that they had actual offices they went to. Apparently, they were all remote, but they did have a location to go to when they wanted to.

While I'd mistakenly believed that my four bosses managed the majority of their clients by utilizing their teams, I'd been schooled on that, too. Due to the sheer size of the company and the high volume of clients they had, there were managers across the globe who were responsible for keeping my bosses up to date, plus Ben, Justin, Landon, and Langston had their own client lists. In fact, my bosses handled the highest-profile clients and a few who had insisted they would only work directly with them.

It was enlightening to say the least. Plus, it made me truly believe that a meeting with all the staff members was necessary. I'd been there for coming up on four months and had no idea the sheer complexity that made up a company of that size. I wanted to learn more, and if I did, I was sure there were others who did, too.

My phone rang at five fifteen and I answered with a cheerful greeting.

"I'm calling to let you know that you have been summoned," Jordan said, his tone filled with amusement.

"Summoned?"

"Yep. So, pack up all your stuff and get your cute little ass up here."

"But it's not five thirty," I said in a hushed tone.

Jordan's tone was just as quiet when he replied, "And I'm sure that's not a problem since Justin is the one summoning you."

"Oh." I glanced at all the closed office doors. "Okay. I'll be there in two minutes."

"Hurry up, sweet cheeks. You don't want to keep the big bad Dom waiting."

After hanging up the phone, I grabbed my purse and my cell phone. I paused momentarily, wondering if I should tell Ben or Langston that I was leaving. I decided not to since they knew that I belonged to Master Parker for the time being. I certainly didn't want to undermine his authority.

I hurried to the front and was greeted by Jordan's wide smile and an envelope he was holding out to me.

"Now scoot," he said, shooing me toward the elevator.

The note on the front of the envelope read: DO NOT READ UNTIL YOU ARE IN THE ELEVATOR GOING UP TO MY APARTMENT.

Feeling slightly giddy, I punched the button for the elevator and waited, doing my best not to bounce as my impatience grew. When the elevator arrived, I was glad to see that it was empty. As soon as I stepped inside, I ripped the envelope open and read the note.

Dear Miss Wagner,

It's come to my attention that you are past due for your yearly checkup. It's imperative that you come in at your earliest convenience. I've scheduled you an appointment for five thirty this afternoon. Don't be late.

Dr. J. Parker

*I expect you to be in character upon your arrival. Punishment will be in order if you disobey.

I was overwhelmed by excitement at the idea of role playing with Master Parker. Jordan had mentioned that Master Parker was prone to this type of play and, well, it looked as though the doctor was in.

Admittedly, I'd never had any sexual thoughts about my doctor or any of my visits. It always felt clinical to me, sometimes even embarrassing, so I was interested to see Master Parker's take on an office visit.

When the elevator opened on his floor, I stepped out and glanced down the hall. Remembering the night they'd fulfilled my fantasy on the beach, I decided I would get right into character. After all, punishment was not what I was in the mood for. However, I would never turn down an orgasm or two.

I hefted my purse up on my shoulder, tilted my shoulders back, and walked toward his apartment door with purpose. Figuring I wouldn't have a key to a doctor's office, I tried the knob to see if it would open.

It did.

I stepped inside to find Ben sitting on the sofa. I wasn't sure what to think at first, but I noticed he only gave me a cursory glance before he went back to reading the magazine he was holding. It honestly felt like I was arriving for an appointment and Ben was a bored patient waiting to go in as well.

Since there wasn't a receptionist to check in with, I assumed I was to take a seat, so I did. I sat in the chair opposite the sofa and reached for another magazine that had been set out on the table. Crossing my legs at the knee, I leaned back and settled in to wait, flipping through the pages.

A solid ten minutes passed before I heard a door open behind me. I didn't turn to look, merely continued my perusal of the magazine.

"Miss Wagner?"

I glanced over my shoulder to see Master Parker in full doctor mode, white coat and all.

"Yes?" I responded politely.

He checked a clipboard. "If you'll follow me, please."

Getting to my feet, I offered Ben a polite smile, then went in the direction of my role-playing doctor.

"How are you doing today?" he asked as he led me into a room.

I hadn't been in this room yesterday, and as I stepped inside, I realized why. This was obviously Master Parker's playroom. Although it was decked out with many interesting items, I noticed there was a mock patient room set up in the corner. Well, technically there were *two* set up and a curtain that separated them. More like a hospital than a doctor's office, but it intrigued me.

"I'm doing well, thank you." I set my purse on a chair near the examination table.

He turned toward a counter and set down the clipboard. Without looking back at me, he instructed me to remove my clothes and put on the patient gown.

"It ties in the front," he added.

If this were real, I would be more than a little uncomfortable changing in front of my doctor, so in order to preserve the scene, I didn't immediately start to remove my clothes. A couple of minutes later, Master Parker turned to face me.

"Is there a problem, Miss Wagner?"

I shrugged shyly. "It's just..." I dropped my gaze to the floor. "I'm a little embarrassed to change with you in the room."

He observed me as though gauging whether I was telling the truth or not, then nodded. "Very well." Grabbing his chart, he headed for the door. "I'll be back in two minutes. Remove all clothing, including your underwear."

"Thank you, Dr. Parker."

He nodded, then slipped out of the room.

As though I was at a real doctor's office, I hurriedly removed my clothing, then put the gown on, tying it in the front as he'd instructed. My butt had just settled on the paper-lined examination table when there was a soft knock on the door before he returned.

Those ocean-blue eyes grazed me momentarily as he set the chart back down on the counter.

"I'm going to do a full physical exam on you today," he informed me, his eyes dropping back to the chart. "It's been quite a while since you've been in."

"It has," I admitted, playing along. "I've been…busy."

I sat with my legs together and my hand firmly on the front of the gown, careful to keep it closed as he stepped around the table. I had to hold back a giggle when he pulled out a blood pressure cuff. The man certainly knew how to get into character. It made the entire interaction that much more stimulating.

After he took my blood pressure, then my temperature with one of those thermometers that rolls across your forehead, he went and noted something in the chart.

"Please, lie back," he instructed as he pulled out an extension on the table and lifted my legs onto it.

I managed to lean back, once again careful to keep my gown closed, maintaining my modesty.

He started by placing his fingers on my forehead, then on the sides of my nose. He lightly pressed down as though checking for sinus pressure.

"Let me know if you feel any discomfort."

I nodded.

He continued his prodding exam, persistent fingers making their way under my jaw, then my collarbone. When he went to untie the gown, heat slammed into me.

"I'll do my best to keep you covered as much as I can," he said, as though he was being professional.

"Thank you," I whispered.

He pulled the gown back, revealing my right breast. His hands were warm and demanding, although they felt almost clinical as they pressed around the soft tissue. It was hard not to be turned on by what he was doing. That was what did it for me, I guess. Knowing he was in charge and I was under his care…it made my pussy throb with need.

"Are you doing monthly breast exams?" he asked.

"I am," I confirmed. And it was actually the truth. My real doctor said it was important, so I followed her instructions to the letter.

"Very good."

His hands were warm as he kneaded my flesh. His fingers brushed over my nipple as he put the gown back in place before performing the same steps on my other breast. My nipples were hard, but he pretended not to notice.

When he was done, he covered me again before jotting something down on his paper.

"When's the last time you had a pelvic exam, Miss Wagner?"

Maintaining the ruse, I shrugged. "It's been a while."

He made another note before returning to the table and pulling out the stirrups. I found it interesting that the man had an actual medical table, complete with stirrups, in his playroom. He was obviously fond of this particular scene.

Gentle hands situated my feet into the contraptions, which then forced my legs wide. Once I was in place, he pushed the extension back into the table. I tried to close my knees, but his big hands slid up to my thighs, gently pressing them open.

"This won't hurt," he informed me. "I'm going to need to open the gown."

I nodded but stared up at the ceiling.

Cool air caressed my skin as he pulled the gown back, revealing my most private parts. Unlike at the real doctor, I was immensely turned on, eager. I wanted his hands to explore me.

"You're rather wet, Miss Wagner," he said, his tone professional as his eyes met mine.

I blushed.

"Is this a normal occurrence for you?"

Where he was concerned, absolutely.

I nodded.

"Well, please relax."

Focusing on my breathing, I continued to stare at the ceiling as his warm hands slid between my legs.

"I'm going to poke and prod a bit," he informed me. "I will just be using my fingers."

Swallowing hard and feeling deliciously naughty, I nodded my understanding.

For several minutes, Master Parker teased my pussy with gentle fingers, gliding over my labia before compressing and rubbing my puffy outer lips. His fingers moved on to my clitoris, where he pulled back the hood, then held the sensitive bundle of nerves between his finger and thumb, massaging it. There was no denying how deliciously wicked his examination was.

He lifted his head. "How many fingers can you usually take in your pussy, Miss Wagner?"

Okay, so *that* was definitely not something my doctor had ever asked. The dirty words made my body tremble. Staying in character, I answered, allowing a slight tremor into my voice. "Mostly one. Sometimes two."

"Very well. I'll start with one, but I'll gradually move to three. I'd like to see how well your inner muscles can stretch."

Oh, God.

Master Parker's finger pushed into me. It was a gradual move, inching in slow and easy, brushing over nerve endings that were now greedy for stimulation.

I held back a moan as he fucked me with one finger. It was a leisurely in-and-out motion, certainly not enough to bring me to orgasm.

"I'm adding a second finger," he informed me as though that was the professional way to handle things. Never mind the fact that he was finger-fucking me in his mock exam room.

I sucked in a breath when he pushed in two thick fingers.

"You're very tight, Miss Wagner. Your pussy's squeezing my fingers nicely."

A real blush infused my face and neck, heat swamping me.

I inhaled sharply, my hips bucking off the table as he fucked me more insistently with two fingers. Then suddenly he stopped.

"I'll be right back, Miss Wagner. I need to consult with my partner. I'd like him to provide a second opinion."

My eyes were wide as I watched him disappear from the room. I hadn't expected this strange turn of events.

That didn't mean I wasn't curious about what was about to happen.

I most certainly was.

FORTY

I REMAINED EXACTLY HOW I was, spread open with my feet in the stirrups, for what felt like a ridiculously long time. When the door finally opened, I held my breath in anticipation.

"I'm sorry to keep you waiting, Miss Wagner," Master Parker said as he entered the room, followed by Ben. "It's been a busy day. I hope you don't mind that I'm going to examine my other patient while I wait for my partners to respond to my request."

I peered over, my eyes following Ben as he moved to the second examination table. His wasn't as fancy as mine, more like a padded massage table with a sheet of white paper laid over it.

"Mr. Snowden, please remove your clothes and have a seat on the exam table."

Master Parker pulled the curtain between us, but he left it open enough that I had a perfect view as Ben began to strip. He obviously wasn't as modest as I was when he went to the doctor because he didn't have an issue shedding all of his clothing. I couldn't look away as he peeled away the layers, giving me an unobstructed view of all that dark skin covering delectably sculpted muscle. I knew if Master Parker were to check me now, he'd find me wetter than before.

"Are you having any issues, Mr. Snowden?"

"I'm having difficulty maintaining an erection for extended lengths of time," Ben said, his voice deep, sturdy.

"How long has this been going on?"

"About two weeks."

"Have you been sexually active?"

"A few times," Ben replied.

"Did you have issues at those times?"

"I was able to come, but not more than once. That's where I'm having the issue."

I smiled to myself. Of course the man wasn't having an issue *maintaining* an erection in order to climax. He was looking to maintain one much longer than that.

"Do you normally orgasm more than once?"

"Yes."

"Please lie back on the table," Master Parker instructed. "I'm going to do a thorough physical exam. Let me know if you feel any discomfort."

Unfortunately, the curtain didn't allow me to watch everything that was going on. I was definitely interested in watching Master Parker touch his submissive.

"I'm sorry, Mr. Snowden," Master Parker said. "If you'll excuse me a moment. I need to return a phone call."

I didn't hear a phone ring, but I wasn't about to call attention to it. The man obviously had a plan and I was eager to see how this played out.

"Sure. No problem."

Master Parker stepped out of the room, leaving me and Ben on the exam tables. We both remained silent for a few minutes, but then I heard Ben move, the shift of his body on the paper-covered table obvious.

The curtain moved back, revealing the sexy naked patient in the room adjacent to mine. His cock bobbed proudly between his legs.

"Do you mind if I keep this open?" Ben asked. "I feel a little claustrophobic with it closed."

"I don't mind," I admitted, trying not to ogle him.

He, however, didn't do the same. I noticed how his eyes slid between my legs, admiring my pussy, which was still on full display.

He didn't visually feast on me for long, though, returning to his table as the door opened.

"I'm sorry to keep you both waiting," Master Parker said as he closed the door behind him. "Unfortunately, my partner is unable to come in for a consultation; however, I think I might've come up with a solution that will help me to make a successful diagnosis."

I wasn't sure who he was talking to, so I kept my mouth shut.

"Mr. Snowden, you mentioned you're having trouble achieving multiple orgasms, correct?"

"That's correct."

With the curtain pulled back, I could see everything taking place beside me as Master Parker approached Ben.

"Let me proceed with my exam first."

It was erotic to watch Master Parker's hands glide over Ben's hard body. He performed the same procedure he'd done on me, pressing on his forehead, the sides of his nose, his jaw, before trailing downward. Ben's response to the man's touch was apparent as his cock thickened nicely between his thighs.

"I see you don't have an issue *gaining* an erection," Master Parker noted.

"No, I do not."

"Good."

Master Parker's hands drifted lower, his fist curling around Ben's cock. He pumped it several times before moving on, fondling Ben's heavy ball sac.

"I'd like to check your prostate, Mr. Snowden."

Master Parker moved over to the counter and pulled out a latex glove and some lubricant.

"Please, pull your legs into your chest. It's not the most comfortable position, but I find it works best."

Ben pulled his legs up and held them with his hands. Master Parker returned and methodically began probing inside Ben's ass. I watched, transfixed by the sight. Ben reached down and gripped his own cock, fisting it tightly.

"Is there any discomfort?" Master Parker asked.

Ben's response came in the form of a grunt.

"Would you like to come, Mr. Snowden?"

"Yes," he hissed.

Master Parker proceeded to finger him, likely fondling his prostate, which I'd heard could be intensely satisfying for a male.

Ben grunted a few times before his cock exploded, spurting on his stomach and his chest.

"Very nice, Mr. Snowden." Master Parker pulled off the latex glove and tossed it into the garbage before handing Ben a towel. "I'm going to check my other patient while you clean up. Once you're done, you may sit up."

Watching Ben come had made me wetter than before and I saw the recognition in Master Parker's eyes when he returned, standing between my legs.

"It would appear that you're quite turned on, Miss Wagner. May I ask what caused it?"

I swallowed hard, remembering that I was supposed to be his patient.

"I…enjoyed watching him come."

"Interesting. I'm going to resume my exam. I believe we were up to two fingers, correct?"

"Yes."

Master Parker inserted two fingers into my pussy, pushing in slightly more insistently than he had before.

"I'm going to tease your G-spot for a moment, Miss Wagner."

Words wouldn't form as those intruding fingers found the sensitive tissue and began rubbing it. The moan that escaped echoed in the room.

"Very nice. Now, I'm going to attempt three fingers," he informed me.

When he added another digit, I felt intensely full, my pussy stretching as he thrust in and out, making my breaths come in rapid pants. I thought for a second he was going to make me come, but he pulled out before I was launched into the abyss.

"You're quite responsive." He moved around to the side of the table, his blue eyes coming to rest on my face. "Would you be open to an experiment, Miss Wagner?"

I wanted to scream, "God, yes!", but I managed to hesitate momentarily, then asked, "What type of experiment?"

"Since my other patient is having issues with multiple orgasms, and you're clearly in desperate need of release, I thought I'd try something that might help both of you."

I glanced over at Ben, who seemed to be chilling while he waited for the doctor to return.

"I'm…okay with that."

"Very good. You may put your legs down now."

After I removed my feet from the stirrups, Master Parker held out his hand and I took it. He helped me to sit up.

"Mr. Snowden, would you mind coming over here for a moment?"

Ben got down from the table and walked over, his rock-hard cock bobbing between his legs. And the man claimed he had an issue maintaining an erection. He'd already come once, for goodness sake.

"Miss Wagner has graciously agreed to help me with an experiment. However, I think it's only fair that we offer her something before she assists in making you come for a second time. Would you agree?"

"I would," he said, his golden eyes meeting mine. "I'm at your service."

"Miss Wagner, I'll need you to remove the gown."

I pretended to want to hold on to it for a moment longer before slowly removing it from my shoulders and letting it fall to the table.

"Mr. Snowden, what do you think of Miss Wagner's body?"

"Stunning," he said, his gaze sliding over every inch of smooth skin.

"When you see her like this, what's the first thing that you think about doing to her?"

"Feasting on her cunt."

My body trembled from the crudeness of his words.

"Miss Wagner, is that something that would interest you?"

I couldn't find words, but my head bobbed up and down in response.

"I'm glad to hear it. Now, would you please lie back again?"

Swallowing hard, I returned to the horizontal position, my legs hanging over the end of the table.

"I'm going to place your feet back in the stirrups. It'll give Mr. Snowden better access to eat your pussy."

God.

I couldn't help the fact that their direct words were burning me from the inside out. It was so hot. The setting, the men, the "experiment." There was definitely something to be said about this role-playing thing.

Once I was situated to his liking, Master Parker rolled over a small stool.

"Mr. Snowden, please have a seat between Miss Wagner's legs. I'd like to observe while you pleasure her with your mouth. Please keep your hands by your sides at all times. In the interest of the experiment, you're only allowed to use your tongue, lips, and teeth. Because of another appointment I have, I'll request that you make her come within three minutes."

I smiled to myself. I seriously doubted that was going to be a problem.

Ben's warm breath fanned over my pussy lips. His tongue then trailed through my wetness, licking and teasing. He didn't seem to be in a rush, which allowed me to savor every graze of his raspy tongue as it made contact with my clit.

Since I was unable to see Ben, I kept my eyes trained on Master Parker. He alternated between watching Ben and me. I could tell he was enjoying this immensely.

Ben moaned and the vibrations shot through my clit, triggering the beginnings of my orgasm. I gripped the table edge with both hands.

"She's close," Master Parker noted. "Send her over now."

Ben suckled my clit, flicking it relentlessly with his devious tongue. I skyrocketed right over the edge into a mind-numbing release.

"Miss Wagner, you come very nicely. I'm pleased."

I was panting, but I managed a breathless, "Thank you, Dr. Parker."

My chest rose and fell rapidly as I tried to gain some sense of balance after that. They left me there on the table as Ben got to his feet.

"If you'll be so kind as to wait right there," Master Parker told him. "I need to perform one more examination, then I'll have you assist me one more time."

Master Parker removed my feet from the stirrups, then pushed them back into the table before taking my hand and helping me to sit upright. I was then on my feet and he was urging me to turn around.

"Please, get back on the table, only this time I'd like you on your knees, Miss Wagner."

I did as he asked.

"Now, place your knees together and I want you to bend over, placing your chest against your thighs, your head on the table."

The position was not one any doctor had ever asked me to get into, but I obliged him, which left my naked behind spread wide and exposed.

I heard the snap of the latex glove.

"I'm going to see how many fingers you can take in your ass, Miss Wagner."

I moaned when he pushed one lubed finger inside me. He began fucking me, rocking in and out in a rhythmic motion that ratcheted up my need. He added another finger, scissoring them and effectively stretching me. When the third finger pushed inside, I grunted as the pain intensified.

"Relax, Miss Wagner."

I tried, but it wasn't easy.

"You have a very tight ass. I'm wondering just how much we can stretch it."

His fingers continued to fuck into me, causing the initial pain to fade, morphing into pleasure. I was riding the sensations, enjoying what he was doing, when he suddenly stopped. The man seemed to have a penchant for doing that.

"Mr. Snowden, if you'll please move to where I was standing."

He discarded his used glove, then returned to my side. Suddenly, the table began to lower as Master Parker pushed a button on the side. I knew that I was now at the perfect height for Ben to fuck my ass. A frisson of fear trickled through me. The thought of Ben's monster cock inside my ass was a terrifying notion.

There was a knock on the door and I nearly panicked, wondering who could possibly be there. After all, this wasn't really a doctor's office. This was Master Parker's apartment.

"While I tend to that," Master Parker said to Ben, "please lube yourself liberally and put some on Miss Wagner's anus while you're at it."

The door opened and Master Parker disappeared. I was so focused on what might be taking place on the other side of the door that I jumped when Ben began lubing my asshole with his finger.

I moaned because, despite the intrusion, it did feel good.

"Such a sweet little ass," Ben said approvingly.

The door opened, my eyes darting over to see who it was. The second Master stepped into the room, my belly did a double flip and my body began to tremble. Simply seeing him was enough to send me spiraling closer to the edge of orgasm.

"It appears my partner was able to etch out a little time for a consultation," Master Parker said, then looked over at Master. "I'm in the process of experimenting. I noticed how incredibly tight Miss Wagner's ass was, and since Mr. Snowden's having specific issues with multiple orgasms, I thought I'd pair them up, see if we can't kill two birds with one stone. You're just in time to watch the show."

Master met my gaze and I saw the flicker of desire in his eyes.

"I'm honored to watch," Master noted, his eyes never leaving my face.

I couldn't keep the smile from my lips. Just having him there made this all the more thrilling for me.

"Mr. Snowden, are you ready?" Master Parker asked.

"Absolutely."

"Please proceed. And remember, I'm hoping to stretch her, so don't feel the need to hurry."

"I will take my time."

Part of me was grateful since Ben's cock was the largest I'd ever had inside my pussy and I wasn't even sure he was going to fit in my ass. If he was rough with me, there was a good chance he was going to do some damage.

"Relax, Miss Wagner," Master said. "It'll make it easier for him to penetrate you."

I exhaled slowly as Ben guided the blunt head of his cock against my asshole. He didn't rush, but he wasn't entirely patient with me either.

Biting my lower lip, I willed my body to relax, to allow the thick intrusion.

"Bear down on me," Ben instructed. "There you go."

"She's tight, isn't she?" Master Parker asked.

"Very. She's a pleasure to fuck," Ben said as he pushed in and retreated slowly.

More lubricant was applied, making it a little easier to take. I think the position also made a difference. Regardless, if I hadn't been so eager and so turned on by the presence of three of my four bosses, it would've been excruciating.

"How does it feel, Miss Wagner?"

I moaned as Ben's pace picked up. "So good."

Big hands gripped my hips, pulling me back with every forward thrust. In, out, in, out. Ben took his time, fucking me slowly, deeply.

"Can she orgasm from anal penetration alone?" Master asked.

"That's a good question."

They already knew the answer to that because Sir had fucked my ass while I was laid out on my desk. There had been no way to disguise my orgasm that day. However, I figured it was all part of the scene.

Several more minutes passed as Ben continued to fuck my ass. He alternated between deep and shallow, but he never picked up the pace.

"Fuck her," Master Parker commanded. "Hard and fast. I want to hear her scream when she comes."

Ben instantly changed his speed, deepening the penetration as he gripped my hips and jerked me back against him. Even as he sped up, I was rocked into a sensual haze, enjoying everything he was doing, the way he controlled me with steady hands, the way he fucked me deeper.

"Open your eyes," Master commanded.

My eyes instantly flew open and I met his stare. The simple eye contact launched me over the edge. I screamed as I came, my body contracting around the thick intrusion.

"Fuck," Ben growled. "So fucking tight."

Within seconds, I felt him pulse, filling me as he came.

Whether it was the adrenaline that flooded my veins or simply the overwhelming sensations that accompanied my orgasm, my eyes closed and I drifted, letting the black void consume me.

FORTY-ONE

IT DIDN'T TAKE ME LONG to figure out that Master Parker was only interested in playing when Ben was around. Granted, he hadn't actually said as much, but considering we did not play when Ben wasn't there, it became evident.

Once I figured that out, relief swamped me. Not because I didn't want to spend some alone time with Master Parker, but I'd been trying to figure him out, wondering if I'd done something to push him away. It made complete sense, but I was a little surprised that Master Parker didn't explain this to me in the beginning. Perhaps he didn't realize he felt that way? Or maybe he simply didn't know how to explain it?

Whatever his reasons, it was much easier to interact with him once Ben was with us. I didn't question it. Sometimes Ben was in Dom mode, other times he was in submissive mode. Regardless, there was a lot of role playing. Things like good cop/bad cop and the dirty little shoplifter, the maid gets caught playing with herself, the virgin librarian sees two guys going at it and gets pulled into the mix. My all-time favorite, though, was the pizza delivery guy walking in while my boyfriend and I were having a hot and heavy session on the couch. Master Parker made a really hot pizza delivery boy. That one was sexy as hell and ended up with me being double penetrated on the coffee table.

And I enjoyed the hell out of every one of Master Parker's ideas.

Only now I could tell something was up because it was Monday morning and Master Parker was grumbling something about having to go on a trip that would take him away from the office for several days. He didn't sound happy about the idea, which wasn't normal for him.

Still, I managed to keep my questions to myself, remembering that in the office, I was their secretary, not their girlfriend, not their submissive, and I didn't want to overstep my bounds.

A few minutes before ten, I went to the back conference room and got the coffee brewing. I opened the blinds, then stood patiently, waiting for my four bosses to arrive.

"It's not by choice, I can assure you that," Justin said as he stormed into the room.

Master appeared a few feet behind him. "Is there anything you need me to do while you're gone?"

"I'm not sure yet. I'll let you know as soon as I figure out what it is I'm doing."

I watched the two men as they went to the coffeepot and each poured a cup.

When they turned back, they both seemed surprised to see me. In fact, Ben was the only one who acknowledged me when he came into the room. Sir was the last to make it and he opted to forego coffee before taking a seat.

"Please join us, Luci," Justin said.

The fact that he used my first name, rather than one of his pet names for me, caught me by surprise.

"Luci?" he said curtly. "Please. Have a seat."

He sounded irritated and I had no idea why. I moved over to my chair and took a seat, grabbing my notepad and pen.

"Something's come up and I have to leave town," Justin informed everyone.

"Is there a problem?" Sir asked, watching Justin closely.

"It's a personal matter. I'll be gone for a while, and at this point, I have no idea when I'll be back."

I looked at Ben, but he was staring down at his hands. If he knew what was going on, he wasn't giving anything away.

"I've instructed my team members on what needs to be done in my absence. There shouldn't be anything left to do, unless they have questions." Justin glanced at me. "Should any of my team members contact you with questions, please refer them to Ben. He'll be handling things in my absence."

"Yes, sir," I said, jotting down the note. Not that I would forget it, but I needed something to do.

"Also, there's going to be a changing of the guard," Justin said. "Obviously, I can't keep her as my submissive if I'm not here. But I'd like to discuss this without Luci in the room. So, let's deal with any other pressing issues first."

Sir informed everyone that he would be out of town on Wednesday, but would be back early Thursday morning. Master said he didn't have any trips in the near future, but if something came up, he'd check to ensure that he wasn't needed to help out in Justin's absence before he made any plans. And Ben said he didn't have anything to discuss.

The next thing I knew, I was being dismissed. And Justin wasn't kind when he grumbled, "That's all we need you for, Luci. Please go so we can continue."

Yep. Rude.

Perhaps I was overly sensitive, or maybe I'd become used to them treating me with a little more respect, but I felt as though they were purposely pushing me away. At least Justin, anyway. Regardless, I squared my shoulders and left the room, closing the door behind me. My heels clicked on the tiled floor as I made my way back to my desk.

I was tempted to see if Jordan wanted to grab some coffee, but I decided against it. As much as I wanted to talk this out with someone who would likely side with me, I wasn't going to do that. It seemed I was back at square one with my bosses again and I was more confused now than when they'd initially asked me to make a choice.

In fact, it was all getting to be too much for me.

No matter how hard I tried, I couldn't seem to get ahead with these men. I tried to be everything they wanted me to be, but it was proving more and more difficult. Especially when I felt as though they weren't giving anything in return.

My hormones were rioting and my emotions were out of whack. I was quickly realizing that Jordan was right. Without open lines of communication, this was going nowhere fast. I knew I couldn't place the blame completely on them, but there was no denying that they were partially at fault.

And to think, things had been going so well. I still reflected back on my time with Sir in a positive manner. The last night, spending it with both Master and Sir, was forever etched into my brain.

However, my time with Justin hadn't proved to be quite as positive. Sure, we'd had some fun when Ben was with us, but Justin and I hadn't been able to connect on a level other than playtime. I didn't think I was to blame for that because, like I promised I would, I'd gone into the situation with my eyes wide open. I'd given it a chance.

Now I was starting to regret my decision.

It was strange that I'd started to feel this way and the fact that it happened with Justin was what got me the most. When I was with Master and Sir, I didn't want things to end. Even when we had our differences, even though I didn't know where I stood with them, there was something different. More accurately, *I* was different with them.

Yes, I cared about Justin and Ben, but not in the same way. They didn't make me feel the way I did with Master and Sir. And it was obvious they wanted something different from me.

Feeling my emotions boiling to the surface, I pulled up my email and shot a quick note to all four of my bosses.

Subject: Appointment this afternoon

I just realized that I had an appointment that I must go to this afternoon. I will be back in the morning.

~Luci

As soon as I hit send, I grabbed my purse and left. Thankfully Jordan was on the phone because if I'd had to talk to him, I would've broken down into tears.

By the time I was in my car, my cheeks were wet and the sobs were making me gasp for breath. I kept my eyes focused on the road and drove straight to my apartment. Once inside, I locked the door, kept all the lights off, and crawled into bed.

What I needed was some time to release all these emotions. Maybe after that, I'd feel a little more normal.

Hopefully.

•

I didn't know how long I'd slept, but when I opened my eyes, it was dark outside. I squinted to see the clock. It was already eight.

Apparently I was tired.

A sudden pounding on my front door had me jerking upright. I wondered if that was what had woken me in the first place. I took a deep breath and decided to ignore it. I didn't want to talk to anyone. It didn't even matter who it was. I wanted to be alone.

More pounding.

My phone buzzed on my nightstand.

Master: *You have two seconds to open this goddamn door or I will break it down. Don't test me, pet.*

I jumped to my feet and rushed to the door. I knew Master was not bluffing and the last thing I needed was for Mrs. Idlemann to call the cops. She was probably already peeking out into the hall from the commotion.

"What do you want?" I snapped when I jerked the door open.

Master walked in, pushing right past me. He closed the door behind him, then pivoted to look at me.

"What the hell is going on?" His tone was tinged with real anger.

"Nothing," I lied. "I had an appointment. I told you that."

"Where was the appointment?"

"What?"

"The appointment, Luciana. Where was it?"

Shit. I hadn't thought that far in advance. I probably should've thought it through, but I'd been too emotional to come up with a lie that would make sense.

"It's none of your business," I barked, spinning away from him.

Before I could make it two feet, Master grabbed my arm and spun me back to face him. Tears flooded my eyes and no matter how hard I tried to hold them back, they wouldn't stay.

When he cupped my cheek with his hand, that was my undoing. I sobbed uncontrollably and shoved my face into his chest, needing his strength, even if only for a minute. This wasn't fair. Not to him, not to me. But I couldn't seem to stop.

We stood there for several minutes while I cried. I tried numerous times to pull myself together but it didn't work. The next thing I knew, Master was guiding me out of the kitchen and into my bedroom.

"What are you doing?" I asked between hiccupping sobs.

He didn't answer, simply undressed both of us before dragging me into the bed with him.

When he pulled me against him, I tried to get away, but he merely banded his arms around me, spooning me from behind.

"Shh," he whispered. "I've got you, Luci. And I'm not letting you go."

I finally gave up trying to put space between us and I let my tears fall. I was grateful he didn't ask questions. At least at first. I didn't get lucky enough that he would hold off forever though.

"Talk to me, pet," he finally probed when my tears dried up.

"There's nothing to talk about."

His words were rough when he spoke. "A lie will get your little ass reddened. Is that what you need?"

I shrugged. "I don't know what I need."

It was true. I had no freaking clue what it was that I needed. Or even what I wanted, for that matter. I was confused and saddened by the way things were going.

"Did something happen with Justin?"

"No," I admitted. I definitely didn't want him to think that Justin had done anything wrong, because he hadn't. At least not on purpose, I didn't think. "It's just…I don't think it's working out between me and him."

"How so?"

I shrugged again. "He seems distant. Like he's purposely keeping me at arm's length."

Master sighed, then pressed his lips against the back of my head.

"Justin's confused," Master stated.

"About Ben?"

"Yes. Things between them…they're more serious than they had been." Master grunted. "He really needs to be telling you this himself."

I managed to turn over so that I could look at Master's face. "He doesn't talk to me. Not about anything. And I thought that was part of how this was done. Being his submissive…I feel as though he doesn't want me."

Not surprisingly, Master didn't respond. I knew he wasn't the type to interfere in other people's business.

"I just wanted him to talk to me."

"Is that why you left today?"

Nodding, I wiped my face with my hand. "He was rude. And I didn't appreciate the way he dismissed me. As though I was merely an object for the four of you to pass between you." Just saying the words made more tears form. "I want more than that."

"From Justin?"

I shook my head. "No. I mean, yes. But not in that way. I want to be friends and I want him to help me explore my desires, but…he's not the one I want more from."

I knew I couldn't elaborate because there was no way I would survive Master walking out of my apartment. He'd been up front about what he didn't want and I wasn't about to push him.

I snuggled up to him.

"Master?"

"Hmm?"

"I'm really tired."

He pulled me closer and rested his chin on the top of my head. "Go to sleep, pet. I've got you."

With the safety and security of his arms around me, I did exactly that.

FORTY-TWO

MY ALARM WOKE ME THE next morning at 5:47 a.m. As was my usual routine, I reached over and hit the snooze button before kicking the blankets off. Oddly enough, the bed didn't feel nearly as cold as it usually did. It was then that I remembered there was a warm body next to me, and I smiled to myself before opening my eyes.

Master was still asleep and I couldn't resist watching him for a few minutes. The smooth lines of his face, the dark stubble on his jaw, the way his thick lashes fanned out over his cheeks. The man truly was a sight to see first thing in the morning. He looked so peaceful.

This was so much better than sneaking in a few extra minutes of shut-eye.

Unfortunately, my alarm went off again and this time, Master woke up, stretching as he wrapped his arms around me and pulled me against him.

"Why're you staring at me?" he mumbled, holding me tighter, as though that would stop me from ogling him.

"Because you're pretty."

He smacked my naked ass, making me giggle.

"You get up too damn early," he grumbled against my ear.

"It's because I have slave drivers for bosses," I teased.

The emotional chaos from yesterday seemed to be at bay, which I was grateful for. I did feel a lot better and I was sure that had to do with the fact that I'd let myself cry it out. That was always a release for me and I figured I should probably schedule time every week to simply sit down and let the tears fall. It would keep me from having an emotional breakdown, anyway.

"I need to take a shower," I told Master as I inched out from his hold.

I didn't want to, but I did have to get to work. As it was, I owed my bosses an explanation for yesterday. What I'd done was necessary for my well-being; however, it wasn't professional. And they didn't deserve me abandoning them like that.

As I was climbing out of bed, Master smacked my ass again, this time making me yelp.

"Make sure the water's hot," he commanded, his voice rough with sleep.

I practically skipped to the shower and turned on the water. I let it heat up while I brushed my teeth. I didn't have much time to spare, so I hurried beneath the warm water, secretly hoping Master would join me. I giggled a few minutes later when he did.

"You're way too chipper in the morning," he groused.

I wasn't usually, but he knew that because he'd spent time with me.

"I'm thinking you need a good fucking to calm you down."

Oh, that sounded perfect. However, it would likely have the opposite effect. If I started off the morning with Master screwing me senseless, there was no way I would not have a great day.

When he jerked me back against him, I moaned. His hands cupped my breasts roughly as he pressed his cock against my behind.

"Put your foot up on the ledge."

I rested my foot on the small shelf I used to shave my legs and hold my shampoo and conditioner.

"Now bend over and put your hands on the wall."

Without hesitation, I did as he instructed when he released me.

I squealed when he pressed his thumb against my asshole.

"God, I dream about fucking this pretty ass." He guided his cock between my legs. "But not this mornin'. Right now, I'm gonna fuck your tight little cunt until you scream."

He did exactly that, and I gave him what he wished for.

•

Master left my apartment after our shower, giving me plenty of time to get ready. I made it into the office at seven thirty and Jordan was standing in the lobby waiting for me. With his arms crossed over his chest, he looked somewhat intimidating. I wondered briefly if that was how his submissive saw him.

"You and I need to have words," he said, his tone firm.

"Why?"

"What happened to you yesterday? You ran outta here like your ass was on fire."

Feeling guilty, I glanced down at the floor. "I'm sorry. I had...to deal with something."

Jordan put his hands on his hips. "What?"

"Personal issues."

He didn't say anything and I realized he was waiting for me to look at him. I lifted my gaze, expecting the backlash. It didn't come and what he did next was probably worse than his wrath.

Jordan pinched my chin gently and held my head so I was looking right into his eyes. "Next time, I expect you to talk to me. We're friends, right?"

I nodded, the movement limited by his hold on me.

"Good. Now, I'm not going to pry right now, but when you're ready, call me. We'll do lunch or dinner or whatever. Just..." I could sense the concern in his voice. "I was worried about you."

Throwing my arms around him, I hugged Jordan tightly. "I'm so sorry."

He hugged me back. "I'm here for you, Luci. If you ever need anything. I know you're going through a lot of emotional crap. That's common when it comes to this stuff."

By *this stuff,* I assumed he was referring to the whole D/s aspect. And he was right. It was an emotional journey, that was for sure. It was likely even more complicated because I was dealing with four Doms, two of whom I was in love with.

"I promise. I'll talk to you next time."

He seemed content with that and I let him go, then offered a quick smile before I headed back to my desk.

As usual, no one was there, so I got the coffee ready to go, then settled in at my desk. I skimmed the calendar, making sure there wasn't something pressing I needed to prepare for. It was clear for the most part, so I moved on to my email.

Ben arrived right at eight, like always. I instantly offered him coffee and he accepted with a smile.

I prepared it to his liking, then delivered it.

"Here you are. And sir, I wanted to apologize for my disappearing act yesterday. It wasn't professional. I know I should've spoken with someone, but I wanted to let you know I will not let it happen again."

Ben seemed taken aback by my apology. He simply stared back at me as though it took some time to process what I'd said.

I was just getting ready to leave when he said, "Have a seat," as he moved his laptop over and nodded toward one of the chairs across from him.

Feeling like a kid in trouble, I slowly eased into the chair across from his desk, my eyes never leaving his face.

"I know you're probably confused about what's going on with Justin."

I nodded.

"He's going through some...things right now."

"Is he all right?"

"Yes. Well, hopefully. His dad's sick."

My eyes widened.

"He's been in a nursing home for a while. Things are going downhill right now, so he's gone home to take care of him."

"I'm so sorry." I had no idea and I felt terrible that I'd been selfish enough to think his issues had been with me.

"Don't apologize. I'm sure he'll explain all that when he has a chance." Ben glanced down at his desk for several seconds. "There's more though."

Swallowing hard, I waited.

When Ben's gaze met mine again, I could see some confusion brightening his golden eyes.

"Justin's come to realize how you feel about Landon and Langston. I think it's causing him some confusion."

I frowned. "I don't understand."

His smile was sad. "This thing we're doing in the office…" His dark eyebrows lifted. "It's always been fun and games. Then you came along and things changed. For everyone. And that's not necessarily a bad thing. It's just…I think he was hoping for more."

"More?" From me? That certainly seemed the opposite of how he was acting.

"It's no secret that Justin's looking for a submissive we can incorporate into our lives. Me and him. One who'll be full time just for us."

Well, that wasn't what I was expecting him to say. "Like a submissive for *his* submissive?"

Ben grinned. "Exactly. But I think the more time he spends with you, the more he realizes it's not going to happen. And that hurts him."

"I didn't mean to hurt him." I honestly didn't. And now my heart ached. If I gave the impression that I wanted Master and Sir more than him, I certainly hadn't meant to. Not in the beginning anyway. Admittedly, things *had* changed along the way, but I wasn't trying to play favorites.

"This isn't your fault, Luci. Not in the least. We all want something different. You should realize that by now. It's the very reason this has become complicated. I think Justin needs time to wrap his head around it."

"Is there anything I can do?"

Those penetrating gold eyes locked on mine. "Yes. You can be true to yourself and your feelings. That's the most important thing. At the end of the day, your happiness is what we all want." He waved his hand. "This all started as fun and games, but it has quickly morphed into something more. We all want *more.* Now, it's just figuring out how to make it work and keep you happy at the same time."

I nodded. "Well, Justin has nothing to worry about. I'm not going anywhere."

"It's not you he's worried about."

"Then what?"

"He's waiting."

"For?"

"For Landon and Langston to get their heads out of their asses and make the next move." Ben sighed. "I'll admit, it's tiresome sitting around and waiting for them to stake their claim."

I shook my head and forced a smile. "Well, that's where he's wrong. There is no next move with them. Master and Sir aren't interested in me that way. We're just…playing."

Ben's brow lifted and he gave me a look that said I was clearly not intelligent enough for this conversation.

When he didn't speak again, I forced myself to my feet. "Is there anything else I can get you, sir?"

"I'm good for now."

I was tempted to ask him if he knew who I was going to belong to next, but I managed to keep the thought to myself. For all I knew, they could very well be deciding to do something different, or not at all. There was no telling with all the chaos going on right now. I was sure my meltdown hadn't helped anything either.

With a quick nod, I returned to my desk as his words ran on a loop in my head. Could he be right? Could Master and Sir want more than what we had already?

I dared not hope, because although they did seem to want to play, Master and Sir hadn't alluded to the fact that they wanted something more. Sure, sometimes I'd felt as though they did, but I was following their lead here.

Again, Jordan was right. Perhaps it was time for us to have a conversation.

•

Master and Sir arrived a few minutes after nine and both headed straight for their respective offices after offering a pleasant good morning as they passed. Knowing I needed to get my apologies out of the way first thing, I went straight for Sir's office once I realized he was going to keep the door open.

"May I come in for a second, Sir?"

He peered up at me from his desk and nodded.

"I wanted to apologize for my behavior yesterday. I shouldn't have run out of here the way I did. It was unprofessional and I can assure you it won't happen again."

He nodded but didn't say anything.

"Can I get you a cup of coffee?" I offered, hating how the silence weighed heavily on me.

"Yes, thank you."

Well, that didn't go as badly as I thought it would. Not as well either. I thought for sure he'd add his two cents.

After I prepared his coffee and delivered it to his office, I was gearing up to go back to my desk when he stopped me with a gentle hand on my arm. I paused, waiting for him to say what he had to say, but Sir surprised me when he got to his feet, then cupped his hand around the back of my neck and pulled me in close.

"I've missed you, sweet girl," he whispered, then pressed his lips gently to mine. "I apologize if I've done anything that might make you think otherwise. I've been simply abiding by the rules."

I hugged him tightly, enjoying the warmth and safety of his embrace. I had missed him, too, more than I could admit aloud. And to hear him say those words...

Well, it certainly didn't help to ease any of the confusion. Between what Ben said earlier and how Sir was acting...I was no longer sure how they really felt about me.

In an effort *not* to put too much thought into what he might mean, I pulled back, offering a smile. "Thank you, Sir."

Needing something to focus on other than my feelings— which had been my issue yesterday—I went to Master's office to offer him coffee. He was on the phone, so I didn't interrupt, choosing to go back to my desk to work.

An hour passed, then another. Phone calls started to stream in, mostly from team members with questions or ideas. Knowing that Ben was already fielding a lot, I decided to help as much as I could. I took detailed notes, offered a few suggestions of my own, then scheduled follow-up calls to check in with those who wanted me to.

My goal was to pitch in as much as possible. Considering the amount of time that I'd worked there, I had caught on to a lot of things. And I knew I had a lot more to offer than simply a decent cup of coffee and the ability to coordinate schedules. Or, of course, the extracurricular activities that I'd enjoyed thus far.

With Justin out of the office, it seemed now was the appropriate time for me to step up.

FORTY-THREE

BOSS MEETING

LANGSTON

"HOW'S JUSTIN?" I ASKED BEN when Landon and I walked into his office that afternoon. We hadn't scheduled a meeting, but I felt it was necessary to check in with him.

"I haven't heard from him this afternoon," Ben said, pushing his laptop away and turning his attention toward us.

I took a seat in one of the chairs across from him.

"Well, when you do, keep us updated, would ya?"

"Of course." Ben sighed. "I know he's tired. Mentally, at least."

"I'm sure this isn't easy for him," Landon said. "They're pretty close, huh?"

"They were. Before his dad's memory started failing him. Now it's hard for him to be around the man. Especially when Carl doesn't recognize him."

I couldn't even imagine. "Let him know we're here for him if he needs us."

Although we were partners, we were still friends. Even if things had gotten a little rough around here lately. The four of us would stick together no matter what. We'd known that since the beginning.

"So, how are things with you? Need any help picking up the slack?"

Ben smiled. "Actually, Luci's been doing a phenomenal job with that. She contacted all of Justin's managers to let them know he's temporarily out of the office and should they need anything they could call her. She asked if she could send out daily updates regarding the things Justin's been working on, to ensure they are being followed up on."

Landon glanced over at me and I knew what he was thinking. Luci was a keeper. The girl didn't let anything keep her down. She was always pitching in, learning whatever she needed to in order to make things simpler around here.

It was one of the many reasons I loved her.

Yeah. I fucking said it. I loved that girl.

"How're things with Luci?" Ben cocked an eyebrow. "Outside of the office?"

"She's doin' all right," I told him, not bothering to pretend I didn't know what he was referring to. "I went to her apartment last night to check on her. She was upset."

"I can understand why," Ben said, his eyes dropping to the desk. "She apologized this morning for storming out the way she did."

"To me as well," Landon noted. "However, I intend to go to her place tonight. Although I appreciate her owning up to it, I have plans to punish her for it." Landon leaned forward. "She ran out for reasons that were not related to work. Therefore, I want to ensure she understands a simple apology won't cut it."

"I think she needs that," Ben replied.

I was surprised by his response. Landon and I had talked earlier and I thought for sure Ben was going to come to Luci's defense when it came to her punishment.

"I agree." And I did. Luci needed to know that her actions meant something to us. And by providing punishment when it was necessary, there would be no way for her to mistake it. "I'm gonna give her a break. Rather than step into the role as her Dom for the next two weeks, I'm gonna hold off. Not that I intend to leave her alone, but I think she needs some time to think it all through."

Not to mention, I needed time. It wasn't easy for me to admit that I was ready to take things to the next level with Luci. I had no intention of getting to the point where Ben would be her Dom for any length of time. As far as I was concerned, that game was over.

Although Luci hadn't been with Justin for long, it fucking killed me to know that she was. Last night, I'd hated to see her cry, but I wasn't disappointed to learn that things between her and Justin hadn't worked out. Landon and I had every intention of stepping up our game with Luci because neither of us could sit back and watch while another man took what we believed was rightfully ours.

However, as I'd mentioned, I wasn't quite ready to take that step. But I would be.

Soon.

FORTY-FOUR

"OH, TRUST ME," I TOLD Kristen. "I'm well aware that I screwed up."

"Did they punish you?"

"What?" I reached into the refrigerator and grabbed a bottle of water. "Why would they punish me?"

Switching the phone to my other ear, I held it with my shoulder and opened the bottle.

"Oh, honey, if you were my submissive, I would've paddled your ass red."

"It's not like that. We were at work."

"Exactly." Kristen's chuckle echoed over the phone. "And since your running out of there had nothing to do with work, you've earned a punishment."

The thought of punishment from one of my bosses wasn't a bad one. No, I didn't look forward to it; however, it would mean— at least to me—that what I did bothered them on a level that had nothing to do with work. And Kristen was right. I'd run out of there because Justin hurt my feelings. Which had nothing to do with work.

"Well," I said, standing tall, "Langston came over last night and he didn't punish me." I chuckled. "Unless you count what he did to me in the shower this morning punishment." I certainly didn't. It had been amazing.

"So, you're having casual encounters with Langston now?"

"He came to check up on me. I was upset."

"Right. Because that's what all bosses do. They go to their employees' homes and spend the night to ensure they're all right."

Fine. When she put it that way...

"Whatever. It's all good now. I apologized."

There was a knock on my door, causing me to spin around and stare at it.

I frowned. "Someone's at my door."

"Well, the polite thing to do would be to answer it."

"Right." I walked over and peeked through the security hole. My breath lodged in my throat when I saw Sir standing on the other side.

Not wanting to keep him waiting, I pulled it open.

"I…uh…need to call you back, Kristen. Sir's here."

"Sir?" She chuckled. "I take it you mean Landon."

Not looking away from his face, I answered Kristen. "Yes."

"All right. I'll let you go. Just remember, if he decides to punish you, you deserve it."

"Okay." I hung up the phone and stared at the handsome man who had now crossed his arms over his chest. "What are you doing here?"

"Invite me in, Luci."

"I'm so sorry, Sir." I stepped back out of the way. "Please come in."

"Thank you."

Oh, crap. He was being far too polite. Kristen was right. I was in trouble and Sir had come over to punish me. Before he stepped inside, he leaned down and grabbed a black bag that he'd evidently brought with him.

Oddly enough, Sir greeted me with a kiss, his fingers trailing down my face as he smiled down on me. I knew that smile. It was wicked.

Yep. I was in so much trouble here.

"Have you had dinner?" he asked.

"No. I just got home, actually."

Sir pulled his wallet out of his pocket, then retrieved a credit card. "Order Chinese and have it delivered."

I nodded, taking the card from his hand.

"Then meet me in the living room."

After confirming what Sir wanted, I grabbed my phone and placed the call. A few minutes later, I had no choice but to head into the living room. I'd done my absolute best not to look to see what Sir was doing. I wasn't sure I wanted to know.

Finally, I shored up my nerve, squared my shoulders, then went into the living room.

"Come." He patted the cushion beside him. "Have a seat."

I walked toward him, my eyes instantly going to the torture implements—as I'd come to refer to them—laid out on the table. Without looking away from them, I hesitantly took a seat on the edge of the cushion.

Shit.

He turned, then pulled me against him, my back to his side, his arm wrapping around my shoulder.

"Do you feel better, pet?"

"Than last night?" I relaxed against him. "Yes. Much."

"Good."

"Sir, I really am sorry for—" I tried to turn, but Sir kept me in place.

"Shh. We'll discuss your punishment in a little while. Right now, I simply want to hold you and talk."

This was more torturous than the thought of him using that evil-looking paddle on my ass.

He pressed his lips to the back of my head.

"Langston mentioned he stayed the night last night."

I sighed. "He did. He was worried about me."

"We all were," he clarified. "And don't think otherwise. He and I discussed who would come over and we decided he would. If I'd had my way, you would've been at our apartment last night and we would've punished you then."

I swallowed hard. "I'm not sure I understand why I need to be punished."

"Really?" He sounded disappointed.

"I mean, sure, I left the office. But…"

"But what? Justin hurt your feelings because he dismissed you from our meeting?"

Well, yes. But now that I heard it from someone else, it sounded a little childish.

"I think I deserve a little more respect than he gave me," I countered.

"Yet you don't think we deserve that same respect when we're in the office?"

"What?" This time I managed to get out of his hold, turning to face him. "Of course you do."

"Yet you let your personal life interfere with work. You ran out without telling anyone because you didn't like what your boss told you to do."

Damn it. Why did he have to be so rational?

"It's hard for me," I admitted. "Keeping my personal life separate from the office. Especially when we're all…" I shrugged.

"When we're all what? Fucking you?" He frowned. "Would it be easier if we went back to before the agreement?"

"Of course not," I blurted. "And that's not what I want. It's just…" I glanced down at my hands. "It's hard for me."

"I know it is, pet." Sir pulled me back so that I was once again resting against him. "So, tonight, when you receive your punishment, you'll have something to think back on the next time you feel the need to run away."

Yeah. I clearly wasn't getting out of this.

•

The food was delivered and Sir and I sat at the kitchen table to share our meal. It didn't take nearly long enough to eat. I would've preferred to sit there all night long rather than come back into the living room, where I was now.

Sir unbuttoned the sleeves on his shirt. I thought for sure he was going to roll them up, but he surprised me when he proceeded to remove it completely. When he was done, he started to unhook his belt.

"I'm going to let you choose," he said, nodding toward the items on the table.

So much for Sir preferring a different form of punishment. Not that I wanted to stand in the corner or be deprived of an orgasm, or even to have to pee in front of him again, but still.

"I'm going to give you twenty licks," he informed me. "You will be counting as I go along. And I'm going to allow you to choose what I spank you with."

I peered down at the items again. There was a wide wooden paddle and a crop.

Sir dropped his belt onto the table.

Crap.

And then there were three.

I looked up at him. "Can I choose for you to use your hand?"

He shook his head. "Not for the first ten, no."

So that meant he would be spanking me with his hand and I only had to endure ten swats from one of these items.

I knew for sure I didn't want the crop. They'd used it on me at the island and that had been a lovely experience, but I knew that sucker could hurt really badly. That left the wooden paddle or the leather belt. Neither of which appealed to me.

"You have five seconds to decide. Otherwise, I'm adding ten more."

"The paddle," I blurted.

"Hand it to me."

With shaking hands, I retrieved the paddle, then took it to Sir. His eyes met mine.

"You know what your safeword is, correct?"

"Yes. It's red."

"Very well. Although this isn't playtime, I will allow you to use your safeword should you need to." He took a step closer and tilted my chin back. "Punishment is not something that interests me, Luci. I prefer never to have to do it. However, I think it's important to establish the roles and you've earned this. Never again will you run away like a scared child, you understand? We expect you to talk to us."

Well, looking back on it now, I got that. However, at the time...

I nodded. "Yes, Sir."

He released me, then took a seat on the sofa. "Come lie across my lap."

Surprisingly, Sir did not ask me to remove my clothes. Then again, I was wearing a skirt and no panties, so he already had access to my bare ass.

It took a minute to get into position, but Sir didn't hurry me. I managed to lie across his lap with my upper body on the sofa, my feet on the floor.

Sir lifted my skirt, his hands grazing my ass, which ultimately had my arousal igniting. Although I was scared, I couldn't help it. This man made me want things I'd never known I could want.

"I want you to count for me. The first ten will be with the paddle."

"Yes, Sir." My voice trembled, as did my body.

Sir rubbed my ass for a minute, warming up my skin.

"Relax. Don't tense your muscles. This *is* gonna hurt more than my hand."

Well, he couldn't say he didn't warn me.

I closed my eyes and focused on my breathing, trying to listen for when he was going to swat me. I breathed in and out, my body instantly tensing when his hand disappeared.

"Count for me," he repeated.

Smack!

Son of a bitch! "One," I hissed through clenched teeth.

That fucking hurt.

Smack!

"Two!" Holy crap. I wasn't sure I could survive eight more.

Smack!

"Three."

Tears were pooling in my eyes, my ass burning as he continued to paddle me and I continued to count. My hands were fisted and I buried my face in the cushion, trying to hold myself together.

When he was finally done, his hand returned, sliding over my skin, holding in the burn.

"Ten more," he stated, his tone even. "You don't need to count."

I sobbed. "I'm ready, Sir."

I wasn't, but I wanted to get this over with. I couldn't deny that I deserved it. I'd done something incredibly stupid and I wanted to be on good terms again. I'd learned from Master that once the punishment was handed out, the transgression was forgiven. I needed that more than anything.

Smack!

Smack!

He seemed to focus on areas that weren't already burning from the paddle. The crease where my butt met my leg, the top of my thigh.

Smack!

Smack!

I was still crying, but now the ache had diminished somewhat, morphing into that same sense of calm that consumed me around Master and Sir.

Smack!

"Color, pet?" Sir massaged my ass, making the sting intensify.

"Yellow. But I'm okay, Sir. Really."

Smack!

I inhaled sharply, wanting to get back to that sense of peace I'd found.

Smack!

Smack!

Smack!

The three hard ones in a row jerked me back to reality.

Smack!

I waited for another, but it didn't come and I realized Sir was finished. Part of me expected his hands to dip between my legs, but they didn't. I was disappointed, to say the least.

When he helped me up, he held me in his lap, wrapping his arms around me. I continued to cry. Not only from the pain but also from everything that had taken place up to this point. I knew I needed more from Master and Sir. I wanted everything they were willing to give me.

Unfortunately, I was terrified to ask.

It seemed as though we were making progress. And that was the very reason I decided to keep my thoughts to myself.

FORTY-FIVE

AFTER SIR SPENT THE NIGHT with me last Tuesday, things returned to normal in the office. Normal meaning that I got to focus on my job and they on theirs. Sir left for a business trip on Wednesday, then returned on Thursday. Justin remained gone all week and no one said when he would be coming back. I hated not knowing what was wrong, mostly because I wanted to be there for him. If nothing else, I considered Justin a friend and I hated the idea of him being alone.

However, it was Monday morning and it was time for me to get the week underway.

Ben arrived as normal. He smiled. I offered coffee. He accepted. Then we got to work.

Master and Sir arrived around nine thirty, but I was on the phone with one of Justin's managers, unable to immediately offer them coffee. Neither of them seemed to mind, coming back out of their offices to get it themselves before disappearing once again.

Now that it was almost ten, I headed to the back conference room and got things set up. At the top of the hour, Master, Sir, and Ben joined me. Still no Justin.

We discussed what was going on and I filled them in on what I knew of the things Justin was working on. Although Ben was the go-to, it seemed he was allowing me to step in and help out. I liked that he was giving me that authority. It made me feel better, knowing that I was contributing more and showing them that I knew what I was doing.

•

For the next week, that was exactly what I did. I filled in where I was needed, not questioning what I should be doing, but rather doing it because it felt right. I fielded calls, answered questions, and became a functional part of the team. Not once did any of my bosses ask me to work naked. In fact, they didn't ask me for anything sexual.

At first, it seemed odd, but I figured they were simply overloaded with work. So, I respected that and went about my business. I was professional, if not a bit aloof. I didn't want them to think I was needy, so I put a little distance between us and went about my day. It helped that I had so much to do and they were depending on me more and more.

Did I miss the interactions? Absolutely. Not only the fun that went along with it but also the intimacy. But I liked that they were respecting me as an equal while in the office. It felt good to be needed for something. Granted, the nights were lonely, and I found myself secretly wishing Master and Sir would show up to surprise me again.

They didn't, although they did talk to me frequently in the office, even texted me in the evenings to see how I was doing. They weren't keeping their distance, but it seemed they were giving me some time to think things through.

"Luci, could you please bring me the notes from this morning's call?" Ben called from his office. "I've misplaced mine and I need to check something."

Grabbing the file folder I'd created for that client specifically, I went into Ben's office and held it out to him.

"I'm so glad you're not nearly as scatterbrained as I am," he said with a huff. He seemed in a rush, not nearly as cool and collected as I was used to. It was obvious something was bothering him.

"Ben?"

"Hmm?" he asked as he skimmed the papers in my folder.

"Have you heard from Justin?"

He looked up at me, and for the first time, I saw the pain in his eyes.

Reacting to the emotions I knew he was holding back, I took a step closer. "What? Did something happen?"

"It's not good, Luci. Justin's father…he's not going to make it."

My throat instantly swelled and it hurt to swallow as I tried to keep the tears at bay. We were in the office and it wasn't appropriate for me to fall apart, but this was not good news and I didn't know how to handle it.

Ben was instantly on his feet, his arms wrapping around me. "It's okay, gumdrop. He knew it was coming."

I shook my head. "But it's not okay. He's alone. He shouldn't be alone. You need to go to him. Why are you even still here?" If Justin and I were in a relationship, I would've been by his side to take care of him.

Ben sighed. "Unfortunately, that's not possible right now. There's too much going on here."

I yanked away from him and glared. "Fuck that. Nothing is more important than being there for him when he needs you. That's what family is for."

There was the hint of a smile on Ben's mouth and that infuriated me more.

"How can this be funny?"

"It's not," he stated, jerking me back into his arms and palming the back of my head. "It's definitely not. I always knew you cared on a much deeper level than you let on."

Wait.

What?

Pulling back, I stared up into his face. "What do you mean? You don't think that I *care*?"

That was possibly the most insulting thing he'd ever said to me. The expression that transformed his features was one that said he hadn't meant to say so much.

I managed to extricate myself from his grip. "Are you saying that no one here believes I care about them?"

"That's *not* what I'm saying," he argued. "However—"

"What?" My voice was way too high to be appropriate for an office setting, but I couldn't help it. I'd spent days crying over these men and they didn't think I cared about them? That was complete and total bullshit.

"It's just that you've kept yourself guarded."

I couldn't believe he said that. Me? Guarded? Hell, from the moment I walked into this building I'd been an open book.

"How do you figure that? If I recall, I've submitted to every single thing the four of you have asked of me. Everything."

That seemed to spur Ben's anger, because his response came out in a rough growl. "It's not all about submission, Luci."

Now I was completely lost.

"Forget I said anything," he grumbled as he turned back to his desk.

I had to assume that neither of us was in a good place to be having this discussion. I was being overly emotional, even I knew that. However, I didn't like what he was accusing me of. And I knew he was hurting because of Justin, but I couldn't refrain from pushing the issue.

"No!" Okay, that was loud. I managed to lower my voice somewhat. "I want to know what you mean by that. Are you saying I've done something wrong?"

He turned to face me and this time his expression was hard. "Tell me the first personal thing that you know about us that doesn't involve anything sexual."

I frowned. "I…" Son of a bitch. I hadn't expected that question. "Give me a minute."

"Take all the time you need," he said in a huff, as though proving his point.

I knew plenty of things about them and I blurted out the first things that came to mind. "I know that Master and Sir have an older sister. I know that their parents are into the lifestyle and have a Master/slave relationship that has remained strong even though they opted to have children."

He nodded. "Well, you've done your homework then." His eyes narrowed. "On Landon and Langston. I wasn't referring to them, Luci. Everyone in the fucking building knows how you feel about *them.*"

Now my anger was growing legs and threatening to race out of control. "I know that Justin has a master's degree in business and that he went to Stanford. I know that...that...he likes to cook, but he's admitted you're a much better cook than he is."

"I guess I was wrong," he said, although he didn't sound sincere.

"No, fuck that!" I yelled. "You don't get to turn this around on me. You don't get to tell me that I don't know anything about you. Tell me one time you've tried to get close to me. When you've showed a personal interest in me. Were you aware that my mother hasn't bothered to call me one time since she came back from her cruise? Even though I've left her several messages?"

His eyes widened and I suddenly felt like shit. This wasn't his business. He was not supposed to be interested in me on that level. It wasn't fair of me to accuse him. No more than it was fair for him to do the same to me.

"Never mind," I said, spinning around only to find Master and Sir standing in the doorway.

Son of a bitch.

This was not good.

Dropping my gaze to the floor, I immediately apologized to them for my outburst. It was unprofessional and fueled by emotion, which seemed to be my downfall these days. However, in my defense, I was worried about Justin. I didn't feel as though he should be alone right now. And it seemed wrong that anyone would put work above family.

Then again, that was my personal view on the subject. Not theirs.

"Pet?" Master's voice was even, almost gentle. "Can I see you in my office?"

Shit.

I nodded, knowing I didn't have a choice.

When I started out of the room, he turned to follow me, placing his hand on the small of my back. I was so angry I wanted to pull away from him, but I didn't. Before we made it to his door, I changed my mind.

"Would you mind if I take a few minutes? I need to…get my emotions under control."

He motioned toward his office. "Take all the time you need. When you're ready to talk, just open the door."

As I stepped into the room and closed the door, I wondered if he'd be okay with me staying in there until tomorrow. Or next week, even. This was all getting to be too much.

No, I probably shouldn't have gone off on Ben the way I had. However, emotions were running high right now, mine especially. It didn't seem to matter how many times I tried to convince myself that this setup was working for me, I knew it wasn't.

Dropping onto the couch, I fell onto my side and hugged one of the pillows. I felt cold on the inside. All this time I'd thought I was doing what they wanted. First, I was shunned by Langston and I'd figured out how to reel in my emotions and to keep them to myself so I didn't overwhelm them. Then I had learned my lesson with Landon, which had taught me to be more attentive. And then everything had gone down with Justin. Between the distance he put between us and Ben's admission that things weren't really working out with me the way they'd wanted…well, I was starting to feel as though it was time to move on.

I sighed. I was being overly dramatic, I knew. In my defense, I was hurting. I'd kept all my feelings bottled up for so long. I should've listened to Jordan. I should've engaged my bosses in open dialogue so at least they would know where I stood. Instead, I'd kept it inside and now I was stuck.

I hated the thought of finding a new job. Not only because the interviews sucked but also because I enjoyed what I was doing here. I was four months in and I didn't want to start over somewhere else. On the other hand, this was more than I'd signed up for. Not the sex or the interactions. I had gone into that with my whole heart. I was referring to this emotional bullshit and the ping-ponging back and forth. That was what I couldn't deal with anymore. I felt like a rubber band being stretched at both ends. Just when I thought I would snap, they shifted me around and started pulling in a different direction.

I hated it.

I remained like that for a while longer, focusing on breathing. It was the only thing I knew to do. I had some decisions to make, but I couldn't do that while I was at work. They deserved my full attention for the remainder of the day. Fortunately, the tears didn't come. I was through feeling sorry for myself. Big girls didn't cry, right?

Getting to my feet, I straightened my skirt and my blouse, then ran my hands over my hair to smooth it. Remembering there was a bathroom, I detoured and took a look at myself in the mirror. I looked fine, maybe a little upset, but not too bad.

"Okay, girl. It's time to suck it up. Stop all the whiny bullshit and…move on." The pain in my chest was intense, but I ignored it. Or tried my best to, anyway.

When I stepped out of Langston's office, the first thing I noticed was three of my four bosses were gathered around my desk talking in hushed tones.

Maybe they were going to fire me. I hoped not, because if I was leaving there, I was going to do it with my head held high.

"Before you speak with her," Ben addressed Langston, "can I have a word with Luci?"

"Sure." Langston and Landon walked toward me. Langston stopped in front of me. "When you're finished, join me in my office."

It wasn't phrased as a question, but I nodded anyway, feeling fairly certain they were going to fire me.

Langston's office door closed and I was left facing Ben.

"Look," he said softly. "I shouldn't've said what I did. You didn't deserve that from me."

I didn't respond because I agreed with him.

He moved closer and took my hands in his. "The only thing I've wanted since the day I met you was for you to be happy, Luci. That's it. No matter what path we ventured down, I've always wanted the best for you."

"I know that," I said, my voice rough with emotion.

"I'm truly sorry for what I said earlier. I'm going through a lot right now." He looked so sincere, my chest ached. "But that's no excuse for me to take things out on you. You've done nothing wrong. In fact, we're the ones who're responsible for this mess we've made. I don't want you to think I blame you."

"Thank you. And I'm sorry, too. I shouldn't be taking things out on you either."

He pulled me closer and wrapped his arms around me. I couldn't resist leaning into him. I cared about this man. No matter what happened from that moment forward, I would always care about my four bosses.

No matter what they thought.

"I'm taking your advice," he stated as he pulled back. "I'm hopping on a plane tonight so I can be with Justin. Even though he says he doesn't need me, I know better. And that's my job to know these things. As his submissive, I owe it to both of us to be there so he doesn't have to be alone."

"I'm glad to hear that. Is there anything you need me to do? I can book the flight or a hotel if you need."

"I took care of it already, but thank you."

Ben cupped my face, then leaned down and pressed his lips to mine in a chaste kiss that made all the love I had for him come to the forefront. Again, I fought the tears, not wanting him to think I was weak.

"All right then. You go deal with Langston and I'll call you tomorrow to let you know how things are going."

"Okay."

I took a deep breath and turned toward Langston's door.

Now for the hard part.

FORTY-SIX

AFTER RAPPING MY KNUCKLES ON Langston's door, I waited for him to respond before I turned the knob and stepped inside. Langston was at his desk, and I was surprised to see Landon in there with him.

"You wanted to see me?" I purposely kept from referring to him by his name or by his honorific. I was through playing this game with them.

It didn't matter that they weren't the cause of my outburst, I knew that it all came down to them. To this thing between us. Or lack thereof.

"I do," he responded, then motioned me toward the sofa. "Have a seat. Let's talk."

He got up from his desk chair and moved over to the sofa. I sat on the one across from him, while Landon moved to sit beside me, keeping a good foot between us. I could sense the tension in the room. It was so powerful it made it difficult to breathe.

"Is there something you need to talk to us about?" Langston prompted.

I sat up straight. "Not at the moment, no."

Perhaps I was being childish, but I honestly didn't have anything to say. Not to them and not to anyone else. I felt as though I'd been discarded and I wasn't about to grovel at their feet. They'd already had months to figure this out. If they didn't know me well enough by now, then that was on them.

Langston's eyebrow lifted skeptically. "Care to explain the argument you had with Ben?"

No, I really didn't, but I couldn't very well tell him that. They were still my employers. "It was a misunderstanding and I apologized to him for my outburst."

"This seems to be a trend," he noted, his eyes narrowed on me.

I shrugged, feeling unapologetic despite the fact that he was right. I was out of control and I was taking it out on everyone else.

"Is something going on that we should know about, Luci?"

I glanced between him and Landon. "I'm not sure what you mean."

"Are you unhappy here?"

"No," I blurted. Damn. That wasn't it at all. "I'm very happy here." My issues had nothing to do with work.

"I've noticed all the responsibilities you've taken on the past couple of weeks," Landon stated. "I have to say, I'm very impressed. And pleased."

I sighed, thankful that he wasn't making this personal, although we all knew that it was. "Thank you. It's been a pleasure to be able to handle more. I'm capable of doing more than answering phones and making coffee." I waved my hand. "And I don't mean that in a negative way."

"Is there something going on in your personal life that you want to discuss?" Langston probed.

As though he didn't already know. It angered me that he was pretending he hadn't spent the night with me not too long ago. I had opened up to him then. Why was he acting like he was in the dark?

God, I hated how sterile this conversation was. It was as though I hadn't spent the past four months getting to know them, the past three being intimate with these men. For some reason, they'd relegated me to the hired help and I wasn't sure why that was.

Or maybe I was doing that. In an effort to put some distance between us, maybe I was the one who was putting up walls, purposely having confrontations. I didn't like that it could be true. That wasn't in my nature.

I shook my head and sighed. "No. There's no issues in my personal life." That was a bold-faced lie, but I didn't care.

If they could sit here and act indifferent toward me, then I could return the favor. I was tired of playing these games and getting nowhere. Sure, I'd signed on for that in the beginning, but as the time had passed and I'd grown to care about these men, I felt they owed me more.

Not that they did. Just because I wanted more didn't mean I was entitled to it.

Neither of them said anything, so I scooted closer to the edge of the cushion. "Do you mind if I go back to work now?"

Langston looked at Landon, then back at me. "Go ahead."

My breath caught in my lungs. Admittedly, I'd been holding out hope that they would take the next step in progressing this thing between us. Unfortunately, it looked as though they weren't going to do so. And I certainly wasn't willing to do it.

Which told me everything I needed to know.

Putting on my secretary hat, I glanced between them both. "If you need anything…"

"Thank you, Luci," Landon said dismissively.

And those words felt like a knife to the heart. Rarely had Landon or Langston ever referred to me by my name, yet it seemed to be a trend today. It hurt more than I expected it to, but I pretended otherwise and made it to my desk.

I noticed that Ben's office was dark, which meant he'd left for the day. Although I felt like shit for how things had gone between us, I was glad that he'd left to be with Justin. The man shouldn't be alone at a time like this.

As I was taking a seat at my desk, Landon and Langston came out of Langston's office and the light went off behind them.

"We're leaving for the day. If you need anything, let us know," Langston said, not even looking my way before they headed down the hallway.

Once again, my anger ignited, but I held it in. Clenching my fists at my sides, I stared at the space they'd vacated.

Knowing I had to do something to keep from losing my shit, I pulled up my email and started going through them one by one. It was only four, so I still had an hour and a half. That would give me plenty of time to take care of any fires, as well as to draft the letter of resignation that I intended to email to them before I left for the day.

My chest tightened just thinking about it. I didn't want to leave, but I felt as though I was causing more harm than good by being here. To them and to myself. Unfortunately, there was no way I could continue working here and have a platonic relationship with them. It would hurt too much.

It was a decision I didn't want to make, and quite frankly, it was possible I was jumping the gun, but something felt really off right now. It was as though they didn't want me here, and honestly, if that was the case, then I didn't want to be here. I had enough self-worth to know that I'd be an asset to any company, didn't matter what my role was.

However, relationships were an important key to a functional work life and it seemed as though I'd worn out my welcome here. Still, I needed to take care of a few things, because I certainly wasn't going to leave them in the lurch. They would find someone to take my place, I was sure of that. Until it was time to leave for the day, I was going to do everything I could to ensure that transition was a smooth one.

FORTY-SEVEN

BOSS MEETING

LANDON

"SHE'S GOING TO DO SOMETHING drastic," I told my brother as we sat in the main-floor lobby of the building we owned.

"That she is," he confirmed, crossing one ankle over the opposite knee as he sighed heavily.

Luci had clearly been pushed to her limits. Her reactions were overly emotional and it hadn't taken long to realize that we were to blame.

In the same regard, though, we had attempted to get her to open up to us. That was one thing the girl couldn't seem to wrap her head around. She was not the type to communicate her feelings. And when we'd taken her into Langston's office earlier, we had tried to pry her open, but it hadn't worked. The girl was nothing if not stubborn.

I peered over at Langston.

Then again, I knew someone else who had that trait.

Put the two of them up against one another and the ending was much like dynamite sealed inside an airtight space. Everything would cave in; there was no other place for it to go. And since Luci refused to look at what was right in front of her face, this was getting to be too much for her.

Then again, the rest of us knew how Luci felt about us. I was well aware of the fact that she loved me and Langston in a way she didn't love Justin and Ben. It was the very reason I'd been holding on all this time, waiting for my hardheaded brother to come around.

I could admit that we'd handled things badly. There was probably a reason this type of office arrangement didn't take place. Had the four of us been looking for one submissive, perhaps it would've worked out. But there had been forces working against each other from the beginning and Luci ended up in the middle of it.

"What do you think she'll do?" I asked.

"Quit."

I sighed, glancing around at the people coming and going from the building. I couldn't even think of a day in the office without Luci there. She'd become such a huge part of our world and I'd come to depend on her. Not only as my secretary but as the woman who made me whole.

Granted, I knew my brother was right. Luci was going to quit. Hence the reason we were sitting right here waiting for her.

"Do you think she'll even read the letter?"

"Doubtful." Langston looked at me. "She's gotten too far inside her head."

That was true. I'd noticed it last week when I had gone to her apartment for punishment. It took a tremendous amount of work to keep her in the moment. She had attempted to drift into subspace at every turn and I had refused to allow that to happen. Although it was my goal to pleasure Luci in ways no one else was capable of, I damn sure wasn't about to let her retreat from me when there was a lesson for her to learn.

Not that it mattered now.

The girl was going to run. And because of that, we were going to put ourselves directly in her path.

This time, she wasn't going to walk away without knowing exactly how we felt about her.

I glared at my brother.

She should've known a long time ago. And I think Langston knew it, too. I could only hope that we could convince her. Otherwise…

I didn't want to think about the alternative.

FORTY-EIGHT

I WAS JUST ABOUT TO open my last email when I heard footsteps coming down the hall. I looked up to see Jordan sauntering toward me with a smile on his face. I tried to mirror it, but it didn't work all that well.

"All alone, I see."

"Yep. They abandoned ship and I'm holding down the anchor."

He laughed. "I don't think it's necessary to hold down the anchor. Isn't that the whole purpose of it being...an anchor?"

I giggled because he was right. "Did you need something?"

He pulled an envelope out from behind his back.

"A little birdy left this with me. Said I was to give it to you at exactly five fifteen."

I glanced at the clock, then back to him. "Who's it from?"

He shrugged. "Don't know and it's not my business."

He placed the envelope on my desk and I stared at it. There was nothing written on the outside.

"Well, I'm about to close it down up front," he informed me. "You want me to wait for you?"

"No, I'm good." I offered a smile. "I've got a couple more things to do and I'll make sure the doors are locked."

"I'll see you in the morning?" I hated that he felt the need to question me. It meant that I was far more transparent than I thought.

"Of course."

"Okay, then. Good night, sweet cheeks."

"Night."

As he walked away, I continued to stare at the envelope. I debated on whether or not I should open it. Normally, I would've ripped it open to appease my curiosity, but I wasn't in the mood for any more games. Not today.

Pulling up a Word document, I let my fingers hover over the keyboard as I tried to come up with how I wanted to word my resignation.

My eyes drifted to the envelope, then back to the screen.

Shit.

Fighting the urge to open the letter, I began typing:

Dear Sirs,

After giving careful thought to the matter, I've decided that it's in the best interest of the company for me to resign my position. I've enjoyed my time here, enjoyed getting to know each of you. It's been an experience I'll never forget. I know I should be giving you two weeks' notice; however, I don't see how that could possibly help matters. I've left a detailed list of my job duties and things that will need to be handled going forward for when you hire my replacement.

Luciana Wagner

As I typed my name, a tear slipped down my cheek. This wasn't how I'd ever envisioned things going, but honestly, it was the best way to handle it. I wasn't the right person for these men. I couldn't keep my emotions from interfering and that was my downfall. They deserved someone who could tend to their needs without entanglements. As it was, chaos had ensued and I knew it was all my fault.

If they were smart, they would keep their playtime limited to the club. It was proving true that mixing business with pleasure was a bad idea.

I copied the details and pasted them into an email. I added the subject: *Thank you for the experience*, then added their names in the *To* field.

Pushing back from my chair, I stared down at the screen before hitting send. My eyes shot over to the envelope. No matter what it said, it wasn't going to fix things. As much as I wanted to read it, it would only make this that much harder.

Rather than risk changing my mind, I grabbed my purse and headed for the lobby. I locked the double doors, then placed my keys in Jordan's desk, pushing them to the far back behind some stuff. I would call him tomorrow and let him know they were there.

I did my best to ignore the way my heart was shattering into pieces, the shards piercing my very soul. As I stepped into the elevator, it became difficult to breathe. This wasn't what I wanted.

Then again, not getting what I wanted was something I was familiar with.

It was time I accepted that fact.

It was time I moved on.

As the elevator descended to the main floor, breathing became more difficult. I was doing my best not to cry. I didn't want anyone to see me breaking down. I would reserve that for when I got back to my apartment. At the very least, until I was in my car.

The second the doors opened on the main floor, my eyes widened when I noticed Landon and Langston standing there. It was as though they knew that I was coming.

Landon held up his phone.

I couldn't see what was on the screen, but I figured it was my emailed resignation. Damn it. I knew I should've printed it off and put it on their desks.

"Going somewhere, pet?" Langston asked, his tone hard, his eyes narrowed on my face.

"I'm going home. Now, if you'll excuse me," I said politely, trying to move around them.

They stopped my progress and redirected me back into the elevator.

"What are you doing?" I hissed. I was trying *not* to make a scene, but they were pushing my limits.

"Where's the letter?" Langston asked.

"On my desk," I snapped. "Unopened."

"Looks as though our little sub is looking for some punishment," Landon stated coolly, his hand curling around my elbow, while Langston did the same with my other arm.

"I'm not *yours*," I countered.

"No?" Landon didn't sound as though he believed me.

"I need to get home," I told them.

They weren't listening and the elevator was going back up to the thirty-second floor.

When I tried to pull away, their grips tightened. It didn't hurt, but it was enough to ensure I knew they weren't letting me go.

When the elevator stopped, they led me into the darkened lobby.

"Go get the letter," Langston instructed me.

"No." I was done with this crap. "I quit. You can no longer tell me what to do."

Landon spun me around to face him, his hand curling around behind my neck, his thumb beneath my chin as he tilted my head back.

"Did you think we only told you what to do because you worked for us?"

Langston left us there, heading down the hallway.

"Yes," I lied. "And I've given my notice. You can find someone else to put up with your crap."

Even as I said the words, I hated speaking to him that way. Although the man thoroughly confused me, he'd never been mean. At least not when I hadn't deserved it.

"Keep it up, sweetness. You're gonna get your little ass paddled."

For whatever reason, I felt the need to push him. This was the most reaction I'd ever gotten out of them and I wanted to see how far they would go. I felt alive for the first time in a week.

"If you think you're man enough," I goaded.

The next thing I knew, I was laid out across Jordan's desk.

"Lift your skirt," he commanded.

I didn't move.

"Do it," he insisted.

I remained still.

"I won't tell you again. Either use your safeword or lift your skirt."

I wanted to defy him, but my inner submissive was terrified he would walk away forever. Although that was what I'd been planning to do, I hadn't expected this.

With trembling hands, I lifted my skirt. My bare ass was on display and I knew if anyone stepped off that elevator, it would be the first thing they saw.

"We'll start with ten," Landon said, his tone harsh. "Count."

Smack!

"One," I ground out, pretending not to be affected although my ass was smarting from the sting. Landon certainly wasn't being gentle.

Smack!

"Ow! That hurts!"

"It's not supposed to feel good. Did you count?"

"Two," I hissed.

Smack!

I sucked in a sharp breath as his hand landed on the bottom curve of my ass. "Three!"

Smack!

"Four," I choked out on a sob.

Smack!

"Five."

The sound of footsteps had me turning to see Langston returning, the envelope in his hand.

Smack!

I squealed from the shock. "Six!"

Smack!

Tears were forming and I couldn't hold them back. "Seven."

Smack!

"Eight." I sobbed, letting the tears come.

Smack!

"Nine." My voice was raspy from the tears clogging my throat.

Smack!

"Ten."

Warm hands caressed my stinging ass before Landon helped me up. He adjusted my skirt, then turned me to face him.

"Are you ready to have a conversation?"

I didn't respond.

"We can go for ten more."

I shook my head. "I'm ready to talk."

"Good, then let's go home."

I had no idea what home they were referring to, but at the moment, I was on emotional overload. I didn't care where they took me or what happened. I needed a few minutes to compose myself.

They flanked me again, each taking one of my elbows and escorting me back to the main floor. We exited the building and headed toward the black truck sitting in front of the doors. Landon passed his keys over to Langston, then joined me in the back seat. I thought for sure they would leave me back there alone to think about what I'd done, but Landon surprised me by buckling me into the middle seat and pulling me against his side.

I relaxed against him, my tears finally drying up. With his arm over my shoulder, I felt the urge to cry again, but I managed to hold it in.

No one said anything during the drive, and it soon became obvious that we weren't going to my apartment. Which meant we were headed to their house.

I wasn't sure how I felt about that.

Part of me was eager to hear what they had to say to me; the other part was dreading it. I wouldn't put it past them to have a sit-down chat explaining why this wouldn't work any longer but asking that I didn't resign my position.

If they did that, I would certainly be leaving the company. Although I considered myself a strong woman, I could only tolerate so much. The thought of watching my bosses move on with their lives without me wasn't something I could contemplate.

At least for now, I had a little time to think about what I wanted to say to them.

God only knew I had plenty on my mind.

•

My ass hurt.

An hour later, I could still feel the sting on my skin. It made it difficult to sit down.

Well, that and the scrutiny of Landon's and Langston's gazes as they watched me from their positions on the sofa.

When we first arrived, they gave me a few minutes alone, directing me to go into Landon's bedroom. I took my sweet time, trying to regain my composure. It wasn't easy when I was presented with Landon's bed. I remembered the last night I was here, when they had both taken me together. It was one of the greatest nights of my entire life.

Finally, I managed to force myself back to the living room, where they instructed me to kneel. Which was where I was now, at their feet, with my sore butt resting on my heels. With every shift, I could practically feel the heat of Landon's hand coming down on me. As angry as I wanted to be at him for it, I couldn't quite get there. I had deserved it.

"Are you ready to talk now?" Langston asked, staring down at me.

I shrugged.

"Not a good answer," he growled roughly.

Sighing, I glared up at him. "I'm not sure what you want from me. I already gave you my notice, so you should be thrilled. You can move on with your lives without having to worry about hurting my feelings."

"And why would we hurt your feelings?" Landon questioned.

Damn it.

I should've known they would back me into a corner with this.

Before I could come up with a reasonable response—one that wouldn't give away everything I felt for them—Langston held out the envelope that had been on my desk earlier.

"I don't want to read it," I said belligerently.

He didn't budge. "I wasn't asking."

Swallowing hard, I took the envelope and glanced between it and them, then back. I really didn't want to read it. I didn't want to know who I was supposed to belong to next because it wouldn't matter anymore. I didn't want to play their games, didn't want to be passed around. My heart was too fragile to endure any more.

"Open it, pet," Langston insisted.

I could feel my throat constricting as tears threatened.

I slid my finger beneath the flap and unsealed it before pulling out the sheet of paper. I took a deep breath, then unfolded it.

Luci,

We're sure you're expecting this letter to tell you who you belong to next. However, that's not the case. It doesn't matter who has the honor of having you for their submissive, that's something we've all enjoyed. The fact of the matter is, we have realized something.

There's no need to do that anymore.

We already know who we belong to.

L & L

My heart nearly burst right out of my chest as I read and reread the letter over and over. The tears started to fall and there was nothing I could do to stop them, even as they splattered on the paper and caused the ink to run.

I couldn't look them in the eye. They weren't telling me who *I* belonged to. They were telling me who *they* belonged to. Had I read the note before I'd sent my resignation, I would've never gotten myself to this place.

Yeah. Even I could recognize that I was far too stubborn for my own good sometimes.

FORTY-NINE

"IS THIS REAL?" I MANAGED to choke out, still staring at the paper.

"It doesn't get any realer than that," Landon said, his voice a mere whisper.

"That is...if you'll claim us." The emotion I heard in Langston's voice broke me open.

My love for these men was the only thing I knew for certain. It was the very reason I'd gotten to the point in my life where I was now. Submission was an act of trust and could be given freely if so chosen. However, it was also an act of love. And in order to give every part of oneself to another, your heart had to be in it.

My heart belonged to them.

Wiping the tears from my face, I looked up at both men. They were watching me, obviously waiting for me to say something.

A smile tilted my lips and I smacked Langston's leg with the paper. "What took you so long?"

A watery laugh escaped as I said the words, more so when they pulled me up from the floor, settling me on their laps. I shifted so that I was straddling one leg of each of theirs.

Landon cupped my face and turned my head so that I was staring into his eyes. He wasn't wearing his glasses.

"I honestly thought there was no one as stubborn as my brother." His voice rang with amusement. "Then I met you."

I couldn't help but smile although I still had tears streaking my face.

"There's one lesson we will be workin' on, sweet girl."

I was pretty sure I knew what Landon was going to say, but I cocked an eyebrow anyway, waiting for him to finish.

"Your need to run and hide isn't something I'm fond of."

Yep. I knew that was coming. And he was right.

"But I love you, Luciana. And I'm willing to put in the effort as long as you are."

My heart flipped, spun, then burst in my chest.

I didn't get a chance to respond, because Langston was turning me to face him.

"I don't consider stubborn to be a bad quality," he said, obviously defending himself. "But I agree that the running will stop."

I could hear the insistence in his tone. Langston was the more commanding of the two and I was okay with that.

"But I'm here, for as long as you'll have me." He brushed his finger down my cheek. "I love you, Luci."

I sniffled, my heart so full I could hardly breathe.

"I love both of you," I told them, glancing between them. "And it's not new for me. I've known it for some time." I forced another watery smile. "But I think you already knew that."

"We tried to get you to open up to us," Landon told me. "Unfortunately, that's easier said than done. Without communication, we'll get nowhere."

He was right. However... "Whenever I tried to open up, even accidentally, you both shut me down."

Landon looked remorseful. "You're right. We did."

"In our defense," Langston stated, "it's not easy for us. We never thought we'd get to this point. You blew in like a hurricane, Luci. Surprising us all."

I could feel the sincerity of his words and my heart possibly missed a beat or two.

"So, you're done runnin'?" Langston asked, his drawl slipping through.

I nodded. "Yes, Master. I'm done running."

Landon grabbed his phone and tapped out a message.

"What are you doing?"

"Reassuring your other bosses that you haven't abandoned us all."

My eyes widened. I hadn't even thought about Justin or Ben. "Wait. What about them? Won't they be angry?"

Langston turned my head so I was looking at him again. "They already know."

Landon put down his phone. "In fact, they've been waitin' for us to figure it out for ourselves."

Ben had pretty much said that very thing to me.

"So, now what?" I asked, not sure what was supposed to happen next.

I mean, it wasn't every day that someone (or two someones) professed their love for me, or me to them.

"Well, first, you're gonna make dinner," Landon said, sounding as though that was the most natural thing in the world.

"Okay." I wasn't opposed to doing that.

"Then we'll eat," he said before glancing over at Langston.

Langston finished for him. "Then, we'll show you the dungeon."

My eyes widened. I'd totally forgotten that Langston had mentioned they had a dungeon in their house. I'd never seen it, not even when I stayed with Landon for those two weeks.

Admittedly, I liked that they weren't making this weird. In most of the romance novels I'd read, they were all about professing their undying love, then getting naked and consummating the relationship. We'd already consummated ours in many, many ways.

Langston glanced over at Landon. "That okay with you?"

Landon shrugged. "Makes sense." His eyes shifted back to my face. "After all, I think a good amount of punishment is still in order."

"Punishment? But…"

Langston put his hand over my mouth. "Dinner first. Then the dungeon." He smiled. "If you're really good, we might even let you negotiate the terms of your punishment."

I nodded, keeping my mouth shut, although I was highly tempted to lick his hand. Perhaps I could give the bratty submissive thing a go at some point in the future. That would sure keep them on their toes.

They helped me to my feet, then urged me toward the kitchen.

"You have one hour to get the meal prepared," Landon informed me.

"Yes, Sir." And with that, I trotted off to the kitchen to do their bidding.

•

I managed to use my hour wisely, preparing spaghetti, meat sauce, and garlic bread for Master and Sir. They seemed very happy with my choices, and while we ate, they talked about work, while I mostly listened in. Every now and then they would include me and I contributed as best I could. It wasn't easy since my mind was already on other things.

Such as this punishment they had in store for me.

Well, that and how things were going to play out from here. Since I had retracted my resignation, I had to be at work in the morning. With Ben and Justin out of the office, I was already trying to figure out what I needed to do to help them out. Plus, tomorrow was Valentine's Day. I needed to do something for them to show them how much I loved them. Since I wasn't used to celebrating holidays, it had completely slipped my mind. However, the idea of spending holidays with them in the future...

"She's thinkin' too much," Master said, his voice drawing me from my thoughts.

"Well, I know how to solve that," Sir informed him. "Why don't I help her clean the kitchen and you get the dungeon prepared."

Master nodded, then got to his feet and left the room. Now that I thought about it, I didn't even know where the dungeon was in this house. I'd been upstairs already, so I knew it couldn't be there. Unless there was some sort of hidden door.

Doing my best not to think about it, I rinsed the dishes and loaded them in the dishwasher after Sir brought them to me. While I wiped down the countertops and the table, he disappeared into his bedroom. When he returned, he was wearing jeans and no shirt.

My heart did that little flutter it had been doing ever since they said they loved me.

I joined him in the living room, then sighed when he placed his hand on the back of my neck and guided me through the kitchen and into their office. Sure enough, there was a door. When Sir opened it, I noticed that it led downstairs, obviously into a basement.

The space was nothing like I expected it to be. I had been envisioning something dark and gloomy, similar to the dungeon floor at the club. While the space was dark, it was far from glum. It was similar to the interior of a barn. The floors and ceiling were covered in hardwood, three of the walls a rich golden-brown while the other was all windows and a set of double doors. A walkout basement, then. It was dark, but I could see there was a patio on the other side of the glass.

There were wooden beams with rustic lights interspersed throughout the room, the beams running both vertical from the floor as well as horizontal across the ceiling. I could identify several things I'd seen at the club, like the giant X thing that I'd heard someone refer to as a St. Andrew's cross. There was also a spanking bench, a large padded table, and plenty of chains, cuffs, and other restraints throughout. Oh, and of course, there was a wall I would be referring to as their torture tools. Various paddles, floggers, and crops were mounted on the wall closest to the stairs into the house.

I couldn't help but wonder how many submissives they'd had there.

"What's on your mind, pet?" Master asked as he removed his shirt, placing it on a hook mounted to the wall.

"Nothing."

"I think it's only fair that we go over the rules," Landon said, leading me over to a set of restraints dangling from one of the wooden beams.

"Strip," Master commanded, his eyes hot as they traveled over me. I couldn't tell if he was angry or turned on.

With trembling fingers, I removed my clothes, doing my best not to look at them. When I turned back, I noticed they were both watching me intently.

"Come here," Master commanded.

I stepped closer, placing my hands in his as he held them out to me.

"First rule," Master stated, his eyes meeting mine as he cuffed my hands to the restraints above my head. "No lying. Above and beyond anything else, we expect honesty at all times. If you don't think we'll like what you have to say, then preface it that way. But do not lie."

I nodded.

"So, do you want to change your answer?" Sir asked as he secured leather restraints around me from behind, circling my thighs, with a strap that wrapped under my butt. "What were you thinking about?"

I hated admitting it because it made me sound petty and jealous, but I blurted out my thoughts. "I'd wondered how many submissives you've had down here."

Master caught my gaze before he dropped to his knees and adjusted the straps around my ankles. "One."

Wow. That sounded far worse than if they'd said many. To have only had one, it meant they likely were serious about her. I tried not to let that bother me.

Master got to his feet, staring down at me. His hand curled around my cheek, his thumb beneath my chin. He tilted my face so that my eyes met his.

"You're the only submissive we've ever had down here."

My eyes widened as his words sank in.

"I once told you that I'd been waiting a long time for you. I don't say things I don't mean, Luci. No matter what you want to believe, I've been nothing but truthful since the beginning."

"Second rule," Sir said, his hands gliding up the backs of my thighs. "From this moment forward, you will not be allowed to have intercourse with anyone else."

I nodded, unable to see him as he again adjusted something around me.

"We share you between us," he continued. "And *only* us. Is that understood?"

"Yes, Sir."

"That means the arrangement at the office is void," Master clarified. "We've already informed Justin and Ben."

They traded places, Sir coming around in front of me as they both worked in tandem to secure me to their liking.

Sir's hands glided over my hips and then my feet were suddenly lifted. From what I could tell, they'd fastened me to some sort of swing. His hands glided higher, brushing the outer swell of my breasts.

"We endured the agreement at the office, despite the fact that we're extremely possessive. Going forward, you belong to us and only us. Your sweet little mouth, that sexy ass, and your lovely cunt have been claimed." As he said the words, Sir's fingers dipped between my legs.

I moaned as he pushed one finger inside me.

"Third rule," Master stated, his arms coming around me from behind, his hands cupping my breasts. "We will all sleep in the same bed. Every night."

That sounded like heaven to me.

"In case it's not clear," Sir added, "you will be moving in with us here at the house. You will also have things at the apartment for the nights we stay in the city. We'll pay the remainder of your lease and both spaces will be as much yours as ours. You can decide which bedroom we should sleep in and even decorate it however you want." He smirked. "Of course, we'll add our own touches as we see fit."

Yes, they did have a penchant for restraints, so I would likely have to work around those.

I nodded, not sure what to say other than okay. I wanted to be with them, morning and night, so I wasn't going to argue.

"Fourth rule." Master swept my hair away from my neck. "You will continue in your role as our secretary; however, your position will be adjusted. You will no longer work for Justin or Ben. They will be seeking a secretary of their own."

Sir picked up where he left off. "We'll be making some modifications to the office arrangement so that we're relocating to another floor. It will give us more…privacy during the workday."

"As well as more space," Master inserted.

I should've known.

Master traded places with Sir, coming to stand in front of me. He stepped in close, his lips gliding against my neck. Sir's mouth brushed the other side of my neck and I found myself sandwiched between them.

"Final rule," Master whispered, pulling back to look directly into my eyes.

I swallowed hard. I could tell, whatever this rule was, that he believed it could possibly be a game changer.

"You will wear our collar."

My heart skipped a beat.

Sir's hands came around as he placed something around my neck. I had no idea what it looked like, but I certainly knew what it meant.

"There are two locks," Master informed me.

I could feel one of the locks click into place. Then Master's hands went around behind me and another clicked.

"There are two keys," Sir added. "We each wear one."

Master met my gaze as he adjusted the collar to the way he wanted it. I'd never been the type to wear much jewelry for the simple fact that it felt too confining. However, the collar felt perfect.

Master stepped back and my eyes were drawn down his torso when he freed the button on his jeans as he continued to speak. "No matter what, you will never be without a collar. If you're not wearing this one, you'll be wearing your play collar. Do you understand?"

I nodded, lifting my gaze to his. "Yes, Master."

"It's a reflection of our ownership," Sir stated, his voice sounding from behind me. "Do you willingly give yourself to us?"

Master moved in closer, his hands on my thighs, while Sir pressed against me from behind. I could feel the hard ridge of his erection pressing intimately between my butt cheeks, while Master's thick cock prodded the entrance to my pussy. I knew what they were going to do and my body was ready and willing.

A tear trickled down my cheek as the love I felt for both of them overflowed from my body. "I do. I freely give you both my body, my submission, and my heart."

Master leaned in and kissed me. "Thank you, pet."

Unfortunately, he didn't linger.

"Do you have any questions regarding the rules?"

"No, Master."

Within seconds, they were both buried inside me. I was filled to capacity by their bodies and their love. They weren't gentle, but I expected nothing less. These men understood me. They knew what I needed, what I wanted, what I craved, and they gave it to me without question.

I moaned as they rocked me between them, their thrusts alternating as they fucked into me, deeper, harder, faster. I tried to hold on for as long as I could, loving the way it felt to be owned by these two men. I wanted nothing more than to spend the rest of my life right here between them.

When I finally gave in to my orgasm, I cried out their names, begging them not to stop. They fucked me harder, faster, their combined grunts carrying me on wave after wave of pure ecstasy. I had no idea how long they fucked me, but I didn't care. I succumbed to one climax after another, knowing that it wasn't merely the pleasure they wrought on my body but the love they were giving me in return that heightened every sensation.

And when they both came, slamming into me at the same time, I knew without a doubt that I would never belong to anyone else.

I was theirs.

And they were mine.

FIFTY

THE FOLLOWING MORNING WASN'T MUCH different than when I had stayed with Landon during those two weeks. Well, with the exception that the three of us had slept in Landon's bed. I hadn't yet decided which room I wanted to be ours, nor did I know how I wanted to decorate it, but I was bound and determined to come up with something.

I learned that they fully intended to change my hours once I was settled into the house. Master insisted that we not get up at the ass-crack of dawn. He said he would rather I work late into the night than have to get up with the roosters. His words.

As long as I was capable of getting my work done, I didn't mind what hours I kept.

Surprisingly, we arrived at the office before Jordan did, and I was a little disappointed. For whatever reason, I wanted him to be the first person I told about what happened. He truly had become my best friend and it was important to me that I share this news with him.

So, after Master and Sir went to their offices and I delivered their coffee, I made my way up front to find Jordan getting his own coffee in the break room.

"Good morning," I greeted.

He turned around, a smile already on his face. The second he looked at me, his eyes widened.

"Holy. Smokes."

Jordan rushed over to me, his hands lifting quickly only to pause right by my neck as he gazed down at the collar I was proudly wearing.

"It's...beautiful."

"I know," I squealed. I still couldn't believe it.

Last night, after they'd carried me up to Landon's bedroom, I'd fallen fast asleep. But this morning when I woke up, I spent a good ten minutes admiring the collar in the mirror. The sterling silver band had an intricate Celtic knot design and went around my neck, but it was relatively loose. Sort of like a necklace, only not as limber as it would've been if it were a chain. There were two locks that connected the back together.

When Master had caught me looking at it, he informed me that it wasn't my play collar. They had one of those that I would wear when at the club. Nothing would ever be hooked to this collar, because it was too delicate for that.

Jordan pulled me against him, throwing his arms around me. I hugged him back.

"I'm so happy for you, kiddo," he whispered. "So damn happy."

"Thank you."

When he pulled back, he stared into my eyes as though trying to read my mind and find out everything that had happened.

"Lunch?" I asked, giggling. "I'll tell you everything then."

"Absolutely."

With another glance at my neck, he smiled and I could tell he was genuinely happy for me. It also reminded me that I needed to call Kristen to let her know. And I had to find a way to tell my mother the news. I wasn't sure what I was going to say to her, but she might want to know that I was moving out of the apartment.

"I have to get back to work," I told Jordan, my brain already scattering in a million directions. "I'll see you at lunch."

•

The day passed quickly, including lunch with Jordan. I told him everything from the beginning, at least the parts he didn't already know. I shared as much detail as I could remember and I answered every question he had. It felt good to have someone to talk to.

Granted, he wasn't all that thrilled that I had tried to quit. He told me if I pulled that shit again, he would be breaking out a paddle of his own.

Shortly after I got back from lunch, Master and Sir asked me to come with them. I followed them into the lobby, then into the elevator. They informed Jordan we would be back soon.

Surprisingly, we only went up one floor. When we stepped off the elevator, we were met with a space that was set up similarly to their office space now. There was a large conference room and a plush lobby. The only difference was this one was not decorated. The walls were white and the floors lacked tile. It was obviously a work in progress.

"We've already designed it," Sir informed me. "They'll be starting work on it next week. According to the general contractor, we're looking at roughly three months before it's complete. And that's pushing it."

I figured Master and Sir had a time frame they were shooting for. They weren't the types who would leave something open-ended.

"The back offices haven't been designed yet," Master said as we walked down the hallway. "We'll have doors here, like downstairs. And we'll have three offices beyond them."

I felt giddy at the thought. "I get my own office?"

"You do," he assured me. "However, we won't have a second conference room, so the open space will be set up for…a recreational area."

I liked that idea.

"We'll let you work with the designer on how you want this space to be. She'll get our input, but we've decided to let you have the final say."

Wow. I hadn't expected that. The only thing I knew I wanted for certain was a little color. Although I liked the modern design, it was a little too sterile for my taste. I was sure I'd come up with something.

"Justin and Ben will be looking to hire a secretary when they return. We'll need you to train whomever they hire."

I grinned, thinking of the training I'd undergone.

Sir pulled me into him. "Not that sort of training, naughty girl."

"Oh, I know," I said sweetly. "I'm sure she'll get *that* training from her two bosses."

"It's possible."

"We might have to do some shifting around for a while," Master said as he walked around the space. "Ben and Justin will be reconfiguring the downstairs offices as well."

I turned around to look out the windows overlooking downtown. Sir placed his arms around me, his fingers playing with my collar.

"With the go-ahead from our structural engineer, we'll be putting in a set of stairs between the two floors to make access easier," he said, his words raspy against my ear.

"Where will Jordan be working?" I asked.

"Where do you want him to work?" Master stepped in front of me, his hands moving to my hips.

"I would prefer that he be on our floor."

"Reasons?" Master prompted.

"Well, for one, he's an integral part of this company."

"True."

"Two," I continued, "he's part of the lifestyle, therefore he knows that discretion is required."

"Sure."

"Three, he's my friend. And four, I will need his help in preparing for the quarterly meetings as well as other conferences that we may have."

"Other conferences?" Sir leaned around to look at my face.

I shrugged. "Come on. You know that the only way to go from here is up. And teamwork is the key to making that happen. Therefore, I see some changes in the future."

Master chuckled. "Is she topping from the bottom?"

I laughed. I'd heard that term before.

"It sounds like it." Sir chuckled.

"You know what happens to bratty little subs who like to top, don't you?"

I put on my most innocent face. "No. What?"

"They get to work naked," he said, moving in closer.

Sir's lips brushed over my ear when he added, "And they get fucked on their desk."

A shiver ran down my spine.

Oh, I was definitely looking forward to that.

Unfortunately, neither of them seemed to be ready to make good on their promises just yet, so we returned to the thirty-second floor. On the way down, I asked them when I would get to relay the details to Jordan. They told me to wait until our next Monday meeting, when Justin and Ben were back. That way everyone was on the same page.

It wasn't easy, but I agreed to keep my excitement to a minimum.

After all, it wasn't like I really had a choice.

•

That night, Master surprised us all by cooking dinner. He said it was his Valentine's gift to me. Granted, they'd had six dozen red roses and three boxes of chocolates delivered to the office, so I think they'd already come through for this holiday.

As for my gift to them... Well, I had taken my limits list and removed all of my hard limits. I knew that Master and Sir would take care of me. I knew they knew my own limits. When I gave it to them, they had both kissed me senseless, letting me know that my gift of submission was all they ever needed. No matter what they said, I could tell they were moved by the fact that I'd given them my ultimate trust.

"Are you staring at me again?" Master grumbled.

I think I'd finally managed to get on his very last nerve when I plopped my butt on the island and watched him work.

"There's a reason I don't cook." If he had been attempting to hide his irritation, he didn't succeed.

"Why's that?" I knew he'd said he didn't like to be in the kitchen, but other than that, I didn't know his reasons.

"Because...I hate to show up my brother."

Sir overheard and laughed. It was a hearty sound that made me chuckle.

"Show me up, huh?"

"Yes," Master said, trying to sound serious, but his smile gave him away.

He looked happy. Happier than I'd ever seen him. It felt good to know that I was partially the reason for that.

Things had certainly gotten off track at the office in recent weeks. I think we'd all known what was going on, but no one did anything about it. There had been a lack of communication, although the three of us knew it was key to making things work. We were all at fault.

But now that they'd collared me and we'd taken the next step, there was significantly less stress.

"Well, if it's any consolation," I told him. "You cook, I'll clean."

Master turned to look my way, his eyes darting over to Sir's.

"Naked," he said absently.

Sir agreed. "I think that's a great idea. From here on out, she's required to clean naked."

"Well, I was thinking more along the lines of she should *always* be naked."

"Always?" I pouted.

"I think we'll need to work on a few additional rules," Master noted as he turned around and tended to whatever it was he was making.

"What's today?" Sir asked.

"Wednesday," I provided helpfully.

"Right. Well, then on Wednesdays, you'll be required to be topless in the kitchen while dinner's being prepared."

Ever the helpful one, Sir came around and pulled my shirt up and over my head. He then released the clasp on my bra and tossed it onto the table.

"There," Sir said as he stepped back and admired my naked torso.

•

By the time dinner was on the table, I was slowly going out of my mind. Turned out that when I was topless, both Master and Sir had wandering hands. Not that I minded, except when they didn't follow through with their teasing.

"I think we should talk about our plans for the weekend," Master tossed out as we were eating.

"What plans?" I asked, suddenly excited to hear what they had in store for me.

"I have the movers scheduled for Monday," Sir stated. "Which means we'll need to get any of your valuables moved before then. They'll handle packing and moving the rest. For the time being, we'll have her stuff stored in your room," he said to Langston. "That way she can figure out what she wants where."

Master nodded as he chewed.

"Okay," I said, trying to keep up. "So we're partially moving this weekend. Check."

"We'll be going to Dichotomy on Saturday night," Master added. "I'll plan to reserve a spot for a scene." He looked at Sir. "We'll have to come up with something to test our little sub's limits."

"Agreed."

They looked at one another and I swear something passed between them.

"What? What's that little thing you do?" I motioned between them. "That silent-speaking thing you just did. What aren't you telling me?"

They both turned to look at me.

"At some point this weekend, we'd like for you to introduce us to your mother and stepfather."

I dropped my fork. Words wouldn't form.

Master said my name firmly, my attention shooting over to him.

I shook my head. "I... What... I..." I couldn't even get the words out.

Sir leaned forward. "Luci, if we're going to move forward, it's important that we meet your parents."

"Both of you?" I blurted.

That was obviously not the right thing to say.

"Last I checked, you weren't with just one of us," Master stated coldly.

I reached for his wrist. "I'm sorry. That came out wrong. I…" I dropped my eyes to my plate and released him. "It's just that my mother is extremely opinionated and she has never approved of anything I've done before. I can only imagine how she's going to react."

"We can handle your mother," Master said reassuringly.

I hoped that was true. More importantly, I hoped that by meeting my mother, they didn't suddenly think that I wasn't worth it. After all, my mother rarely had anything good to say about me.

Then again, for all I knew, she could be ecstatic about the news. Someone to take me off her hands so she would never have to worry about me again.

I frowned, but I managed to look at them. "I'll call her tomorrow, set up a time for us to go over there. I'll have to find out what day Jim's off."

They seemed content with that answer.

Master motioned toward my plate. "Now finish eating so we can watch you clean naked."

Well, at least I had something to look forward to.

FIFTY-ONE

HOLY CRAP.

Holy crap.

Holy crap.

That was the only thing that I could think as we walked from Sir's truck up to my mother's front door on Friday evening.

It wasn't the best way to start the weekend in my mind, but my mother had informed me that Jim was working all day Saturday and would likely be sleeping on Sunday, so if I wanted to visit, it would have to be Friday night.

And here we were.

"Relax, pet," Master said, gently squeezing my shoulders.

"You haven't met her," I mumbled under my breath as we made our way up the stairs. If he had, he would know that relaxing wasn't an option.

I knocked on the door and I could feel Master and Sir staring down at me. I figured when they went to visit their own parents, they probably had a key to the house or perhaps Mel and Jeremy would merely have the door unlocked to welcome them.

Not my mother.

She did not want me having a key to her house and not once since I'd moved out at seventeen had the door ever been unlocked when I came over for a visit. Scheduled or not.

A few minutes later, the door finally opened and Jim stood there. His eyes instantly widened as he glanced between Master and Sir.

"Luci? Is everything okay?" He sounded concerned.

"It's great," I said, putting on my best smile.

When he pushed open the screen door, I stepped inside.

"I'd like you to meet…Landon and Langston." I motioned toward my stepfather. "This is Jim Wagner."

Master and Sir both held out their hands to greet Jim. My stepfather looked dumbfounded, but he had the decency to shake their hands.

"And how do you know Luci?" Jim asked them directly.

"I met them at work," I tossed out, not quite ready to announce that they were...whatever it was they were to me.

"Your mother's in the living room," Jim announced, his gaze bouncing between the three of us. Clearly, he did not know what to think.

We followed Jim through the small dining room and into the living room at the back of the house. My mother was sitting in her chair watching television, seemingly unfazed that I had arrived. I could tell she hadn't been home long, probably settling in for the evening.

"Mother." I said her name loud enough to get her attention.

She turned her head, but then jerked upright. "Luci? What's wrong?"

Geez. Why did they keep asking that? It wasn't like Master and Sir looked like serial killers.

I glanced back at them.

Okay, fine. They were intimidating, sure. But harmless.

"Did something happen?" she asked, clearly wanting me to answer.

"No, Mom. Everything's fine." I peered over my shoulder at Master and Sir. "I just wanted to introduce you to my... This is Landon and this is Langston." I turned back and motioned in her direction. "And this is my mother, Terri Wagner."

They both moved toward her, offering their hands. She shook them hesitantly, her eyes never leaving their faces. I couldn't tell what she was thinking, but whatever it was, it wasn't good. Her brows were pinched and she was frowning.

"It's nice to meet you, ma'am," Sir said politely.

I noticed that Master didn't say anything at all.

"Please, have a seat," she said, motioning to the sofa.

Reluctantly I sat down, Master and Sir sitting on either side of me. It was incredibly awkward and I didn't know what to do with my hands, so I fidgeted for a few seconds before Master reached over and grabbed my fingers, pulling one of my hands into his lap. Of course, my mother noticed and followed the action before peering up at me.

"Can I get you anything to drink?" Jim offered.

"No, thank you," Sir told him. "We actually have dinner reservations in a bit. However, we thought it would be appropriate to stop by and officially meet Luci's parents."

I could tell my mother was trying to figure out the punchline. It wasn't every day that I brought a boyfriend home with me, much less two. In fact, I had *never* brought a boy home to meet my mother. Even now that I was sitting in front of her, the idea terrified me.

"And how exactly do you know Luci?" My mother looked confused.

Master and Sir both looked at me. I knew they were waiting to see if I would admit to our relationship.

"Landon and Langston are...my boyfriends," I blurted, shocked and slightly proud of myself.

There was a deep groove in my mother's forehead as she stared at the three of us for a moment. Then, surprisingly, she started laughing.

Now I was the one who was confused. "What's so funny?"

"Your...boyfriends? Plural?" She laughed even harder.

Granted, her chuckles died a quick death when Sir reached for my other hand, linking our fingers together.

"Oh, my God. You're serious." My mother's face turned a bright red. "Luci, this is absolutely unacceptable."

And there it was. I knew that this was a bad idea.

"Actually, Mrs. Wagner, we didn't come to get your approval." Master's tone was rigid yet civil.

That threw my mother for a loop.

"We simply felt that it was important to officially meet you," he continued. "And to let you know that Luci will be moving in with us."

"Both of you?" My mother's mouth hung open a little.

"Yes, ma'am," Sir confirmed.

"How long have you been dating…them?" she asked, her eyes narrowed on me.

"Three months," I admitted.

"Three months! And you're moving in with them?" Her voice was reaching a fever pitch.

Sir glanced over at me and Master. "Would you mind waiting out in the truck? I'd like to have a conversation with your mother."

"No," my mother snapped. "That's not necessary. I don't even want to know what depravity Luciana is a part of. I take absolutely no responsibility for her…ridiculous decisions."

Before I could plan a counterattack, Master pulled me up from the sofa and led me toward the front door. I pulled on his hand once, but he held firm, forcing me to follow him.

"Come on, pet," he said softly. "Let Landon handle this. The man's quite adept at dealing with unruly people."

I was so embarrassed I started to cry. I couldn't believe my mother would react like that. It wasn't like I hadn't suspected what she would say or do, but *that*…

She called me depraved and it…it hurt.

When we got to the truck, Master opened the back passenger door but he didn't urge me inside. He turned me to face him, cupping my head in his big hands.

"Look at me, Luci," he insisted.

I opened my eyes and tried to focus through the watery haze of tears.

"I know it didn't go the way you wanted it to," he said softly. "But it was imperative that we meet them. I think you'll find that, in the future, you'll have a chance to repair the relationship with your mother."

"You're wrong," I said on a sob. "It's a lost cause."

"It's not," he assured me. "However, if she would've found out that you moved in with us and you didn't bother to tell her about the relationship, she would've been just as angry."

It was true. She would have. And then it would've been my fault.

Master tilted my head back a little more, locking eyes with me. "One thing you need to know about me and Landon…we're not embarrassed about what we want." He fingered my collar. "We've waited our entire lives for you, Luci. And we're not ashamed to admit it. If that's not something you want, then you need to tell us now."

I grabbed his wrists. "I'm not ashamed either," I said, praying he would believe me. "I'm not embarrassed about being with the two of you. In fact, I'm proud of that. I'm just…I'm embarrassed that my mother doesn't love me."

Master leaned down and pressed his lips against my forehead. "Your mother loves you in her own way. If she didn't, she wouldn't have let you come over today. A strained relationship is still better than no relationship at all." He pulled back so I could see his face again. "Luci, your mother's selfish. She thinks about herself first and foremost. Nobody's perfect. But that's on her, not you."

I had never thought of it that way.

I heard the front door open and I turned to see Sir walking out. He shook Jim's hand and then sauntered down the steps to the truck.

"Come on," Master urged. "Let's go have dinner. We'll talk more when we get there."

I agreed, although I wasn't sure I wanted to know what my mother had to say when I wasn't there.

•

They took me to a fancy restaurant. I wasn't quite dressed for the occasion, but no one seemed to mind. We were led to a private table in the back corner, away from most of the other patrons. While the waiter bustled about, bringing water, then wine, and finally taking our order, I sat patiently, wondering if Landon was going to tell me what happened.

And then when he finally did, I wished he hadn't.

"She'll come around," Landon said, holding my hand in his. "She doesn't know how to feel, Luci. You've admitted that you didn't have a close relationship with her. This is her way of dealing."

I fought the tears back because he was right. My mother rarely had anything to do with me. There was no reason I should care that she didn't want to talk to me.

"It's fine," I finally said, knowing they were trying to comfort me. "I don't care."

And that was mostly true. I didn't *want* to care. It wasn't like I needed her blessing. I was going to be with Master and Sir regardless of whether she approved or not. I guess somewhere inside was still a little girl who had hoped her mother would show at least a little affection toward her.

I drank a little more wine than I was used to, but it helped to ease some of the pain. I even managed to make it through dinner without bringing the subject up again. Master and Sir carried the conversation, obviously knowing I was still hurting, but respecting my need to pretend it hadn't happened.

"Would you care for dessert?" the waiter offered after clearing our plates away.

"We would," Master said, surprising me. He wasn't the dessert type.

The waiter disappeared, then returned a moment later with a tray full of various sweets. He pointed them out with a brief description of each.

"I'll have the chocolate mousse," I told him.

"Very well." He looked between Master and Sir. "Anything for you?"

"No, we have other plans for dessert," Sir stated, his tone serious. "However, we will have coffee."

I couldn't help it, I chuckled. The waiter's ears turned red and he forced a smile before heading back to put in the order.

"Other plans for dessert, huh?" I teased.

Both men turned their wicked gazes on me and I felt the full brunt of their sexiness. Perhaps it was the wine, or maybe it was merely them. I didn't know and I didn't care. I was just happy to be there, to have them beside me.

I felt one warm hand travel up my left thigh. Another hand moved up my right. At the same time, they forced my legs apart, hooking their feet in front of my ankles to keep me from closing my legs. Thank God there was a tablecloth.

"We're going to see how well you can behave," Master whispered, his mouth against my ear. "While we tease that pretty pussy."

A lightning bolt of heat shot straight up my spine.

"Now, remember where you are," Sir said, his hand trailing higher on my right thigh. "There are plenty of people in this restaurant, a few probably watching you right now."

My eyes scanned the room, trying to figure out who could possibly be watching me.

Warm fingers teased my pussy, casually grazing my clit. I swallowed hard, doing my best not to moan. That *would* draw attention to myself.

Master repositioned my leg so that my knee was hooked over his thigh. Sir did the same so that I was forced to inch my butt forward, giving them better access.

The waiter returned to pour the coffee, and while he was standing there, someone pushed a finger deep into me. I jerked but forced a smile as the waiter looked at me.

"Do you need anything else for now?"

"No," I squeaked. "I think we're good."

"Your dessert should be out momentarily."

"Thank you."

That mischievous finger remained buried inside me, teasing me relentlessly. Based on the pressure on my right thigh, I was pretty sure it was Sir's finger, but I couldn't be sure because another finger began grazing my clit.

"There's only one rule, pet."

I locked eyes with Master as the finger on my clit began pressing insistently.

"I can't come?"

He smiled, but it was a devilish grin. "Oh, you can come. But no one here can know. So if that's what you choose to do, then I suggest you disguise it well."

I wasn't sure that was possible.

The waiter returned with the chocolate mousse. He set it directly in front of me and offered a quick smile before disappearing. I was pretty sure he knew what was taking place beneath the table.

"Eat up, sweetness," Sir urged, his teeth nipping my ear. "Because when I get you home, I'm going to have my dessert."

Swallowing hard, I silently willed him to tell me what that meant.

He kissed my neck. "I intend to have you sit on my face so I can lick this sweet pussy until I've had my fill." As he spoke, he added another finger, pushing deeper into me. When he brushed my G-spot, I whimpered. In an effort to hide my reaction, I grabbed my spoon and took a bite.

I was grateful when they sat up as though nothing was happening. They continued to lean toward me, speaking softly, as though this was just a regular conversation. All the while, they were fingering me and teasing my clit to the point of distraction. At one point, I simply held the spoon up to my mouth, forgetting to take a bite until Master chuckled.

"Let us know when you're finished," he informed me. "That way I can take you out to the truck and get started on my dessert."

Oh, heavens.

They were too much.

I pushed my half-eaten dessert away, then waved my hand for the waiter.

Sir laughed, sitting up straight as he instructed the waiter to bring the check.

Ten minutes later, we were in the truck. I was in the back seat with Master while Sir was driving.

"Lift up that skirt," Master ordered as the truck was pulling out of the parking lot.

My body was on fire and I was desperate for attention. I didn't balk at his request, hiking my skirt up.

"Turn on the light," he ordered Sir.

The dome light came on, practically spotlighting my bare pussy.

Master placed his arm over the back of the seat behind my head.

"Let me watch while you tease yourself."

Crap.

That wasn't what I was hoping for. I needed to feel his touch. However, it was obvious he was purposely making me wait.

While I watched the cars move by us, I let my hand drift down between my legs. It didn't even matter that someone could possibly see me. I began teasing my clit, working myself right back to the precipice they'd held me at in the restaurant.

"Don't come," Sir commanded from the front seat. "The rules have changed now that we're on the way home."

Damn it.

They were sadists, I was sure of it.

I did my best to tease myself slowly, but Master felt the need to pitch in. He used my own fingers against me, but never giving me enough. What should've been a quick drive home felt like an eternity.

Once we stepped into the house, Master picked me up. I had to wrap my arms around his neck and my legs around his waist and hold on. He seemed to be moving with purpose as he strode through the kitchen and into the living room.

Sir wasn't far behind.

When Master put me down, he instantly began tugging my clothes from my body. Sir did the same with his own and then Master disrobed. Within minutes, we were all three naked and Sir was lying on the sofa.

"Sit on my face," he commanded roughly. "Let me taste that sweet pussy."

There wasn't an ounce of modesty left in me at that point. I simply needed to come, so I straddled Sir's head, staring down at his face as he wrapped his arms around my thighs. His tongue rasped against my clit and I cried out.

Master stood in front of me, stroking his cock while I bucked on Sir's face, trying to launch myself over. He held back just enough to keep me hanging by a fragile thread.

"Put my cock in your mouth," Master demanded, his hand sliding into my hair.

I didn't hesitate, leaning forward and taking Master's thick cock into my mouth. I wrapped my lips around him, then allowed him to take over. He fucked my mouth, driving deep while holding my head in place. I whimpered and moaned as Sir tormented my pussy with his wicked tongue. I was on the verge of tears, desperate to come, when he finally, *finally* gave me what I needed.

As though they had choreographed it ahead of time, Master pulled his cock from my mouth while Sir shifted me off him. Then Master was lying flat on his back. He positioned me so that I was facing away from him, pulling me down onto his cock. He thrust up into me, making me cry out again. And this time, Sir used my mouth for his own pleasure.

I was lost to the sensations, overcome by the fierce need I could feel emanating from them. They needed me as badly as I needed them. And it wasn't long before we all succumbed to our own desires, filling the room with our combined moans and groans until we collapsed in a heap.

The night certainly ended on a better note than it had started on.

FIFTY-TWO

THE CLUB SEEMED EVEN BUSIER than it had been the first time I was there. Everywhere I looked, there were people. They filled the sections of the main floor, some talking, some laughing, even a couple of Doms checking out the submissives in the holding area.

The music was even louder than I remembered it being.

That or I was simply enjoying myself more.

Yeah. That was probably it.

Before we left the house, Master and Sir had removed my silver collar and replaced it with a sexy lace one that had two locks on the back and a hook on the front. To my surprise, when we stepped inside the club, they had hooked a leash to it and kept one hand on it at all times.

I probably should've been appalled, but I wasn't. In fact, it turned me on.

Granted, if they made me crawl around like a dog, I would probably have to have some words.

Tonight, I was wearing a sexy leather halter and a matching skirt that Sir had given me after we had showered together. I'd been surprised by his request, but when he insisted on washing my hair and my body, I hadn't been able to come up with an excuse. And while he had finished in the shower, I had gotten out and Master had dressed me.

Needless to say, it was a side of them I'd never seen before. One that I happened to be quite fond of. Sure, they'd always been attentive, but tonight they had paid particular attention to taking care of me.

Rather than boots like last time, they had instructed me to leave my shoes at the front desk, which I did without question. It wasn't until we got inside that I realized none of the submissives were wearing shoes. I figured it had to be some sort of theme.

While Master and Sir talked to people they knew, I followed behind them, the leash dangling from Master's hand. People were looking my way and I wasn't sure why. I figured it was likely due to the fact that I was collared by the two sexiest Doms in the place.

At least that was my reasoning. Truth was, I wasn't worried about why they were looking at me. I was here for Master and Sir and that was all. Their rule for tonight had been simple: obey. It was all encompassing, but hey, I was up for a challenge.

As we made our way across the floor, I stopped when they stopped. It wasn't until I heard a familiar voice that I peeked between them to see Kristen with her submissive. I was about to call out to her when I remembered the protocol. Here at the club, she wasn't my friend. She was a Domme and it would've been disrespectful to her, as well as to my masters, for me to react to her like that.

They spoke to her for a few minutes, then separated and moved me between them.

"Luci, say hello to your friend," Sir instructed, placing his hand on the back of my neck.

"Hi." It was hard, but I held back my excitement.

"Well, aren't you looking lovely?" Kristen eyed my collar. I could see a hint of concern mixed with a genuine amount of happiness.

Yeah. We probably had some things to talk about. The last time we'd chatted had been the night Sir came over to punish me. I'd texted her to tell her that things were fine and that I wanted to see her, but we hadn't had time to schedule anything. Now that she saw the collar, I was sure we'd be making that time really soon.

I wanted to squeal, but I kept myself in check.

Master pressed his lips against the side of my head. "Very good girl."

His praise made my body hum.

"Will we be seeing you scene later?" Kristen asked, her question directed at Master and Sir.

"We'll be in the dungeon tonight," Sir informed her.

Kristen's eyes met mine. "I look forward to watching."

I offered her a smile but remained where I was. When Master and Sir began moving again, I walked with them.

"Master Ramsey," Sir greeted, holding out his hand and shaking the Hollywood Dom's hand.

Unlike last time and my impolite reaction, I kept my eyes down, my focus on Master and Sir. I was bound and determined I was not going to let them down tonight. The fact that I was wearing their collar meant something to me and I wanted to make them proud. Perhaps I wasn't the most experienced submissive out there, but I knew what my masters expected of me.

"Glad to see you could come out tonight," Master Ramsey said. "I see you've got…"

When he paused, I looked up and noticed he was eyeing my collar.

His smile widened and he held out his hand to Master, then Sir, shaking with them. "Congratulations."

Apparently collaring a submissive was quite the reason to celebrate.

"I can't necessarily say I'm surprised," Master Ramsey joked. "It's been a long time since I've seen you with a submissive. I'm happy to see one has finally captured you both."

I think it was the other way around, but I wasn't about to argue. The fact that I belonged to them, and them to me, wasn't something I was going to dispute.

"Have a good night," Master Ramsey concluded, then moved on to talk to someone else.

Master and Sir led me toward the stairs, stopping a couple more times to talk. By the time we were heading down the stairs, I was trembling with anxiety. I had no idea what they had planned for me tonight, but I was eager to find out.

When we reached the bottom floor, I realized there was a crowd gathered in the far corner. Master led me over there, with Sir not far behind. People seemed to move out of the way as Master strolled toward the front.

My surprise was back when I saw Jordan with his submissive. He was using the violet wand again and people were standing around in awe, including me. Although he was utilizing the same tool he'd used on the island, his scene was completely different. His submissive was naked and restrained to a St. Andrew's cross. The blindfold covering his eyes likely made it all the more stimulating since he had no idea what his master was going to do next. I was quite fond of the blindfold, I could admit.

Master finally escorted me away from Jordan's scene and into an empty alcove on the far side of the room. It was roped off, which I took to mean it had been reserved. There was nothing in the space to give away what Master and Sir intended to do to me, which only heightened my intrigue. I was eager to find out.

•

Thirty minutes later, Master and Sir had successfully removed my clothing and restrained me with my arms above my head and my legs spread wide. The position forced me to remain on my toes. I was naked and on display for anyone who cared to watch, but my attention was solely focused on them. For the first time, I was completely in the moment, not paying any mind to the people who were gathering around us. They didn't matter.

And sure, it had taken months for me to understand, but now I could see exactly what Master and Sir had been teaching me along the way.

"Are you ready, pet?" Master crooned in my ear, his breath warm against my skin.

I shivered. "Yes, Master."

"Do you know what we plan to do to you?" He placed a blindfold over my eyes, then secured it behind my head.

"No, Master." I had absolutely no idea, but I trusted them.

Something grazed my back and my spine straightened.

"What do you think that is?" he asked.

"The flogger."

"Very good, pet. Are you still eager?"

"Yes, Master." I didn't care what they did to me. I was looking forward to it because I knew they were going to give me every ounce of their attention.

I heard something buzz in front of me and I jerked in response.

Sir chuckled. "Do you know what this is?"

"It sounds like a vibrator, Sir." On steroids.

"It's a Hitachi," Sir explained. "Also known as a magic wand."

Something pressed against my mound, then it clicked on and I jerked again. The vibrations were in no way subtle. It made Big Red and the bullet vibrator seem like amateurs. Holy crap. It was intense.

"Tonight, sweetness, we plan to break you in right."

I shivered again. His voice was raspy and deep, echoing through the space.

"Are you ready for us?"

"Yes, Sir," I said, loud enough to be heard by anyone nearby.

"Very good." He pressed his lips to mine.

Master's voice came from somewhere behind me. "What is your safeword, pet?"

"Red, Master."

"Do you have any questions?"

Only one. "Am I allowed to come, Master?"

Several people chuckled and I felt my ears heat from my embarrassment.

"Yes, sweet girl," Sir confirmed. "You are allowed to come as many times as you'd like."

"Thank you, Sir."

Swallowing hard, I remained still, my hands gripping the chain that dangled between the wrist cuffs. I focused on keeping my body straight in an effort to please my masters.

I waited for a few seconds, my body thrumming with excitement. However, nothing happened. I could still hear people talking at a distance. I even noticed the rustle of clothing around me, but no one touched me.

I was just about to call out when hands were suddenly behind my head, the blindfold being loosened. I frowned, worried I'd done something wrong and my masters weren't pleased with me.

When the blindfold came down, that was when I saw them.

Master and Sir were each on one knee before me.

I stared down at them, confused.

"It's no secret that Landon and I have spent a lifetime waiting for our perfect mate. For the woman who would complete us in every way. The submissive who would draw out our instincts and our need to control and protect. Never in a million years would we have expected for that beautiful, amazing creature to come to us."

"But you did," Sir said, seemingly picking up where Master left off. "You showed up in our office one day, eager and willing to please in ways you hadn't even realized at the time. You stood there before us, so sweet, so beautiful that we instantly knew that you would belong to us."

Master cleared his throat. "You took a journey that led all three of us to this moment, perhaps the only time you'll see us on our knees."

Several people chuckled and I smiled, tears filling my eyes.

Sir continued, "You honored us by accepting our collar, by giving us your heart and soul to go along with your submission, and we vow that we will never take that for granted for as long as we live. Along with our collar, we would like you to wear our ring."

They both lifted one hand, each holding something out toward me.

"Luciana Wagner," they said in unison, "will you do us the most incredible honor of being our wife?"

I nodded, choking back the happy tears that threatened. "Yes," I whispered. "Absolutely, yes."

And there I was, restrained and naked, staring at the most incredible men on the entire planet.

My Master.
My Sir.
My future husbands.

FIFTY-THREE

"I THINK I WAS MOST surprised to see Mel and King there," I told Ben, giggling as the memory swamped me.

It had only been two days since Master and Sir surprised me with a very unconventional proposal at the club. I hadn't been expecting it, but I wouldn't trade that single moment for any. And to find out they'd been planning it, which was the very reason Kristen, Jordan, and Master and Sir's parents had attended, had been the icing on the cake. I'd learned that they had even ensured that Master Ramsey would be in attendance.

"I wish we could've been there," Ben told me, smiling down at me. "And trust me, it wasn't easy when Landon requested our presence. Unfortunately, we had to stay there, so we had to turn him down."

"I completely understand." Although I wish they could've been there, too.

Ben had just arrived in the office a few minutes before. I was so happy to see that they were back. It could've been under better circumstances, sure. I had learned the sad news of Justin's father's passing last night. Master and Sir had felt the need to warn me, prior to coming into the office this morning. I was glad that they had. I didn't know Justin's father, but I had still cried for Justin.

The funeral would be held on Thursday, and we would all be attending. Until then, Justin had felt it necessary to come home so he could spend a little time focusing on work. I figured it was more of a distraction than anything. I couldn't imagine the pain he was suffering.

"But I do have one question..." Ben cocked his head to the side. "Which one of them will you marry?"

Grinning, I shrugged. "We haven't decided that yet. Since that's merely a legality, I don't know that it matters."

"Well, I'm sure you'll figure it out." He laughed. "Or, more accurately, Langston will tell you how it is."

Yep, Master was nothing if not up front about how he wanted things. Then again, so was Sir. The fact was, I didn't know and I honestly didn't care. They wanted it for legal reasons, to ensure that I was taken care of in the event something happened. I, personally, just wanted to be with both of them and having to choose which of them to marry was more than I cared to deal with.

Footsteps sounded and I looked up to see Justin walking toward us. He looked a little worse for wear, but still just as handsome as always. When he came over to my desk, I instantly got to my feet. I wanted to hug him, to offer my condolences, but I paused, not wanting to be overly emotional if he needed space.

He seemed to know what I was silently asking for, because he offered a small smile, followed by, "Come here, princess."

I rushed over to him, throwing my arms around him and hugging him tightly. "I'm so sorry about your dad."

"Thank you." He ran his hand down my hair, his arms holding me to him. "He's in a much better place now."

I had learned from Master and Sir that Justin's father had suffered from dementia and it had progressed at a rapid pace in the past year or so. To the point the man had no idea who his family was most of the time, yet Justin and his brother had made a point to take care of him until the very end. My heart broke for him.

Justin pulled back at the same time Master and Sir came out of their offices.

"I hear congratulations are in order," Justin said, reaching for my hand and lifting it up to inspect the rings. His eyes then darted to the collar and he smiled.

"Looks like a lot of changes are taking place around here," Ben noted. "Good changes."

I smiled. It was true. I'd never been happier.

Justin looked at me. "Have you set a date yet?"

"We have not. Not officially anyway."

"We're hoping for June, maybe July," Sir noted. "Our mother's insistent on making this a grand affair."

I giggled, remembering Mel's excitement. She had approached me after the proposal, once Master and Sir had finished the scene. They'd laughed at me when they realized I thought the proposal was all they'd intended to do to me. Needless to say, I got intimately acquainted with that magic wand and Master's flogger. In fact, it had taken some time for me to come down from my subspace high, but then everyone was there to congratulate us all.

Justin glanced between Master and Sir, then back to me. "So, are we still on for the Monday meeting?"

"Absolutely," I told him with a grin. "And I have a ton of updates."

"Have you placed an ad for another secretary?" Justin asked.

"Not yet, but I've got it prepared." It wasn't like it was difficult. I was going with their tried and true: REQUIREMENTS TO BE PROVIDED AT TIME OF INTERVIEW.

Surely, someone would be interested.

Perhaps a sweet little submissive whose world would be changed when she had the opportunity to work for some fabulous Doms.

Granted, she wouldn't be as lucky as me. I'd been trained by four.

The next girl would only get the pleasure of two. But two was good.

I glanced over at Master and Sir.

Two was very, *very* good.

EPILOGUE

FOUR MONTHS LATER, JUNE

"HOW ARE THE INTERVIEWS COMING along, pet?" Master asked when I returned to my desk that afternoon.

I grimaced at the memory of the last two interviews. "Not very well."

In an effort to find the person who would be an asset to the team, Justin and Ben had requested that I handle the initial interviews for those interested in the secretary position. I'd been at it for two solid months, talking to one person after another, hoping they would be a perfect fit for my previous bosses. I'd even enlisted Jordan's help, but to no avail.

In the interim, I was still working for all four of them, although we had officially moved to the thirty-third floor now that the renovations were complete. Granted, they were just starting on the changes to the thirty-second floor, so there was still a lot going on. I continued to hold out hope that the next applicant would be the one to waltz in and blow our minds. Unfortunately, that had yet to happen.

Perhaps I was being too picky, but I wanted someone whose personality would mesh well with all of us. But I was also seeking someone who had the potential to become more for Justin and Ben. That was more difficult to find than I'd originally thought. I had liked one girl, a sweet little blonde fresh out of college, but Jordan had vetoed her before I could send her resume along to Justin and Ben. After a lot of discussion, I'd conceded. My best friend thought the girl was too young and far too immature. Looking back on it, I had to agree.

"We've scheduled one more for this afternoon. She should be here any minute," I informed Master. "Hopefully, she'll fare better than the others."

"I'm sure it'll all work out the way it's supposed to."

Footsteps sounded outside in the hallway and I continued to watch my office doorway until Sir appeared. He came to a stop beside Master, glancing between us as though trying to figure out what we were discussing.

I sighed. "I was just telling Master that the interviews aren't going well."

He nodded his understanding. "Maybe you need a little motivation."

My insides warmed instantly. I'd gotten familiar with my masters' motivational techniques, and I had to admit, I was quite fond of them.

"Yes, Sir," I agreed.

Before he could insist that I do something, my desk phone rang. I snatched up the receiver and put it to my ear.

"The next applicant is here," Jordan informed me.

"Thanks. I'll be right up." I sighed when I hung up the phone. "Unfortunately, duty calls."

Sir lifted an eyebrow. "Then we'll merely relocate. She'll have to wait."

My eyes widened, but I didn't argue when Sir took my arm and we started toward the front. I heard Master's footsteps close behind.

When we stepped into the lobby, I instantly greeted the young woman. "I'm sorry, but I need to meet with my bosses for a few minutes."

"Oh, sure," she said sweetly, her eyes scanning Master and Sir before a huge grin took over her face. "Take your time."

Oh, Lord. That was the last thing she should've said. Master and Sir would certainly do that now.

"I'll be right back." I turned to find Sir holding open the door to the conference room. Rather than panic, I walked right in. I knew that Jordan and the applicant would hear anything that took place, and perhaps they would see the shadows as well, but it wasn't my place to argue with what Sir wanted. He was my Dom; therefore he made the rules. I merely abided by them.

"Start by undressing," Sir instructed. "And I'll be back in a minute."

Sir slipped out of the room, but Master didn't follow, instead choosing to lean against the wall near the door. He watched as I undressed, his eyes never leaving me.

"Present yourself," he instructed.

I did as he requested, kneeling in front of the conference table as I waited for Sir to return.

A few minutes later, the door opened, then closed. Their feet finally appeared in front of my eyes and two hands settled on my head.

"Stand and greet your masters, sweet girl."

I got to my feet and smiled brightly.

They laughed.

I couldn't help it. I enjoyed their attention and anytime I got it, I was sure to let them know. Granted, I got a lot of attention. Having two men—two Doms, at that—tended to keep a girl busy. Not that I was complaining.

"Up on the table," Sir instructed.

I hopped up on the conference table that was very similar to the one downstairs, only it had a wooden top, not glass. When Sir had ordered it, he had specifically said he wanted something "extremely sturdy." He got what he wanted. We had tested it out a few times already.

Sir instantly settled me into the position he wanted me. I was on my back, my feet flat on the wood top, knees bent and pointing skyward. He proceeded to secure my legs, using straps, connecting my ankles to my thighs. He then used another strap to pull my knees in close to my chest, while spreading them wide so I was completely exposed.

"Comfortable?" he asked as he cinched the strap tighter.

"Yes, Sir."

"Good."

Master moved around so that he was standing opposite of Sir. He situated me so that my head was hanging off the side of the table, his cock at mouth level.

Apparently, he wasn't wasting any time.

Warm hands ran up my thighs.

"Do not come, pet," Sir insisted. "Not until we give you permission."

"Yes, Sir."

"And remember, there are people out there who can hear every moan you make."

I'd learned long ago that my masters were always challenging me. I was past the point of promising to be quiet because I knew they would merely see that I did the opposite.

My two masters provided me with a very nice distraction. Sir's mouth feasted on my pussy, licking, suckling, and teasing me until I was moaning around Master's cock, which impaled my mouth over and over. They worked me over good before alternating positions. Then Sir's cock was fucking my mouth and Master was driving me wild with his tongue.

They did this several more times, offering me pleasure while taking theirs. They would bring me right to the brink, then pull back. Clearly, they knew that withholding wasn't my strong suit.

When Sir was once again between my legs, I heard the distinct buzz of his magic wand as he powered it on. My body tensed.

"Sir?"

"Yes, pet?"

"May I come?" I knew there was no point in pretending I could hold off. Not with that brutal vibrator they enjoyed using on me.

He pressed it against my clit and I whimpered. That damn thing was the devil of all vibrators.

"You may come, pet. But not until Langston does."

I swallowed hard, opening my mouth as Master fed me his cock. The vibrator pressed firmly against my clit as I sucked Master into my mouth. I whimpered and moaned as the pleasure slammed into me. The position I was in allowed Master complete control to use my mouth and I gave it to him freely. He began fucking my throat, his hands kneading my breasts. I could tell he wasn't holding back and I was eager for him to come. Mostly for selfish reasons, of course.

Sweat dotted my skin as I raced to the edge, hanging on by my fingernails. I was so close to bursting, I could hardly contain myself. The pleasure bordered on pain.

Finally, Master's hips stopped moving.

"Come for me, little one," he commanded as his cock pulsed in my mouth.

I swallowed him down as I could, then I let out a muffled cry when my orgasm detonated.

They traded places, gave me the same instructions, and several minutes later, I was coming again while Sir shot into my mouth.

Afterward, they released the restraints, then helped me up before massaging my entire body from neck to toe.

"So, are you motivated?" Sir asked, brushing my hair back from my face.

"Absolutely, Sir." I was always motivated.

He chuckled. "I meant motivated to find a secretary for Justin and Ben."

"Oh." I grinned. "Of course." Then my eyes widened. "Crap! The applicant."

"Don't worry!" Jordan yelled from the other side of the door. "She's gone. I think your moaning freaked her out."

I couldn't help it, I laughed, despite the blush that overtook my face. Jordan had apparently heard everything.

Sir looked at Master. "I'm not sure I believe her. She sounds sincere, but..."

Master shook his head, then moved around behind me. "I'm not sure I do either."

Sir grinned. "Maybe you need an extra...push."

"If it pleases you, Sir," I said with a giggle, my mouth watering when he began to unbutton his shirt.

After all, I would do *anything* to please my master

♥ ▫ ▫ ▫ ▫ ♥ ▫ ▫ ▫ ▫ ♥

I hope you enjoyed Luci's story. These characters pulled me in and kept me suspended for so long, I felt as though I truly got to know them. Of course, I also feel as though it's not over for Justin and Ben. They've got to find their own submissive. And they will. Soon.

Want to see some fun stuff related to the Office Intrigue Duet, you can find extras on my website. Or how about what's coming next? Find more at: www.NicoleEdwardsAuthor.com

If you're interested in keeping up to date on any of my series, as well as receiving updates on all that I'm working on, you can sign up for my monthly newsletter.

Want a simple, *fast* way to get updates on new releases? You can also sign up for text messaging. If you are in the U.S. simply text NICOLE to 64600 or sign up on my website. I promise not to spam your phone. This is just my way of letting you know what's happening because I know you're busy, but if you're anything like me, you always have your phone on you.

And last but certainly not least, if you want to see what's going on with me each week, sign up for my weekly Hot Sheet! It's a short, entertaining weekly update of things going on in my life and that of the team that supports me. We're a little crazy at times and this is a firsthand account of our antics.

ACKNOWLEDGMENTS

First and always, I have to thank my wonderfully patient husband who puts up with me every single day. If it wasn't for him and his belief that I could (and can) do this, I wouldn't be writing this today. He has been my backbone, my rock, the very reason I continue to believe in myself. I love you for that, babe.

Chancy Powley – This was a tough one, I know. It tested our friendship and I hope you know that you mean the world to me. I thank you for everything you do for me, all the wonderful suggestions and ideas, and especially for letting me bounce mine off you.

Allison Holzapfel – Our friendship has grown stronger the past few months and I'm so glad that I have you. This book tested all of us, but I thank you for the time and dedication you put into reading it and giving me your input. The book is better because of it.

Amber Willis – You don't particularly care for BDSM romance, but you dug in and powered through. I thank you for all you do for me, and for being my friend.

Karen DiGaetano – You're probably the fastest reader I've ever met, and I thank you for taking the time to read through this book – twice – and for giving me your input. Thanks to you, I decided to elaborate some and add a few more perspectives. The book is certainly better because of it.

Wander Aguiar and Andrey Bahia – You two are class acts in every way. Thank you SO much for giving my characters life. Working with you is a true pleasure and I look forward to what the future has in store for us.

Thank you to my proofreaders. Jenna Underwood, Annette Elens, Theresa Martin, and Sara Gross. Not only do you catch my blunders, you are my friends and it is an honor to call you that.

I also have to thank my street team – Naughty (and nice) Girls – Your unwavering support is something I will never take for granted. So, thank you Traci Hyland, Maureen Ames, Erin Lewis, Jackie Wright, Chris Geier, Kara Hildebrand, Shannon Thompson, Tracy Barbour, Toni Thompson, and Rachelle Newham.

I can't forget my copyeditor, Amy at Blue Otter Editing. Thank goodness I've got you to catch all my punctuation, grammar, and tense errors.

Nicole Nation 2.0 for the constant support and love. You've been there for me from almost the beginning. This group of ladies has kept me going for so long, I'm not sure I'd know what to do without them.

And, of course, YOU, the reader. Your emails, messages, posts, comments, tweets… they mean more to me than you can imagine. I thrive on hearing from you, knowing that my characters and my stories have touched you in some way keeps me going. I've been known to shed a tear or two when reading an email because you simply bring so much joy to my life with your support. I thank you for that.

About Nicole Edwards

New York Times and *USA Today* bestselling author Nicole Edwards lives in Austin, Texas with her husband, their three kids, and four rambunctious dogs. When she's not writing about sexy alpha males, Nicole can often be found with a book in hand or making an attempt to keep the dogs happy. You can find her hanging out on Facebook and interacting with her readers - even when she's supposed to be writing.

By Nicole Edwards

The Alluring Indulgence Series
Kaleb
Zane
Travis
Holidays with the Walker Brothers
Ethan
Braydon
Sawyer
Brendon

The Austin Arrows Series
The SEASON: Rush
The SEASON: Kaufman

The Bad Boys of Sports Series
Bad Reputation
Bad Business

The Caine Cousins Series
Hard to Hold
Hard to Handle

The Club Destiny Series
Conviction
Temptation
Addicted
Seduction
Infatuation
Captivated
Devotion
Perception
Entrusted
Adored
Distraction

The Coyote Ridge Series
Curtis
Jared

The Dead Heat Ranch Series
Boots Optional
Betting on Grace
Overnight Love

The Devil's Bend Series
Chasing Dreams
Vanishing Dreams

The Devil's Playground Series
Without Regret
Without Restraint

The Office Intrigue Duet
Office Intrigue
Intrigued Out of the Office
Their Rebellious Submissive

The Pier 70 Series
Reckless
Fearless
Speechless
Harmless

The Sniper 1 Security Series
Wait for Morning
Never Say Never
Tomorrow's Too Late

The Southern Boy Mafia Series
Beautifully Brutal
Beautifully Loyal

Standalone Novels
A Million Tiny Pieces
Inked on Paper

Writing as Timberlyn Scott
Unhinged
Unraveling
Chaos

Naughty Holiday Editions
2015
2016

BECAUSE NAUGHTY CAN BE OH SO NICE.®
LTD